"I loved this book, s
immersed in the history of the time!

~

"This book is a sweet and clean romance."

~

"I loved that real emotions and struggles were
involved as it made you relate to the characters."

~

"The suspense amps up in this second
installment. And wow are there some twists."

~

"I read the book in one sitting without
stopping, every line of the book pulls the other
one and does not allow the reader to stop."

~

"Falls Ends the oath is a touching
story, this is a must read!"

~

"Paul Feenstra has written such a
compelling story centered around the simple
herdsman that I'm drawn to this series."

~

"This story will grab you on the very first page"

~

FALLS ENDE SECUNDUS

by

Paul W. Feenstra

Published by
Mellester Press

Books
by
Paul W. Feenstra

Published by Mellester Press.

Boundary

The Breath of God (Book 1 in Moana Rangitira series)

For Want of a Shilling (Book 2 in Moana Rangitira series)

Falls Ende eBook series

Falls Ende – The Oath   (eBook 1)
Falls Ende – Courser   (eBook 2)
Falls Ende – The King   (eBook 3)

Falls Ende – Primus Book 1
(Print version of eBook compilation 1, 2 & 3)

Falls Ende – Secundus Book 2

Falls Ende – Secundus
First published in 2019 by Mellester Press

ISBN 978-0-473-47184-2 Soft Cover
ISBN 978-0-473-47186-6 Hard Cover
ISBN 978-0-473-47187-3 Kindle
ISBN 978-0-473-47185-9 epub
ISBN 978-0-473-47188-0 ibook

Published in New Zealand. A catalogue record of this
book is available from the National Library of New
Zealand.Kei te pātengi raraunga o Te Puna Mātauranga
o Aotearoa te whakarārangi o tēnei pukapuka

With heartfelt thanks.
Cover Images, beti bup
Edited by Jill Davis

http://www.paulwfeenstra.com/
Falls Ende © 2017 Paul W. Feenstra

Falls Ende – The Oath © 2017 Paul W. Feenstra
Falls Ende – Courser © 2018 Paul W. Feenstra
Falls Ende – The king © 2018 Paul W. Feenstra
Falls Ende – Primus © 2018 Paul W. Feenstra

Falls Ende – Secundus © 2019 Paul W. Feenstra

Published by
Mellester Press

Falls Ende Secundus

Book 2

Men never do evil so completely and cheerfully as when they do it from religious conviction.

Blaise Pascal

19 June 1623 – 19 August 1662

CHAPTER ONE

Exeter, Devonshire, England 1167 A.D.

The priest slowly straightened, placed both hands against his hips and arched backwards to ease his discomfort. He closed his eyes momentarily, then opened them and refocused on Bishop Immers as the ache slowly subsided.

"Are ye sure, is this everything?" the bishop asked again as he stared at the assortment of goods laid out in orderly piles before him.

"Aye, Yer Grace." The priest sighed quietly. "All of Oswald's and Durwin's personal possessions have been removed and the rectory is now empty except for fitments."

Bishop Immers clasped both hands behind his back and slowly walked alongside the chattels removed from Mellester's church rectory. His eyes flicked from item to item, he missed nothing. "What are these?" he asked, pointing at one pile.

"They are articles I've deemed worthless and will be handed to the wretched, Yer Grace."

The bishop nodded but wasn't satisfied.

"And those are personal things and will be returned to their respective families ... and this other large collection belongs to the church." Priest Benedict pointed helpfully.

Bishop Immers was perturbed. In reflex, he unclasped his hands and reached for the pectorale that swung from a silk cord around his neck, his fingers sensually caressing the fine jewels inlaid into the crucifix as he pondered his dilemma.

The church wanted title on the land where the Falls Ende gristmill was being built at Mellester Manor. Previously deemed derelict, and if not cleverly outmanoeuvred by Sir Hyde Fortescue, Lord of Ridgley Manor, the Church would now be in possession of Falls Ende and he'd be humbly receiving papal blessings in gratitude for his fine acquisition.

Through levies, the mill represented a steady, long-term source of income, however, and according to the Church, its current tenant, Herdsman Odo Read, had a tenuous and illegitimate grasp on the title. Bishop Immers knew if he dug deep enough and persisted, opportunity existed to wrench the deed from him... *but how*? He fondled the pectorale... *God would provide. But where to look*? He stared blankly at the items collected from the rectory. A polite cough from Priest Benedict brought him from his reverie.

"Have ye found anything that relates to the herdsman, Odo Read?" The bishop raised an eyebrow with some expectancy and a measure of divine hope.

"Ah, we did find this, Yer Grace." Benedict stooped to retrieve a scroll and cringed as he felt a twinge shoot up his spine. He did his best to hide the malaise from the bishop and helpfully untied the ribbon and unrolled it before handing it over.

Bishop Immers quickly read the letter. "An unfinished missive... is of no importance... Although I do wonder what interest Durwin had at the convent?" He returned the scroll to Benedict. "What else?"

Priest Benedict walked to a pile of sundry odds and ends, slowly crouched and carefully lifted a pyxis. Constructed from wood, the pyxis was old and scarred, one side was slightly charred and many of the corners were chipped. He placed it on a nearby table as the bishop curiously stepped over to peer closer.

The pyxis was almost a foot in length and not quite half a foot in width and height. It had a small brass face-plate attached to the front with a hole for a key. "Belonged to Oswald, Yer Grace. There is no key and it isn't locked."

"Where did ye find it?"

"Methinks, discarded. T'was beneath a pile of furniture," replied the priest.

Bishop Immers opened the hinged lid and saw only a solitary folded parchment inside; he reached for the document, unfolded it and began to read.

The cool wind whistled through Exeter's expansive Cathedral Church of Saint Peter as Priest Benedict continued to rub his afflicted back.

A small smile formed on Bishop Immers face. He tossed the parchment back inside the box. "The sentimental writings of a lonely priest to his son. Silly old fool. Burn it, Benedict, along with all of Oswald's other things."

"As ye command, Yer Grace," Benedict bowed his head.

"And the other goods ye wish to give to the wretched, burn them too. I will inform Durwin Babcock the elder and he can send someone to retrieve the possessions of his deceased son." Bishop Immers spun to leave when he had a thought. He touched a finger to his chin. "Wait! The pyxis." He turned back to face the priest. "Give the pyxis and the letter to the herdsman. It may well be a good idea for him to see we are acting in good faith. I would hate to see the young man bear any ill feelings towards the Church," smirked the bishop. "The epistle and pyxis have no value to me."

"Very well, Yer Grace." Benedict dipped his head in supplication as he watched Immers walk away. When the bishop was no longer visible, the priest shook his head and relaxed. The physical, arduous work demanded of him by the bishop was not the work of a clergyman. Ever since he'd been assigned as Mellester's new priest, he'd been tasked with emptying the entire contents of the rectory and transporting everything all the way back to Exeter, just so the bishop could inspect them. For some unknown reason he was fixated on Falls Ende and finding a way to obtain title on that piece of land owned by Herdsman Odo Read. As far as Benedict was concerned, it was a futile waste of time and effort.

Much to everyone's astonishment, Bishop Immers recently gifted three pounds to the renovation of Mellester's church, while speculation and idle gossip suggested he did so only to avoid a scandal that may have involved Priest Durwin Babcock, the younger. Priest Benedict couldn't care less for chin-wagging and preferred to be as far removed from the close scrutiny of Exeter's bishop as possible. As Mellester's church was currently undergoing renovations, he wanted to return to the village and ensure the House-Wright and his men were not skylarking and were delivering quality work as promised.

He'd heard much about the gregarious young herdsman who held title on Falls Ende and had yet to make his acquaintance. Immediately upon returning to Mellester, he'd look forward to delivering the pyxis to him as instructed and form his own unbiased opinion on the nature of the young man.

The sun had yet to fully rise and already the good people of Mellester stood in small groups alongside the road that passed through the village. They watched in curious fascination as a long column of fully armed knights, followed by sergeants, squires with spare horses and wagons departed the manor. Trailing them were dozens of archers and men-at-arms on foot.

"I count 'bout five score, that's a lot of men," said Odo.

Both Herdsman Odo Read and Reeve Petrus Bodkin stood at the bottom of the carriageway that led up to Mellester's manor house and watched the procession depart.

"Here comes Sir Gweir and Mellester's knights now," offered the reeve.

They both turned their attention to the impressive figure of Mellester's lord, resplendent in his finest armour and doing his utmost to keep his destrier under control, riding towards them. Not content to walk, the horse pranced and sidestepped, eager to be allowed to run. Villagers, fearful they were too close, stepped back as the war-horse veered closer to where the reeve, Odo and a few others stood.

"Keep Odo away from trouble, Petrus!" shouted Sir Gweir as he rode past.

"I'd suggest ye do the same, milord!" shouted the reeve in reply.

"Do yer have the cheese?" yelled Odo to the lord.

Sir Gweir waved in reply, as did most of the fifteen knights who rode under his banner.

"What cheese?" the reeve asked.

"For the king, my gift," replied Odo. "He wanted our cheese, so I had Cheesemaker Gerald make some for him."

"Cocky sod," said the reeve shaking his head.

"I guess I'll have to be nice to ye, as ye fancy yerself as lord now, at least until Sir Gweir returns," said Odo with a grin.

"Aye, and best yer don't forget it," laughed the reeve in response.

"Come with us, Odo!" yelled Sir Renier as he rode past with his sergeant, Thomas Roundtree riding alongside.

Odo grinned.

"Charlotte may not approve," replied the reeve with a smirk.

Sir Renier waved farewell then spurred his horse to catch up to the others.

"Make sure ye return Thomas, ye owe me another archery lesson!" Odo shouted.

Thomas grinned, "Ye still owe me a mead!" Then he too charged after his master.

King Henry II called on his lords to assemble an army. Wishing to assert dominance over Irish Kings and Norman warlords, he hoped to deploy at least five hundred mounted knights, four thousand men-at-arms and archers, and set sail for Ireland departing from Wales as soon as conveniently possible.

In compliance, his lords began marshalling their forces. They gathered in small numbers and rode from manor to manor collecting more and more men along the way. In the region of Devonshire, all forces, including Mellester's, would finally gather at Ridgley Manor before setting out for Wales under the flag and command of Sir Hyde Fortescue, one of the kings most trusted friends and confidantes.

Manors were not left totally unprotected; a few knights and men-at-arms still remained here and there. Even though some were injured, old or inexperienced, the lords still needed to know their manors were safe in their absence as no one knew when they would return.

"I expect we'll have some peace and quiet now all the knights have gone," said the reeve as he watched the last man man-at-arms disappear into the distance.

Odo nodded. It felt strange to see all the knights leaving.

Both men turned and began walking back to the village to begin their day. Ahead was Mellester's church. Already the House-Wright and his men were clambering over the exposed roof beams in preparation for replacing the roof.

"Oswald would be pleased and smiling to see a new roof being built, wouldn't ye say, Odo?" The Reeve stopped to watch.

"I didn't think there was anything wrong with the old one."

Reeve Petrus gave Odo a withering look.

"Aye, I suppose he'd be crowing about it," Odo acquiesced. "If were even possible for him to smile."

"Ye need to go easy on him, Odo, he was yer da."

"Well, then he shoulda acted like my father instead of a cantankerous old goat."

"Perhaps ye should try acting like his son," added the reeve raising his eyebrows.

Odo was used to the reeve needling him and ignored the taunt. He attempted to change the subject. "I have to admit, Lord Ridgley surprised me by having the bishop pay coin for the roof and renovations."

Reeve Petrus laughed, "Don't underestimate Sir Hyde. Even for a greybeard, he's a cunning sod."

Odo joined in the laughter.

The reeve's eyes were constantly moving. Fully competent, he was attentive to the daily happenings of Mellester and its people. It was his job to ensure the lord's lands and serfs were managed productively and efficiently. When the routine and balance of manor life was misaligned, he was the first to know. So, when he saw a figure running frantically through the village, he paid attention. "Here comes yer apprentice, Daniel, what's got under his skin?"

Odo turned from the men working on the church and saw Daniel running through the village towards them. Both men waited in silence as Daniel pulled to a stop.

"Odo, one of the cows has died!"

"What? How?" cried Odo.

The reeve's expression hardened.

"Did someone kill it? Brigands? Who would–"

"No, Odo, t'was just layin there on the ground in the byre," interrupted Daniel. "Wasn't me Master Odo, I did nuttin, honest."

Just as Daniel described, one of Odo's prized milking cows lay dead inside the byre. A quick external examination revealed no visible signs as to the cause of death, but there was evidence of a few small lesions on the cow's flanks and back.

Odo stood back and with hands on hips, looked down at the dead animal. He shook his head in bewilderment.

"Murrain[1]," whispered Reeve Petrus. His expression was grim.

Odo shook his head, "No, it can't be, my animals are without sickness."

"Find Cathal, bring him here as fast as ye can, Daniel, and say nothing about this to anyone, ye hear me?"

"Aye, Reeve Petrus," Daniel nodded and climbed over the wooden rails to leave.

"And hurry," added Odo. He waited until they were alone. "I don't understand, what could cause this if it weren't murrain, Petrus?"

"No need to worry yet, wait for Cathal, he'll know why it died, and yer bother might be fer nought."

Both men were still staring at the carcass when Cathal and Daniel entered the byre a short time later. Cathal didn't speak and looked at the animal carefully. With ease, he leapt over the wooden rail and approached the head of the cow. He squatted and pried its mouth open to inspect inside.

"What killed it, Cathal?" asked Odo.

The Irish seer didn't respond and turned his attention to peer inside the cow's nose. Finally, he stood and moved to the rear end of the cow and looked at its filthy excrement-covered hindquarters.

"Murrain?" questioned the reeve.

---

1   *A plague or infectious disease affecting cattle that results in death.*

Cathal slowly stood, scratched his beard for a moment and climbed back over the rail. "I will return soon." Without another word he walked out of the byre and was gone.

"Well then, he was helpful," said Odo. "Now I need to figure out what to do. This isn't good Petrus."

"Aye, lad, we do have a problem."

"Grab a couple of spades, Daniel; we have to bury it as soon as possible."

Reeve Petrus didn't move. "Odo, until we know what caused this death ye can't be selling milk," instructed the reeve with seriousness.

Odo's head whipped around. "But it could be anything, reeve, it may not be murrain–"

"Listen to me Odo, ye know more than anyone what this could mean. We have to be careful. People could get the sickness and die."

Odo looked down at his feet; he knew the reeve was right. "Aye, I know, reeve... this could ruin me."

"And it could destroy Mellester," added Reeve Petrus.

CHAPTER TWO

Priest Benedict hurried from Exeter and returned to Mellester as quickly as possible. Mainly he was concerned about the House-Wright and ensuring he was doing a good job on the church renovations. The other reason was to put some distance between himself and the disagreeable bishop.

On arrival he'd laboriously unpacked the wagon and found the pyxis that was to be given to the herdsman. As it wasn't late, he decided to call on the young man he'd heard so much about.

Odo wasn't in a particularly social mood and his disposition didn't improve when his discussion with Charlotte about the dead cow was interrupted by an untimely door knock.

Charlotte opened the door to find a middle-aged man standing in the entranceway carrying a wooden box. He was of average height, slightly greying hair and had an open, expressive face. She recognized him immediately as she'd seen him packing a wagon at the rectory a week ago and guessed he was Mellester's new priest.

"Mother Read?" asked Priest Benedict.

"Nay, ye are mistaken, I am Charlotte Read and have no children," she said returning his smile.

"Then forgive me, Bishop Immers was incorrect. I am Benedict, and

Mellester's new–"

"Away with him!" bellowed Odo, hearing the man introduce himself. The last thing he wanted was to engage with another sanctimonious cleric. He'd enough problems to deal with.

"–priest," finished Benedict.

"Perhaps you should return on the morrow," Charlotte suggested.

"Tell 'im, my tithes are met and we give to the wretched already!" yelled Odo.

Charlotte looked apologetic.

"Ah, then in God's eyes ye are generous. However, I come here not to discuss church affairs, but rather more personal ones." Benedict continued with his smile. "If you'd rather spend some time discussing redemption then I can avail myself to you at another time?" He winked at Charlotte.

Odo twisted in his seat to look towards their unexpected visitor. "What affairs?"

"Best ye come in, Priest Benedict." Charlotte moved to the side and allowed him to enter.

"How can we help ye?" she asked once he was inside and seated.

Odo looked on with suspicion.

"Ah yes, Bishop Immers asked that I organise the possessions of Priest Oswald and Priest Durwin. I found this pyxis in the rectory buried beneath a pile of furniture, and the Bishop kindly suggested I hand this over to ye." Benedict stood and reverently passed the box to Odo.

Odo was puzzled; he'd never seen the box before. It wasn't beautiful or expertly crafted as some he'd seen; it was ordinary in every respect and even showed signs of excessive wear and damage. One side was scorched from fire and the other side was battered. It looked old and worthless.

"Open it, Odo," instructed Charlotte, impatient to see what it contained.

"A key isn't required," volunteered the priest when he saw Odo look at the brass face-plate.

Carefully Odo opened the lid, and from the light of candles, Charlotte and Odo saw a single folded parchment.

"I can read it to ye if ye wish," volunteered Benedict wanting to be helpful.

"We can both read English," smiled Charlotte.

Benedict looked surprised. *Commoners who can read?* "Oh, but ah, that may prove difficult for it is written in Latin."

"I can read some Latin," offered Charlotte.

And Latin? That's unheard of, he thought. Benedict returned her smile.

With care Odo unfolded the document. Oswald only taught him to read English and the strange words on the parchment meant nothing to him, he handed it to Charlotte.

"Is from Oswald," she said quickly.

Odo urged her with a nod to begin.

She turned back to the distinctive penmanship and the familiar script. The distant memory of Oswald's Latin lessons returned to her easily. In practice, she silently mouthed the words before speaking aloud as Priest Benedict curiously waited to see if the young woman could indeed read Latin as she claimed.

She cleared her throat and began with uncertainty. "To my last –

surviving son, Odo. If ye are – deciphering this, then I have passed and already and – stood before almighty God in – judgement. I have sinned in – abundance, and sorrowfully, heaven will not be my – terminus, for my soul will be damned to an eternity in hell. A just reckoning for my evil – undertakings."

"Doesn't surprise me," said Odo dryly.

Priest Benedict ignored the barb and nodded in approval. He was impressed, the young woman was indeed capable.

Charlotte gave Odo a cold look before returning to the letter and continuing. "I have – grieved that I was unable to provide ye with the most – salient – endowment of all, the – avuncular love of a father. While my trusted friends Godwin and Hetti offered ye love and accepted ye as their own, may they forever be blessed, they are not of yer blood. My love fer ye, Odo, is – bestowed unto ye through these words and in this pyxis. It is my – invocation to ye to accept this love, and with persistence, may ye dwell upon these words and heed my precept ~ fer love lies within. Love is my legacy. Blessed be to yer. Anon, yer father." Charlotte sniffed and wiped away a tear before handing the letter back to Odo.

The room was quiet. Priest Benedict felt awkward and stood to leave. "I uh, I shall let ye enjoy yer gift and yer ruminations." He turned to Charlotte, "Well read." He dipped his head in acknowledgment.

Lost in thought, Odo was silent a moment longer, then slowly stood. "Thank ye Priest Benedict, I apologise for my earlier rudeness. It was kindly of yer to bring me this, it hasn't been a good week for us."

"Think nothing of it," he nodded and stepped to the door. "If yer wish to discuss salvation and the empty coffers of the church, we can talk again soon," he quipped, and gave Charlotte another wink.

"Aye, I'm sure ye will," smiled Odo.

The priest departed and Odo slowly exhaled. "What is this all about?"

"I don't know, Odo." She still held the letter and stared at it.

"He seems a pleasant fellow, for a priest."

"Aye, he does."

"That is a strange letter, could ye have read it wrong?"

Charlotte shook her head, "Nay, I've read these words many a times but not in this order, was almost like Oswald prepared me by making sure I knew those words."

"What does he mean by decipher?"

Charlotte shrugged.

"Read it again."

Before she could begin there was a loud clatter at the door.

"That be Petrus," said Odo recognising the sound of the reeve's staff striking the door.

Reeve Petrus stood at the door and behind him stood Cathal. "We need to talk, Odo." The reeve offered no customary smile as he usually did.

The four sat around the table in Odo and Charlotte's cruck house.

Odo turned to Cathal. "Where did ye disappear too?"

Cathal was fixated on the pyxis that sat on the table before him. He didn't reply.

"Out of the goodness of his heart, Bishop Immers decided to give me a letter that Oswald wrote. And Mellester's new priest, Benedict, discovered it in this box," volunteered Odo seeing the interest in the pyxis.

"Anything of importance to ye?" asked the reeve.

"Nay, it is a puzzling letter."

The reeve nodded. "Cathal has something to tell ye. Cathal?" All heads turned to the Irish fili but he wasn't listening and focusing entirely on the pyxis that sat on the table before him.

"Cathal!"

Slowly the Irish seer tore his eyes away from the box.

"Tell Odo what ye learned," instructed the reeve impatiently.

"Ye said ye'd be right back, and ye've been gone for two days," interjected Odo.

"Aye, that I have," he finally began. "I didn't believe the sickness was caused here at Mellester." The Irishman adjusted the robe he wore and repositioned himself on the seat. "For sickness and pestilence to fester there must be other things."

"What things?" Odo asked.

"Imbalanced humours. Earth, air, fire and water. How do imbalanced humours become so?" he turned to study the faces of Odo, Charlotte and Petrus. They all shook their heads. "The balance here at Mellester is good, so from whence does it come?"

"From the wind?" volunteered Charlotte.

"Aye, and that is what I thought."

"Wind?" Odo repeated. "How about water?"

"Aye, even water," Cathal responded. He leaned forward. "I'm told the wind comes from the south this time of year. Two hours ride, south of Mellester is the cause. Herdsman Byram, ye know this man?"

"Aye, and he'd not be a herdsman's arse," Odo spat.

"His herd is all but dead!" said Cathal.

"Nay, it can't be!" He was here only days ago, said all was well.

"One or two still live, but the murrain comes, borne on the wind. I believe this pestilence is known as Steppe Murrain."

Odo's mouth opened. He knew of this sickness, a herdsman's worst fear.

"Have more of yer cows become ill?" Reeve Petrus asked.

Odo shook his head, "Nay, not as of this morn."

"They will," Cathal replied with finality.

"What can I do? Can I move my herd, keep them away from the wind, perhaps keep them in the byre till it passes?"

Petrus shook his head. "Odo, ye know it won't work. As Cathal said, the danger is from other herds who have the murrain. People could catch the sickness, and not just from yer cows, from someone else. Cathal, how many other herds have the sickness?"

"I have seen sign of pestilence in many cows, but as yet none have died other than from Herdsman Byram. I believe many cows will succumb and die soon," Cathal replied.

"Do ye know of a remedy?" asked Odo.

"I'm told some use dill, but..." Cathal shook his head. "I've yet to see if it works."

Everyone was silent as they digested Cathal's ominous words.

"And what happens if we wait and do nothing?" asked Petrus, looking to Odo and Charlotte.

No one replied.

"People could die," continued the reeve with gravity. He made eye contact with Odo and waited for the young herdsman to respond.

Odo toyed with a spoon that lay on the table. Everyone waited for him to speak. They all knew what he was mulling over. Finally, he looked up, his expression grim. "Then we must cull them all, not just my cows, but all of them," he said despondently. "Is the only way to prevent the sickness from becoming worse and spreading."

Petrus and Cathal had already discussed this and they knew what Odo suggested was the only sensible response.

"What will I do?" Odo placed his head in his hands. "This is my life … our dream … it will destroy us."

"Oh, Odo." Charlotte reached over to embrace him.

The reeve scratched the back of his head as he thought of the affect it would have on the locals. "What will happen to Mellester?" He turned to Charlotte. "Yer father will have no milk to make cheese." He shook his head. "All the people that milk yer cows, Odo, they will have no work and no coin to buy food. The waggoneers, the tavern, this affects everyone. This scourge affects us all," he added quietly.

Charlotte realised she still held Oswald's letter. Rather than see it damaged, she lifted the lid on the box and placed it inside.

Cathal watched her. "There'd be an ill wind…"

The three of them looked at the Irishmen but said nothing.

"And fire… fire, Odo. Ye are in danger. Fire will come."

It was the reeve who spoke first. "What is this nonsense ye speak of?"

"There are signs and I have seen them. Ye must leave here Odo take all yer worth and begone for a while. It *will* be so."

"I can't begone, not now. What is this doggerel ye utter?" Odo asked.

Cathal shook his head and shrugged. "I know nothing more."

Charlotte looked hard at the seer. "Ye speak in riddles, Cathal."

"Aye, and they come to me in riddles too."

No one spoke.

"On the morrow, I will speak with other herdsman," said the reeve breaking the silence. "They won't be happy when I tell 'em to destroy their herds."

"We will have to burn them," said Odo as he looked at Cathal and reminded of his warning of fire.

CHAPTER THREE

Bishop Immers was inside his cathedral fidgeting with a prayer rope he was given by a Coptic monk some years previous. As intended, he used it to remind himself to pray and it was that time again. Presently his thoughts were tuned to the daunting task of raising funds to have his cathedral rebuilt. It was old and not as prodigious as other more recently built cathedrals. The thirty-three knots on the prayer rope slipped through his fingers in a repeating cycle of abstract motion. With a heavy sigh, he decided to offer another prayer and seek help in finding a wealthy benefactor, or perhaps three, then finish his prayer with a request on a pardon, or unsparing leniency, for his numerous sins with the ardent hope that a generous remission on punishments would be considered when he was judged before The Almighty.

He turned into the nave and began walking to the bema, near the altar, where he would pray, when raised voices made him stop and look behind. What he saw gave him pause. Immediately his heart began to beat faster. He swallowed dryly, his prayer beads forgotten.

Ignoring the pleas of a priest, six fully armed knights in chainmail strode into the atrium, their footfalls loud on the stone floor as they marched, spurs rattling, towards the nave.

"The Bishop is occupied!" cried the priest, trying unsuccessfully to halt their advance. Two armed guards stood helplessly by as the knights pushed past.

Immers watched a moment longer. The cause of his growing anguish was the bright red cross emblazoned over the white mantle they wore. The six men were not ordinary knights, these were Templars.

"I will see these men!" shouted Bishop Immers to the priest. His heart began beating even faster and he felt his face flush red in foreboding.

The young priest stopped waving his arms, stood aside, faced the bishop and bowed his head. "As ye wish, Yer Grace."

Ignoring the priest, the Templars strode in synchronised time towards the waiting bishop. On entering the nave, the six men each took turns and dipped their fingers in holy water and as one, dropped to a knee in genuflection, crossed themselves, rose, and walked with absolute composure and confidence to the waiting bishop.

"Yer Grace, Bishop Immers?" asked one, older than the others and obviously the commander.

Bishop Immers forced himself to smile and nodded. "I am." He offered his hand, and the knight kissed the episcopal ring with practised ease. "Hail, good sirs, how may I be of help?" Immers warily studied the men before him. They were seasoned fighting men, nearly all bore scars and their mail, filthy from travel. Each wore an impressive sword with gauntlets tucked into belts. While these men may be travel weary and tired, their eyes were sharp and clear – they were formidable soldiers and not to be trifled with. *But what are they doing here?* Where Templars went, trouble followed, and these fighting monks were renowned for their exceptional abilities and untold wealth. The bishop had a fleeting thought that the Templars could contribute handsomely to his new cathedral.

"Yer Grace," repeated the commander, his voice authoritative and peremptory. "May we spare a moment of yer valuable time to confer, perhaps more cloistered?" It sounded like an order and not a request.

Bishop Immers noticed the knights all rested their hands on the hilt of their swords, their heads in constant motion searching for threat and danger. "Of course, but an appointment is customary, is it not?" Feeling more at ease, Bishop Immers felt no qualms about asserting himself to these men. While they frightened him, he was still a bishop and here ruled supreme.

The commander's eyes flashed briefly but he remained silent and continued to look at the bishop, expecting a reply. Tired of waiting he spoke again. "The rectory will suit, Yer Grace."

For a heartbeat or two Bishop Immers considered denying the request, after all he resided at the manor and not the rectory, but... It was curiosity and not good nature that saw him finally accede.

"Very well, follow me," said the bishop sounding vexed. While the Bishop retained a small force of armed men, only a few were on duty and they would be ineffectual against Templars. There was little he could do but acquiesce to the commander's imperiousness.

Bishop Immers excused the hearth wife and once alone with his unwelcome guest, turned to face him. His heart still beat furiously, his hands were damp and he was frightened. He knew of Templars and no good would come of their visit. Automatically his hand caressed the pectoral as he waited for the commander to speak.

With the exception of the older knight, one other Templar stood guard at the door, while the others waited outside. Unknown to Bishop Immers, the six Templar knights were also accompanied by six sergeants, also experienced and competent fighters, who presently encircled the rectory.

"I am Sir William Marshal, 1st Earl of Pembroke," said the older knight. "I represent His Holiness the Pope and belong to the Poor Fellow-Soldiers of Christ and from the Order of the Temple of Solomon."

Bishop Immers nodded as if this introduction was a normal occurrence. *What could Templars possibly want here,* he wondered for the umpteenth time?

"We seek a man and believe ye may know of him and his whereabouts," stated Sir William, forgoing any pleasantries.

"I am but a humble servant of the Church and will do all I can, Sir William. Who is this man ye seek?"

"His name is Odo Brus." The Templar watched the bishop carefully for any reaction.

Feeling immediate relief that a previous misdemeanour wasn't being scrutinized, Bishop Immers shook his head. "I know of no such person. Why is it ye honour me with this request?" He turned in puzzlement to quickly glance at the other knight near the door.

"Because we believe ye do know of this man, he is a priest and is commonly known as Oswald."

Time seemed to stop for the bishop. He swallowed thickly and sought a moment to gather his wits. *Oswald, Odo Brus?*

"Bishop?" reminded Sir William.

"I'm sorry, I have no such priest in my diocese," finally said Bishop Immers, deciding there was nothing to gain by helping these men.

If the Templar was disappointed, he showed no reaction.

"Why is it ye seek him, what has he done to deserve the attention of the Pope and such gallant men as yerselves?"

"Before we arrived here, Yer Grace, we passed through a number of manors, and were told, more than once, that ye knew of this man, Odo Brus or Oswald." Sir William wasn't happy, his jaw tightened and his eyes bored into the bishop.

Under the piercing gaze of the Templar commander, Bishop Immers suddenly felt a generous measure of benevolence and a change of heart. "Perhaps ye misunderstood me, Sir William, Oswald is not a priest in my diocese, he is deceased."

The Templar commander glanced quickly at his associate. As Bishop Immers observed, the knight at the door stepped towards his commander and conferred in hushed tones before returning to his station.

"That is unfortunate." Sir William nodded and looked thoughtful for a moment before continuing. "And where would his possessions be? Where could we find them?" He took a small step closer to the bishop.

To Bishop Immers, the step was an implied threat. "It appears that good fortune smiles upon the Poor Fellow-Soldiers of Christ this day, I have all his belongings here where they are to be destroyed."

"Show us, take us to them. Now." For the first time, Sir William expressed some excitement. He again turned to the knight at the door, the eye contact and affirmation an indication to the Bishop that whatever these men sought was very, very important.

Bishop Immers mind worked furiously. What was it the Templars were so anxious to find? The only thing of real value would be a holy relic of some description. Many existed and although some were fake, others were very real and people would travel for days and then pay coin to see a fine relic on display or better yet, touch it. He licked his lips. If it were more than a simple relic, then the Pope would want it. The person who brought such an important and valued treasure to His Holiness would receive many thanks and blessings. Here was opportunity he couldn't ignore.

The Templar knights eagerly followed the bishop as they re-entered Exeter's cathedral through a side door. An elderly monk on bended knee was wearily scrubbing the granite floor with a brush, a bucket of filthy water at his side. With the monk blocking access into the cathedral, Bishop Immers paused momentarily, then cuffed the monk and pushed past him, his knee driving into the shoulder of the man. The aged monk, unable to keep his balance fell onto the wet floor, knocking the bucket over as he reached forward to protect himself. Immers gave the monk a cursory glance, and scowled before continuing on, muttering under his breath.

Sir William reached down and assisted the frail monk to his feet. Although seemingly unhurt, the monk held his chest and was in some discomfort. In fear he'd slip and fall, Sir William carefully assisted him to a stone bench seat a short distance away and gently eased the man down.

"Thank ye, kind Sir," wheezed the toothless monk, "I shall be fine."

"Are ye sure?" questioned the Templar.

The monk nodded as colour began to slowly return to his waxen face.

"Have ye no homage?" yelled the commander at the back of the disappearing bishop.

Seldom was Bishop Immers spoken to so curtly. The knights lacked the deportment he expected and showed him little or no respect. Their visit was an intrusion and he'd be more than happy to see them on their way, but on the other hand, there may be opportunity. "Everything you see on this pile belonged to Priest Oswald." Bishop Immers waved his arm dismissively at the pile of articles to be destroyed.

With the exception of Sir William who watched anxiously, the five templars began combing through the small collection of Oswald's possessions. After a thorough search, and a few hushed words, they stopped and looked at their commander and one by one shook their heads.

"Are ye sure this is everything?" asked Sir William. "There is more, is there not?"

"Well, uh, I believe this is everything taken from the rectory, Sir William."

"Then nothing has since been taken from here?" Sir William stepped closer to Bishop Immers, he stood only a foot away and looked down at the man. He didn't believe him. "What was taken?" the Templar hissed.

If Bishop Immers had any intention of offering deceit to the Templar knights, the thought disappeared quickly as the Templar commander loomed over him. "It was only a worthless letter, the rantings of a lonely priest." He shrugged. "Of no value."

"Where was the letter found?" Sir William's voice rose, his patience wearing thin.

Bishop Immers was becoming genuinely concerned. "In an old pyxis."

Immediately the Templar knights gathered around Immers eager to learn more.

Sir William bent at the waist, his head inches from Immers. He spoke slowly as if questioning an unruly child. "Then where is the pyxis now?"

Bishop Immers mind worked furiously. *The templars wanted the pyxis badly. It must contain something of immense value, could it be a significant holy relic - or something more? If he could retrieve the pyxis from Benedict, before these knights did, then personally deliver it to the Pope...*

"This is unknown to me, but I can find out. I will send messengers out and–"

"So ye don't know who has the pyxis?" asked Sir William. The tone of his voice left no doubt he found the bishops excuse less than convincing.

"Oh, I do, I do, but I sent him to deliver letters to manor parishes, he could be anywhere. I can send messengers to each parish to locate him and order him to return here immediately."

"How long will this take?"

"A day or two, not longer," appeased the bishop feeling buoyed by the restoration of his confidence.

Sir William scratched his chin as he considered his options. He turned to his men. "The horses are fatigued, they need rest."

As one, they nodded.

Focusing his attention back on the bishop, Sir William asked the question Immers hoped he wouldn't. "Who is this person that has the pyxis?"

"A priest."

"Who?"

Immers swallowed. "Priest Benedict."

"And where is Priest Benedict's final destination?"

The bishop sought a way to turn this to his advantage, but the knight commander was relentless.

"Bishop?"

"M...Mellester Manor."

"Never heard of it." Sir William exhaled. He was tired. They'd been searching for the pyxis for almost two years. He and his men were mentally and physically exhausted and needed rest. They were so close, so close, and this rapacious self-serving bishop stood in their way.

The Templar Knight took a step away in frustration. If the bishop only knew that what the pyxis contained and how it was the last single piece, one of many, that would lead them to the ultimate... He couldn't share that with the bishop because this was Templar business, their responsibility, it was solely their *métier*. Nothing would stop them from fulfilling their mission. *Nothing*.

He stepped back to the repugnant man. "We will wait two days, ye have two days to deliver the pyxis, Bishop Immers," said Sir William. "We will take advantage of yer hospitality and remain here at the cathedral. Please have someone show us where we can rest."

The relief was almost overwhelming. "It is my honour to have ye as my guests, and I will see that ye are well taken care of," offered Immers. It would now suit him to keep the Templars here for as long as possible as he'd already formulated another plan.

Within the expanse of Exeter Cathedral, clergy were busy arranging quarters for the twelve members of the Poor Fellow-Soldiers of Christ and of the Order of the Temple of Solomon. During the confusion, Bishop

Immers informed a cleric he would be visiting the abbey next door where he would be arranging for messengers to be sent to recall Priest Benedict.

Truth be told, the bishop had no intention of doing that. He had a different reason to visit the abbey.

Once welcomed into the abbey and seated before the abbot, a dear and trusted friend, Bishop Immers politely discussed pleasantries.

"And what really brings yer here, Yer Grace? I can see yer a little distraught."

"Aye, and it is of much importance to the Church, Abbot Andrew. Have ye seen my guests who insolently invaded the cathedral?"

Abbot Andrew nodded. "The Templars? Word travels quick."

"I require ye to do something fer the Church and the success of this approbation will require me to immediately attend to His Holiness with a prized gift of limitless value, a treasure. It requires some delicate handling of a sensitive nature and I would prefer that the means ye go about performing this task be done quickly and quietly. No one must know."

"Of course Yer Grace." Abbot Andrew leaned forward.

"I need yer to send a handful of men, not clergy, to Mellester Manor and retrieve a pyxis that contains a letter from Priest Benedict. He may not have it any longer and already given it to Herdsman Odo Read."

"The same herdsman that falsely sits on land the Church should possess?" the Abbot queried incredulously.

"Aye, the very same."

Abbot Andrew chewed his bottom lip as he thought. "And if the herdsman has the pyxis and is unwilling to return it to the Church?"

"I do not care what it takes; the Church must have that pyxis, at any cost."

"At *any* cost?" the abbot queried. He inclined his head.

The Bishop made eye contact, waited a heartbeat or two, then nodded.

"Hypothetically, Yer Grace, if in the pursuit of this pyxis the herdsman were to yield to an unfortunate accident that would take his life, would not the Church also take possession of Falls Ende?"

Bishop Immers smiled, he'd already had a similar thought. "Aye, such an accident would surely benefit the Church greatly. But, dear Andrew, this must be done quickly, immediately, as I fear the Templars are not patient men and if there is delay, they will attempt to visit Mellester and obtain the pyxis themselves. This must not happen." He gave the abbot a steely look. "On retrieval of this holy relic, I will immediately depart for Campania[2] from Exmouth."

"What of resistance, defenders at the manor?" asked the abbot.

"Fear not, Andrew," smiled Immers, "All knights have departed for Ireland at the bequest of the King." He reached across to the abbot, handed him a bulging purse and rose to leave.

"I will send word to ye on the outcome, and will keep the pyxis here with me, at my side."

"Very well and God's blessings to yer, Andrew." Bishop Immers patted the Abbot's shoulder and quickly left the abbey to return to the rectory.

In Exeter's Cathedral, Sir William was discussing his concerns.

"Then ye don't trust the bishop?" asked Sir Hugh.

---

2   *Pope Alexander III was in exile in Campania, Italy.*

"Nay, I saw it in his eyes, I fear he will attempt to wrest the pyxis from us," said Sir William.

"Then we shouldn't dally, and be on our way."

Sir William rubbed his face with his hands. "We will not wait two days, we leave for this place called Mellester and find Priest Benedict on the morrow. See to it everyone is informed and ready."

CHAPTER FOUR

At Falls Ende, on the land owned by Herdsman Odo Read, villagers toiled tirelessly with the grisly task of slaughtering and disposing of Odo's beloved cows. The sombre mood reflected the seriousness of this calamity and how it would ultimately affect them all.

After each cow was killed, it was dragged into a large pit. A pile of wood, soaked in pitch, lay at the bottom of each hole and then carcasses were carefully stacked on top of each other. Already dead cows filled two entire holes. A third was being prepared, while a fourth pit was being dug. When the wood in each pit was set alight and the carcasses burned, the remains would collapse onto themselves and eventually be covered over with soil.

Charlotte, her mother and sister stood some distance away. With the help of village women and children, they handed out water and food when the men required it. It was hard work, everyone was exhausted and the mood, mournful. Most of all for Odo.

He worked harder than anyone, his distress obvious to all. They weren't just animals to Odo, these cows were his and Charlotte's future and he'd nurtured and cared for them their entire lives. He knew them all, each uniquely familiar and now he'd helped to slaughter and incinerate them. Most were pregnant. His experiment in breeding bigger more productive cows would never be realised. It was devastating; the end of a lifelong dream.

He'd risen early, the eastern sky only just beginning to lighten when he set out alone with his shovel and began to dig the first pit. Word spread, and before the sun had fully risen, more and more volunteers arrived to lend a helping hand. Community spirit was strong, but sombre. Words weren't needed; everyone felt the same and the men and women of Mellester, under the reeve's oversight, came together in this time of need. Odo was heartbroken, this was the most gut wrenching thing he had ever experienced.. His own tears mixed with soil he threw from the hole he dug. They fell on still warm bodies after he'd killed them, and they ran onto the grass that fed and nourished his once healthy herd. He was heartbroken and disconsolate.

Today, Odo's deierie farm was razed, tomorrow, he would join with others and do the same thing all over again to another herd owned by a different farmer. Reeve Petrus estimated that in four days' time all cows within the area would be dead, burned and buried.

Much to everyone's surprise, Mellester's new priest also helped and he worked resolutely. Despite his ailing back, he laboured and sweated selflessly with the rest of them. He informed the reeve that his father raised many cows, and as a boy he'd learned much. "I can toil in the fields as any man can," he offered and lent his body willingly.

At midday he stopped working and gathered the villagers together. The people of Mellester needed no urging and beneath a sunny sky, two hundred men, women and children under the guidance of Priest Benedict prayed for the murrain to end. They prayed to be spared from the pain of starvation and they prayed the sickness wouldn't strike them down.

On Cathal's affirmation, Reeve Petrus announced they must not eat the meat or drink the milk, and certainly, they must not feed other animals from the affected cattle. This provided some argument, but Reeve Petrus, as eloquent as ever, managed to silence all resistance and nay-sayers.

Charlotte kept a close protective eye on her husband. When she saw him struggle and look skywards in despair, she went to his side and offered comfort and emotional support. She felt as he did, but she knew that at this time he needed her strength and resolve, she had to be strong. Without her, he told her later, he would never have made it through that evil day. Odo was sullen and despondent. His lifelong ambition of being the finest deierie farmer in England was over. If not for Charlotte, his life would have ended.

It wasn't just about losing his animals; he felt a responsibility towards others. He could no longer employ Daniel, Mother Rosa, and a dozen other milkmaids. Charlotte no longer worked at her father's Cheese Shoppe, and in replacement, Cheesemaker Gerald hired Mother Rosa's daughter. As Gerald no longer had cow's milk to make cheese, he had no further need of her. The disastrous effect of the murrain rippled through Mellester and other manors like a hurricane and Odo assumed the burden of guilt. He felt the loss and carried the weight on his shoulders.

Four immense columns of smoke billowed up into a darkening sky and Odo stood and watched morosely as tired villagers slowly walked home. Many came to him and said a kind word, others patted him on his back and walked silently away. Tears streaked his filthy face as he looked on, Charlotte at his side, her arm linked through his. They didn't speak, they didn't need to, they each knew how the other felt.

Leaning on his staff, Reeve Petrus stood some distance from the fire and watched Odo and Charlotte. He felt their pain and sadness and vowed he would do all he could to help the gregarious young man he respected and liked so much.

It was decided to keep watch over the burning carcasses lest someone try to drag one away for food. Reeve Petrus felt it his duty to remain with Odo until the fire took hold and once everything was well alight, they could leave.

Charlotte shivered in the cool early evening air. "I will retrieve my cloak," she told Odo. He'd decided to dig the pits as far away from the village as possible and it was some distance to walk back to their home.

"Let me, I will go, stay near the fire," he volunteered. Odo stared at the spade he held, and in disgust threw it aside. Without another word he began to trudge back down the gently sloping field towards their home. Unsure, Charlotte was thinking of going after him.

"Let him," offered the reeve as Odo walked away. "He has some thinking to do."

"My heart breaks fer him, but this," she pointed to the fire that slowly consumed the carcasses, "this is so tragic and I'm deeply worried about him."

"Aye, but knowing Odo, he will use this time and as always, bounce back," said the reeve doing his best to offer comfort.

Charlotte shivered again. She was unwilling to stand too close to the fire. The smell of pitch and burning flesh made her feel queasy.

As Odo approached their home, he noticed a flickering light from a candle seep from a gap beneath the door when there shouldn't have been any. Someone, a villager was inside his home. He barged inside and stopped in his tracks.

Inside, stood four men, ruffians, outlaws; they paused in surprise as he entered. "What do ye want, out with ye?" he shouted in anger. On a normal day he may have reacted differently but today wasn't normal and already at near emotional breaking point, he snapped. With no concern for his own safety, he lunged at the nearest sneering scoundrel. Caught by surprise, the ruffian fell to the floor and Odo, in a blind rage, began pounding him with his fists before he was dragged away and kicked repeatedly.

Odo curled up into a ball to protect himself from the beating he received. The ruffians, believing he had no fight left in him, finally paused. It was all Odo needed. Again, with no regard for his own well-being, he launched himself at the nearest man, grabbed him by the legs and pulled him to the ground. In a fury, he hammered at the man's face and landed blow after painful blow.

They tried to pull him off, but Odo recklessly threw his body from side to side and kept moving, each time managing to slip from their grasp. At one point he slammed into the table almost knocking it over. The thick candle slid down the table to land on the dry rushes that carpeted the floor.

Odo was young, in superb physical shape and remarkably strong, but it wasn't enough. He couldn't fight four men and the short brawl ended when he was brutally struck across the head by a chair. He lay bleeding from a nasty head wound and mindless. During the mêlée, all attention was focused on Odo and not the candle which lay on its side. Already the dried rushes on the floor began to burn.

"He's barmy!" cried a ruffian as he spat out a broken tooth and wiped blood from his nose. He gave Odo another kick for good measure.

"But where's the box? We gotta find the box."

"We've looked everywhere…"

"An now we 'ave a fire." The ruffian spat more blood from his mouth.

They all turned to look at the rushes as small flames reached upwards. "Leave it, let 'im burn, bastard deserves it."

One outlaw saw the Welsh longbow in the corner, his eyes widened. "I'm taking that bow wif me. Is worth a bit it is, not leavin it 'ere to burn."

"Aye, the box ain't 'ere, we looked everywhere. We'd better scarper b'fore someone comes."

The flames licked higher and begun to take hold.

Charlotte stood with her arms wrapped around her shoulders. "Where is he?"

Reeve Petrus stared into the roaring flames.

"He should've been back by now," she said with worry.

Petrus turned away from the fire and took a few steps and casually looked back down towards Odo and Charlotte's home. Still dazzled by the brightness of the fire, all he saw was darkness. He held his arm to shield his eyes from the firelight and looked again. He thought he saw flames. He rubbed his eyes and peered into the darkness. "Fire! Charlotte, yer house is aflame."

Charlotte ran, and with the help of his staff, Reeve Petrus did his best, but a painful quick walk was all he could manage. Within seconds Charlotte was gone.

Alerted by smoke, villagers began throwing buckets of dirt and water over burning walls. Flames spread quickly, and neighbouring thatched rooves began to smoulder and then ignited in a flash. When Charlotte arrived, the village was in pandemonium.

"Where's Odo?" she yelled to anyone close.

It was Huntsman Seth who ran up to her.

"Where's Odo?" she repeated.

"I last saw him in the field."

No one else had seen him either.

"He may be inside!" she cried. "And we need to turnout the animals."

The bleating of sheep, goats and the frightened whinnies of horses could be heard over the panicked yelling of villagers.

The flames and heat near the front of the house and doorway were too intense and Seth couldn't approach safely.

"The rear!" she shouted.

"See to the animals, Charlotte, I'll find Odo." Before she could protest, he sprinted away.

She wasn't going to listen to him. She needed to get to Odo! Thankfully the fire had yet to spread to the rear part of the house, and the animals, although showing the first signs of panic, were for the time being relatively safe. Her immediate concern was for her husband. She went to chase after Seth when a hand firmly grasped her shoulder.

"The animals, Charlotte!" said the reeve sternly. He pushed past her and went to help the huntsman, leaving her alone with her fear.

Charlotte paused in indecision; she wanted to find her husband, but Seth and the reeve were near the door and blocked access into her house. She turned away from them as one of the horses kicked savagely at a stall. Simultaneously the sheep and goats began to bleat and climb atop each other in growing panic. Sobbing, she reluctantly ran back towards the rear of the byre towards the pens that housed them, quickly unfastened the gate and released them into the paddock. She turned towards the horses while Seth and the reeve searched for Odo.

The roar of flames grew louder as the fire took hold. Outside, villagers screamed, their cries of alarm and distress swelling above the crackling blaze that was taking hold inside the house.

Seth paused a moment as flames began to lick beneath the stout wooden door. Already the heat was intense. With his arm he protected his face as he raised a leg to launch a powerful kick. With a mighty crash the door flew open and fed by the draught, the fire surged. The far wall and roof were consumed by hungry flames; already bits of falling debris began cascading down. He kicked burning remains away from the door and entered, the reeve a reassuring step behind. He found Odo sprawled on the floor, his hair singed as small pieces of burning remains and ash fell from the roof and landed on his back. He lay unmoving, like a bloodied corpse.

"He's here, I found him!" Seth yelled, then coughed as smoke threatened to overcome him.

Charlotte screamed. "Odo!" she cried and began to run towards them from the other side of the byre.

The reeve knew Charlotte only too well and knew she would come. He risked a quick look over his shoulder "Stay away, Charlotte. It's too dangerous!" he warned, shouting above the roar of hungry flames.

Amica began violently kicking in his stall as smoke began to fill the byre through the open doorway. Charlotte paused as Sally also began tossing her head in agitation. The reeve and Seth were now inside and she couldn't see anything but fire. Reluctantly she turned her attention to the stallion. His eyes looked wild, he was terrified. He kicked again, splintering wood.

Showing no outward sign of the fear she felt, Charlotte carefully approached the frightened stallion and spoke calmly and slowly. His ears twitched at the familiar sound of her voice. Cautiously she undid the gate latch, pushed it open and quickly stood back. With no hesitation, the panicked courser charged out of the byre, the sound of his hooves lost to the roar of the blaze. Next she released Sally who lumbered out, following Amica to safety. Now that the animals were out of harm's way, she could finally turn her attention back to Odo.

Thick smoke billowed into the byre, and flames, fed by the draught from the open door, continued to leap up the walls devouring everything in its path. Ignoring minor burns from glowing embers, ash and flaming remains that fell on them like a deadly rain, Seth and Reeve Petrus, coughing and hacking from smoke inhalation, half stumbled, carried and dragged Odo from the wreckage that had once been Odo and Charlotte's modest home.

Charlotte saw Seth and the reeve carry Odo awkwardly from the house. He was out! She felt the relief, but *how badly was he hurt*? Her heart pounded and blood coursed through her veins - nothing else mattered and no one or anything would prevent her from helping Odo; her thoughts were only of him. Overcoming fear, and with no concern for her own safety, she ran from the horse's stall towards the Seth and the reeve.

This time she wasn't sent away. With her help, they managed to escape the inferno and safely move Odo into the field behind the byre and burning homes. His face was caked in blood, his clothes smouldered, his hair was singed and he was still mindless. Odo didn't move, but he was breathing and at least he was alive.

Galvanised into action, and fearful the fire would spread, frenzied villagers began to throw water and sand on raging flames from outside. More and more people came to assist, they ran in all directions, colliding with one another spilling water and achieving little. It was confusion and fear; it was havoc.

With Odo out of harm's way, the urgency was to prevent further damage and stop the fire from destroying the entire village. Reeve Petrus and Seth left Charlotte alone with Odo, and went to assist with fighting the fire. The reeve expertly coordinated people and assigned tasks. Through the organised efforts of the villagers under his direction, the fire was quickly brought under control and to everyone's relief, extinguished.

Three homes were completely destroyed, including Odo and Charlotte's, but fortunately, their byre was only partially burned. Other than Odo, no one was hurt. The harsh reality and extent of the damage would be revealed by the sun's early morn light.

Reeve Petrus was angry. He'd tried to piece together what happened that caused the fire and all he learned was that four men, strangers, were seen leaving Mellester after hearing a commotion from Odo and Charlotte's home. Including Charlotte, no one knew anything more.

Priest Benedict, covered in soot, insisted Odo be brought to the rectory where he could be cleaned and his injuries assessed. Charlotte assisted as best she could and with the help of the priest, tended to Odo's severe head wound. Much to Charlotte's worry, he hadn't stirred.

Cathal was nowhere to be found.

Throughout the night the four large fires in the field continued to burn, the smell of burned meat and pitch occasionally wafting down to the village, an unkind reminder of an uncertain future. The village fire could have been worse, and thankfully many homes were spared. Regardless, Reeve Petrus was beside himself in outrage at what had happened.

CHAPTER FIVE

A young man-at-arms found Reeve Petrus supervising the repairing of damaged homes. The three burned cruck houses, including Odo and Charlotte's, were completely destroyed and already men pulled charred debris from the structures to transport it away in wagons.

"Reeve, ye need to come," instructed the man-at-arms. "There are knights here, they are at the rectory."

"What knights?" he questioned. The reeve knew all knights in the area were now well on their way to Wales. "Can't be," he added.

"Well these knights have a red cross on their front, don't they."

If they wore a red cross on their mantle and over their mail, then the reeve knew exactly who they were. "Templars."

"What?"

"Templars."

"Well, there'd be six of them wif sergeants, reeve, and they'd be surrounding the rectory."

Templars? What would Templars want in Mellester? thought the reeve. He left instructions with the men demolishing the homes, and with the man-at-arms at his side, stomped off as quickly as he could towards the rectory at the other end of the village. He was in a very disagreeable mood.

Just as the man-at-arms told him, he saw the rectory surrounded by armed men dressed entirely in black. He knew that only full Templar

Knights wore the white mantle with the red cross that symbolised martyrdom. The men outside the rectory wore all black; they were Templar sergeants. "Go back to the manor, assemble everyone but remain there until ye hear from me, understand?" instructed the reeve to the young soldier.

"Should we send a message to Sir Dain?" enquired the soldier.

Prior to leaving for Ireland, Sir Gweir assigned Sir Dain as military commander during his absence.

The reeve shook his head. "Nay, but have a rider ready, just in case."

"Aye, as yer command, reeve," the young man replied, and eager to assist, ran off.

Reeve Petrus walked towards the entrance to the rectory when a Templar sergeant stepped in front, blocking his access.

"What is this? Move aside!" demanded the reeve indignantly, his patience wearing thin.

"Yer can't be goin' in there," informed the sergeant.

"I'll go in there if I choose, make way!" The reeve took in the appearance of the Templar sergeant. Although not yet knights, these sergeants were still formidable. They were all seasoned soldiers and he needed to be cautious. The sergeant had his hand on the hilt of his sheathed sword.

"Step away, Sergeant!" commanded the reeve in his most authoritative voice. He took a step forward and he had no intention of stopping

With speed the sergeant unsheathed his sword and moved back a step to create space. Petrus saw another sergeant making his way towards them also unsheathing his sword. He didn't have the time or the will to stand here jawing or sparring with these men.

It was unlikely that the sergeant had ever heard of Petrus Bodkin. If he had, then he may have chosen a more sensible course of action.

The reeve wasn't wearing a sword; the only weapon was his staff and the sergeant incorrectly surmised that the man before him used the staff only as a walking aid and therefore didn't pose a threat.

Before the sergeant could react, the staff spun upwards in a blur and connected with the elbow of his arm that wielded the sword. It was a single hard blow and delivered so quickly the sergeant couldn't react. The nerves of the elbow were struck hard. Three things happened simultaneously; the sergeant howled in pain, his fingers opened involuntarily and his sword clattered to the ground. Reeve Petrus pushed past the stunned sergeant and entered the rectory only to surprise the Templar knight standing inside near the door.

Ten pair of eyes turned as one to the unexpected entrance of Reeve Petrus Bodkin.

The reeve took in the scene before him. Odo lay on a cot with Charlotte at his side. The new priest, Benedict, stood near Charlotte and faced an older, senior Templar knight. Another five templars were spread out in the crowded room. The one near the door where Petrus just stepped through wore an astonished look of surprise and was about to draw his sword.

"What is going on here!" demanded the reeve before anyone could speak.

"Petrus?" exclaimed a voice from the shadows.

The reeve turned to the voice and a Templar knight stepped into the light. Reeve Petrus recognised the man immediately. "Sir Hugh!"

Charlotte remained silent and appeared nervous in the presence of six

Templar Knights.

Before anyone could say a word, the sergeant, clutching his elbow entered the rectory.

"Wait outside!" commanded the older, senior knight curtly.

The sergeant gave the reeve a bitter look before obeying the order and returning to his position guarding the rectory .

"This is my old friend, Petrus Bodkin. We trained together many years ago; he's one of the finest swordsman I've ever met," said Sir Hugh Paduinan, addressing the senior knight and introducing him to Petrus.

They cautiously shook hands.

"No longer, Hugh, an injury took care of that." Petrus pushed his foot out. "I was kicked by a horse, damaged m' knee. T'was the end for me."

Sir Hugh stepped towards the reeve and they embraced.

"Ye must have some skill, the sergeants outside were given orders not to allow anyone to enter," said Sir William. He gave the reeve careful scrutiny.

"Aye, and he wouldn't be the first to misjudge me, methinks not the last either." The reeve noticed the Sir William looked extremely tense. "And as my lord, Sir Gweir, rides with the King, then the manor falls under my responsibility. I am the reeve, how can I be of assistance to ye?"

Sir William took a big breath. "Our business is with Priest Benedict and concerns the Church, not this fine manor. Perhaps if ye and the woman would kindly wait outside, we will conclude our affairs and be on our way."

The reeve looked towards Odo who appeared to be still benumbed. Charlotte, he noticed looked tired and stressed. He nodded. The last thing he wanted was to find himself in a dispute between Templar knights and the

Church. "Very well. Come Charlotte, a bit of fresh air will work wonders on ye."

Feeling the tenseness in the room, Charlotte didn't argue, and quietly left with the reeve. "How does Odo fair?" he asked once they were outside.

A few villagers gathered near the rectory to watch the unusual sight of Templars in their village. They kept their distance, wary of unfriendly sergeants who stood guard outside.

"He's hasn't stirred, he lays there as if he's asleep. I don't know what to do," she replied wiping her eyes. "Have ye seen Cathal?"

"Nay, haven't seen him since yesterday morn. I will find him and have him tend to Odo."

She nodded and wiped her eyes.

"And of these men inside, did ye hear anything about what they want? Why are they here?"

"Nay, but they don't know who Priest Benedict is."

Just then the door opened and Sir Hugh stuck his head out. "Petrus, could ye return with the lady?"

Petrus nodded. "Well now, what's this all about then?" he asked as he entered the room.

"Be seated," instructed Sir William when they were inside.

"I'll stand," replied the reeve. He nodded to Charlotte to sit.

Once seated, Sir William took another chair, dragged it close to her and sat down. "No need to be frightened, lass, we mean yer no harm. But Priest Benedict tells me ye may be able to help us."

Charlotte looked back to Odo laying on the cot. He hadn't moved. She risked a quick glance at the reeve. He smiled, offering reassurance.

"How, milord?" she replied nervously.

The Templar knight commander nodded. "I believe a day or so ago, Priest Benedict brought ye and yer husband a pyxis, a box."

Charlotte looked thoughtful and said nothing.

"It is of extreme importance to the Church that we find this pyxis, do ye know where it is?" continued the knight. In reflex, the other knights stepped closer, eager to hear Charlottes reply.

"Is at home. Why do ye want it? It belongs to Odo, is from his father, Oswald."

"Charlotte, the box isn't there, there are no remains of it, the box is gone," replied the reeve. "Everything burned."

"What is this?" cried Sir William. "Then where is it?"

"One moment, Sir William." The reeve's voice contained an edge Charlotte had never heard before. "Last night there was a fire. Odo, who lays there," the reeve pointed, "was struck by four outlaws and his house set alight. I saw the box the evening before last, and it sat on the table–"

"As did I," confirmed Priest Benedict.

"Aye, and that was where Odo left it – on the table," added Charlotte.

"And I never saw the remains of it when I was there this morning. Or it was stolen by the outlaws."

Sir William stroked his grey beard. "We need to look at the house, or what is left of it, and search thoroughly for it."

"Why do ye want the pyxis? It belongs to Herdsman Odo Read," asked the reeve. "Yer can't just come here and do as yer please. Ye'd be no better than the robbers who hurt Odo!" Petrus wasn't having a good day, and he wasn't happy with the attitude of the Templars at all.

"Forgive me, Reeve, we have been searching for the pyxis for two years, we tend to become rather obsessed with it," replied the knight commander. "May we search through the home and try to locate the pyxis or its remains?"

The reeve was about to reply when Charlotte spoke first. "Ye are welcome to look for it, as yer say, and if yer do find it, then remember, it belongs not to ye, it belongs to Odo, and he's poorly right now. Do yer understand me, milord?"

In spite of his foul mood, Petrus couldn't help but grin.

"Of course," Sir William dipped his head.

"Reeve Petrus, could ye show them the house? I will remain with Odo."

"Aye, best yer stay here, Charlotte."

Led by Reeve Petrus, six templars and four sergeants walked through Mellester village. The remaining two sergeants stayed with their horses at the rectory. Intimidated by the sight, people made way for the procession. The reputation of the religious order of fighting monks was legendary and word quickly spread. The men who strode through the village were hardened, tough soldiers and Mellester's residents were wary and untrusting.

Sir William Marshal, 1st Earl of Pembroke walked beside the reeve. He could see the unusual activity of men removing charred debris. "What happened here?" he asked.

"Last evening, strangers, the brigands we spoke of earlier, ransacked the house of Odo Read. No one knows what happened, because the young man on the cot in the rectory is still mindless. The brigands set fire to Odo and Charlotte's home and fled. They left him to die inside the burning house. Another villager and I were able to drag him to safety, but alas, he suffered a severe blow to the head and has not yet recovered."

"So ye do not know the reason why these men came?"

Reeve Petrus stopped to face the templar commander, "Has your visit here anything to do with these brigands?"

"We are not familiar with any brigands and have never been here before; we came from the north and stopped first at Exeter–"

"Bishop Immers?" interrupted the reeve.

Sir William nodded. He turned away and looked into the distance, as he considered the bishop's duplicity.

The Templars decided not to wait for Bishop Immers to recall the priest and they departed Exeter early the following morning. It appeared as though the bishop was being deceitful, as he predicted.

"Is the bishop involved in this?" asked the reeve as if reading his thoughts, his voice again took on a hard edge.

The knight turned to the reeve. "I'd hoped this had nothing to do with him, but now I am in doubt."

They resumed their walk and ahead of them they saw the destruction. Three cruck houses were completely demolished, and a few others had their rooves damaged. Already men clambered over them replacing thatch.

"This is Odo's home, or where it once stood," the reeve pointed. Most of the byre that was once attached to the cruck house still stood.

"Where was the pyxis?" asked Sir William.

Petrus walked towards the hearth and stopped. "Here, this was where the pyxis sat on the table." The charred remains of the table were scattered at his feet.

Sir William indicated for his men to begin searching. The reeve stepped closer to where the corner of the house was, looked around and scratched his head.

"Something ails ye, reeve?" asked Sir William, seeing Petrus looking puzzled.

"Aye, Odo had a yew bow and quiver, it is not here, and there are no embers. The entire bow would not have burned."

"Why would a herdsman have a yew bow?"

"Ah yes, Sir William, yer see, Odo Read is not an ordinary herdsman as ye will come to find out. Do yer see out there?" The reeve pointed towards the field where Amica was grazing.

"The black courser?" asked Sir William.

Petrus smiled, "How many herdsman do ye know who own such a fine beast."

Sir William scratched his beard. "A magnificent animal. I too would like a stallion such as this. Why would a herdsman—"

"The courser is a killer and Odo alone can ride him."

"But what of the fires that burn yonder?" Sir William pointed to the still smouldering remains of the incinerated cow carcasses.

"We have a cattle sickness, Steppe Murrain, and we had to cull Odo's herd. That is what burns."

"Times are tough for Mellester," answered the templar. "I am woebegone, the young herdsman suffers so. He has lost his cows, his house—"

"And the pyxis," finished the reeve.

Sir Hugh approached both men and shook his head. "Nothing, there is naught here that suggests the pyxis burned."

"Then God smiles upon us," answered Sir William. He crossed himself. "The pyxis survives and someone has taken it. It seems the outlaws who caused this wilful damage may yet possess it. Have the sergeants search the entire area where these homes once stood, then we will return to the rectory. I wish to ask the priest a question or two about the bishop.

CHAPTER SIX

They were all inside the cramped space of the rectory. Priest Benedict was outside supervising the repairs to the church roof. Sir William was standing over Odo looking at his head wound and minor burns. "I have seen trauma such as this, and by God's grace, they survive. Fear not m'dear, I am sure your man will be hearty and hale. We will pray for his recovery."

Charlotte looked up and offered the Templar commander a smile. "Thank ye, Odo needs all the help he can get." She turned back to her patient and looked thoughtful. After a moment of silence she twisted around to face Sir William directly. "Why is this box important to ye? It contained only a letter from Oswald to Odo. The letter has no value to ye."

Reeve Petrus listened intently. Her question was also on his lips.

Sir William looked at Charlotte and saw a beautiful young woman; he saw her intelligence and strength hidden beneath naivety and innocence. The young injured herdsman was blessed to have such a fine lass.

The search for the pyxis was exhausting and consuming and for two years they'd travelled from the east, across Europe to Scotland, then indirectly south to Mellester. Their mission was secret, known only to themselves and even His Holiness the Pope was not totally aware of what they sought. He couldn't divulge all, but it would be immoral to seek advantage of her and lie. There were enough people telling untruths throughout the land, he didn't want to be another. The people of Mellester were good, honest and hardworking. In spite of all that happened here, it would be wrong to be deceptive and forswear to them. He shifted his gaze to the big man standing nearby. Sir Hugh spoke highly of the reeve. In the short time they'd been in Mellester, he'd come to like him. He was honest and disciplined and cared a lot for the people of this manor. That much was obvious. The lord here was fortuitous to have such a trusted reeve.

Sir William weighed his options carefully. He dragged a chair over and sat down close to her. "The pyxis contains a clue to something of great importance to the Church and Christianity, perhaps more than anything else in existence. It, however, contains nothing of benefit to ye, except only to us, for it is just a piece of information. If ye found it by accident, it would have no value, but to us it would complete a piece of a puzzle. For this, we would offer ye a fine reward."

"But it contained only Oswald's letter," repeated Charlotte.

"The letter belongs to ye, we seek not that letter. The pyxis contains more."

"And the bishop knows this?" asked Reeve Petrus.

"He knows only that we seek the pyxis, not what it contains. But now I suspect he believes that the pyxis contains more, only because he knows we seek it."

"The bishop is a conniving leech, if he can line his pockets, then he will," offered Petrus.

"Aye, I agree. Bring me, the priest, Benedict," commanded Sir William to his men.

Priest Benedict stood in front of Sir William.

"Tell me about Bishop Immers, what type of man is he? Does he serve God Almighty before himself, or does his piousness extend only to his purse?" asked Sir William.

"He is a man of God, an apostle–"

"Enough! That is not what I seek. Ye will offer me the truth or I will have ye hung from the rafters of yer church if yer lie to me!" Sir William's eyes blazed. No one doubted his threat was real.

Charlotte and Reeve Petrus watched apprehensively.

The priest looked down at his feet to collect himself, then looked up and squarely met the gaze of the Templar knight. "I find Bishop Immers an odious man and as ye say, interested only in his exalted position. I have found him to be covetous and devious."

Sir William nodded. "Thank ye, before God, the truth is best, fer ye *will* be judged. But what ye say is what I also believe. Could the bishop have sent outlaws here?"

"Through the abbot," replied Priest Benedict. "Abbot Andrew avails himself to the bishops bidding, this way the bishop's hands remain unsoiled."

Sir William turned to Sir Hugh, "When the bishop insisted on a delay of two days, that was merely a ploy. While we remained resting in Exeter, the bishop sent men here." He faced the priest again. "Tell me, were ye tasked with visiting other manors before arriving here with the pyxis?"

The priest shook his head.

"Then we need to return to Exeter and speak with the bishop. He must have the pyxis. We leave immediately." He turned as if to leave.

"Wait!"

All heads turned to Charlotte. She slowly stood and looked up at Sir William; if she felt intimidated she didn't show it. "The pyxis does not belong to ye or the Church, it belongs to Odo. If ye find it, then ye have a moral and noble obligation to return it here before ye do anything. Odo will decide what to do with it."

"But he is sick, and—"

"Then ye had better pray for a quick recovery, had ye not?" Charlotte's cheeks glowed red.

The reeve knew what the Templar was thinking. "If I may say more?"

Sir William was displeased. Seldom had he been spoken to in such a way, yet the young peasant woman was correct. And now the reeve...

"I showed ye his courser outside, ye remember?"

Sir William nodded, curious to where this conversation was headed.

"Then ye know Odo Read is not yer normal herdsman. What ye don't know, is Odo Read has King Henry's ear."

Sir William's jaw dropped.

"Aye, the Church tried to rob Odo before and failed. Be warned, Sir William, if ye act as Bishop Immers has done, the King will hear of it. The thing about Odo Read, he doesn't listen and he doesn't accept the word 'no.'"

Sir William looked away from Petrus and Charlotte and turned to stare at the unmoving form on the cot. "Let us all pray he recovers quickly."

Charlotte and the reeve exchanged a fleeting glance.

"We shall take our leave and rest assured, will return here with the pyxis when we retrieve it," said Sir William to them both. "Ye have my word as a devoted man of God."

Priest Benedict watched. The conversation was like a revelation to him, and now he understood why he was sent to Mellester. Bishop Immers wanted him to report back on happenings here at the manor. Now he felt morally conflicted. *He had a duty as a priest to obey the bishop and minister to the people, but when the bishop was corrupt...*

A short time later the Templars rode out of Mellester and headed towards Exeter. Benedict exhaled. "As a military order of monks, I find a self-righteous imperiousness to them."

Reeve Petrus nodded. "I agree, don't trust the sods."

"Will they return with the box?" asked Charlotte.

"I hope so, not much we can do if they don't." The reeve studied the priest. "Ye have no love for the bishop, do ye?"

Benedict looked uncomfortable. "As a simple priest there is little I can do but obey my bishop, I serve at his pleasure. But nay, I care not for the man. I am happy to be as far removed from him as possible, but he makes it difficult."

"Why?" Charlotte asked.

"Because he requires me to administer to the good people of Mellester and report to him on anything that involves Falls Ende and Odo."

"Then ye serve the bishop?"

"All priests serve their bishop, but in my heart I serve God, and will always do what is right by him. The bishop only makes it more difficult for me."

"Then ye are a spie[3]?" asked Charlotte.

---

3   *Spy*

"I am happy if the bishop believes this, but … as an intelligencer, how do I report to him and not abuse the trust from the people here, including ye and Odo?"

"Then we can only hope the Templars inform the Pope about Bishop Immers," added the reeve.

Odo groaned.

"Odo!" cried Charlotte as she returned to the cot where he lay.

He didn't stir, the groan nothing more than an involuntary noise. He remained still, unmoving.

Petrus stepped up to her and placed a hand on her shoulder, "He will heal. Despair not for Odo is hale and it will take more than a blow to his head to stop him."

Charlotte looked up, her eyes glistened.

"I will leave ye in the care of Priest Benedict. I have to ensure Herdsman Garrick is culling his cows." The reeve paused. "Charlotte, where will ye sleep, with yer family?"

"I think it best Odo and Charlotte remain here. I will bed down in the church, there is a place I can sleep," generously offered the priest.

"Aye, that be pitying of yer," nodded the reeve.

"Thank ye kindly, Priest Benedict," Charlotte replied.

While the reeve ensured all Herdsman Garrick's cows were culled, men began rebuilding the cruck homes destroyed in the fire. For Charlotte, the night was long and lonely. Odo didn't stir and she was becoming more worried. There was little she could do other than tend to his burns and be there for him when he woke.

The next morning saw no change when Reeve Petrus briefly came to visit. Before he said farewell, he promised to return again later.

CHAPTER SEVEN

Bishop Immers' face soured at the news. He drummed his fingers on the armrest of the chair he sat on in the abbey. "Send them back out," he demanded. "I want the pyxis. It must be there somewhere and the Church must have it."

Abbot Andrew inclined his head. "Of course, Yer Grace. And of the Templars? What do ye expect they will do, return here? Surely when they fail to locate it, they will seek ye."

"Aye, that they will." His fingers continued to tap the armrest. "I will plead innocence; they have no cause to suspect me. Although it seems they trust me not."

Abbot Andrew raised his eyebrows in surprise.

"They didn't wait here for the two days but left early in the morn," added Immers with some petulance.

"Ye believe they will accept yer word and happily be on their way after they speak with ye?" asked the abbot.

The tapping stopped. "I have done nothing, my word as bishop will suffice. If they persist with unpleasantness, then I can always refer them to ye, can I not?"

The abbot fought to control his reaction. "As yer wish, Yer Grace. I'm sure yer actions always serve the best interests of the Church."

"And where are the brigands now? In an alehouse? Whoring?"

snapped Immers, his mood still sour.

"Nay, they wait for instructions, Yer Grace. They will be informed to return to Mellester, as ye request."

He stroked the fine jewels inlaid into the pectoral that hung from around his neck with almost sensual pleasure as he considered his options. "Do ye truly believe what the Templars seek is seminal? Or am I wasting coin for, for what?"

The abbot thought carefully before replying. "If the Templars have twelve men searching all over England and the known world for … uh, something, then Yer Grace, I expect it has immense worth. Trust yer feelings."

Bishop Immers released the pectoral and began tapping on the armrest again. "How many men can you find to go back to Mellester?" Before the abbot could reply, Immers continued. "It would be best to have enough capable men to search for the pyxis in every cruck in Mellester and then prevent the Templars from taking it once they find it."

The abbot swallowed. "Yer Grace, ye would require many men, perhaps … two score, and such an undertaking would be costly, would it not?"

The bishop stopped his tapping. "We may never have such an opportunity again to return such a prized relic to the Church. The Templars seem to act independently of the Church and if they retrieve it first, rest assured they will keep it. If I bring such a grand prize to His Holiness, then surely he would be eternally grateful." Bishop Immers met the gaze of the abbot. "See to it, make sure there are enough men and send them to Mellester immediately, before the Templars return."

Abbot Andrew dipped his head, "As ye wish Yer Grace."

"The herdsman, what became of him?"

"He may have perished in the fire. Seems the young man was untypically violent and required subjugating. He was left benumbed on the floor of his cruck as fire ravaged his home."

"Is he dead, or isn't he?" Immers snapped losing patience.

The abbot shrugged.

Bishop Immers stood and glared at his old friend. "Then I suggest ye find out!"

"Of course, Yer Grace."

"And as this is costing me more than a penny or two, it would serve this diocese well to obtain title on Falls Ende." He raised an eyebrow.

"I concur, Yer Grace," smiled the abbot.

"There are no knights there; the manor is unattended except by a handful of aging men-at-arms, cripples and boys. With all the men ye will send, they'll have no problem searching every cruck in the entire village."

The abbot nodded in servile acquiescence.

The bishop stood to leave. "See to it, Andrew!"

Charlotte was studying Odo carefully. His breathing was irregular and his eyes seemed to move, but why wouldn't he wake, she couldn't fathom. During the night he cried out, but wouldn't respond when she talked to him. She'd stayed awake the whole night and was exhausted.

She decided to close her eyes just for a minute but she must have fallen asleep and never heard Reeve Petrus enter. His voice startled her. When she turned her head to face him, she saw Cathal standing beside him looking disturbed.

"Any change?" asked the reeve as Cathal approached Odo's cot.

"He yelled once during the night, nothing more," she said wearily. "Cathal, why won't he wake?"

The Irishman chewed his lip for a moment before bending down to inspect the wound on Odo's head. "I warned him of an ill wind, did I not? Ye both were there, why did ye not listen?" he shook his head in pity. "Now look at him."

"Cathal, Odo needs yer help, please," she pleaded.

"Ye can bring in a barber, have him look at the scalp, maybe bone is pressing onto his head," he offered.

"Is that what ye suggest?"

"Nay, it would kill him. There are no barbers here who I would allow to do that." Cathal moved a chair and sat in front of Charlotte. "The danger now is not from the injury, it is from humours. The imbalance grows stronger each day."

"I don't understand, he doesn't look worse."

"Is he eating food and drinking water?" he asked.

She shook her head.

The longer he goes without water the more danger he is in."

"Then what can I do to help him, because he won't swallow water or food."

Cathal leaned forward and gently took Charlotte's hands and placed them on Odo's hand. "Wet his lips, put a few drops of water in his mouth.

Gently rub his hands, his arms and face, touch him constantly. Talk to him, whisper to him of things where ye both laughed and made ye happy. Do not stop."

"Can he hear me and feel my touch?"

"Aye, I believe he can. It will help him to wake. Ye too, Petrus, ye are a friend and can talk to him too when she sleeps."

"What do I have to say to 'im? Talking about cows will make him miserable."

The Irishman fixed the reeve with a virulent look. "Talk to him of good times and remind him of the laughter ye shared."

"Will he live?" she asked.

"Methinks he will." Cathal nodded, offered a rare smile and sat back in the chair.

Charlotte was softly rubbing Odo's hands when Cathal began to sing. It was the same song he'd sung to Odo and the reeve in France, and one he knew Odo loved.

She listened as his soft melodious voice filled the rectory. Reeve Petrus leaned against the wall, folded his arms and closed his eyes. She turned back to Odo, currently lost in the dark recesses of his mind.

Cathal's voice was smooth and almost haunting; he swayed in a gentle rhythm as he sung of fair-headed maidens and eyes that sparkled blue. Her own eyes welled, and she longed to stare into Odo's eyes that shone with the warmth and love she knew all too well. Her fingertips gently stroked his arms then moved up to caress his face and she knew within her heart he could feel her and hear Cathal's silky voice. She bent low, her lips inches from his, her breath offering him life as he breathed her in. A tear spilled onto his cheek and as she gently brushed it away, Odo's closed eyes twitched. Another tear fell, and with Cathal's lilting ballad filling her with emotion, she lay her head on his chest and unable to hold back any longer, she cried. It began with a single sob, and within moments it became a torrent of pent up helplessness and frustration. Her back heaved as she buried herself into Odo's unresponsive body.

Reeve Petrus opened his eyes and as he watched her, he fought to control his own feelings that threatened to overwhelm him. He blinked away a tear as Cathal's song came to an end, and the sound of Charlotte's sobbing filled the room. Neither man was sure what to do. Petrus glanced at Cathal and inclined his head towards the door, a subtle signal to allow her privacy. Quietly, they made their way to leave.

"Don't go, please," Charlotte implored as she composed herself. With one hand she wiped her eyes and stood, but still held Odo's hand firmly and looked to both men earnestly.

Curiously, the reeve and Cathal waited. They could see she was struggling to collect herself.

"Odo and I spoke of this and we want to see this done," she said. Her voice gaining in strength. "Cathal, how long before we can have cows back on our land?"

"Imbolg, Saint Brigid's day, when the equinox falls upon us once more, the murrain will have passed and it will be safe."

Reeve Petrus nodded in agreement at Cathal's estimated nine months.

Charlotte took a calming breath. "Very well." She looked to the reeve. "I will have Daniel begin to make a fence, we will assign a third of the land at Falls Ende for the people who will suffer because of this pestilence.

Without money, they will likely become hungry and need food. They may use our land to grow late crops so that they will not be without. Is there still time to plant?"

"They will have no coin to pay yer, Charlotte," he responded.

"Nay, we do not want coin. This is to help them, the land is theirs to use until the spring equinox. We have no use for all the land until we can obtain a new herd."

"Aye, there are some late crops to plant." He paused for a heartbeat or two. "This is kindly of ye, Charlotte."

"Is Odo's idea, this is what he wants. If any villagers do not have coin to pay for seed, we will give them coin to pay for them. It is our wish."

"I will see to it. Again, ye are charitable, Charlotte." Reeve Petrus smiled and stepped outside.

Cathal glanced at Odo, turned back to Charlotte, held her gaze a moment as if he wanted to say something, then he followed the reeve.

"Is there anything ye can do? Ye must have something in yer bag of tricks … can't yer give the poor lad one of yer special potions?" asked the reeve once he was outside.

Cathal looked skywards

"Have yer nothing to say?"

"What can I do? He can't eat or drink." He shook his head and walked away scratching his head.

The six Templar knights and sergeants stopped near the outskirts of Exeter to water their horses before continuing on to the cathedral. As the sergeants tended to their animals, the knights discussed their plan.

"I find the bishop to be contemptible," volunteered Sir Hugh.

"As do I," replied Sir William. "We have come far, we are tired and now we are so close. Bishop Immers is our final obstacle."

Heads nodded in agreement.

Sir Hugh looked perplexed. "Why would the priest give the pyxis to the herdsman? Is this not irregular?"

There was a moment of silence as the knights pondered the question.

Sir William's eyes opened wide. "Of course... We have been so fixated on the pyxis we ignored the obvious."

All heads turned to him.

"The herdsman Odo Read is the son of Brother Odo Brus."

"But he lives just as a simple herdsman..." stated Sir Hugh.

"Nay, not just a simple herdsman, far from it," added Sir William.

"And does the bishop have the pyxis? Do we know this, are we sure?" asked Sir Gualdim Pais.

"Alas, we do not," offered the commander. "Methinks a conversation with the abbot before we speak to the bishop might be wise." Sir William signalled to his sergeant to ready his destrier. "We should not tarry, let us first visit Abbot Andrew."

A short time later all twelve men approached Exeter Cathedral. Rather than enter, they skirted around the rear towards the abbey. As customary, the sergeants started to dismount and secure their horses before the knights entered the building. However, a shout altered their plan. From a rear doorway, a lone figure appeared and began to run frantically from the abbey and head towards town, only a short distance away.

The knights and sergeants had been together for two years, they were an efficient team and knew their commander only too well. He gave only a head nod, and his sergeant responded quickly. Sir William repositioned his belt and shifted his sword before placing his hands on his hips to observe.

The sergeant's courser charged off in chase of the errant figure. With ease, he unsheathed his sword as his quickly moving horse bore down on the fleeing man. At the last moment, the sergeant, a skilled horseman, leaned precariously to his right, bent low, and with his sword, tapped the ankle of his quarry. Immediately the man tumbled to the ground as the courser slid to halt.

Despite their fatigue, the knights laughed. They never tired of seeing this delicate manoeuvre performed. They waited patiently as the sergeant encouraged his escapee to limp back to where the knights waited.

"What is the meaning of this!" cried the man, somewhat indignant at the rough treatment.

Ignoring the question, Sir William appraised him. "Ye are a bit long in the tooth to be rushing about, are ye not?"

The captive studied a cut on his hand from when he fell. It was minor, no more than a scratch, noticed the commander.

"Ye have no right, Bishop Immers shall hear of this!" he admonished, wiping his palm on his tunic.

"Please accept my humble apologies," offered the commander, "my sergeant will be punished." He gave his sergeant a steely look and in return the sergeant managed to look suitably remorseful.

"And can we assist ye to yer destination, sir? Forgive me, I know yer name not."

"I am the abb– What do ye want?" asked the man quickly correcting himself.

"Ye wouldn't be Abbot Andrew, now would ye?"

Abbot Andrew hadn't known what to do when he saw the Templars approach, but he thought it would be wise to make himself scarce. "Bishop Immers sent ye to me, did he not?"

"And now why would he do that?" asked Sir William.

Sir Hugh stepped up to his commander and nudged him and turned back to look towards the abbey. A good number of men, friars, monks and others were gathering outside. None looked to be in a good mood, their scowls and angry murmurs obvious.

Unbidden, a couple of sergeants repositioned themselves and stood between the knights and the abbey, creating a barrier. Sir William wasn't concerned. While outnumbered, he doubted they would make a move against his men.

The abbot, feeling buoyed by the overt support of his men, was feeling more confident. He turned to walk away, until a sword pressed into his chest prevented his from leaving. "I suggest ye remain here a moment longer," warned Sir Gualdim.

"Abbot, I understand ye may have provided some help to the bishop and sent some men to Mellester..." Sir William walked around Sir Gualdim, whose sword tip still remained pressed into the chest of the abbot, and stood directly in front of him. The tall knight bent slightly at the waist and looked into the shifty eyes of the abbot and spoke slowly and forcefully. "Where is the pyxis?"

The abbot shook his head. "I know not of what ye speak. Unhand me! I am a pious, peaceful man devoted to God, ye have no right…"

Sir William saw the abbot's men slowly moving forward. He still wasn't concerned; they were unarmed and stood no chance against experienced Templar knights. It wasn't until another nudge from Sir Gualdim alerted him to impending danger from the opposite direction. From town, a large group of twenty or so men were watching. A few men, observed the commander, carried swords.

Again, Sir William wasn't overly perturbed. Six Templar knights and sergeants could easily deal with an unruly mob of unskilled yeoman and merchants. He just didn't want to see bloodshed. "I must know where the pyxis is," appealed Sir William focusing his attention back on the abbot.

Bolstered by the sight of local spectators, the abbot became haughty. "Ye have no business here, be off with yer."

Sir William was in a dilemma. The safest course of action to avoid any violence would be to move into the abbey, but he didn't want to leave their horses. If he left a few sergeants to guard the valuable destriers, they'd soon be overwhelmed if the mob became hostile and turned their attentions on them.

For two years they'd been searching, two years of frustration and chasing false trails. This mission was the most important thing they would ever undertake. They couldn't be thwarted by a lowly godless abbot. *Not now*, he thought with a grimace.

"If ye don't tell me where the pyxis is, you will die," said Sir William quietly. His eyes bored into the abbot's.

The abbot laughed.

The knight commander pushed aside Sir Gualdim's sword and unsheathed his own. "Where is it?" he hissed.

The abbot risked a look towards the mob.

Many of them were armed with a variety of weapons and they weren't happy at seeing their friend, the abbot, being questioned by Templars. Uncertain as to what to do, they'd paused in indecision. Templar knights posed a serious problem, and wisely, no one was foolish enough to want to fight them. Regardless of the loyalty they felt towards their friend the abbot, friendship and allegiance extended only so far. In addition to shouting, some began hurling rocks from the safety of distance which separated them.

Sir William glanced quickly at the mob and made a quick decision. "Hold fast!" he commanded his sergeants. To his brother knights, he gave a nod. Five Templar knights unsheathed their swords, spread out on foot to block the advance of the rabble. With a sigh, he turned back to the abbot and expertly flipped his sword so it pointed down and drove it into the abbot's foot.

The abbot screamed.

"Tell me, where – is – the – pyxis?" again ordered the Templar commander between clenched teeth.

"They, they didn't find it," sobbed the abbot. He tried to lower himself to the ground but with a single hand, Sir William held firmly to his tunic and kept him standing.

"Where are these men now, the ones who ye sent to Mellester?"

Abbot Andrew was about to pass out, and received a thorough shake.

"Where are they?" repeated Sir William. He began contemplating putting his sword through the abbot's other foot.

"Bish—Bishop Immers demanded they return to Mellester."

Sir William released the abbot to collapse on the ground, sheathed his sword and strode confidently to his men who were dodging rocks and other missiles.

"We leave now," he told his men.

"Where?" asked Sir Hugh as he swayed to the side to avoid a projectile.

"Back to Mellester, and quickly."

CHAPTER EIGHT

Charlotte was asleep and lay partially on top of Odo when Reeve Petrus entered. He paused at the door and shook his head. He'd hoped to see some improvement with Odo, but nothing had changed. Charlotte stirred and sat upright.

All of a sudden, Cathal appeared at the door carrying a small bowl. He pushed his way past the reeve and walked towards the cot where Odo lay. "Don't just stand there, help me turn him over onto his stomach," he ordered the reeve. "Charlotte, keep his head steady as we roll him."

"What ye got there, a potion? Ye told me he couldn't eat, what will ye do with it, push it up his arse?"

Charlotte turned to the reeve and frowned.

As instructed, the three of them managed to reposition Odo so he now lay on his front.

"What are ye doing, Cathal?" Reeve Petrus asked.

"T'was Charlotte who gave me the idea," Cathal replied as he stepped to the fire and pulled a glowing ember from the hearth. He dropped it into the bowl with other items it contained. "I need a blanket, quick, quick!"

Charlotte retrieved a blanket as the reeve looked on in puzzlement.

"I'm going to rouse his mind."

The dried substance in the bowl began to smoulder and pungent smoke filled the air. Cathal told Charlotte to carefully lift Odo's chin as he draped a blanket over Odo's head. He eased the bowl near Odo's nose and ensured the smoke from the smouldering bowl did not escape.

"What will that do?" Reeve Petrus queried.

"I want Odo's mind to hallucinate. Become more active so he will awaken. When I saw Charlotte breathe onto him, it gave me an idea."

"Then what is this potion?" Charlotte asked. "Because it odorous."

"Is from the east and known as Ma, ye call it hemp," offered Cathal as he raised the blanket for a peek to ensure the cot wasn't in flames.

"Hemp!" exclaimed the reeve.

"Aye, but not the normal hemp," Cathal replied, "this hemp is potent."

They waited in silence as the hemp continued to smoulder, its distinctive smell filling the rectory.

Upon hearing a commotion and raised voices outside, the reeve walked to the partially open door to peer out.

Priest Benedict was being roughly pushed towards the rectory by three sword-wielding ruffians. The door was flung open and the reeve was jostled aside as the priest was aggressively propelled in by two strangers. A hasty look outside saw other men spreading out through the village. The third stranger remained outside guarding the door.

"Who are ye?" asked a ruffian as he entered. His sword carved through the air causing the reeve to quickly step back. "Answer me, dammit!" he yelled.

"I am Mellester's reeve, by what right to do ye have to be here?" Petrus challenged.

The dastard[4] laughed, ignoring the question. "And looks what we

---

4   *A dishonourable or despicable man.*

'aves ere, then." He looked from Charlotte to the figure hidden under the blanket. "Who'd he be?"

Charlotte was about to answer when the reeve imperceptibly shook his head.

"He was kicked by a horse. He's hurt bad," volunteered Petrus. He hoped to keep Odo's identity from these men.

The outlaw's attention switched to Cathal and he pointed his sword at him. "What are ye, a barber?"

He didn't answer.

"Who'd he be?" The ruffian directed the same question to Priest Benedict who was looking flustered.

"Aye, he'd be a láech[5]," replied the priest.

Another of the ruffians was staring at Charlotte and licking his lips.

"An her?"

"She'd be helping the injured man," replied Petrus. He wasn't wearing his sword; all he had for defence was his staff. In the cramped confines of the rectory, there was nothing he could do. "What do ye want here?" Outside, in the village he could hear yelling and screaming. He seethed. "What are ye doing in Mellester?"

Again the dastard ignored the reeve's question, stepped closer towards Odo and removed the blanket.

"That's 'im, the herdsman!" cried the second ruffian tearing his eyes away from Charlotte.

"Why is he sleeping?"

---

5   *Láech, (Irish – Latin orig) doctor.*

"His head, he was hit hard on the head and he hasn't woken," Charlotte replied, keeping her composure.

"He shoulda been dead," said the ruffian leader as he raised his sword above Odo. He tensed a moment before he drove it down.

"Nooo!" Charlotte yelled.

In reflex, the reeve lunged towards the ruffian but was too far away and totally helpless. Before he took a second step, the other outlaw pressed a sword into his back. Petrus froze and could only watch in horror.

Cathal, still seated beside the cot, surprised everyone. The sword began its descent and in a well-timed move, he reached up and struck the ruffian's wrist with his fist. The sword fell harmlessly onto the bed. Without pausing, Cathal's leg shot out and kicked the ruffian behind the knee causing him to twist as the leg gave out. Cathal jumped from his seat and stood defiantly as the man collapsed at his feet. "Ye want to be cursed? If ye kill him, ye and all yer families will suffer for eternity!" He pointed a finger at each outlaw and glared, wide-eyed at the man on the floor before him.

Fearful, the man scooted away. Cathal turned to the cot and retrieved the fallen sword and with contempt, tossed it to the floor beside the quickly retreating ruffian. "Ye will not harm or lay a finger on him!"

The intruder slowly stood and rubbed his wrist where Cathal struck it. Without taking his eyes from the Irish fili, he bent down and retrieved the sword.

Charlotte was tending to Odo when the guard outside stuck his head through the door. "Everythin' alright?"

"Get back outside," snarled the ruffian feeling more confident now his dignity and sword were returned to him. Still mindful of the peculiar láech, he took another step further away to keep his distance.

Unconcerned, Cathal directed Charlotte to resume supporting Odo's head as he pulled the blanket back over him.

Reeve Petrus was as surprised as anyone; he'd never seen the Irishman move in such a way and with such deadly efficiency without a weapon.

In the village, more intruders were busy searching through cruck homes for the pyxis they sought. Systematically they went from home to home. Anyone resisting was pushed aside and their homes ransacked.

Cries from outside were becoming hysterical and panicked. "What do ye want here?" the reeve asked the ruffian leader. He was becoming more frustrated as there was nothing he could do.

"We come for the box, didn't we?" he snarled, "Where is it?" His head swivelled around the room, searching for the mysterious pyxis they sought.

Reeve Petrus was livid. These were the same men who'd burned the crucks and hurt Odo. "What box?"

"The box, he," the ruffian pointed to Priest Benedict. "gave the herdsman."

Charlotte looked up and glared at the ruffian. She was furious. "So ye did this to Odo!" She released Odo's head and stood, her anger evident as she pointed to the ruffian. "It was ye in our home who set fire to it!"

"Well, my little lovely, got spirit, don't ye." He laughed. "Where's the box, cause it ain't in yer home, now is it?"

She glared at him. "Leave us, begone!"

"Give us the box and we'll be on our way."

"It was on the table. That's where it sat, where Odo put it. Why do ye need it, only contains a letter?"

"Don't ye go a' worryin 'bout it, just tell me where's it at?"

She shook her head in exasperation. "I don't know! If it isn't there, then I just don't know." She looked to the reeve for an answer.

Reeve Petrus clearly remembered seeing the box sitting on the table, so if it wasn't in the house and the Templars and these ruffians didn't have it, then where had it gone? He shrugged his shoulders.

"Yer lyin to me." The ruffian stepped closer to her and kept a wary, watchful eye on the Irishman.

"I wouldn't do that if I were ye," advised Cathal without looking up. "Best fer ye if ye leave her be."

The ruffian gave her a firm push and sent her back to her seat. "Sit down!" he snarled.

Cathal heard enough. "Out! I want yer to leave, out with yer!" he yelled, his uncharacteristic outburst surprising everyone. He made eye contact with the ruffian leader and spoke slowly and forcefully. "I saw a sign earlier, and it didn't look good. If ye want to survive, best yer make use of the door. This village is cursed by murrain, and ye will suffer because of it. Begone, away with yer!"

The ruffian heard of the murrain that plagued the area, but now this peculiar long-haired druid gave him pause and frightened him. He called to the man outside guarding the door. "Stay here with them, no one leaves." He stomped outside, only too pleased to be in the fresh air.

Outlaws pushed protesting villagers out of their homes and into the square and each house was painstakingly searched. Most men were working in the fields and were unaware of what was unfolding in the village.

Women, children and elderly posed little threat to the brazen outlaws who acted with total impunity. Any wooden boxes that were found were placed on the street and then inspected to see if they matched the description given to them. So far they had not found anything closely resembling what they sought.

From the safety of the manor, a man-at-arms observed the strange goings on in the village and reported what he saw to the steward.

From atop the hill where Mellester's manor sat, Steward Alard watched. "Assemble and arm all the men," he ordered, the instruction unfamiliar to the man-at-arms at his side. He wondered if Reeve Petrus was aware of what was happening. Was he still in the fields, where was he?

Steward Alard's concern was for the safety of the villagers, but he also had a responsibility to protect the manor. The sooner he could locate Sir Dain the better.

Sir Gweir, Mellester's Lord of the Manor, decided Sir Dain was not able to fight with his men in Ireland, insisted he remain behind and appointed him as temporary commander. He lived a short distance away from Mellester and already a rider was on his way to inform him.

The steward could see small figures waving swords, but the distance was too great to determine details. Occasionally he could hear a cry or shout as someone argued and remonstrated against the intruders. He wondered when they'd turn their attentions to the manor.

"Do ye think we should shutter and secure the manor, steward?" asked the man-at-arms.

"Aye, best see to it," replied Steward Alard with a heavy sigh.

Children were crying and held tightly to their mother's skirts as armed men shepherded them from their homes. Some resisted and were roughly pushed outside to stand in fear as strangers entered and searched through their meagre belongings.

Before long, men toiling in the fields became aware that something peculiar was happening in the village. Word spread quickly, and soon they hurriedly began to make their way back. At the Falls Ende grist mill, stonemasons and other workmen alerted to shouts of alarm, downed tools and headed to the village. At first, and in curiosity they walked, then ran as they heard yells and children screaming.

Reeve Petrus tried his best to see outside and count how many men were there. The outlaw kept a watchful eye on him and didn't allow the reeve to move. It was cramped inside the rectory, and although Petrus knew he could easily disarm the ruffian, he couldn't position his staff, nor was there room to swing it. The reeve was patient and he knew the opportunity would present itself. But what then? He was vastly outnumbered. He only hoped Steward Alard was aware of what was happening and would do something.

"Who sent yer here?" asked the reeve. "Was it Bishop Immers?"

The outlaw didn't reply.

"T'was him, was it not? Yer know ye will swing fer this. When the lord returns, he'll have yer, he will."

"Shut it, or I will," came the reply. The outlaw was distracted and staring out the door. He could hear a commotion from within the village.

Cathal and Charlotte continued to attend to Odo and Priest Benedict sat on the floor in the corner.

"What harm will it do to tell me, eh?" pushed the reeve. "Ye'll get yer coin and be off, what does it matter. Was the bishop who sent yer?"

"It wasn't Bishop Immers, was it?" the priest asked, breaking his silence.

The reeve's eyebrows furrowed. *Then who*, he wondered?

"Aye, I knows who it was that sent yer all here," continued Priest Benedict.

The ruffian turned away from the open door to face the priest. He looked uncomfortable, the guilt obvious.

"I thought so. It was Abbot Andrew, t'was him, I know it was." Benedict twisted his head and looked up at the reeve. "And it was the Bishop who told the abbot to do it."

A shout from the street caused the ruffian to move closer to the doorway.

"Villagers are returning," yelled the outlaw leader.

Without a word, the ruffian ran from the rectory. The reeve and Priest Benedict followed him outside and into the chaos.

CHAPTER NINE

Lyman Webb was worried. Things were quickly growing out of control. More and more of Mellester's men were arriving from the fields to confront his people and they were finding it more difficult to keep them under control. Further enraging villagers, he'd caught his men stealing and taking valuables from homes. One young woman was raped, two women were beaten and now at either end of Mellester, skirmishes broke out and a handful of villagers returning from the fields were wounded as they tried to push past his men to get to their families. For the present, they controlled the entire village, but not for much longer as more and more inhabitants were arriving.

The odds were changing - and not in the outlaws' favour.

The instructions he'd been given by Abbot Andrew were simple; search every cruck and find the pyxis. *Do not* pillage. Tracking down suitable men at short notice who would obey and follow his orders was difficult. Essentially he'd assembled multiple outlaw gangs and promised them they'd be well paid. Some were now fighting amongst themselves over stolen items, and they no longer listened to him. Consumed by greed, they were out of control.

Nearly all, if not most of the crucks were searched. They'd uncovered many boxes, some contained valuables that were pilfered but nothing that resembled the pyxis as described to him. It was now time to leave.

He called to Robert, one of his trusted men who just appeared from inside a cruck. His face bled from where a woman scratched him. "Time to scarper, we can't hold 'em any longer."

Robert nodded, placed his fingers to his mouth and whistled. The piercing shriek was the signal to the outlaws who rampaged through Mellester to leave. Immediately outlaws appeared from homes and began running towards their horses.

The reeve was furious. As much as he wanted, there was nothing he could do. Outlaws were everywhere and if he manged to overcome one, or even two, they'd retaliate in moments. He watched the leader mount his horse as others followed suit. He seared their faces to memory, he'd exact his revenge.

"Do ye know him?" asked Petrus pointing to the outlaw ringleader.

Priest Benedict shook his head. "I've seen him in Exeter, but do not know his name."

"I'll remember him," offered the reeve, his grim expression an indication of his anger.

The outlaws were finally leaving Mellester. As they mounted their horses and rode away, one last straggler, arms full of stolen goods was desperately running through the square towards his horse. A woman was assailing him and the ruffian was doing his best to ward off her blows as he ran. She didn't give up and try as he could, he couldn't shake her off with his arms full.

Reeve Petrus stepped down from the rectory as the ruffian went to pass him. Too busy trying to protect himself from the angry woman, the outlaw never saw the reeve or his staff. In a flash, the staff flew up and connected with his head. The blow knocked him backwards and he fell to the ground, scattering her possessions everywhere. The woman immediately fell to her knees and set-upon him, alternately striking him and gathering her valuables. In moments she held up a small purse. Her toothless grin contrasting the tears that ran down her face.

Priest Benedict went to her assistance.

"Th' bastard took it, he did. Got it back though," she said to Benedict before hawking at the unconscious man.

More and more villagers began assembling near the reeve. Understandably they were outraged and upset. Strange men, outlaws had invaded their homes, assaulted them, hurt them, and stolen from them. Women and children were crying and their infuriated men sought answers. A few people began kicking the outlaw, but Petrus didn't want him killed. He had questions for the man.

"Stop!" he yelled. "I want to question this man and find who they are and who sent them, if ye kill him now, then I can't talk to him. Return to yer work and yer homes, help yer neighbours. The outlaws have all gone, it's over."

"I can't pay me rent, they took all m'coin, reeve, what am I gonna do?" cried one.

An upwelling of anger rippled through the people of Mellester. Many suffered a similar fate.

"Aye, they took everything!" yelled another.

The shouting grew in intensity, they wanted revenge.

"If ye don't do anything, then we will!" yelled a threatening voice.

Fists were raised in solidarity and pumped angrily in the air.

"Ye'll do no such thing!" came the unexpected voice of authority.

All heads turned to see Sir Dain and an assortment of mounted men-at-arms and archers standing behind them.

Someone laughed. "With a dozen of ye?"

Including the partly disabled knight, there only twelve of them. In the distance Reeve Petrus saw Steward Alard descending the carriageway from the manor, with him were another half a dozen men-at-arms. It brought their total to eighteen.

"Go about yer business, I wish to speak with Reeve Petrus!" ordered Sir Dain.

The commanding voice of the knight broke the spell. Villagers looked uncertain and turned to each other for support. Orders from a respected knight were to be obeyed and not questioned.

Much to the relief of the reeve, the crowd reluctantly began to disperse.

The prisoner was taken to the gaol behind the manor and Sir Dain spoke at length to the reeve. Their biggest fear was that the outlaws would return. As the knight began preparations for Mellester's defence, the reeve returned to the rectory to speak to Cathal and Priest Benedict about tending to the injured.

Charlotte sat on a chair and held Odo's hand as the reeve spoke to the Irishman.

Suddenly Charlotte felt Odo's hand pull from her grasp. She turned to look down at him and saw him blinking.

"Odo!"

Cathal and Petrus quickly stepped closer.

"Odo? Odo, can yer hear me?" She reached across and held his face in her hands.

Cathal handed Charlotte a mug with water. "Give 'im this."

Odo stirred, his eyes slowly focused on Charlotte but he said nothing.

Carefully she lifted his head for him to drink from the mug. He groaned and winced as she placed a hand to support him. He took a mouthful, then another and quickly drained the mug. He closed his eyes and within moments was asleep.

Cathal reached down and placed a hand on Charlottes shoulder. "He'll recover, and be fine. Now he needs time to heal."

Overcome, she buried her face into Odo's chest.

"Sleep, Charlotte, Odo needs yer strength and love. You've hardly slept in two days."

She raised her head and reached up to place her hand on his. "Thank ye Cathal, yer magic potion worked."

"No m'dear, t'was the will of yer man."

Reeve Petrus breathed out a sigh of relief.

Three thoroughfares led into Mellester village. The major road headed east and west and passed by the very northern end of the village near the church. The other smaller road dissected the length of the village and ran perpendicular to the main road and headed up towards the River Eks, near Falls Ende where it narrowed and met with the bridge and the riverwalk. Two men-at-arms stood guard near the bridge, two more were positioned on the western approach to the village on the main road, and another two were on the eastern side. Their role was to provide advance warning if the outlaws returned. Sir Dain took other precautions and built barricades that blocked horse access into Mellester's main street, but would it be enough?

If the outlaws did return, then that was another matter. He would defend Mellester with his small force to the best of his abilities. He had four archers, and including himself, there were four knights and nine men-at-arms. Not enough to withstand a determined effort by two-score outlaws who wished to pillage Mellester, but certainly enough to cause them a problem or two. Needless to say his small ineffectual group of defenders was somewhat apprehensive at the possibility of a fight against superior numbers.

When the men-at-arms stationed as lookouts on the western approach to Mellester heard the sound of approaching men on horseback, apprehension turned to alarm and in fear for their safety, they fled back to the village.

Sir Dain was frantically issuing instructions to his few men. Archers were positioned on roof tops on either side of the village road and men-at-arms wielding pikes stood nervously behind the barricade. At the opposite end of Mellester, villagers were being quickly escorted towards the bridge and safety. If the situation worsened, then they were told to hide in the forest beyond. At risk of aggravating Odo's injury, Cathal advised that he not be moved. Priest Benedict was with them. Charlotte was at his side and slept.

Reeve Petrus stood with Sir Dain behind the barricade and waited. It wasn't long before the unmistakeable sound of approaching horses could be heard. The reeve strapped on his sword, leaned on his staff and waited.

"We can do nothing more, reeve. Is in God's hands now," said Sir Dain.

"Priest Benedict will be pleased to hear that," he replied dryly.

The sight of twelve fully armed men on horseback filled the road. There was a collective sigh of relief, it was the Templars.

"Hail, good sirs," greeted Sir William from his horse as he surveyed the improvised defences, "Are we not welcome?"

After the introductions were made, Sir William glanced around the empty village. He looked unhappy; all this was because of the pyxis. "Did they find it?" he asked.

Reeve Petrus scratched the back of his neck. "I saw some carrying boxes as they ran from here, but I don't think it was the same one that Priest Benedict gave Odo. This is why we think they may return."

"How were they armed?"

"Just swords," offered the reeve.

"Archers?" inquired the Templar.

"Only one, and it was Odo's stolen bow."

Sir William looked thoughtful as he contemplated his next move.

"This pyxis that is so important to ye, why do ye want it?" asked Sir Dain.

"It has value, but only to us," replied the Templar commander after a moment's pause.

"Then these men who came here, why do they want it? It must also have value to others?"

"We know they were sent here by the abbot in Exeter," replied Sir William. "It has importance to the Church."

"Then that is where those men have gone, back to Exeter."

"Aye," said the Templar knight. "We are weary, our horses need rest and we will return to Exeter, of that ye can be sure. In the meantime, we will rest here for the night."

"Of course, Sir William," offered Sir Dain feeling more comfortable having the Templars in Mellester.

"The, uh, herdsman, how does he fare?" asked Sir William.

"He woke earlier, drank some water and now sleeps," replied Reeve Petrus.

"Then that is cause to celebrate." Sir William looked genuinely pleased at this turn of good news.

CHAPTER TEN

Odo was ravenous and Charlotte was spoon feeding him a broth made by Mother Rosa. He'd woken from his sleep a short while ago and seemed no worse for his injury other than some minor burns and a very sore head. Overjoyed, Charlotte couldn't stop jabbering and told Odo all that happened while he slept.

The news of the Templar visit came as a surprise and he wasn't convinced he would give them the pyxis if they ever found it. When the reeve came to visit, the conversation turned to cows.

"All cattle have been culled, Odo," informed the reeve when Odo asked.

His despair was hard to conceal as the reeve detailed how all of Sir Gweir's cows were slaughtered and incinerated. "Then Mellester has no cows?" Odo asked seeking confirmation.

"None," agreed the reeve. "Nor other farms around Mellester as well."

"Cathal says we can put cows back on the land after the equinox, Odo," Charlotte volunteered, hoping to lift his spirits with some good news.

"Where is he?" Odo asked.

"Soon as he knew you'd woken, he disappeared again," replied the reeve. "He's a strange one." Petrus shook his head in puzzlement at Cathal's habit of vanishing.

Their discussion was interrupted by a knock on the door. Priest

Benedict opened the door to find two Templars outside. More Templars encircled the rectory.

"We heard the herdsman awoke. May we speak with him?" asked Sir William.

The priest stepped aside and allowed Sir William and Sir Hugh to enter. Sir Hugh greeted the reeve warmly and both Templars stood in front of the cot where Odo lay.

"I have Sir William and Sir Hugh here to see ye," said Priest Benedict.

"Forgive this late intrusion, but because we will leave for Exeter in the morn, I wanted to have a word with Herdsman Odo before we depart," said Sir William.

Odo was taken back. Templar knights were legendary and spoken about in tales of bravery, chivalry and unsurpassed fighting ability. Never in his wildest dreams could he have ever imagined that Templar knights would seek him out.

"How can I be of help to ye?" Odo asked with some trepidation. He still lay in the cot.

Charlotte removed the bowl and scooted her chair aside so Odo could see the knights more clearly.

"I've heard some remarkable stories about ye," volunteered the Templar commander.

"As I have heard many a yarn about Templars," Odo added, his voice a little scratchy.

Sir William managed a smile and looked around the room before continuing. "Perhaps I could speak with ye privately?"

"These people are my trusted friends."

"I have things to do and must take my leave. I do need yer help Benedict," the Reeve suggested.

"And may I join ye, Petrus?" asked Sir Hugh.

The three men exited the rectory leaving Charlotte, Odo and Sir William alone. Charlotte offered the knight commander a chair. Odo found himself staring at the red cross on the mantle of the knight and thought about what it represented.

"I knew yer father," Sir William suddenly said surprising them both. "I'm told he became the priest here in Mellester."

"Aye, he was," answered Odo, wondering where this conversation was headed.

"He was a sullen, grumpy man," added the Templar.

Odo tried to laugh, but doing so hurt his head and throat. He winced. He took an immediate liking to the Templar. "We can't disagree with yer there, milord."

"Did ye know he was a Templar?"

"No! That's not we were told. He was an archer!" Odo said proudly.

Charlotte held Odo's hand tightly.

Sir William looked at the floor for a heartbeat or two. "Ye are very much like him. I see yer temper and determination the same as I saw in him. But Odo was always a Templar. What happened to him was unfortunate, and changed him.

"Odo? His name was Oswald," interrupted Odo after a moment.

The Templar shook his head. "Nay, his real name was Odo Brus, and it seems ye were named after him. Do ye know of his name?"

Odo looked at Charlotte and shook his head. "We never really did know him, did we?"

"So it seems."

The Templar looked on for a moment and then continued. "It was important to him that people did not know he was a Templar because of the secret he was burdened with."

"What secret was this?" Charlotte asked taking the words from Odo before he could speak.

"The box, the pyxis, isn't it?" Odo added.

Sir William nodded.

"Tell me, Sir William, did Oswald steal the pyxis?" asked Odo.

The directness of the herdsman's questions caught the knight off guard. Most commoners were respectful to nobility to the point of being fearful. This young man showed no reservations about what he asked or how he spoke. Sir William allowed himself a smile. The young herdsman spoke to him like an equal. He'd thought what he'd heard about the herdsman and initially believed they were nothing but exaggerated stories, but now, it was obvious, he was comfortable speaking with nobility and not easily intimidated. *He is certainly the son of Odo Brus*, thought the Templar. Sir William considered his response and discarded any thoughts about lying. Like the young woman, he wouldn't speak untruths. Sir William shook his head. "No, he came by the pyxis justly. But it was always his desire to see the Templars obtain it."

"Then why give it me if he could have given it to the Templars?"

Sir William shook his head. "I do not know."

"I do, is in the letter," Charlotte said.

Both men turned to her.

"Oswald wanted Odo to have it because he knew the value of it and he trusted Odo to make the right decision over it."

"I have not seen this letter, so I cannot say."

"Perhaps, Charlotte. I would need to hear the letter read again," Odo suggested.

"Aye, Odo, if we had it."

Sir William cleared his throat. "When we find the pyxis we will return it to ye, I give ye my word on this. I ask ye in the name of the Church and the holy spirit that you allow us to keep it." He looked closely at Odo. "We, the Poor Fellow-Soldiers of Christ and the Order of the Temple of Solomon will offer ye a reward fer the pyxis. I expect this may also provide ye with some help with the problem ye have with yer cows."

Odo's face clouded over. "I will think on this, but for now it is for nought, for ye do not have it and I know not where it is."

"When ye went home, the night the outlaws were there, did ye see it on the table where ye left it?" Charlotte asked.

Odo thought carefully. "Nay, for I recall the outlaws saying they could not find it. They asked about the pyxis but I was too angered to pay mind to what they said."

"I think they possess it. They must do, fer who else would have it?" stated Sir William. "We will return to Exeter in the morn and, God willing, find this pyxis."

"I wish ye luck," said Odo with a yawn.

Sir William stood. "And I wish ye a quick recovery, Odo." He turned to Charlotte and dipped his head in respect. He caught himself in time and almost called her, milady. As he left the rectory he couldn't help but feel the young couple were the most unlikely commoners he'd ever met. Then he corrected himself, the herdsman was born of noble blood.

Over the next couple of days, things almost returned to normal in Mellester. Other than the loss of all Mellester's cattle, the people cleaned up after having their homes pillaged, the homes that were burned were being rebuilt and those who were injured were lucky they only suffered minor wounds. Work continued on the church and the masons were hard at work at Falls Ende working on building the mill.

Each day saw an improvement in Odo and he was up and walking for short periods. He still suffered from occasional spells of dizziness and a lingering headache, but each subsequent day saw an improvement. Charlotte never left his side; they were inseparable.

Cathal had not returned and no one had seen him.

Apprentice Herdsman Daniel began to build a fence to separate pastures from where crops were to be planted. Villagers were helping, working and cooperating together in healthy spirit. They weren't happy, but for now, they were taking steps to ensure they wouldn't starve for food.

Sir Dain and Reeve Petrus decided that six men-at-arms would be in the village at all times patrolling and making sure if the outlaws returned, there'd be someone able to resist them until others arrived in support.

All of this was costing Odo and Charlotte considerably. While they had ample coin put aside, they had no income other than the rent they received from Falls Ende and their savings were depleting quickly.

Odo was despondent. The evenings were the worst, and each night when they talked about their future, Odo's despair worsened. His mood soured and he fell sullen and quiet. It was difficult for Charlotte. She knew the reason for his sadness, but there was nothing she could do to lift his spirits. After two days of his deteriorating mood, she was at her wit's end.

Priest Benedict continued to sleep in the church and insisted that Odo and Charlotte remain in the rectory until their home was rebuilt. They were alone. Odo was in a disagreeable mood and not talking, and Charlotte, unwilling to provoke his wrath over something insignificant, remained quiet.

A knock on the door broke the tension. Before she could rise and greet the caller, the door flew open and Cathal appeared carrying a sack. With his foot he kicked the door closed and paused in the middle of the room.

"Do yer always enter uninvited?" Odo asked, testily.

"Would ye have not made me welcome?" replied Cathal.

Well, aye, but…"

"Then ye should save yer bitterness for those worthy of receiving it," Cathal advised dismissively. He winked at Charlotte.

"What have ye, a brace of rabbits?" asked Odo hopefully as he pointed to the sack.

Cathal ignored the question and looked to Charlotte and then Odo. His expression hardened. "I warned ye of an ill wind, did I not?"

Odo remained silent.

"Answer me, Odo!" Cathal's voice rose.

Charlotte felt a chill.

"Aye, ye did," Odo finally responded. He made eye contact with Charlotte who looked apprehensive.

"And what did ye do about it?" Cathal raised his eyebrows as he waited for a reply.

Odo shrugged. "We did nothing, Cathal." His voice took a softer tone, his bravado fading as he understood how serious the Irishman was.

Cathal nodded. "There wasn't much ye could have done, but pack all yer belongings and hide in the forest. If ye had, yer wouldn't have been knocked silly."

Odo frowned. Cathal was correct.

"Do ye ever wonder why I came here to Mellester?"

"Aye, I have done. Charlotte and I have talked about this a time or two and questioned it."

"It was a sign I received in France. Before ye came. Then another sign and each day came another and another. I did not know whom it was I was waiting fer until I saw ye in the camp of Sir Renier. Then I knew it was ye."

Odo's mouth opened.

"I know not what creates the wind or makes grass grow. I know not why fire is hot or the sky blue. I accept these things because I know it to be so and is beyond question." Cathal paused a moment. "Just as I do not question why I must be near ye to keep yer safe."

"What say ye?" Odo was surprised. "Ye came here to Mellester to keep me safe?" he repeated.

"Aye, and Charlotte too."

Charlotte slid her chair close to Odo. Despite his earlier foul mood, he reached for her hand.

"Ye must trust me, the both of ye. What I do, I do fer ye both." Cathal leaned forward and met the gaze of the young couple before him. "I do not act fer myself, and I accept this task because it is asked of me. I do not have quarrel over this, for it is my destiny and yers to be linked to me. Do not ask me for answers, fer I have none. I do not expect ye to have answers either."

They both nodded and returned Cathal's piercing stare. After an age, he turned away and reached down for the sack. Odo and Charlotte were transfixed and followed his hands as they disappeared into the coarsely woven bag. With the utmost care he pulled out the pyxis.

Charlotte gasped; both her hands flew to her face. Odo's mouth opened, he was speechless.

"I kept it safe. I knew they would come." With the pyxis held in both hands, the sack slipped away. "I pondered the quandary of this box." He raised both hands and lifted the pyxis above his head, then with force threw it downwards. The old wooden box smashed and wood splinters flew everywhere. The pyxis was completely destroyed and beyond repair.

Ignoring the pain in his head, Odo leapt from his chair, followed a heartbeat later by Charlotte. They stared, shocked, at the remains of the box. Cathal stood unmoving and a small smile played across his face.

"What have ye done!" cried Odo.

Cathal bent down and rummaged through the debris. He extracted a document and handed it to Charlotte. She immediately recognised it as the same document she read over a week ago. Cathal sunk to his knees and began to sort through the remains and pried apart the bottom of the box and carefully extracted another document that was hidden in a narrow false bottom. He slid it out from between two pieces of wood and stood. Without looking at it, he handed it to Odo.

Odo was stunned.

"This is what the fighting monks seek," Cathal's voice only a whisper.

Odo's hands shook with anticipation. With care, he unfolded the vellum[6] and stared at what was written on it. Charlotte moved to stand beside him so she could see.

"Wh-wh." Odo cleared his throat. "What is this, I understand it not?"

Charlotte looked equally puzzled and shook her head. "I have never seen anything like this before, do ye know, Cathal?"

Odo handed the single piece of vellum to the Irishman who looked at it in mystification. He stared at the unfamiliar pictographs. The single sheet contained a series of precisely drawn symbols and shapes. There were letters, but not arranged in any recognizable order. The entire document was a code. He shook his head in consternation. "These small pictures are a language I know nothing of, but the fighting monks do. This is what they seek and what they hold so dear to them."

"This is holy?"

"Aye, I expect so," Cathal replied.

"It has no meaning to me," Odo said returning to his seat.

Cathal handed the document to Charlotte.

"Read Oswald's letter again," Odo asked.

Once seated, Charlotte began to read the letter. "To my last surviving son, Odo. If ye are deciphering this, then I have passed and already stood before almighty God in judgement. I have sinned in abundance, and sorrowfully, heaven will not be my terminus, for my soul will be damned

---

6   *Prepared animal skin or membrane used as a material for writing on.*

to an eternity in hell. A just reckoning for my evil undertakings. I have grieved that I was unable to provide ye with the most salient endowment of all, the avuncular love of a father. While my trusted friends Godwin and Hetti offered ye love and accepted ye as their own, may they forever be blessed, they are not of yer blood. My love fer ye, Odo, is bestowed unto ye through these words and in this pyxis. It is my invocation to ye to accept this love, and with persistence, may ye dwell upon these words and heed my precept ~ fer love lays within. Love is my legacy. Blessed be to yer. Anon, yer father."

The room was quiet.

"Then this piece of vellum is Oswald's gift?" Odo asked

Cathal nodded. "The letter is an instruction to ye to find the gift. If ye replace the word 'love' with 'gift' ye'll see the instruction clearly. Read the last part and replace love with gift, Charlotte."

Charlotte cleared her throat. "My *gift* fer ye, Odo, is bestowed unto ye through these words and in this pyxis. It is my invocation to ye to accept this *gift*, and with persistence, may ye dwell upon these words and heed my precept ~ fer *gift* lays within. *Gift* is my legacy. Blessed be to yer. Anon, yer father."

Odo nodded. "I see it now."

"And what do we do with this?" Charlotte held the vellum up. "Cathal?"

"I cannot influence yer; this is yer decision and choice, Odo."

"Do we inform the Templars? Charlotte asked.

"I think we should," Odo replied slowly, but it does not mean they will have it, but it is only fair to tell them we have what they seek so they can stop looking fer it. It is wrong to hide this from them. What happens afterwards depends on what they say and do."

Cathal smiled. "Ye are a proper and just man, Odo."

Odo grimaced at the acknowledgement. "We need to hide and keep it safe." He scratched at his head. "I have an idea."

"And how can we tell the Templars without drawing attention to this and risk Bishop Immers and the outlaws finding out and returning?" Charlotte asked.

"If ye allow me, I will go to Exeter and inform the fighting monks and request they return to Mellester to speak with ye."

"Aye, a good idea, Cathal." Odo turned to Charlotte who nodded in support.

A short time later Odo and Charlotte were walking up the carriageway to Mellester Manor. They carried a bundle wrapped in cloth. The large door at the hall's entrance, normally guarded, remained unattended, but locked. Odo used his fist to bang on the door. Not hearing a response, he thumped again until he heard a noise from within.

Eventually the door creaked open and Steward Alard stuck his head out. "Odo, is good to see you hale, are ye well? And greetings Charlotte."

"I am feeling better, thank ye, Steward Alard. May we speak with ye?"

The door opened wider and the Steward allowed them to enter.

Once inside and seated at a bench, Steward Alard looked in question to them both.

CHAPTER ELEVEN

Bishop Immers was unusually subdued and sat miserably in a cold, austere room at the rear of Exeter's cathedral. Alongside him was Abbot Andrew; neither appeared to be in good spirits.

Sir William towered over them both and demonstrated surprising emotional control as he fought to keep his anger in check. A pulsing vein on his neck was the only indication of his volatility. Sir Hugh, only a step away, did little to hide his scowl or disgust from the two seated men.

"Ye dishonour the Church and what it represents, yer own greed came before the good folk of Mellester and ye persist in obstructing our sanctioned quest." Sir William's piercing eyes flicked from one man to the other. "This shall come before his Holiness, and I will ensure he learns of yer deceit, yer greed and impiety." He turned away from both men and began pacing. "I have vowed to defend the Church with my life, as have all my brothers. We have forsaken a normal life and embraced a selfless, pious existence of devotion. In doing so, we wield a sword and vowed to protect what is so sacred to us and the Church. The enemies of the Church shall perish by our hand!" He paused and turned to face both men again. "I will smite thee without guilt!" His face reddened at the passionate outburst. "And ye are an enemy of the church and thus, my enemy!"

The bishop looked fearful while the abbot, unable to meet the accusing stare of the Templar, turned away.

Sir Hugh took a step closer. "Where is the pyxis? What have ye done with it, fer if it was in Mellester, it no longer is."

Sir William took a moment to collect himself and observed as Sir Hugh began to pressure the bishop and abbot.

Abbot Andrew sat forward and eased his heavily bandaged foot into a more comfortable position. He opened his mouth to reply when he felt the bishop's hand on his arm.

"While ye search for this mysterious pyxis, ye cannot lay a hand on me or the abbot. In doing so would likely mean the pyxis may slip from ye grasp forever."

The sound of a sword unsheathing filled the room. Sir Hugh reached behind and placed a restraining hand on the chest of his commander. "Not yet, Sir William," he breathed, "We must have strength. The time will come when these men will face judgement. Until we find the pyxis, we must resist the temptation, these men cannot be harmed."

Bishop Immers managed to smile.

The cords on Sir William's neck stood out as he fought to regain control of himself. He knew Sir Hugh was right, because he'd preached those very same words to him before arriving at the cathedral.

"The good folk of Mellester have been plundered," began Sir Hugh, turning once again to face the bishop. "The recompense shall come from yer purse." He pushed a finger firmly into his chest. "And ye will see it done."

Both the bishop and the abbot were discomfited.

"Ye will not interfere with Mellester, its inhabitants and especially Herdsman Odo and his woman," said Sir William as he took a step towards the seated men. "God help me, if I find ye have disobeyed me, I will hunt ye down and ye will discover the Templar wrath. There is nowhere ye can go to escape us." He took a step backwards. "Come," He indicated to Sir Hugh. "Let us rid ourselves from these despicable heathens." Both men strode from the cathedral, their heavy footfalls loud in the expanse. They walked from the oppressiveness of the church into the fresh air and felt its immediate relief.

Daylight succumbed to the inevitability of darkness, the point where it was neither day or night and a precarious gloom settled over Exeter. Sir William paused and Sir Hugh, at his side stopped and looked to his commander in question.

"It is too quiet," whispered Sir William. "Something is amiss," his sixth sense alerting him to potential danger. In reflex, the Templar knight unsheathed his razor sharp sword. His eyes probed the gloom as Sir Hugh also withdrew his weapon. They stood silently, almost back to back with swords ready and listened.

Normally, the cautious Templars would have formed a defensive perimeter around the Cathedral, but tonight they were exhausted and believing it safe, Sir William ordered his men to rest while he and Sit Hugh went to confront the bishop and abbot. The other Templars and sergeants were in the abbey, but the abbey was some distance away and they needed to walk around the cathedral's bounds to reach it. For now, it was only the two of them.

The sound of approaching footsteps was the first signal. From the growing darkness, men appeared. They wielded swords and swaggered towards the two Templars, buoyed with the confidence coin and mead gave them.

Recognising the threat and with unspoken precision, both Templars positioned themselves so their backs were against the cathedral wall and stepped away from each other to create room to swing their lethal swords. Sir William controlled his breathing, it slowed, yet his mind was alert, and his reflexes honed to perfection.

If the superior number of men who confronted the Templars believed this confrontation would be easy, they were sadly mistaken. But ten armed men against two were odds that even the Templars had to take seriously. They couldn't discount anything; this is why they still lived.

Lyman Webb directed his men to spread out and not bunch up. He knew he'd only achieve success if he could force the knights apart. Attack them singularly, one at a time. In the growing darkness the white mantle and red cross the Templars wore made them easily distinguishable, but since it was also an insignia of bravery, valour and storied victories, it created a measure of unease and fear amongst his men.

The outlaws became nervous. Their earlier courage, fortified by alcohol and their self-assurance bolstered by numbers had waned considerably. They now warily approached the two Templar knights.

"Together, lads," instructed Lyman, trying to boost their confidence.

The outlaws were only a few paces from the waiting Templars.

Without any apparent signal, both knights simultaneously sprung forward in a coordinated attack of whirling steel and clashing swords, surprising their ill-trained adversaries. The outlaws incorrectly assumed the knights would stand in defence and not become the aggressors. As quickly as it begun, the knights stepped back. Before them, four men lay on the ground; blood seeped through torn clothing to run in rivulets, spreading into small pools on the dirt beyond the consecrated confines of Exeter's cathedral.

Uncertain, the remaining outlaws withdrew a step, their shifty eyes darting to their fallen accomplices. Lyman was stunned at the ferocity and determination of the Templars. He rallied his men. "Keep together, attack together!" he yelled. "There'd be only two!"

The retreat halted, and after a brief pause and further encouraged by Lyman, they cautiously stepped forward.

Sir William and Sir Hugh had still not spoken. With wisdom borne from experience, they cast their eyes at the outlaws, flicking from man to man, each instinctively searching for the most experienced of the swordsman who would be their target when they next attacked.

This time more coordinated, but with less confidence, the outlaws advanced. As before, the Templars struck again. They twirled and spun, their swords arced through the half-darkness and with exactness they found and struck their enemy. The Templars were also hit, but lacking force or accuracy, the blows glanced harmlessly off chainmail without drawing blood.

"Back, go back!" yelled Lyman seeing how the Templars' initiative in attacking his men was proving to be successful. Two more men lay bleeding on the ground. Those who could, scooted or crawled away, their pitiful cries going unheeded. Lyman told his men to withdraw a little further, but he wasn't finished yet, he still had a plan. He turned his head towards the gloom and shouted "Now!"

Sir William was puzzled and wondered why the outlaw shouted. Then it dawned on him. Before he could yell a warning to Sir Hugh, he heard the unmistakeable sound of bowstrings as arrows were launched. In reflex he twisted his body and dropped to the ground as he shouted a warning to his brother Templar.

A handful of arrows hissed through the night. Most clattered off the stone cathedral wall behind them. Sir Hugh, in the process of emulating his commander was still lowering himself to the ground when an arrow struck his thigh. He grunted and fell to his knees. Immediately Sir William prepared to defend his brother Templar with unquestioned loyalty. Another volley of arrows was sent towards the two Templars, but in the gloom, and with the knights crouching low, the arrows were ineffectual and posed no threat.

Cathal arrived in Exeter and was making his way to the Cathedral to find the Templars when he heard the distinctive sound of clanging swords. With curiosity, he dismounted, tied his horse to a fence and cautiously approached.

What he saw angered him. Outlaws in superior numbers were attacking two Templar knights. In the gloom, he observed the Templars begin their deadly first attack, but a noise behind the outlaws drew his attention. He carefully crept closer and saw a half dozen archers. He was too distant to prevent the first flight of arrows, but he saw them launch a second and his blood boiled. From behind and unseen, he stealthily approached as the archers notched new arrows to their bows.

He struck quickly. His leg shot out, and struck one archer, then a second. His form moved with graceful vehemence and more men collapsed clutching at limbs.

Confused by the commotion, the remaining archers saw only a single unarmed adversary, yet the manner in which he attacked was at the same time irregular and flawlessly effective.

Seeing the Templar on the ground trying to extract the arrow, Lyman decided to signal another flight of arrows. With his men at a safe distance he again yelled, "Now!"

Nothing happened.

"Shoot!" he cried in frustration.

There were still three swordsmen to defeat and Sir William stood and faced them fearlessly before deciding to attack. Sir Hugh, lying on the ground, twisted and pulled at the arrow and managed to extract it from his leg. Blood flowed freely from the wound but there was little he could do about it until later. Eager to rejoin the fray, he rose cautiously to his feet.

Something was wrong. Lyman took a tentative step backwards in retreat. The other remaining outlaws also had considerable doubt and their resolve wavered. Without prompting, they eagerly followed Lyman's example. One step became two, and then three. With the enraged Templar quickly bearing down on them they fled.

Cathal was breathing hard and stood over four men who clutched at their legs and other body parts. In fear for their safety, the two archers still standing ran away.

Cathal began to kick the fallen bows away from each man when he saw Odo's yew bow and quiver. He picked them up and turned to look behind. A Templar knight approached.

"Ye did this?" asked Sir William with incredulity as he watched Sir Hugh limp towards the four injured archers to stand guard. *How could a single unarmed man wreak such havoc*? he wondered.

"Aye," shrugged Cathal.

"Why did ye risk yer life to help, and with what, where is yer weapon, fer ye didn't use that." He pointed at the longbow.

"I came at the bequest of Master Odo and I have no need to carry an instrument of death when my body can serve such a purpose. And this..." he held up the bow, "belongs to Odo, t'was plundered from his home."

Sir William stared at the finely crafted Welsh longbow and wondered how the herdsman came to be in possession of it. "Praise God, none of them could use it," he exclaimed. He turned to keep a watchful eye in case the outlaws regrouped and decided to attack.

Cathal began to walk towards the other Templar who was inspecting his wound. "Let me see to yer friend."

Sir William bent down and retrieved a discarded bow and studied it briefly before snapping it across his thigh. "Is but a hunting bow," he said in disgust and followed the stranger.

"How are ye called?" Sir William asked when he caught up.

"I am Cathal."

Sir William stopped. "The fili, the same who is known throughout, in France?"

"Aye, and other places."

"Your name, it is familiar to many."

"I wish that were not so," he replied.

"Why did ye help us?" repeated Sir William as Cathal offered to look at Sir Hugh's injury.

"Because I came to Exeter to seek ye out."

Sir William's brows furrowed.

"I bring a message for ye, if ye are Sir William?"

"I am he."

Cathal nodded. "Then Master Odo asks me to inform ye, he has the pyxis ye seek."

Both Sir William and Sir Hugh's eyes widened.

"Surely ye jest," said Sir Hugh.

Cathal shook his head.

It took a moment for both Templars to absorb the news. "Are ye sure, could ye be mistaken? asked Sir William not daring to believe this part of their quest could finally be over.

"It is as I said." Cathal replied.

"And how did the herdsman retrieve the pyxis, for it was lost to him?"

Cathal sighed, and stood. "The wound is minor and will mend quickly," he offered, then paused for a couple of heartbeats. "I brought him the pyxis, it was in my care."

"Ye had it! An, and the herdsman knew of this?" stammered Sir William.

Cathal met the gaze of the Templar commander. "The pyxis is the possession of Master Odo, it is not fer ye to question him. And nay, he did not know I had it."

Sir William and Sir Hugh were dumbfounded.

"Be warned, Sir Knights, that ye will act with honour, ye will not forsake righteousness to satisfy yer need to obtain what the pyxis contains."

Sir William was trying desperately to control his quickly beating heart. The discovery of the pyxis was beyond belief and now this strange seer had the audacity to advise him of honour. Yet the peculiar man did so, not out of his own self-interest, but in concern for the young herdsman he called 'Master.' "I have already given my word to Herdsman Odo. Rest easy, for we are not his enemy or yers."

"Then yer seek his good health and wellbeing?"

Sir William was about to reply, then stopped and thought about the question before answering. "Perhaps ye are wise above all others, Cathal. Nay, we have a mission to retrieve the pyxis, that was foremost in our minds. People like the herdsman who are in the way of our quest … is easy to cast them aside with nary a thought. But we seek him no ill will."

Cathal nodded, "Then Sir Knight, may ye think wisely on how yer treat Master Odo."

"Aye, it will be as ye say Cathal, ye have my word."

"And of the bishop and abbot, t'was them who set the outlaws upon us," interrupted Sir Hugh. "What shall we do with them?"

"There is little we can do for the moment. To kill a bishop, even one who is evil and acts without God in his heart, will create complications we do not want. However, I will ensure the Pope hears of them both, although I struggle with the temptation to return inside and run both men through. But, humiliation by the Pope's hand is punishment enough and I hope to see that day."

"Then we leave for Mellester in the morn?" asked Sir Hugh.

"Aye, soon as possible."

"Where did he go?" asked Sir Hugh glancing around. "He's gone."

Both Templars peered into the darkness; of Cathal, they saw no sign.

CHAPTER TWELVE

It could have been a beautiful day, the sky was blue, the sun shone brightly, yet all was not well in Mellester. Felt by everyone, a dark cloud hung over the hamlet, and in its depressive shadow, fear and worry cruelly mouldered. Odo leaned over a fence rail and fed carrots to Amica who noisily crunched the treats. Ahead, he could see Apprentice Daniel and several villagers helping to finish the fence line that would divide his main pasture. Already some were digging and preparing the ground for planting late seasonal crops.

Odo predicted that during the coming winter, villagers would starve if steps weren't taken to ensure everyone could be fed. With no work or coin, how else would they obtain food?

He turned away from the fields and looked towards the village and saw the gaping maw where his home once stood. He shuddered. The sadness was consuming; he couldn't shake the oppression, and the loss of his prized animals was like the death of family.

He longed to see fat milking cows grazing contentedly on his land. It had been his dream since before he could remember, and up until a fortnight ago, he'd achieved it. And now, he had nothing, it was gone. He had no home, no cows and no hope of ever recreating what he once had.

Cows were valuable and expensive. He had no coin to replace his herd, and if he did, it would be sometime before his land was safe from the murrain to allow cows to graze on his pastures. He felt Charlotte wrap her arms around his waist.

He turned to her.

Her hair, the colour of summer wheat, shone in the morning light. Even her face, tanned, vibrant and unblemished, glowed with healthy vitality. She was the most beautiful woman he'd ever known and he never tired of looking at her. He felt his heart quicken as her eyes probed his.

She knew him better than he knew himself. She could read his moods and understood his strengths and weaknesses; she was so much a part of him, they were like a single entity. He felt her scrutiny; it was like she could read his mind. He sighed. She deserved so much better than what he'd been able provide for her and it made him feel guilty for his recent churlish behaviour.

"I know, Odo," she said barely above a breathless whisper. "You don't have to feel bad, we have each other and somehow we will survive." She leaned forward; the top of her head touched his chin.

He breathed her in, her smell, her essence. She completed him, and he understood then he hadn't lost everything. While their home had burned, their cows killed, he still had Charlotte, and nothing would ever take her away from him. He felt better and breathed out the anguish that he'd allowed to permeate through his being; he held her tightly, frightened to let her go.

Amica snorted, his nose mere inches from them. They pulled apart in laughter. The courser's ears twitched, his eyes focused on something in the distance. With his sleeve, Odo wiped his face and looked behind. Walking towards them were Templars, their sergeants, Cathal and the reeve. His heart began to beat faster.

"Have trust and faith in yerself, Odo," she whispered again sensing his reaction.

"Aye, but can I trust the Templars?"

"Hail Master Odo, Charlotte!" greeted Sir William with a big grin. "Is good to see yer up and about."

"Aye, and causing no end of mischief and misery," offered the reeve as he stepped up.

Cathal stood to the side and watched everyone warily. He didn't smile, but then he never really did. He made eye contact with Odo and nodded, the only indication everything was well.

"I feel better each day, but still suffer from pain in my head."

Cathal's eyes narrowed slightly.

"I'm sure it will pass," offered the Templar commander.

Charlotte observed that Sir Hugh wore a bandage on his upper thigh. "Did ye meet with an accident?" she asked.

Sir Hugh smiled, "Is but a scratch, nothing more."

"It will need tending, or ye risk corruption," suggested Cathal speaking for the first time.

Sir Hugh nodded and looked with some expectation at his commander. Behind, the other knights shuffled their feet. They too were anxious.

"Uh, I understand ye have the pyxis," said Sir William, unable to contain himself any longer.

"In a manner, I do."

The reeve looked puzzled. *What is this all about*? he wondered.

Sir William breathed out in relief. Behind him, a few knights murmured. "Then perhaps we can speak?" asked Sir William with excitement creeping into his voice.

Odo nodded. "Do ye object if we go to the manor?"

"It suits us to talk there," added Charlotte. "Cathal, Reeve Petrus, we would like ye to come too."

Within a short time, the group was outside the manor house. A man-at-arms led the sergeants with their destriers to the stables and showed them where they could rest and sleep. The heavy door to the great hall was open and with Reeve Petrus and Sir Hugh leading the way, they entered.

Steward Alard was seated at his writing desk and stood to welcome everyone. Sir William spoke briefly to his fellow knights and with only Sir Hugh remaining, they left the hall to stand sentinel outside. The Templars trusted no one.

Odo introduced Steward Alard to the Templars and then, at Alard's invitation, they sat at a large table near the dais at rear of the hall.

"It may be a good time to see the pyxis," suggested Sir William without preamble.

Sir Hugh was seated beside him and nodded enthusiastically.

Odo gestured to Steward Alard who then rose from his seat and disappeared through a door only to return a moment later carrying a bundle wrapped in cloth. Sir William and Sir Hugh exchanged a glance of confusion.

Steward Alard placed the bundle on the table and unwrapped the cloth to gasps of horror. In unison, both Templars leapt from their seats.

"What is the meaning of this?" cried Sir William. They stared in disbelief at the remains of the pyxis.

Odo did his best not to smirk. "Ye wanted the pyxis. Here it is, or what's left of it. I apologise for its condition." Odo spared a quick glance towards Cathal. "But sadly it met with a mishap."

Sir William leaned forward and immediately began to search through the broken pieces of wood. Sir Hugh stared as if in a trance.

Odo nodded to Charlotte who stood. In her hand she held Oswald's letter. Sir William stopped rummaging through the debris. His mouth clenched tightly as he looked towards her. Odo noticed the Templar's hands shook. For the first time he realised what the pyxis meant to these men. It wasn't just a lost item they were trying to find. It represented a lifetime of dedication, sacrifice and years of searching, traveling, and following clues and leads. Driven by their faith and belief that they would eventually locate what meant so much to them, and the Church, and here it lay. He felt a measure of pity for them. "Milords," Odo began respectfully, "Please be seated. Charlotte will first read to ye the letter Oswald wrote."

Reeve Petrus was equally fascinated and was seated beside Charlotte, while Cathal eased himself to the bench beside him. Petrus recalled what Oswald's letter said, but he knew not that Odo had since found the pyxis, and was disappointed to now see it destroyed. He turned to Cathal, hoping for an answer.

Cathal leaned to his side, "Wait," he whispered.

"You read Latin?" asked Sir William with incredulity when she finished reciting the letter.

"Aye, Oswald taught us both to read English, but I had no interest in learning Latin, and so he taught just Charlotte," replied Odo proudly.

"Brother Odo was always a sly fox," Sir William offered in response, "But there is more, is there not?" he asked with growing impatience.

"What is this? Brother Odo?" the reeve looked in question.

"Oswald was not his real name, Reeve Petrus," volunteered Charlotte. "Is Odo Brus."

The reeves jaw dropped. "I know of this name, it is known to many, but fer the life of me I cannot recall why."

Sir Hugh cleared his throat, eager to continue. He leaned forward.

The reeve looked at Odo hoping to refresh his memory.

"Aye, there is more," continued Odo ignoring the reeves open mouthed gaze, "As Oswald wrote, the pyxis also contained a gift. We found that if we exchanged the word 'love' for 'gift' then the letter had a more obvious meaning."

"May I see," Sir William asked.

Charlotte handed him the letter, and with Sir Hugh watching over his shoulder, they read the letter and transposed the words.

The Templar knight nodded, "And ye found the gift?" he asked with some hope.

"Aye, we did, but we needed to destroy the pyxis to find it. The gift was carefully hidden."

"Then please, let me see it?" Sir William pleaded.

"One moment, milord," Odo replied tersely.

Reeve Petrus finally closed his mouth. He was spellbound and leaning forward on the table just like Sir Hugh, listening intently. Cathal sat back, and looked unaffected. Steward Alard was attentive and remained silent but watched the proceeding with barely constrained curiosity and some disbelief.

"I want to ask ye, what will ye do with this gift, what is its purpose?" Odo questioned.

Sir William licked his dry lips. "If this gift is what we believe it to be," he turned to Sir Hugh quickly, "then this is a piece, a single part of a paradox that we hope will assist us to find something of, uh, greater importance which has been, uh – misplaced. Its worth, its value is beyond comprehension and will have a profound effect on the Church and even the entire Christian world as we know it." The Templar took a big breath and spoke slowly, barely beyond a whisper. "There is nothing, nothing that is worth more. Not all the gold in the entire world gathered together can equal it."

Steward Alard shook his head. *Incredible*.

Reeve Petrus mouth dropped open again.

Odo stared at Sir William. The hall was deathly quiet.

"I will offer ye recompense," croaked Sir William breaking the silence.

Odo stood. "It isn't about a reward; I care not for such things." He shook his head. "Through my father, I am burdened with the responsibility of deciding if ye are worthy of receiving it, or are ye caught up in, in–" Odo searched for the right words and turned to Cathal for support.

The Irishman sat with his arms folded and just nodded his head in encouragement for him to continue.

"–untruths, selflessness, and greed," Odo continued. "Just like Bishop Immers, and so many others like him. "Are yer intentions to better us all through this gift, or will yer purses bulge and provide the Church with even more riches and treasure?"

Charlotte stared at Odo. She couldn't believe he spoke this way. His passion and belief was so profound and unselfish, it made her feel ashamed. She'd previously thought of Oswald's gift and what it meant to her and Odo in terms of a fat purse and a financial reward. But here in this hall, in front of all these men, he thought not of himself, but for others. She felt her eyes moisten as she proudly watched him.

Again the hall was deathly quiet.

Sir William cleared his throat and spoke softly. "May I see this gift, please?"

Odo looked to Steward Alard. After a brief hesitation, he nodded and reached into the folds of his tunic and extracted the single piece of vellum and placed it carefully on the table in front of Sir William and Sir Hugh.

Neither said a word. Both men just stared at it wide-eyed. Sir William eventually tore his eyes from the document and looked up at Odo.

"Open it, have a look." Odo sat down.

With reverence, the Templar knight reached forward and slowly unfolded the vellum. When he saw the pictographs he gasped and immediately crossed himself and recited a brief prayer. Sir Hugh followed his example. Both men appeared overcome. Sir William coughed.

Odo made eye contact with the steward who reached across and retrieved the precious vellum.

"Ye have yet to answer my question, Sir William," stated Odo.

Sir William was having difficulty composing himself. He looked up and exhaled. "It is not easy to put emotions into clear words when you've spent years overcoming obstacles and putting aside feelings."

Odo acknowledged him with a smile and allowed him to continue.

"When I committed myself to the Church, I did so with the belief that I was doing the right thing for a just and holy cause. I stand by my decision, for I still believe in the greater good. Just as ye do, Odo. Yer father's gift will strengthen the Church, and in doing so make it pure again. There is no room for men like Bishop Immers or Abbot Andrew. Brother Odo's gift will help restore belief and the pure love of Christ." Sir William stood and leaned forward across the table towards Odo. "If ye have faith, then there is only one decision for ye." He remained standing and locked eyes with Odo.

The sound of creaking wood broke the silence as the reeve shifted position.

"Will ye tell us why this document is worth so much to ye?" Odo asked.

Sir Hugh coughed.

"Master Odo, we are sworn to secrecy, I'm unable to tell ye what ye wish to know," said Sir William. His voice contained an edge. It was obvious to all, he wouldn't share his secret.

The hall was again silent.

It was the herdsman who spoke first. "May I consult with my friends, Sir William?"

The Templar inclined his head, "Come, Sir Hugh, let us check on the horses."

When the Templars departed, everyone seemed to relax. Reeve Petrus shook his head. "Odo, what have ye done? It is like the fate of mankind rests upon yer shoulders."

"Aye, and if we are to believe the Templars, then it does," added Charlotte.

"Steward Alard, what say ye?" Odo asked.

The steward had his face in his hands. He removed them and looked thoughtful for a moment. "I wish I knew their secret; why won't they tell ye?" He scratched his neck. "I, I don't know. If ye do not turn the gift over, what will happen?" he replied rhetorically.

"Is there a reason why I should *not* hand it over? Do we trust the Templars?" Odo asked as he searched the faces of his friends. "I believe Sir William; I think he will act with honour."

"I don't trust them at all, they serve no one but themselves," added the reeve. "If ye say no, they will just take it and there will be nothing anyone can do to stop them."

"It is as Steward Alard says. If ye do not give them the gift, ye will never know the good that it could bring. If ye give the templars the gift, and yer trust in them is fer naught or abused, then it is not yer fault, for ye tried," said Cathal.

Steward Alard and Charlotte nodded.

Odo turned to the reeve. "Have ye more to say why I shouldn't give them the gift?"

"I speak from my heart Odo, nothing more."

"Very well, I have made up my mind."

Sir William and Sir Hugh returned and stood before Odo. Reeve

122

Petrus watched in amazement. Here were two venerable Templar knights, standing meekly before a herdsman waiting for a decision as if their very lives were at stake. And Odo was managing this entire situation as if he were a lord, born from nobility. *Perhaps he is,* thought the reeve.

"Before ye speak, Odo, regardless of the outcome, I have the utmost respect in ye. If Brother Odo Brus were alive to witness this, then he too would be proud of ye. I am honoured to make yer acquaintance and yer goodness and honesty will always remain with me as inspiration."

Odo's cheeks reddened. Before he could reply, a noise near the doorway caused all heads to turn. Four Knights Templar and their sergeants entered the hall. They stood guiltily near the door. As much as their commander, they too wanted to hear what Odo would say. Sir William was about to order them to leave.

"Let them remain, Sir William, if it is true what ye told me, then their desire to know the outcome is as strong as yer own.

"Very well," he replied.

Odo took a cleansing breath and turned back to Sir William. "We have discussed this gift and what it means to ye and I believe Oswald, er, Odo would want ye to have it. Why he left this decision to me, I do not know when he could easily have given it to ye himself." He made eye contact with the Templar commander. "It is yers."

Sir William looked upwards, crossed himself and began to silently mouth a prayer. In unison all the other templars and sergeants dropped to a knee in genuflection and began to recite their own.

"Thank ye, Odo, I thank ye, my brothers thank ye and so does the Church." He dipped his head in a show of respect.

Odo looked to Steward Alard who produced the vellum document and with both hands, carefully handed it to the Templar knight.

Sir William couldn't prevent his hands from shaking, and after a quick glance at the cryptic symbols he placed the document inside his tunic. "Thank ye, Odo, thank ye all." He lowered his head again, then faced Odo. "Uh, may I speak with ye outside?"

"I trust my friends–"

"Nay Odo, just ye," the Templar insisted.

Odo looked unsure.

"Ye will come to no harm."

Both men stepped outside the hall and slowly walked in silence around to the front of the manor that overlooked the village, Falls Ende in the distance and the forested hills beyond.

"The murrain has struck ye hard, has it not?" queried Sir William.

"Aye, I've lost most everything, and almost my life." Unconsciously his hand went to his head and touched the fresh wound.

"I spoke earlier of a reward. The Templars no longer wish to call it a reward, but we wish to bequeath to ye a gift. After much discussion we believe ye will accept this gift and use it wisely. Ye are a good and noble man, Odo, ye deserve this gift." Sir William reached into his tunic and extracted a folded piece of vellum, almost identical to the gift document found in the pyxis. He held it up for Odo to see. "This was created some time ago for the single purpose of purchasing the pyxis. This is for ye, with the blessings of the Poor Fellow-Soldiers of Christ and from the Order of the Temple of Solomon. Please accept it with our gratitude and respect."

Odo took the proffered document and carefully unfolded it. What he saw made no sense. It appeared similar to Oswald's pyxis document and contained pictographs or symbols. Some were triangles, others random shapes. He recognised what looked like signatures at the bottom. He turned back to Sir William who was grinning.

"And what do I do with this? I am sorry, Sir William, I do not understand?

"Aye, ye'd not be the only one. It is a letter promising to pay the bearer, that is ye, Odo, the amount that is promised. Deliver this document to any Templar castle and they will give ye the coin or gold. But do not destroy it, guard it with yer life."

Odo wasn't sure about keeping it and was about to return it when Sir William raised his hand.

"Nay, I will not accept it, so ye cannot return it. While yer father left ye a gift, then so do we. Think of this as the Church's gratitude."

"If ye are generous enough to present me with a gift, and if I was so fortunate to receive five or ten pounds then I ask that ye give this to the good people of Mellester who were robbed. Many had things taken from them, coin, simple possessions meaningful to them, so they should receive this gift, Sir William."

The Templar knight smiled. He lifted his chain mail and revealed a heavy purse tied to a belt. "If I were to gift ye twenty pounds, Master Odo, then I would give ye this purse."

Odo's eyes widened in surprise, then he looked thoughtful and chewed his bottom lip. He nodded. "Thank ye, Sir William, but how much have the good soldiers of Christ given me?"

125

It was obvious Sir William was enjoying himself. "The Templars will tell ye." He finished with a laugh.

"I don't understand what is happening, why give me such a large amount of money and why is this pyxis cipher of such value? He shook his head slowly from side to side. "What is it ye seek?"

Sir William took a step forward and looked out over Mellester. He could see small figures putting the last finishing touches to the church roof. People walked through the busy hamlet, while further and yonder, men could be seen toiling in the fields. Odo stepped up beside the knight.

"I long to return to a life like this, Odo. I could make my home here, Mellester is perfect. Ye are a unique young man and are fortunate. People, good people believe in ye and naturally follow ye. The reeve, he is a good honest man. Cathal, ever peculiar but a wonder and gifted in so many ways, he is truly blessed. Even Priest Benedict, he too has faith, not only in our almighty God, but in ye, Master Odo. Yer beautiful woman, Charlotte looks at ye with pure love, and is a joy to behold." He turned from the spectacular view and looked deeply into Odo's eyes. "Our gift to ye is more than ye can ever imagine, but this gift we bequeath to ye, in comparison to what we have sought for many a year is naught. We expected to acquire the pyxis from an episcopate and in doing so, needed a great deal of coin to entice a possessive bishop to part with it." He took a breath. "I cannot tell ye what we seek for I have sworn an oath, but when we find it, as God is my witness, it will be because of you. Our gift alone can never fully repay ye, Odo." Sir William held out his hand and both men shook. "And now we can leave here and complete our quest," said Sir William, "it has been a long journey for us all and I am weary."

Odo's heart threatened to explode from his chest as he processed what the Templar told him. After a moment of silence he asked. "Where will ye go?"

"First back to Exeter to speak with the bishop and the abbot. I have some harsh words for both men and then we ride to Brycgstow[7], where we will find a ship to take us to Scotland and then to France."

Odo didn't know what to say, he was still reeling.

"Come, let us return to the hall. And Odo?"

Odo turned to Sir William.

"Two things. First, learn to defend yerself and yer family, use that Welsh bow, it may save yer life one day."

"Aye, Reeve Petrus badgers me about it constantly." Odo looked guilty.

"Yer have time, have ye not?" Sir William raised an eyebrow.

Odo nodded.

"Best not to tell anyone, other than those ye trust with yer life about what I gave to ye. Many a shameless filcher will look to improve his repute by taking that tally and will kill without lament. Be on yer guard, Odo, the burden of wealth is as vexatious as indigence."

A buoyant Sir William left Mellester's hall, Reeve Petrus returned to matters that required his attention and he departed, which left Charlotte, Cathal and Steward Alard in the hall.

"Ye did an honourable thing Odo, and I am proud of ye," said the steward when they were alone.

Cathal watched but said nothing.

---

7   *Modern day Bristol*

"I'm proud of ye too, Odo, many men would have taken the reward and thought nothing of what that peculiar document represented," complimented Charlotte.

Odo looked guilty.

"Ye did, he offered ye the reward and ye took it didn't ye?" laughed Charlotte.

"I had no choice in the matter, Sir William insisted I take it, but he called it a gift and not a reward."

"Let me see?" Charlotte asked.

Odo produced the folded vellum document and Charlotte looked at curiously. "What is it? It looks similar to the one ye gave Sir William."

Cathal leaned over to inspect it.

"I know what it is," offered Steward Alard, "I have seen similar documents before."

"Then what is it?" inquired Odo.

"Templar knights are a perplexing group. Originally they protected Christian pilgrims who visited Jerusalem from plunderers who wished to rob them while they travelled. They devised a system where someone could exchange valuables with them at one location and receive a document acknowledging its worth."

"Much like a quittance?" asked Charlotte.

"Aye, exactly. However, if ye present that same receipt to Templars at a different town, they return to ye the value of what's written on the receipt," continued the steward.

"So pilgrims wouldn't need to carry a fat purse that could be stolen," added Odo.

The steward nodded in affirmation. "What ye have here, Odo, is a warrant from the Templars."

"Fer how much?" Charlotte asked.

Steward Alard laughed. "If the value of the warrant clearly stated the amount, then it would likely be thieved. That cipher can only be read by Templars, so only they know what the value is."

Odo looked puzzled. "Then I must take this warrant to Templars to find out?"

Steward Alard smiled.

"But where?"

Cathal sat forward and spoke for the first time. "The Templars have castles everywhere; ye can take this receipt to the closest one."

"I think it is clever," said Odo. "Is a good way to protect yer coin. I wish I had used the Templars when I went to France. If it hadn't been for Reeve Petrus, I would have had my purse stolen."

"The Templars have a place in Somersetshire called Combe Templariorum," offered the steward.

"That isn't too far to travel," Odo said quietly.

"Are *we* going to Somersetshire?" Charlotte asked. The tone of her voice left no doubt Odo wouldn't be leaving without her.

CHAPTER THIRTEEN

The grim news caught everyone by surprise. Sir Hyde Fortescue, Lord of Ridgley Manor, was slightly injured in battle shortly after arriving in Ireland. At the time it hadn't been serious, only a minor arrow wound, however rather than heal, the wound festered and became corrupt. Against all Sir Hyde's protestations, King Henry insisted he return to Ridgley Manor to mend, but instead of healing, his condition worsened. Weak and racked by fever, he was unable to rise from his chamber and now, according to word, death was the likely and expected outcome.

Shocked at the discovery of Sir Hyde's condition, Charlotte and Odo asked Cathal if he would attend to the powerful lord. Perhaps with his unique healing skills, he could do what others couldn't, or so Odo hoped. Cathal readily agreed and without delay departed Mellester Manor. Meanwhile Charlotte and Odo finalised plans to visit Combe Templariorum, a Templar castle in Somersetshire where they hoped to learn the value of the warrant given to them by Sir William.

"Is too far to travel in one day," warned Reeve Petrus. He wisely counselled they head towards Taunton, in Somersetshire, an old town where they could safely spend the night before continuing on the next day. Even though he felt there was little likelihood they would experience any trouble on their short journey, he wasn't thrilled they chose to travel alone.

The reeve knew only too well the fickle mood of commoners and nobility, and seeing a freeman riding such a beautiful horse would arouse suspicion and even resentment, "Take Steward Alard's document proving ye own Amica," he advised.

Odo needed no further prompting, although Charlotte raised another valid point. "Odo, both the Templar warrant and the proof of ownership for Amica should be kept in a safe place while we travel. If God forbid we are robbed..."

"Then where is such a place? What do ye advise?" he asked as he groomed Amica in the byre.

Charlotte lightly scratched the stallion's forehead. She looked around. "Inside the saddle?"

When Odo was given the stallion by Sir Gweir, he was also given the saddle, bridle and other tack. Sir Wystan preferred the traditional knight's saddle, similar in design to the Roman saddle, with high pommels in front and cannels at the rear. Mellester's former lord also preferred longer stirrups, instead of shorter stirrups many knights still used. This made for easier riding but less mobility when mounted. The saddle tree was constructed from wood, but strengthened by steel and stuffed with wool and covered in leather. When alive, Sir Wystan may have had numerous character flaws, but his expertise on horseback was unquestioned, if not brutal in method.

Charlotte eyed the saddle that lay across the wooden railing. "Perhaps we could hide them inside the saddle?" she repeated.

Odo stepped away from Amica to look carefully at the saddle. He tipped it up on its end and studied the rear thoughtfully. "Aye, s'pose we could," he said as he placed a finger through a fold of the leather into the inside. "In here will work."

It was agreed, and after rolling and individually wrapping both the Templar warrant and the receipt for Amica tightly in leather, Odo stuffed the two small cylinders into the inside of the saddle where they were completely undetectable and safe.

The following morning, with Odo riding Amica and Charlotte riding the placid hackney, Sally, they said farewell and departed Mellester under a cloudless sky and a promise of warm weather. It was a beautiful day and both horses had a spring in their step, enjoying being away from the constraints of the paddock where both animals normally grazed. Charlotte was not an expert on horseback, although she was somewhat competent and sensibly knew her limitations and abilities. Forgoing skirts, they were similarly dressed. For practicality, she wore woollen breeches and a capuchin but Odo remarked it did little to hide her beauty .

The cloud of misery hanging over Odo seemed to lift and his mood changed once clear of Mellester. Laughter came easily, and the pain in his head that had plagued him daily, faded away. Both of them were happy, in love and it showed. They waved to those they passed, offering cheerful greetings and kind words to everyone. Even Amica seemed to be in good spirits.

It was mid-afternoon when Charlotte challenged Odo and Amica to a race. "First to that tree," she pointed to the solitary landmark in the distance. "Ye must allow me to go first, then count to thirty before ye begin," she laughed.

Odo readily accepted, although Charlotte's unfair advantage made it challenging. Sally lumbered off as Odo began to count. He stopped after ten, then waited until he thought Charlotte and Sally were far enough away before he allowed Amica to spring forward and surge after them.

Sally wasn't really a galloper, more of a plodder, but she did her best and Charlotte looked behind to see Odo laying low over Amica's neck as they sprinted towards her. It would be a close finish.

The tree was only a short distance ahead when she saw two figures standing in its shade. She pulled Sally to a stop early and waited for Odo to arrive. Amica was tossing its head as he slid to a stop beside her. Odo saw the men beneath the shade of the branches.

"Hail friends!" came a voice.

"Hail, good sirs!" replied Odo. "Keep behind me," he advised Charlotte as he nudged Amica a little closer to better see the two men.

As they approached, it was clear to Odo one man was a knight. The other man was immense, a brute, and towered over the knight but wore the livery of a sergeant. A single horse was hobbled and ate grass a short distance away. Odo cautiously kept himself between Charlotte and the two strangers.

"Is a lovely day to be out," greeted Odo.

"This day could have fared better," replied the knight while looking at Amica. "Misfortune has struck a cruel blow and my horse suffered a broken leg … she lies yonder past the corner in the road."

Odo grimaced. A broken leg on a horse was irreparable, and the knight would have had to put the beast out of its misery. "I'm sorry, for yer loss. I am Herdsman Odo and this is my wife, Charlotte."

Charlotte nodded but kept respectfully silent.

"I am Sir Ector and bound for Ireland to join the king's forces. This is

Jagger, my sergeant."

The huge man smiled warmly at Odo and nodded to Charlotte.

On closer inspection, Odo saw he had a youthful face but he certainly was no youth. The man was abnormally large – a veritable giant. "Ye are late to be going to Ireland; my lord left some weeks ago."

"I suffered injury in France and could not leave with the king until mended," replied Sir Ector, taking a casual step closer to Odo. "We are headed to Wales to catch a ship. Or we were."

"I hope ye fare well, milord, but now we must take our leave as we have somewhere to be."

"Ye have an impressive horse," complimented the knight as he took another step. The sergeant followed.

Odo was becoming uncomfortable. "Thank ye, milord," He gave Charlotte a quick glance.

"Is very unusual to see a villein on such a fine animal." Sir Ector turned to his sergeant and said something neither Odo nor Charlotte could hear and then faced them again. He wasn't smiling.

"I am a freeman … is there a problem, milord?" Odo asked, feeling stirrings of anxiety.

The knight turned back to his sergeant and suddenly cuffed him over the back of his head. Finally, and with obvious reluctance, the sergeant strode forward and quickly reached for Amica's bridle. Before Odo could react, the knight unsheathed his sword. "I suggest, Herdsman Odo, that ye dismount. I will take possession of this beautiful horse. I am in need of a courser and God has answered my prayers and so provided. Unmount!" The sword arced up, its sharp point within striking distance of Odo's chest.

"The horse is mine, I have–"

"Don't!" Charlotte hissed.

Odo looked at her in question.

"No, Odo, ye can't say anything," she whispered, and shook her head.

"Have yer something to say?" asked Sir Ector overhearing her.

"This is my horse!" appealed Odo. "Yer can't take him, it is theft."

The knight was becoming angry. "Are ye challenging me, a mere serf defying a knight?" His expression hardened and his eyes bored into Odo. "Remember yerself."

"Sire?" questioned the sergeant.

"Hold the horse fast, idiot!"

The sword tip pressed against his chest and he could feel the sharp point through his clothes. "The horse belongs to me and I am a freeman!" Odo repeated defiantly. He was struggling to control himself, the cold steel a reminder his life hung in the balance. He knew the knight could eviscerate him with one simple slash.

The sword remained steady, unwavering.

"Then ye are insolent and disrespectful of yer betters."

"Nay, milord, just protecting what is rightfully mine." Odo began lifting his leg to unmount.

"I will take this animal, and ye won't stop me."

"Then milord, leave me the saddle," Odo appealed.

"I can't do that, my saddle lays beneath my horse. Dismount!" Sir Ector tensed, ready to strike.

Jagger, the sergeant, seemed to anticipate his master. "Nay, sire!" he yelled.

Sir Ector lunged, his sword thrust forward, but Odo slid backward from Amica's back and landed safely on the ground. The sword swished dangerously close.

The stallion was fighting with the sergeant and pulling his head back, but Jagger was strong and held him secure. In panic, Amica began to sidestep away from the knight as he prepared to mount. "Hold him still, want-wit!" Sir Ector shouted angrily at the sergeant.

Odo took another step backward as Amica tried to lash out with his rear hooves. The knight was an experienced horseman and easily anticipated Amica's flailing legs. He sheathed his sword and quickly placed a foot in a stirrup, and before Amica could react, hopped twice and smoothly launched himself up and into the saddle. Amica raised his head and screeched, then with the knight trying to maintain control, they took off down the road. Odo could hear the knight's laughter.

The big sergeant turned to Odo and stared wordlessly. It appeared he wanted to say something and then thought better of it. He shrugged, shook his head, then turned and ran to his horse to remove the hobble. Odo squatted on the road with his hands to his head as the sergeant rode after his master.

Sally foraged for grass on the roadside as Charlotte and Odo sat huddled together.

"I'm so sorry, Odo, if I hadn't told you to not say anything, then we wouldn't be in this mess." Her eyes glistened as she looked into her husband's face.

Odo shook his head. "If the knight would have seen the Templar warrant, he would have taken it, of that ye can be sure. There was no way we could have proved we owned Amica without revealing the warrant."

"I should have kept quiet–"

"Ye did nothing wrong, Charlotte, ye may have saved us. We will go to Taunton and report the theft. Then we can prove to everyone Amica is ours."

"If we can get near the saddle, and how do we do that?" she asked.

A short time later, with Charlotte seated behind him on Sally, they headed towards Taunton where they hoped to find Sir Ector and Amica.

CHAPTER FOURTEEN

Summoned by Steward Alard, Reeve Petrus entered Mellester's great hall to find Priest Benedict and Sir Dwain already seated and waiting for him at one of the benches.

"Why the long faces?" the reeve asked pleasantly, seeing their frowns.

Steward Alard waved an arm for him to be seated. "Petrus, we have a problem."

The reeve looked up, his own smile faded and he nodded in acquiescence. "Aye, I've been hearing about it for days now."

"When Sir Gweir departed for Ireland, he ensured the manor had ample funds. He even made sure Sir Hyde had provided his share of the costs for the Falls Ende mill in advance," stated the steward. "But now, after all that has happened with the murrain and the robbery, the villagers cannot meet their rent." He turned to the priest. "Benedict, has the church received all its tithes?"

"Nay, not since I've arrived here. Most people have been unable to give. It preys on my mind because soon I must tell Bishop Immers."

"As I thought," replied the steward. "The manor has not been receiving income, and I have been using reserves to pay for manor expenses. In another twenty days, I will have no more coin, the coffers will be empty. Construction on the mill will have to stop unless we can find a way to recover the money that was stolen by the brigands, and then some."

"The bishop will require the Church receives tithes before the manor does," the priest offered. "I know this because of the plight of other poor manors who failed to meet their tithes. Bishop Immers declared the Church comes first."

"It was the bloody bishop who was behind the theft in the first place," volunteered the reeve angrily.

Sir Dain scowled and grunted in agreement.

"Aye, and the manor isn't generating any coin…" said the reeve. "Then we will have to halt construction. The manor can ill afford to pay for the mill when coin is needed elsewhere."

Everyone nodded in agreement.

"But how long will it take before the manor becomes productive again?" asked the steward.

"As far as animals go, we can safely begin grazing cows after the equinox. It could be a cold and hungry winter for many," said the reeve.

"Could be worse," replied Steward Alard, "at least is only nine months distant."

"Nay, ye are wrong. Tell me, from where will the cows come from? There are no cows within miles of here, they've all been culled. Who has the money to purchase cows?" He looked from face to face and received no response.

"Is Ridgley Manor suffering as we are?" asked Sir Dwain.

"Nay, the murrain has not struck Ridgley Manor, not yet," volunteered Petrus. "And perhaps it will not strike there."

"And they have more varied ways of generating income," added Alard. "I will go to Ridgley Manor and seek counsel with Steward Baldric; he may offer the benefit of his acumen.

Reeve Petrus leaned forward on his elbows and stared at the roughhewn wood of the bench top. He knew Mellester couldn't survive the winter if something weren't done. *But what?*

The three horsemen slowed as Odo yelled in greeting. "Hail to ye, I seek the bailiff, do ye know where I can find him?" Odo impatiently asked the approaching men.

Just ahead of them was their destination of Taunton. Here at the town's outskirts, the air was rank, discarded refuse lay in stinking piles either side of the road near a large ditch that surrounded the town. Rats scurried over the rubbish, oblivious and uncaring of the newcomers who stood gathered in the centre of the road. Odo and Charlotte rode as fast as Sally could carry them until they saw the three horsemen riding from the town. They paused and waited as one man, better dressed than the others, walked his horse closer.

"What do yer need the bailiff for?" he growled. His eyes darted to Charlotte and lingered.

"My horse was stolen, and I wish to report the theft. Perhaps you saw the thief ride this way?" Odo asked with some hope.

The man's expression changed. "Then ye'd be Herdsman Odo?"

Odo was immediately suspicious. "Ye have me at a disbenefit, good sir. Ye know my name, but I know yers not."

The man smiled for the first time. "I am Bailiff Ernoul Granger, the man ye seek." Before Odo could reply, he continued. "We have matters of importance to discuss."

"Oh, and why is that, do tell." Odo could feel Charlotte gripping him tighter. He knew she was as concerned as he was.

The bailiff laughed and turned briefly to the men behind him. "He wishes to know why?" They shared his mirth and began laughing. "Do ye think we welcome all travellers to the good town of Taunton personally, that we stand here with open arms to congreet ye and yer woman?"

Odo tried to take measure of the man.

"Ye have saved me considerable time, Herdsman Odo, fer I have left the repose of my burgh to find ye. Come, let us ride back together and ye can tell me why it is ye seek Taunton's bailiff?"

The two men accompanying the bailiff moved behind Sally to bring up the rear while Bailiff Ernoul rode alongside them.

They rode past the ditch and over an old bridge, through the town's gates and headed towards a market up ahead. The town wasn't as large as some as Odo had seen, but for Charlotte, it was huge. Every now and then they could see glimpses of a castle that peeked ominously above the houses and a church spire that rose to dizzying heights. A few people stared curiously at them, and the bailiff nodded in greeting to some he passed and ignored the taunts of others. Odo explained in detail how Sir Ector stole his horse and the bailiff listened and remained silent, preferring for Odo to talk.

Bailiff Ernoul directed Odo down a side street and towards the castle. Once inside the inner bailey, Bailiff Ernoul indicated for Odo and Charlotte to dismount. Never had Odo been inside a castle before and both he and

Charlotte stared incredulously at its size.

One of the men who accompanied the bailiff stepped up to Odo and grabbed his arm. "This way."

He tried to shake off the man's grip, but the bailiff's man held him firmly. "What is this!" cried Odo as he tried to free himself. "Leave me!"

"Ah, yes, I forgot to tell ye," exclaimed Bailiff Ernoul, "I've arrested ye for theft. Seems ye stole a knight's horse. Doesn't look good fer ye and I don't expect that will sit well with the court." He gave Odo a disparaging look.

"Ye can't be doing that," cried Charlotte as she stepped in front of the bailiff, "he has not stolen anything, ye are mistaken."

"Away with yer, he'll 'ave his chance to explain to the court."

The bailiff tried to step around Charlotte, but she wasn't having any of it. She wouldn't let him walk around her. "This is wrong, and ye know it!"

He grabbed her and pushed her roughly aside. "If ye don't leave, then I'll lock ye up as well! Be off with yer, wench!"

Each of the bailiff's helpers had one of Odo's arms and began leading him away. "Charlotte!" he yelled over his shoulder, "yer know what to do!"

Charlotte's heart pounded in her chest. Her face flushed, her anger vehement, she wanted to scream; she was helpless against these men. There was nothing she could do. She clenched and unclenched her fists and tried to calm her breathing as she watched Odo being led inside Taunton Castle.

Behind Mellester's manor house, on the far side of a large courtyard, lay a cluster of buildings that provided housing for men-at-arms, knights and guests. Additionally, there was a smithy, stables, a workshop, storage rooms for food and a few other necessary structures. The gaol was in the last building which was also used for storage and housing the pillory.

No one saw the reeve enter the gaol; there were no guards posted to watch over the prisoner as all available men-at-arms were in the village keeping watch for the return of the outlaws. The prisoner was well taken care of and given a fine meal once a day and he had plenty of water. He had want for nothing except, perhaps, his freedom.

When the reeve came to visit, he wanted nothing more than to question the man and confirm who sent the outlaws to Mellester and why. Petrus wasn't in a congenial mood when he first spoke to the outlaw and it didn't improve any with the prisoner's belligerent, obsequious attitude.

The outlaw's reluctance to share information prompted the reeve to take matters into his own hands. The key to the gaol cell was hanging from a hook near the large doorway and Petrus quickly unlocked the steel door and entered the cell carrying only his staff, and faced the smirking inmate.

Not long after, Petrus locked the cell, replaced the key on its dedicated hook and quietly left the building with distressing knowledge. It was now confirmed Abbot Andrew had hired the outlaws on the express wishes of Bishop Immers. The prisoner, who now regretted his unsocial behaviour, had eventually talked as the reeve knew he would. He gave his name as Seth and presently lay battered and bleeding on the stone floor of Mellester's fine gaol.

Reeve Petrus gave the matter a great deal of consideration and decided there was only one viable option. He informed Steward Alard that he had matters to attend to elsewhere. He would be absent for three days and leave on the morrow.

He strapped his sword around his waist, tied his staff to the saddle and before the morning sun fully rose, rode from Mellester Manor. His mood was dour, his face grim and his disposition determined.

The sun was directly overhead when Petrus rode into Exeter and he headed immediately for the cathedral.

Bishop Immers, with one of his clerks, was currently reviewing new levies that he would impose over his diocese. This was an ongoing dispute with his clerics and priests; they always claimed the parishes were poor and could ill afford to contribute more which prompted some vociferous debate. As Immers insisted, a new cathedral needed to be built. He had a small retinue of soldiers that needed to be paid and of course, he had to pay for the exorbitant tastes of his bloated clergy who wasted his valuable coin on the unnecessary and frivolous. Increased tithes, he reminded them time and time again, were the only sensible alternative.

An interruption gave pause to his trenchant homily, which offered some needed respite to the attending cleric.

"Yer Grace, ye have an unannounced caller," informed the young priest at the door.

The bishop twisted to face the priest. "Who is it?" he grumbled testily.

"Ah, Yer Grace, it is Mellester Manor's reeve, Petrus Bodkin."

"Tell him to go away, I'm indisposed."

"Yer Grace, I have informed him of this, but he insists that he speak with ye."

"I have no time fer rabble, see him away!"

"As ye wish, Yer Grace." With delicacy and sensitive to the bishop's temperment, lest he be offended, the priest shut the heavy door with nary a sound.

Bishop Immers turned back to the cleric who thought he'd been reprieved from a further haranguing. "How is it possible for the Church to administer to the parishes if we are ill-kept, hungry, in rags and slatternly? It is God's desire to see the Church preside over–"

The door flew open and banged into the wall with a crash. Petrus winced inwardly; he didn't intend to fling it open with such force. With his staff firmly in his grasp, and unbidden, he limped inside and faced the bishop. "Excuse my interruption, Yer Grace, but I have an important matter to discuss with ye. I–"

"How dare ye disrespect the sanctity of the Church and disobey my instructions! Have ye no reverence? Be gone!" The bishop's face turned scarlet with anger.

Petrus, readjusted his belt and took a deep breath. *Too late to stop now*, he thought, and took another step closer to the bishop. "I think it best we speak now, then I'll be on my way, Yer Grace. It won't take long." The reeve did his utmost to keep his voice moderated and his tone even.

Bishop Immers looked up at the reeve and saw his grim expression. He flicked his fingers at the cleric, who gathered his scrolls and quickly exited the room. In the doorway, stood the young priest. The Bishop gave him a nod, and the priest shut the door and hurried away to call the guards.

"Ye have no cause to interrupt the sanctified work of the Church, I will give ye a moment and then ye will go." He raised a jewel encrusted hand

and waved it dismissively at the door. "Guards have been summoned, so be brisk."

Reeve Petrus gave the bishop a cold stare. "I've been told that ye were behind those responsible for the robbery at Mellester. Much was taken and–"

"I will not sit here and listen to false accusations!" The bishop's fist thumped on the table.

"I wouldn't be here if they were false, Bishop," Petrus interrupted. "I'm here because the good people of Mellester suffer because they have no coin to meet their rent or tithes – they will starve. The murrain–"

"Ha," exclaimed the bishop, "The murrain, a pestilence from God, a gift to the unworthy."

The door was again thrust open and banged against the wall. A man-at-arms strode in and paused.

"See him off!" instructed the bishop.

Unperturbed, Reeve Petrus stood his ground. He stepped closer to the bishop and leaned forward. "I'm here to have ye repay the coin taken from the good people of Mellester. All of it! And I will see it done." The reeves eyes were slits and a vein throbbed on his neck.

The man-at-arms unsheathed his sword and took two steps towards the reeve.

Reeve Petrus was enraged and required all his self-control to not strike out at the simpering bishop.

The unsuspecting man-at-arms was no match for the experienced reeve and he felt the wrath of his ire. Without turning, the reeve's staff whipped up and struck the guard solidly between his legs. It was a hard and cruel blow, meant to stop the man-at-arms and indeed the ploy worked. The guard crumpled to the cathedral's floor gasping, his sword clattered uselessly away, quickly forgotten.

"Ye will suffer fer yer actions, how dare ye!" Bishop Immers glared.

"Mellester's good folk deserve better, ye will repay what was taken, of that ye can be sure," hissed the reeve.

Two more guards rushed into the room. Reeve Petrus turned to face them. "Go away, this concerns ye not. I warn ye both."

"Kill him!" snarled the bishop as he backed up against the wall. "Kill him! He has threatened my life!"

Both guards unsheathed their swords and without hesitation, attacked the reeve.

With lightening quick reflexes, the reeve thrust his staff at the first onrushing guard hitting him squarely on the chest. Clutching his injured ribs and winded, the guard sank to his knees. Petrus dropped the staff and unsheathed his own sword. He straightened and appeared relaxed and unfazed by the unfolding drama. His sword angled down and pointed to the right, halfway between both his left and right leg. The guard launched into an unimaginative lunge, and with the sword tip aimed for the reeve's heart, he advanced quicker than what was considered wise. It was a foolish inexperienced manoeuvre, and with little effort, the reeve countered easily. His sword flicked up twisted around the oncoming blade and deflected it. With his free hand, Petrus grabbed the tunic of the lunging guard, pulled him close and gave him a good head-butt. He joined his friend slumped on the floor. The reeve kicked the swords away and turned back to the bishop, he wasn't even breathing hard.

"I will make ye suffer–" the bishop sputtered.

"Ye will do no such thing except return to the people of Mellester the coin you stole. I want that coin in Mellester in seven days. On the eighth day, if I don't see that coin, I will return here for ye, and yer army of lads won't stop me." His eyes bored into the bishop's before finally turning to leave.

"I will see you drawn and quartered first!"

"Perhaps, but ye will return the coin ye stole." The reeve used his foot to push a guard back down to the floor who was trying desperately to stand. He picked up his staff and limped from the room. His next stop was an alehouse.

CHAPTER FIFTEEN

The room was small, dark and windowless. Dirty rushes covered the floor and a tallow candle sat on a small wobbly table pushed against a grimy wall. The candle flickered constantly, protesting against a cold draught that snaked its way through the building and into her room. Other guests at the inn, their raised voices seeping porously through paper-thin walls weren't seeing eye to eye and their disagreements, so full of anger and hate, and no longer private, seemed trivial and unimportant and pervaded her assiduous introspection. Charlotte sat on the horse-hair stuffed mattress and stared sightlessly at the yellow, smoky and agitated flame of the candle.

On leaving Taunton Castle, she had spoken to a few local merchants and learned that the Lord of the Manor of Taunton, was in fact Henry of Blois, the Bishop of Winchester. In proxy, he assigned a seneschal who would preside over the manorial court to be held at the week's end. Odo was to be judged, not by the Lord of the Manor, but by a seneschal, a judiciary who was by all accounts a fair and just man. This gave her some measure of hope. However, when Odo yelled at her, "Yer know what to do," he meant that she needed to locate that despicable knight and find the saddle that contained the receipt from Steward Alard proving Odo owned the black stallion.

After leaving the merchants, she quickly found the Swan Inn as recommended. It had modest tariffs and was suitable – only just. With Sally securely stabled and fed, Charlotte now needed to find a place where knights would find suitable lodging. She stood, blew out the candle and exited the inn to find herself on Taunton's main thoroughfare known as the Parade.

It would soon be dark, and she knew not to tarry. Dressed in breeches and a tunic, she attracted little attention and began searching for the finer lodgings that a knight would seek. It was astounding how many there were and at each place she visited, the proprietor shook his head and dismissed her. No one knew of Sir Ector or Jagger, his sergeant. She returned to the Swan Inn dispirited, but she wouldn't give up, not yet. There were more places to visit tomorrow. With her heart aching for Odo, she finally fell asleep, exhausted.

Filthy stinking straw covered most of the floor. Each of the six men locked inside the Taunton castle's gaol found a suitable place to sit, as far away as possible from the others, and contemplated their destiny as men do who are resigned to the foibles of feudal law and judgment from the manorial court. A couple of men spoke to each other and swapped stories of how they came to be incarcerated. Others preferred silence and solitude and didn't engage in conversation. Odo was morose and grieved; again he'd been taken advantage of by those who prided themselves on their honour. All that separated those dishonourable men from the men in the gaol was noble distinction, a man-made division. Nobility wasn't a birth right that assured superiority. Odo knew men, poor men, with hardly two pennies to rub together who demonstrated honour and selflessness to an extent that surpassed many knights he'd encountered. Yes, there were some nobles who were kind and generous, but born into gentry was not the deciding factor. From this day forward he, reminded himself, I will judge a man by his actions and not by the size of his purse or lofty title.

He missed Charlotte and was worried for her. He hoped she'd found safe lodgings and would quickly begin to search for Sir Ector. From what Bailiff Ernoul said, the punishment for horse stealing was severe. "Don't expect leniency," he said. "The court is fair, and for the guilty, punishment is swift and without mercy." Comforting words he didn't need to hear.

The dark, dankness of the gaol was oppressive. Water dripped from one wall and ran into cracks on the stone floor and disappeared somewhere below. Rats came and went with impunity, their brazen excursions into the confined space were risky; if caught, they'd most likely be eaten by those who'd been here longer. The incarcerated at Taunton's gaol were responsible for feeding themselves and if you had coin, a halfpenny could purchase a simple meal a day for just three days.

Odo shifted his position and wrapped his arms around his knees. The hard, cold stone offered little in the way of comfort and he knew that he had no option but to believe Charlotte would come through for him. He rested his head on his knees and turned his thoughts again to all the things in his life that made him happy. Charlotte, his cows... and then he remembered, he didn't have cows anymore.

She'd been to every lodging in Taunton and no one knew where Sir Ector and Jagger were quartered. One washerwoman she talked with heard he was living with friends, with other knights at a nearby manor. It was a futile, time-wasting search.

Again she sat on the mattress in her room at the Swan Inn. After traipsing through Taunton's streets and narrow thoroughfares all day, the silence broken by loud conversations and revelry in adjoining rooms only added to her exasperation. She knew Taunton's seneschal, Steward Cederic, would hold court in two days' time. Perhaps the best option would be to return to Mellester and have Steward Alard write a new proof of ownership document. If she hurried and left Taunton early, she could be in Mellester, get the document and be back in Taunton the night before Odo was due to appear before the court. It was her only viable option, and so emboldened, she lay her head down and fell into a troubled sleep.

"Steward Alard ain't 'ere, he'd be at Ridgley Manor." The man-at-arms guarding the door to Mellester Manor's great hall blocked access.

Charlotte clutched her head. "Nay, this can't be…"

"Best ye move along."

"When will he return?"

The guard remained silent.

"Please, it's important," she appealed.

He sighed. "On the morrow more'n likely."

"And Reeve Petrus, where is he, I need to speak with him?"

"Aye, well yer see, he'd be gone too."

"Gone? Where has he gone?"

The guard shrugged.

Charlotte was crestfallen. *And Cathal was at Ridley Manor too, everyone had gone*. She turned to walk away then stopped as an idea came to mind. "Who is governing the manor?"

"Sir Dain, he'd be inside."

"Can ye let me see him? It's about Odo, he needs help," she pleaded.

The man-at-arms looked uncertain. However, he was aware that Herdsman Odo Read was seen favourably by Mellester's nobles. He relented and led Charlotte into the hall where Sir Dain sat at a bench talking with a young squire.

Sir Dain scratched his beard after hearing Charlotte's plea. "I will send a messenger to Ridgley Manor, and have Steward Alard create what ye need. I advise ye return to Taunton with fastness and wait for the messenger to arrive. All will be well, Charlotte," offered the knight with a warm smile.

"Thank ye, milord." Charlotte dipped her head. "Ah, milord, could ye not write such a document, something to take to the court?" She looked up at him with a measure of hope.

"Alas, I cannot, my... uh, my arm... uh, it suffers still." He looked apologetic. "And it is doubtful Taunton's seneschal will acknowledge me in court, I know not of him, nor he of me."

"Then, milord, I shall return to Taunton at first light and wait at the Swan Inn."

Sir Dain nodded. "Fear not, all will be well."

Reeve Petrus Bodkin's eyes blinked open. Without moving his head, he stared up at the night sky. Stars blinked briefly as they always had and always would, then temporarily disappeared as clouds obscured them again. He was cold, thirsty and hungry and racked in pain. He wasn't sure how long he'd lain here, but he suspected longer than a day. His tongue flicked over blood encrusted lips. Water, he needed water.

He tried to piece together what happened, but his recollections were murky. The only thing he knew with certainty was he would die here.

When he first woke he discovered he lay in a muddy ditch. No doubt his assailants believed him to be dead and discarded the body where no one would find it. Unable to move without excruciating pain, he managed to shift his body enough so that his head now rested partially against the side of the ditch. From time to time, rats, the size of cats scurried over him and thankfully spared him no time. At first he tried to strike at them with an arm, but moving it was agony. After a while he gave up and let them do as they pleased. He screamed for help, but his cries were lost to the wind and went unheeded. He figured that the men who attacked him at the inn threw him into the ditch, presumably on the outskirts of Exeter, knowing he'd never be found.

Oh yes, he knew who they were. They were the same men who'd ransacked and robbed Mellester. He saw them at the inn after leaving Bishop Immers and recognized their leader. Someone called the man Lyman.

It was at the Inn when he was struck brutally from behind and fell to the floor where he was set upon by a handful of violent men. There was little he could do to protect himself and couldn't recall anything else before waking in the ditch.

He'd explored his injuries with the emotionless patience of a man resigned to death. He began with his head and the numerous wounds that initially bled profusely and had eventually clotted and then stopped. His neck was sore but he could move it in incremental amounts. Ribs were broken, perhaps two or three. Any movement caused shooting pains so intense he saw white. His previously injured knee was reinjured and he knew he had a broken bone on his good leg. His right wrist was swollen and also possibly broken and his left shoulder was damaged somehow. The biggest concern was the knife wound in his side. It still bled and he knew festered implacably. He closed his eyes and hoped death would come soon – he was so thirsty.

Crows circled Ridley Manor, their incessant cackling disquieting for many. Cathal had been attending to Sir Hyde who was now stable, but not out of danger. Even after much care and attention, the minor arrow wound continued to moulder and eventually the smell of death pervaded Cathal's senses. Sir Hyde was delirious and Cathal wisely informed those close to the ailing lord that the injured arm would have to be removed. All heads nodded; those consigned with his care contended that a barber be called to perform the procedure. "Absolutely not!" Cathal insisted. There wasn't a barber within miles of Ridgley Manor he'd entrust to remove the arm without killing him. "I will do this task," he informed them with finality. "At least then he stands a chance of surviving."

For two days after Cathal removed the arm, they'd cared for Sir Hyde and feared he would not last the night. But surprisingly he did, and then the next day and night as well. Time to heal and constant care was what Sir Hyde needed, but there was little more Cathal could do. However, unable to sleep, Cathal walked the outside perimeter of Ridgley Manor's great house, unsure to the cause of his unease. When the messenger came last evening and informed Steward Alard, who was visiting Steward Baldric, of Odo's dilemma in Taunton, the feeling of apprehension only worsened. His first impulse was to leave Ridgley Manor immediately and deliver Steward Alard's document to the seneschal himself and come to Odo's need. But a nagging, persistent feeling told him otherwise and this was the patent cause of his qualms.

Cathal trusted his instincts as few men did. He couldn't explain or answer why when asked. There was a force and an energy that existed that he could rely and depend on. It wasn't whimsical or arbitrary; the energy was pure, honest and powerful. He felt it as a man feels pain or love - you can sense it, feel it, know it is there, but cannot expound on. To the Irish fili it was self-belief and an undeniable faith he trusted.

As dawn broke over Ridgley Manor, Cathal stood at the stone wall surrounding the manor house and looked skyward. Circling crows were perplexing, their agitation unusual, and he felt the knot of anxiousness begin in the pit of his stomach. Without a second thought he turned from the crows and sensing urgency, returned to the stables where he slept and fetched his bag, extracting a small leather pouch from inside.

He squatted, loosened the tie that secured the bag's contents and upturned it. Bones scattered randomly onto the hard packed dirt. He bent down to inspect how they fell and spoke quietly in unintelligible whispers. He stared for some time, muttering occasionally, then scooped them up, carefully replaced them and walked back to the wall and looked up. The crows had vanished. He waited and stood alone. He felt the foreboding like a descending blackness greater than before, but he wasn't sick. He felt the need, but not its touch. He heard a calling but no voice. He stood patiently, a solitary figure listening for something yet to be heard, because he knew it would come. It was time to leave Ridgley manor.

CHAPTER SIXTEEN

It was the same young squire that she saw talking to Sir Dain that brought the document from Steward Alard. She was relieved and gushed with heartfelt thanks when he handed it to her. Now she hoped that the court would act with integrity. The squire, having fulfilled his duty, bid her farewell and set out to return to Mellester where he was needed, while she returned to her squalid room to wait for morn.

The room where freemen were judged was beside the castle; an unremarkable room with bench seats arranged in such a way that people could observe the proceedings without interfering, as tended to happen on occasion. Two men-at-arms stood at the entrance and two more stood guard near a table where the seneschal would sit. About a dozen people were already seated and talked quietly amongst themselves. Of Sir Ector, she saw no sign, but expected he would attend.

After a long wait, a door at the rear of the room opened and another man-at-arms led six manacled prisoners in a long procession into the room. Odo was last in line and he looked dreadful. When she saw him look around the room, she stood and waved the letter. He smiled in return but appeared dispirited. She tried to sit closer and talk with him, but a guard shooed her away. He tried to speak, but was struck by a vine stick wielded by a guard. He could only twist his head and look at her, his eyes sorrowful and pleading.

Finally the seneschal entered, followed by a cleric, and Bailiff Ernoul Granger brought up the rear. Charlotte shifted her attention to the seneschal, Steward Cederic. He was a rotund man with a grave expression and little eyes. Her eyes were drawn to a large misshapen mole on his left cheek that bounced up and down as he spoke, the dark blob seeming to move on its own accord. She tore her gaze away from the steward and searched the room – still no sign of Sir Ector.

The proceedings began without a fuss and the first arraigned man was accused of beating a merchant senseless. When given the opportunity to speak, he claimed to have purchased a steel pot from a merchant and when put over a fire it melted. When the merchant failed to return his coin, the man hit him with the pot repeatedly and would have killed him had onlookers not intervened.

Steward Cederic spoke little and listened attentively. Bailiff Ernoul offered his perspective from time to time and within moments the steward arrived at a decision. The guilty man was sentenced to one day in the pillory and the merchant was required to return the coin he took for the defective pot.

Charlotte, engrossed in the proceedings, failed to see Sir Ector stride into the room. It was when the bailiff nodded in greeting to the knight that she first saw him. He walked to the far side of the room, sat on a bench reserved for nobles and slouched with detached arrogance. His appearance caused a stir; it wasn't often a knight appeared at a manorial court. She didn't know if he saw and recognized her. Of his sergeant, she saw no sign.

The next man to be judged by Steward Cederic had killed a man in a drunken brawl over a woman. As per usual, it was dealt with quickly and efficiently and the man was sentenced to a flogging.

And so the morning went. The fifth man to face the court was accused of being a vagrant, a man without a home. If the bailiff's expression was anything to go by, this was a serious offence in Taunton. Charlotte had never conceived the possibility that a man would have no home. When asked to explain himself, the accused began to inform the steward how he was deposited in Taunton by a large eagle and was waiting for the bird to return to take him back to his lands in a place no one had ever heard of. Most spectators found this amusing and laughed. Steward Cederic didn't; his austere expression remained unchanged, his face grim.

He whispered to Bailiff Ernoul then to the cleric recording the proceedings and passed judgment. "Ye will forfeit the use of yer left hand!"

The spectators didn't react. The punishment for being without a home was serious, but the guilty man seemed incapable of understanding that his left hand would be removed. He politely thanked the steward.

"Herdsman Odo Read, ye are called before the court to face the charge of horse theft!"

The court spectators stirred. To deprive a noble of his horse, a trained and expensive courser, was indeed consequential.

Odo shifted his position, and looked quickly at Charlotte.

Bailiff Ernoul quickly explained the circumstances and turned to the knight. "Please tell us what happened, Sir Ector?"

Sir Ector made it seem like he apprehended brigands and took Amica from a dangerous outlaw. He recognised the horse because he was well acquainted with Sir Wystan who owned it. It was a remarkable animal he told everyone, a vicious bad tempered beast offset by incredible beauty – an unforgettable horse. Upon the death of Sir Wystan how could a commoner, a mere herdsman afford to purchase such an expensive horse, he asked, his voice loud and assured. Charlotte was livid and wanted to present the steward with the document she had. Odo shook his head. Not yet.

Sir Ector finished his embellished tale and sat smugly.

"Herdsman Odo Read, ye have the privilege to explain yourself to this court before I decide yer punishment," instructed Steward Cedric.

Charlotte almost choked. *Odo was already judged guilty?*

Odo had days to mull over how he would explain himself, and Charlotte had confidence he would do so quite well. Her heart swelled with pride as he stood.

"Milord," concluded Odo, "It seems the ownership of the horse is really what is in question. I have a document to show ye all that the horse belongs to me."

"Oh?" Steward Cederic inclined his head, "Bring me this document."

Charlotte stood. "I have it, milords."

"Who are ye?"

"This is my woman, Charlotte, milord," Odo informed them.

The steward extended a fleshy hand and curled his fingers repeatedly, indicating for Charlotte to bring it over.

She stepped to the table where the steward sat and handed it to him and returned quickly to her seat.

It was quiet as the steward read Alard's proof of ownership letter. The cleric craned his neck to read; the bailiff, unable to read, sat back and stared at Odo.

Her heart pounded in her chest as she waited. She risked a look at Sir Ector. He winked at her.

"I am not acquainted with Steward Alard, although I am familiar with his name. I understand he is a good and just man," said Steward Cederic. His mole bounced as he spoke. "If I understand what ye said correctly, ye received this horse as a gift from the Lord of the Manor, Sir Gweir?"

Sir Ector snorted in derision.

"Aye, milord," Odo replied.

"But this document," he held it up and waved it, "was only created yesterday." He looked puzzled. "I cannot accept this as complete proof of ownership. It does, however, make me question it."

Sir Ector laughed.

"I can explain, milord," Odo stated.

"Quickly, now," said the steward waving his hand.

"I hid the original proof of ownership document in the saddle that sat on the horse. Because Sir Ector took the horse with the saddle, I was unable to show it to ye. This is why Charlotte returned to Mellester Manor to get another, milord." Odo turned to Charlotte for confirmation. She nodded enthusiastically.

Sir Ector scoffed. Others began to laugh.

"And ye say, the original warrant is hidden inside the saddle?"

"Aye, milord."

"Then, Sir Ector, where is this saddle?" asked Steward Cederic. The mole bounced in perfect time.

The steward needed to be careful. If what the herdsman said was true, and Mellester's Lord did indeed gift the horse, then he needed, with absolute certainty, to ensure there was no room for an error of judgement. Sir Gweir, Mellester's Lord, swore allegiance to Sir Hyde Fortescue, a powerful lord, and not one to risk upsetting. If Sir Ector had taken the horse from the herdsman in error, then he risks dishonouring the knight. This particular case was not about right or wrong, or who'd committed the actual crime, it was about passing judgement in such a way where he didn't offend powerful lords. No matter how he adjudicated, nobility would be offended. He needed to tread carefully.

"My sergeant is tasked with cleaning it, milord, it isn't far away. But what this commoner says is twaddle. Ye can't go believing *his* word over mine. Ye don't know if that letter is real and ye must ignore it. He stole the horse from Sir Wystan." He raised an arm and pointed at Odo. "He's a thief, and should be drawn and quartered!"

The bailiff nodded in quiet reflection while a few spectators began shouting at Odo. The punishment for horse theft, as most knew, is to be drawn and quartered. Body parts were sent to outlying communities as a stark reminder of the penalties of such a heinous crime.

Odo felt unwell.

Steward Cederic sighed. "If we are to resolve this, then, Sir Ector, can ye bring to me this saddle. That will solve everything."

Both Odo and Charlotte nodded in agreement.

Sir Ector stood and glared at the steward. His honour had just been challenged. His hand grasped the hilt of his sword. To Charlotte it looked as though he would unsheathe the weapon and strike the steward. The men-at-arms took a step toward the knight. Charlotte held her breath as the room fell deathly quiet.

"Bailiff Ernoul, perhaps ye could retrieve the saddle," suggested the steward breaking the tension. Everyone relaxed as Sir Ector returned to his seat and glared at Odo.

Sir Ector reluctantly gave instructions to the bailiff on where to find the saddle and asked him to tell his lazy sergeant to also return to the court and attend to him. Bailiff Ernoul left the building with a man-at-arms and promised to return as soon as possible. Steward Cederic and the cleric left the room and would return when the bailiff arrived with the saddle, meanwhile, all the prisoners were taken back to the gaol. Charlotte sat alone and frightened.

It was a repeat of earlier, except only one prisoner was escorted into the room. Odo looked at Charlotte and smiled. She didn't feel his optimism. Someone must have sent word out because Sir Ector arrived moments before the bailiff. He looked around the room in consternation, but his sergeant had still not arrived. Steward Cederic and the cleric entered, followed by, much to both Charlotte and Odo's relief, a man-at-arms carrying the saddle. He placed it on a table in front of the steward and stepped back. More people filed into the room until it was almost full. Sergeant Jagger was not amongst them.

"Has anyone tampered with the saddle?" asked the steward, the mole on his face moving as if it were alive.

The bailiff and the man-at-arms shook their heads.

"Herdsman, would ye please retrieve the original document from where ye hid it?"

Odo stood and held up his manacled wrists. A nod from the steward and the heavy clamps and chains were unscrewed. Odo gave Charlotte a quick look and walked confidently to the table, only two steps away. To see better, people began to stand as Odo flipped the saddle upside down and poked his fingers between the leather flaps underneath.

He changed position and pushed his hands into the saddle and into the wool stuffing. After a short while he pulled his hand out, it was empty and didn't contain the leather bound documents. People began to laugh. Charlotte's hand covered her mouth.

He tried again, and thrust his hand, deep into the saddle and felt blindly for the two tubes he'd placed there only a week ago. He knew they must be there, they had to be, but weren't.

"Well, where is it herdsman?" asked Steward Cederic.

Sir Ector who was standing began to laugh. "The word of a herdsman isn't worth the cow shit he eats!"

Everyone began talking, speculating. Odo stood despondently with his hands at his sides as he tried to fathom what happened to the leather tubes. He looked at Charlotte and shook his head. They were gone.

Bailiff Ernoul was laughing along with Sir Ector; others joined and soon everyone was enjoying Odo's obvious discomfort. He dug his hand back into the saddle for another attempt.

"Keep looking lad, yer might find yer brains!" someone shouted.

Steward Cederic wasn't laughing. "Sit!" he commanded.

Odo returned to his seat and everyone followed suit. The grin on Sir Ector's face returned. Charlotte looked at the floor and shook her head. *Where were they, where had they gone, could the bailiff have taken them?*

Would the Templars create a new document for them if this one were lost?

"It seems, herdsman, that yer document has mysteriously vanished. I was prepared to consider your argument with some seriousness–"

"Flog 'im first fer lying, then have him drawn and quartered!" shouted Sir Ector.

Steward Cederic looked at Odo, his face clouded over. "–and I am in agreement with yer accuser, Sir Ector's suggestion is apt."

"No!" Odo yelled. "Someone took it! I put it there myself, not seven days past. Now it is gone, ye have my word."

"Yer word isn't worth much – Thief!" cried Sir Ector.

"So it shall be. Flogged, then drawn and quartered," informed Steward Cederic. The manorial court was over and punishment meted out.

Charlotte was devastated, her eyes filling with tears as she looked down at the floor hoping for answers.

The main door to the court opened. Late afternoon sun streamed in, momentarily bathing the room in bright daylight. When the immense figure stepped into the doorway, filling almost the entire space, he paused, blocking the sun from the room. The room immediately darkened.

"Where the hell have ye been?" shouted Sir Ector.

Jagger stood uncertainly in the doorway. All heads turned and all conversation stopped.

"Ye were supposed to be working, what were ye doing, skylarking around? Yer useless pillock."

Jagger took a step into the room and latched the door behind him. Immediately, the room returned to its prior gloominess.

"Well? Answer me!" shouted the knight with no regard to who

overheard.

"I, uh, I was away thinking, sire," Jagger answered.

Odo looked up at the huge man, his own despair temporarily forgotten. Sir Ector spared no opportunity to publicly belittle his sergeant, and yet the sergeant seemed to be defying his master. What was going on?

Sir Ector laughed, "Ye, think? Nay, it isn't possible fer ye to think. Wait outside for me."

Jagger remained unmoving.

"I said – outside!" Sir Ector was angered.

"I was listening outside," said Jagger ignoring the order from his master, his voice crisp and articulate. "I heard the steward say the herdsman is to be flogged and then drawn and quartered as the steward says he stole that horse."

"Idiot. Outside!" Sir Ector was becoming more agitated; he was being made a fool of by his sergeant.

"It isn't right. With respect, the steward is wrong, the herdsman didn't steal the horse, it says so here." Jagger held up the leather tube Odo had been searching for. "I found it in the saddle when I was cleaning it."

"Bring it here," ordered the steward.

"He's nothing but a simpleton, an idiot… get out or I'll take to yer with a whip!" shouted Sir Ector.

Jagger ignored the insults and walked towards the table where the steward sat. He handed over the tube and turned to Odo. "What we done was wrong, I told him it was wrong when we saw ye and yer woman ride up that day. But–"

"He lies!" screamed Sir Ector. He stomped forward towards Jagger and this time he did unsheathe his sword. "Get out!" The sword scythed through the air only just missing the sergeant as he leaned to the side to avoid the blade. Quicker than the eye could see, Jagger unsheathed his own sword and defended another slash.

"Stop this at once!" bellowed Steward Cederic.

"I – am – defending – my – honour," yelled Sir Ector as he advanced, his sword a whirling blur as it descended on Jagger time and time again. Yet with each thrust, lunge or swipe, the sergeant parried and defended himself with expertise. For such a large man, he was remarkably agile.

In panic, people began pouring out of the building, preventing the men-at-arms from entering. Benches were overturned and the hurried exit soon became pandemonium. The two men-at-arms at the rear of the room remained motionless. They were ill prepared to deal with the rage of a volatile and highly skilled knight. Surprising everyone, the enormous young man defended himself with relative ease. Yet not once did he counterattack or attempt to strike his master. He held his ground then slowly inched forward, forcing Sir Ector backwards.

Odo was frozen in shock; Jagger's revelation was a boon. He felt Charlotte's hand through his arm pulling him away to safety.

Sir Ector's face was flushed and his attack became nothing more than wild hacks and thrusts reflecting his anger and frustration. He was being humiliated by his sergeant. Jagger managed to advance another foot forcing the knight to step backwards again. He never saw the bench lying on its side and he tripped over it, sprawling in a heap onto the floor. Men-at-arms rushed in with their own swords drawn and disarmed both Sir Ector and Jagger. Order had been restored.

Steward Cederic's face was scarlet, his anger obvious to all as he read the original proof of ownership document Steward Alard created for Odo. Sir Ector quietly seethed and was seated with a man-at-arms standing either side. His sword, and Jagger's, lay on the table top in front of the bailiff. Jagger sat on the other side of the room guarded by the other two men-at-arms. Odo was seated and this time Charlotte was permitted to sit beside him. Other than the bailiff and cleric, no one else was allowed back into the court room.

The steward looked up and shook his head. "Ye made an error in judgement, Sir Ector. I find no reason to uphold the conviction on the herdsman. He is free to go."

Odo felt the weight of the world lift from his shoulders. Charlotte grabbed his hand and squeezed.

"Sir Wystan was a friend, a brother," spat Sir Ector.

"Perhaps he was, but ye are a brave knight and be best that ye continue on yer journey to Ireland –"

"No he isn't." Jagger spoke.

The steward raised his eyebrows, the mole following in an upward trajectory.

"Sir Ector feigned injury in France to avoid having to fight for the king in Ireland. He is a coward!"

Sir Ector leapt from his seat, but the two men-at-arms pushed him back down. A sword pressing into his chest offered him no alternative than to comply.

"That is quite an accusation."

"And be the truth, milord. Oh, aye, he was injured, a minor wound, but he purported it was worse."

"Then that is a matter for the Lord of Taunton to take up with King Henry. I urge ye to find a way to leave Taunton as soon as possible, Sir Ector, ye may have outstayed yer welcome here. The bailiff will tell ye where ye can purchase a horse. This day is done. See the herdsman receives all his documents and his horse."

Two men-at-arms escorted Odo, who carried the saddle, and Charlotte, who held the leather tube containing the receipt, to a large manor house near the outskirts of Taunton where Sir Ector lodged. It was there they found Amica who snorted when he recognized Odo's voice. The men-at-arms urged them to leave quickly lest more angry knights take offence at their presence. It was plain to see that Amica had been well looked after and did not appear to have been hurt by the antics of Sir Ector. They led him out of the stable and headed back towards the Swan Inn. As yet, neither Odo nor Charlotte had spoken about what was mostly on their minds. They couldn't, in fear the men-at-arms may overhear.

The men-at-arms left Odo and Charlotte at the Swan Inn stables; finally they were alone. Amica munched happily on hay beside Sally, and Charlotte flew into Odo's arms. Neither spoke. They held each other tightly, both acutely aware how close he'd come to death.

When Odo opened his eyes and was finally able to pry Charlotte away, he saw him. Jagger stood at the stable's entranceway. The sergeant didn't move; his enormous arms hung loosely at his sides. His sword that seemed so large and lethal when he defended himself from Sir Ector seemed small, like a child's toy as it hung from his belt.

CHAPTER SEVENTEEN

He heard it, not once but again.

"Holy, holy, holy is the Lord of hosts; the whole earth is full of His glory!" He kept his eyes firmly closed and wasn't sure if he was even able to open them if he wanted. He was frightened, unsure, like a boy facing his first test of manhood. He then felt it, a delicate whisper of touch, the gentle rustle of feathered wings as they brushed against him. Even through closed eyes he felt tears of joy, he knew then he stood before God. The sound of feathered wings and songs of praise could only be Seraphim, angels surrounding the divine throne. He was about to face judgement. He stood before the Almighty and not at the gates of hell.

If his mother could see him now, she'd be shocked. She'd always warned him, "Hell will be your salvation, ye naughty boy," she'd told him, wagging a finger in his face. He wanted to laugh but couldn't.

He raised his arm to wipe his eyes, and felt a stab of pain; his body tensed involuntarily causing more shooting pains to envelope him in a flash of brilliant white. He began to sob and cried for joy, for love, and he cried for all he'd ever suffered through. His tears ran freely down a blood encrusted face, too many to wipe away, and he cried for all those souls who'd suffered by his hand. *Yes, I'm ashamed*, he wanted to cry to the world, but couldn't.

Judgement was cruel, merciless.

He felt it again. The Seraphim stirred, this time when they touched his face, it was almost sensual, he felt their love. It was reassuring. Again the touch... he sighed. It hurt.

Forgive me! he shouted in thought, words he was unable to speak and desperately wanted to yell. He cried shamelessly as a young boy would to his father. He bared his soul, and with it, a lifetime of guilt washed down his face. *I'm so sorry*! he screamed in silence.

The pressure on his face increased, he felt the fiery breath of Seraphim, he knew they loved him, he knew God loved him. The touch meant so much. He wanted to open his eyes but was so frightened. He couldn't.

Water, water, how did they know? Could they read his mind, think his thoughts? He welcomed it and with some effort opened his mouth a little and felt a single drop of cool water splash onto his tongue in an explosion of sensory delight and relief. Another, then another. Like a dog he lapped at it, then a torrent, he swallowed. *God blessed him*, thought the reeve. Then it went black.

Odo turned to face the giant, Charlotte, took a half step to stand partially behind him. "I wish to thank ye, for what ye did. Ye saved my life," Odo spoke first.

Jagger remained quiet and motionless. His eyes flicked from Odo to Charlotte and then back again. He swallowed. "One thing bothers me." He took a step closer to the couple. "Why would a herdsman receive a gift of such a valuable courser from the Lord of the Manor?" He took another step and walked towards Amica, stepping past Odo and Charlotte.

"He will kick!" warned Odo as Jagger approached Amica's

hindquarters.

Amica continued to munch on hay, his ears twitched and Jagger reached out and gently stroked his rump. The stallion ignored him. Both Odo and Charlotte looked surprised.

"I thought about this after I found that leather tube. Ye must be a good man, fer an honourable lord would not do such a thing for no reason and just for any commoner. Or perhaps ye were fortunate or just lucky?"

Odo didn't have anything to say... he let the sergeant talk.

"Not all nobles are good men, ye saw Sir Ector and how he tormented and slated me. Something he took great pleasure in."

Charlotte moved from behind Odo and began to slowly walk towards the young man who stood at ease near the stallion. "Some men are cruel and seek pleasure from creating and seeing pain on others. We know this only too well, as I think ye do too."

Jagger nodded. "And some men are good men... Why else would a herdsman have a Templar document?" He turned from Charlotte to look at Odo. "I don't think ye stole it, nay, for such a document cannot be stolen, this was given to ye."

Odo was about to approach Jagger to explain how he came by the document, when he raised his hand. Odo froze, his mouth open, when he saw what the sergeant held.

The giant revealed the Templar document, still wrapped in leather, in a meaty hand, and held it up so that Odo and Charlotte could easily see it. "I know of these, my own father used Templars to transport coin from one place to another." He searched Odo's face; probing, looking to take measure of him. "Then this is valuable to yer, is it not?"

"Aye, it is," nervously croaked Odo. He felt Charlotte squeeze his arm.

The giant nodded. "I think it is best others do not know of it." He lowered his arm, extending it out towards Odo.

Fearful the giant could hear his pounding heart, Odo stepped closer and took the proffered leather tube. "Thank ye, Jagger. Ye are a decent and honourable man." Again for the second time that day Odo felt overcome with relief.

The giant's eyes were slits as he stared at the herdsman. "So, through good fortune ye receive the stallion, then ye have that Templar document. Who are ye, Master Odo?"

"I think we need to go inside and sample the proprietor's fine ale," Odo suggested in response.

The three of them sat in a corner of the Swan Inn, and each sipped from a tankard of ale. While the Inn was reasonably busy, customers kept their distance and left them alone to talk in privacy. Word quickly spread about the young giant with the impressive skills. No one wanted to interfere with him.

"Ye have yet to answer my question," Jagger reminded Odo.

"Men see Odo's goodness and seek to take advantage of it," offered Charlotte. "Odo has been fortunate too, and helped people and been rewarded."

Jagger nodded and looked thoughtful.

"Ye could have kept that Templar document, yet ye chose to return it to me, why?" Odo drained the tankard and looked at Jagger, waiting for his reply.

He shrugged, "Why not? It was the right thing to do."

"Will ye still travel to Ireland with Sir Ector?" asked Charlotte.

"Nay, Sir Ector has released me. He no longer wishes for me to serve him. He believes me unworthy and that I can no longer be loyal to him." Jagger took a big breath and exhaled slowly. "I was looking fer a reason to leave long ago, but have nowhere to go, no home, and without a master, then I have nothing."

Odo laughed, "Yer master wasn't very happy this morning when ye wouldn't listen to him in court and go outside like he wanted."

"Aye, but I am not sorry, I did what was proper." Jagger placed the tankard on the table, then leaned forwards. "Where are you headed towards?"

"We are bound for Combe Templariorum," Odo answered.

"And ye travel alone, with that Templar document?" whispered the giant.

"Aye, and we thought it was safely hidden," added Charlotte.

For the first time, Jagger laughed. "Then I shall journey with ye, and make sure ye come to no harm." He raised his tankard.

Odo and Charlotte stared at each other.

Cathal built a slightly raised platform of wood. A large fire burned fiercely only a few feet away. Flames leapt into the evening sky accompanied by sparks that shot upwards and away like fairies. Inside the depths of the fire lay rocks, heating.

Reeve Petrus lay on the platform only scant yards away from where Cathal found him. He thought him dead, perhaps he had died, but a flicker of life, had returned or remained. So faint, so weak.

With infinite care and patience, the Irishman first cleaned the blood from his face, and then gave him a little water. It gave the reeve strength, it helped. But the danger was the knife wound.

While Petrus was again insensible, Cathal built the platform, constructed an elementary roof shelter and built the fire. He found two sturdy poles and strapped them together and tied a blanket between each pole. It was unavoidable, and the reeve in his delirium screamed as Cathal slowly managed to drag him onto the makeshift stretcher. It was difficult, for the reeve was not a slight man and carried considerable weight.

Once the reeve had settled down, Cathal used his horse to drag the stretcher up the bank onto flat ground near a large tree and eased him gently onto the platform. The platform was to assist in balancing the reeve's humours.

It was cold and damp where the reeve had lain for such a long time. Keeping him off the ground and rolling hot rocks beneath the platform would create heat and dryness. The crude roof would prevent dampness from settling on him. Cathal knew if he was to save the reeve's life he must first make him stable and create balance.

Again he carefully gave the reeve water, not too much but just enough and then began removing the reeves clothing. The knife wound was nasty and already looked to be defiled. By the light of the blazing fire's dancing flames, Cathal squatted on the ground beside Reeve Petrus Bodkin and wondered how he was going to save him.

The lands beyond Taunton flattened out and the riding was fun, if not exhilarating. Even Sally, with Amica on one side and Jagger's destrier on the other seemed encouraged by such distinguished company and seemed to have more spring in her step. A man as large as Jagger needed a horse capable of carrying him yet, he rode with a lightness and ease that surprised Odo. He was masterful on horseback, no wonder Amica liked him.

After a good meal, and an even better sleep, Odo was no worse for wear after his ordeal in Taunton's gaol. The following morning saw him refreshed after Charlotte convinced him he needed to remove some of the suspicious clumps of matter that clung from his body. He sat inside a horse trough, with knees drawn to his chin as Charlotte scraped and washed. She even managed to wring out his clothes, and he wore them damp as they set out on their thirty mile journey.

"Is the Templar document the reason ye wish to visit Combe Templariorum?" asked Jagger as he snacked on pork and cheese. They sat beneath the branches of a large oak tree as the horses rested.

"Aye, it is," Odo answered as he watched Jagger. He was astounded at the amount of food the young man ate. "Have ye been here before?"

"Aye, many a time. Ye'll be wanting the Preceptory, that be where the Templars do all their work."

"Do ye trust them?"

"The Templars? Aye, with coin."

It was late afternoon when they rode into the small town. They found lodging and decided to visit the Preceptory the following morn.

Odo and Jagger talked. To Charlotte it was bewildering that both men, each from such different backgrounds and upbringing saw the world almost exactly the same. Jagger explained how he was always bullied when a child. Older children, sons and daughters of knights and noblemen saw Jagger purely as a target. As he grew older, they saw him as being soft, because he preferred to be quiet and not be the focus of attention. He came to learn that honour held little meaning for those who had so much.

As he explained, Sir Ector used him because of his family's wealth, for Sir Ector was wanting in wealth and lacked honour. "It wasn't all bad," he said. He'd received five years of intense and valuable training that few other knights could offer. While Sir Ector was a fallacious man, he was an expert swordsman and a gifted teacher when abstinent.

Odo told Jagger all that recently happened to them both and how the murrain was the reason all his cows had to be culled.

Lest someone overhear, Jagger leaned forward and whispered, "Then this bishop ye speak of is not a good man?"

Charlotte laughed, "He is a lecherous toad," she replied quietly.

"From what ye tell me, this man who wishes to have yer land, uh, Falls Ende, will stop at nothing. Then ye are both in danger. How can ye protect yerselves and each other? Yer friend the reeve has shown ye the way of the sword, has he not?"

Odo shook his head.

"Odo was given a bow and had one lesson from Thomas, one lesson!" she began to chuckle, "and that ended miserably."

Odo rolled his eyes.

"The arrow flew twenty feet, would have been less if it weren't fer the wind."

Jagger saw Odo's face and burst out laughing. Charlotte joined in.

"I have a proposition, Master Odo," stated Jagger once he had control of himself. He turned to look at each of them carefully. "Let me continue to journey with yer. I can keep an eye on yer and keep ye safe. I will decide fer how long, when I see Mellester Manor."

"I can't deny we need all the help we can get. We've been unlucky, Jagger. Recent times have been unfavourable to us and we welcome yer help, but we have no coin to pay fer yer."

"Ye are the son of a lord, a noble. How will that look to yer family? It will create problems," she added.

"Problems fer who? Not fer me. I have nowhere else to go, what am I to do but help someone in need, and ye do need help. Ye are both good people. I don't need coin, I need honesty, respect and a cause."

They talked long into the night; Charlotte was surprised Odo spoke so willingly and freely to the likeable giant. In turn, Jagger spoke of his life and the pain he suffered. Both men had previously suffered and the bond between them grew.

At first Charlotte was a little apprehensive about him. She thought it was her natural distrust of nobles, but after a while, she saw Jagger differently. He confided in them with emotion, at one point he wept as he told how he'd been treated as a child. His mother had been cruel, their servants no better, and a privileged life was nothing more than torment. She listened as he spoke and came to understand him.

He explained that he had vowed never to suffer from the malice of others, and he learned how to defend himself. Because of his size and strength he found it came easily to him and he worked harder than anyone to become masterful.

In the beginning Sir Ector was kind and understanding – a natural teacher. As the years passed and the knight squandered his wealth, his temperament changed. He became bitter and abusive and recently, Jagger told them, he'd decided to leave the knight's service as soon as he had somewhere to go.

"Now ye have somewhere to go," smiled Odo. His eyelids were heavy, he'd drunk too much. Charlotte wasn't in much better shape and they retired to their rooms, exhausted.

CHAPTER EIGHTEEN

"Mellester's Reeve is dead, Yer Grace," said Abbot Andrew matter-of-factly.

Bishop Immers raised his eyebrows in response to the good news.

"His body lies in a channel some miles from Exeter, and it, uh, will be some time before it is found. Crows and vermin now feast on his remains."

"Can the man's unfortunate death be linked to ye? His horse?"

"His horse and possessions were left in the area, there is no link to us," replied the Abbot with a reassuring smile.

"To us?" Immers face clouded over.

"I misspoke, Yer Grace," answered the Abbot hurriedly.

The bishop gave the abbot a hard look, then noticed the man looked weary. "Your foot ails ye still?"

Abbot Andrew nodded, "I will never walk properly again."

Bishop Immers managed a sympathetic look and then changed the subject. "Our prayers *are* being answered, Andrew."

The Abbott raised his head in interest.

"Sir Hyde Fortescue is near death, he may not recover from the wound he received in Ireland and Sir Gweir... well, last I heard he is still hale. But in his absence, Mellester is weak and unprotected. With the death of its reeve, then that really leaves only the meddlesome herdsman."

"Aye, I see yer point, but if I may, Yer Grace, what of the Templars?"

The Bishop waved his jewelled hand dismissively. "They are gone, and they have little interest in anything outside what fills their coffers. Ye won't hear from them again."

Abbott Andrew nodded in servile agreement and hoped the bishop was right. "But the herdsman, Yer Grace, I know the Church would benefit greatly if he succumbed to an unfortunate mischance."

"He has no guardians; this is the best time to deal with him." The Bishop offered the Abbott a smile.

"He and his woman were seen leaving Mellester over a week past, on horseback. They have yet to return, Yer Grace."

The smile vanished. "Oh?"

The Abbott looked at his master and waited.

"If the young imposter and his woman are on some journey, then it may serve the Church's interests if he never returned, what say ye, Andrew?"

"Of course, Yer Grace."

"He rides that stallion, he wouldn't be difficult to recognise... could ye send a man out, find the herdsman and uh ... resolve our dilemma?"

"One man?"

"Herdsman Odo has already cost the Church significantly, unless ye feel two men would be suitable then perhaps ye pay his stipend?" The bishop raised a single eyebrow.

"Oh no, Yer Grace, one man as ye advocate is most frugal and wise."

"Very well, Andrew, see to it. The next good news I expect to hear is the untimely misfortune of the young herdsman." The Bishop stood to leave.

Cathal tied wooden splints to the arm and right leg of the reeve. The left leg had a severe break; jagged bone broke through the skin and needed to be taken care of immediately. It took Cathal a while to prepare what he needed, and after infusing a medley of herbs for the reeve to inhale and a piece of tightly bound leather to bite on, he firmly pulled the lower portion of the leg down, separated both broken pieces of bone and then aligned the leg and pushed both parts together. He wasn't gentle and needed to be forceful if the leg had any chance of healing properly. He took no pleasure from the task, and when the reeve screamed, he winced in compassion. Cathal knew the pain was unbearable, but it had to be done. Now senseless, beads of sweat lined Petrus' face and his breathing was even shallower than before. Luckily he was successful after the first attempt and the leg realigned perfectly. He quickly bound the leg to two additional splints he'd made and set about addressing the next task. Cathal knew the body now needed to heal; this was the most crucial part because if the reeve's condition worsened, he'd most certainly die.

As the reeve slept, Cathal scoured the countryside for plants and herbs he needed. It was then he found the reeve's horse and staff. Another turn of good fortune, he mused.

With a mortar and pestle he made a paste from the assortment of leaves and roots he'd collected and filled the knife wound with the concoction. Wood was plentiful and with a raging fire to drive away damp, the reeve lay unmoving, barely breathing and more dead than alive.

Cathal hadn't slept all night, and even though it was early morning, he lay beside the fire and hoped to sleep for a short while, then replace the poultice over the knife wound with a fresh mixture. He hoped the reeve would still be alive when he woke.

Mounted Templar Knights, with their sergeants carrying spare lances only a step or two behind, charged ahead in a tight formation. The sound of dozens of destriers storming across the countryside was impressive, if not a little frightening. Odo, Charlotte and Jagger watched from the road. A Templar knight, possibly a commander, began yelling at his men as the force pulled to a stop. Within moments, they were off again, this time the advancing coursers were even closer together, a tighter line.

"The Templars train here at Combe Templariorum," informed Jagger.

"Why was the knight yelling, what did the others do wrong?" Charlotte asked.

"Gaps or spaces in an advancing line of horses or men is dangerous, is a place of weakness and a skilled adversary looks for those gaps. These Templar Knights know better, but they were being lazy, this why he yells."

"Fer what reason do they train, is there going to be a battle and who will they fight?" Odo asked.

Jagger shook his head. "I don't know, perhaps for a hastilude."

Odo furrowed his eyebrows; this was a word he was unfamiliar with.

"Martial contests, like a *tornement*," Jagger explained.

Odo nodded.

"So, for more important reasons, I have heard that the Church will bring war in the east to regain Christian land that Moslems have claimed. Some knights say that everyone will be called on to defend the Christian faith from them."

"Will ye go if called upon?" Charlotte asked.

"I am not a knight, and not in the service of a knight nor have I sworn fealty to a lord or king. I think I will not be called upon unless something changes."

Odo was nervous; the Templar warrant was foremost on his mind. He looked at the building in the distance. "Is that the Preceptory?"

"Aye, that is where we need go," assured Jagger. "Ye will go inside, hand yer warrant to a dismal cleric. They'll not be genial and will ask ye a question or two to make sure ye are who ye say ye are, then hand over yer coin and shoo ye out. Is quick and easy."

Charlotte exchanged a look with Odo and smiled. "I find it hard not knowing what the Templars have gifted ye."

"Then we should find out." Odo squeezed Amica with his legs and he took off in a slow canter. Sally did her best to keep up and Jagger, as usual kept to the rear.

A Templar man-at-arms with a nasty looking pike barred them access. "State yer business!"

Odo cleared his throat. He was used to this, having experienced similar in France. "I am here with a Templar warrant" he said with confidence and showed the guard the document. Jagger had quietly ridden up and now stopped, almost between the guard and Odo. The guard spared Jagger a second glance; seldom had he seen such a large man.

"Ride around the rear, someone will take care of yer horses." He gave Sally a long look.

"Thank ye."

The Preceptory sat on the outskirts of the village and was still under construction. From the look of things, it was far from complete. Craftsmen were everywhere, piles of stone and wood were heaped in various places, while men with hand carts moved stone from one heap to another. To Odo it looked chaotic.

Another man-at-arms, without the cumbersome pike, led them from the stables into the interior. It was busy and men were everywhere.

"Everyone believes Templars are just fighting knights, this is not so," whispered Jagger as they entered a large room. Scribes sat at tall sloping writing desks, more men-at-arms stood guard at each doorway. No one paid them any attention.

"This way," informed their guide as he led them to a central desk where a steward sat.

Odo knew he must be patient, a valuable lesson he'd learned in France. Charlotte stood slightly behind at his elbow. Jagger on his other side, stood half a step back.

The steward looked up with a typically bored expression, glanced at Odo, then fixed his eyes on Jagger for a little longer, then quickly moved to Charlotte and back to Jagger for a second look. Finally he wrested his gaze from the giant and looked at Odo in question.

"I, uh, I have a warrant," said Odo with less confidence that he wished. He handed the document to the steward.

With care the steward unfolded the warrant and glanced at it quickly. His expression changed and he stood from his seat. "From whom did ye receive this?"

Odo knew this was a test because Sir William explained his name was on the document. He instructed him on what questions would be asked and how to reply.

"From Sir William Marshal, 1st Earl of Pembroke, milord."

Odo felt a nudge and turned to Jagger. The big man shook his head, and bent down and whispered, "He isn't a lord, he's a monk."

Odo felt his cheeks redden.

The steward looked over the document again. Satisfied, he looked up. "Be seated," and pointed to a bench along the far wall. "I will return."

Odo and Charlotte sat as asked. "Here we go, now we have to wait three bloody days while these jesters take their time," groused Odo.

Charlotte held his hand while Jagger remained standing. They waited.

Within a short time the steward returned with two men-at-arms, "Follow me, please."

Please, silently mouthed Jagger.

Odo couldn't help but grin. *A courteous steward*?

The procession was led through a hallway and they entered another room. A man sat behind a large table. Odo had never seen such a room before, his mouth opened in wonder. Beautiful paintings and tapestries hung from the walls. There was furniture, soft and luxurious, and even things made of silver. Charlotte's head swivelled from side to side. Jagger kept a single pace behind Odo, surveying the room quickly. The two very attentive guards remained at the doorway, wary of the guests.

The man rose from behind the table. He was dressed simply in a flowing tunic adorned with the typical Templar white mantle with a red cross, but the fabric was finely woven and almost shone. The steward stood to the side, tactfully out of the way, but available if needed.

"Hail, Master Odo. I am Preceptor Lucius, and we welcome ye to the Preceptory of Combe Templariorum, the present home in this region to the Poor Fellow-Soldiers of Christ and from the Order of the Temple of Solomon. Who are yer friends?"

Odo cleared his throat. "Hail, Preceptor, this is Charlotte, my wife, and this is Jagger."

The preceptor nodded to them each and indicated for them to sit. Both Odo and Charlotte had never sat on anything like these chairs before, they were padded, soft, and covered with a beautiful fabric. He could see Charlotte was enjoying it tremendously.

Much to his surprise, he felt Jagger's presence as he moved to stand directly behind him. Odo twisted quickly to look. Jagger stood like a sentinel, like a gigantic immoveable statue. It was an unusual feeling, but also reassuring, and it made him feel safe. Other than Godwin, no one had ever protected him, other than perhaps Reeves Norman and Petrus, but not like this. This was different and certainly welcoming. Charlotte looked at him and gave him a wink.

"Now then, ye have me at a slight disadvantage. It will take some days to collect the coin ye require. I trust ye want it all, that is why ye are here?" the preceptor asked.

Odo swallowed, he'd lost his voice. "Aye," he managed to squeak.

Preceptor Lucius looked at the looming figure of Jagger and gave a barely perceptible smile. "And ye have no doubt brought more men and a sturdy cart with ye?"

The room was filled with an expectant silence. Odo coughed.

"Preceptor Lucius, I have no understanding of what is happening here…"

Preceptor Lucius leaned back in his chair, his fingers steepled beneath his chin.

"… Sir William gave me this document, I know not what it contains or of its value. I didn't even want it. But Sir William insisted and Jagger is a friend, not a guard. I, I am at a loss, sir," Odo gushed.

The preceptors smile grew larger. "Sir William told me that I would enjoy yer company, he said ye were…" the preceptor paused as he sought for the right word. "…uh, gregarious, and different from most other men he'd met. I tend to agree with him." The preceptor leaned forward. "Tell me, is it true ye travelled to France and met with King Henry?"

Odo heard Jagger's sharp intake of breath. He hadn't told him about that.

"Aye, I travelled with Sir Renier, Reeve Petrus and Thomas, and I met with the King."

"At a ceremony?"

"Nay, we met alone," added Odo. He remembered to heed King Henry's warning to not speak of what was discussed.

"And ye are a Freeman, a herdsman?"

"Aye, well, nay, we had a murrain and my cows were all culled, so I am without," replied Odo despondently.

Preceptor Lucius nodded, "Aye, Sir William told me of this. And yer head, I understand ye were attacked and suffered injury?"

"All is well, mostly. Each day is better, milord."

The preceptor nodded again, clearly enjoying this conversation. He leaned back on his chair. "Sir William spoke highly of ye, Odo. He thinks ye would have made a fine Templar Knight, much like yer father."

Odo laughed, and then felt Jagger stir at the latest revelation.

The preceptor's smile vanished. "What ye have done fer our order, fer Christians, is far beyond anything we can ever do to repay ye, Odo. We are in yer debt, and yer have our thanks and blessings."

There was another gasp from behind him.

Odo met the eyes of Preceptor Lucius.

"Then ye would like to know what the Knights Templar have granted ye?"

Odo noticed Charlotte held his hand again, he felt her squeeze. He nodded, his voice failed him.

CHAPTER NINETEEN

The ditch where Cathal found Reeve Petrus was a short distance from a stream, a minor tributary to the river Eks. Convenient for Cathal, everything he required to tend to the reeve was nearby. He woke after a short nap and thankfully found the reeve had not passed away while he slept. His breathing was shallow, but of more concern was his temperature. He felt too hot. To the fili, this was another humour imbalance and immediately he set off for the stream where he retrieved some water and soaked a cloth. Now he needed reduce the reeve's body temperature and restore the balance.

Cathal was worried, being hot was a problem and alluded to corruption in the wound. He placed the wet cloth over the reeve, cleaned out the knife wound and repacked it with a fresh poultice. The wound did not appear to have worsened any, he sniffed it and thankfully he smelled nothing foul. A good sign.

After doing all he could for Petrus, he went out to check the traps he'd set earlier that morning and found two rabbits. He returned to the campsite and within a short time had a rabbit stew bubbling away. They both needed to eat, and Cathal would take a portion of the cooked stew, and by using the mortar and pestle, turn it to pulp and feed it to the reeve in small amounts.

As Cathal stared into the flames and then deeper into the hot glowing embers, a sense of unease permeated through his body. There'd been signs, growing indicators he couldn't ignore – Odo was still in danger.

He sat cross-legged and motionless in front of the fire. His breathing slowed and his chest barely rose. Occasionally an insect would land on him, on his face, hair or a shoulder and then fly away. The Irishman didn't react. Emboldened, birds pecked for nearby food and ignored the inert form that sat in meditative repose.

Around the campsite Cathal created, the natural order of life returned to its basic essence. The reeve stirred, groaned, then remained silent. Above them, clouds drifted past, and shadows lengthened. It was some time before Cathal moved. He eased himself to his feet, stretched and then attended to his patient. With surprising tenderness, he dripped water into the reeve's mouth, wiped his face and stood back.

Cathal knew he couldn't leave Petrus alone while he went to find help. No one knew they were here, help for him wasn't coming anytime soon and he knew that with absoluteness. If Petrus were to survive, begin to heal and recover, then he needed to remain motionless for long periods of time. Movement would slow healing.

He bent down and touched the reeve's face, the balance was good. He lay his head on the reeve's chest. His breathing was regular. He cleaned out his wound, and sniffed. Again, the parity was good and the trauma appeared less red and inflamed. Cathal nodded and began mumbling and speaking in strange tongues as he fetched a sliver of bone and thread from his bag. With care he sewed the wound closed, packed a fresh poultice around it and stood back to observe and think.

He knew what needed to be done. With bowl in hand, he walked away and searched for the special ingredients required. He was going to make the reeve sleep.

Earlier that morning, Birney Beekman rode from Exeter on a fine horse; he was well-dressed and carried a small bundle strapped to the rear of the saddle. He attracted no unnecessary attention and those tending to crops who watched him pass by believed him to be clergy or a merchant. He carried no sword, but he was armed with an assortment of knives and a variety of lethal potions guaranteed to kill. He wasn't a pleasant man, but when the need arose, he could be amiable, polite, and to the unwary, even friendly.

Birney Beekman wasn't a merchant or clergy, he was simply a man tasked with doing a simple job. In this instance his employer demanded that he locate and kill Herdsman Odo Read and make it look like an accident. Birney couldn't be happier, this was an easy job, and one that paid handsomely well.

His instructions were to pick up the trail of the herdsman north of Mellester Manor, as he and his woman were seen travelling in that direction over a week past, and had not since returned. Birney whistled merrily as his horse carried him deep into the countryside.

"Before I tell ye, Master Odo, I would like to have a quick word. If Charlotte and Jagger could take a little walk, have refreshment …?" Preceptor Lucius turned to the steward who walked over.

Odo's eyes widened. "Charlotte and I don't have secrets–"

"Is some personal wisdom and ideas I wish to impart on ye, Odo, nothing more."

Charlotte nodded, while Jagger looked reluctant to leave. She grabbed his arm and with the steward leading the way, they exited the room.

The preceptor rose from behind his desk and walked around and sat on the chair vacated by Charlotte. "Our Order is in possession of fine lands in the southern area of England," began Preceptor Lucius. "We manage that land as a lord over his demesne. It is in our interest to ensure that land is used productively."

This was a subject Odo was familiar with and understood. He felt more at ease. He nodded and the preceptor continued. "Sir William explained how ye had been breeding cows, that ye wanted, uh…"

"I wanted my cows to produce more milk and be able to use the land more efficiently," Odo explained with his normal enthusiasm.

"Aye, and we agree with ye, Odo. We would like to see ye succeed, if ye succeed, then so will others, our lands will also become more productive – if ye show us. If farms are productive and producing, then people are happy, earning money and all tithes are met. Do ye follow?"

"Aye, it is what I have always believed."

"And so I understand and we wish to help. This gift ye have received from us is to help ye achieve this. We expect, that ye will use our gift wisely; we are in essence investing in ye. And Odo?"

He looked inquisitively into the face of the preceptor.

"We will keep an eye on ye, know this. Because dark forces lay in the shadows."

Odo's face clouded over. "Bishop Immers?"

"Aye, I know all about the bishop and his activities, but that is a Church problem, and one we hope to fix. We want ye to farm cows and be happy."

"But the murrain! I have no cows, I have no—"

A harried knock on the door interrupted him.

A steward stuck his head around the corner. "We are in need of ye, Preceptor, an agitated merchant …"

"I will be there soon, have him wait, offer him wine, and have Mistress Charlotte and Jagger return." The preceptor turned back to Odo and continued. "We know about the murrain and what happened to yer cows, we see it as an opportunity fer ye."

Odo was puzzled.

"Are ye familiar with Frisia?"

"Frisia? I met a Frisian captain, he took us to France," Odo replied. "But what is special about Frisia?"

The Preceptor stood, "Cows, Odo, their cows."

Odo's eyebrows knitted together. *Cows*?

"Frisian cows."

He'd once heard something about Frisian cows, if he could only remember.

Again a knock, and the door opened and Charlotte and Jagger entered and stood silently waiting as the preceptor continued.

"Now then, let us return to yer warrant, ye said ye wanted it all?"

Odo's mind was working furiously, he didn't understand. Charlotte stepped up behind him. Jagger stood slightly to the side and listened intently.

"Aye, uh – nay, fer I know not what I have been given." Odo shook his head in the confusion of the moment.

Preceptor Lucius moved to stand in front of him and bent down to place both hands on his shoulders. "Odo, the Poor Fellow-Soldiers of Christ and from the Order of the Temple of Solomon have gifted ye … six – hundred – pounds."

Jagger caught Charlotte as she collapsed, his own cry of surprise mingled with hers.

The preceptor, in shock at Charlotte's reaction stepped back as Odo leapt up and rushed over to her. Jagger carefully eased her to the chair.

"Fetch water!" the preceptor told the steward who rushed away.

Charlotte shook her head as she regained awareness only moments later. "Is this…" She took a breath. "Is this true, do ye jest, Preceptor Lucius?" she immediately asked, seeming no worse from her light-headedness.

Pleased to see Charlotte fully coherent, the preceptor's face looked sombre. "On the word of our Order and all we believe and have faith in, six hundred pounds is yers. Odo and Charlotte Read, ye are now very wealthy, congratulations."

Odo hadn't comprehended what just happened. His mind a whirling maelstrom of confusion, abstract thoughts and memories. His first thought was of all those years ago when he and his father Godwin stood before Mellester's lord when Godwin received title on Falls Ende. The look on his father face, a look he'd never forget. Odo now felt as Godwin must have. Tears cascaded freely down his face… cows, a future and Mellester's people fed and happy. He cast aside the dark shroud of recent events and with tear filled eyes, beamed at Charlotte.

Charlotte stood, and with Jagger's help stepped to Odo and wrapped her arms around to hold him tightly. They stood together as one as the preceptor and Jagger watched awkwardly. With a matter to attend to, Preceptor Lucius departed the room with the steward, the men-at-arms followed.

Jagger was seated, his elbows rested on massive thighs and he shook his head. "I'm a young man and have only lived two score years or so. I have seen much, journeyed far and witnessed things no man should ever see. But never, never have I experienced such as this." He lifted his head and turned to Odo and Charlotte still clutched tightly together. "Odo, who are ye?" He shook his head again, still unbelieving. "Six hundred pounds! The King! The Knights Templar treating ye like royalty! What more is there to ye?"

"I think ye will find out soon enough," replied Charlotte wiping her eyes as she separated herself from Odo.

Odo hadn't said a word, he couldn't. The amount of six hundred pounds wasn't a lot of coin, it was an inconceivable amount. He looked at the ground at his feet and shook his head in disbelief.

Preceptor Lucius re-entered the room followed by his guards. He was grinning. "I only wish Sir William could see yer face."

"Did Oswald know? Did he know this would happen and did he know the value of the pyxis?" Odo asked.

"I knew him briefly, I was young at the time. But he was well thought of and respected as a good, honest and pious man." Preceptor Lucius looked into the distance and took a deep breath. "And quite a reputation…"

Odo was staring at the preceptor.

"I think he did know, or would have known. He could have given the pyxis to the order at any time. Instead he chose to wait. He wanted it to be yers, of that I have no doubt."

"I feel unworthy of this gift, Preceptor."

"We can help ye Odo, we want to help." He took a step back. "Now then," he clapped his hands once. "How much coin do ye think ye will need, Master Odo?"

Odo turned his gaze to Charlotte for support. "Uh, fifteen, nay, twenty pounds?"

She nodded.

"I think ye need one hundred pounds," offered the preceptor.

"One hundred?" Odo cried. "That is a lot of coin."

"Aye, but ye will need to purchase a new herd, and other things will ye not?"

"Other things?" he questioned.

"And I don't think it wise ye travel back through Taunton with so much coin when yer leave here, ye need to go directly to Mellester."

"He speaks wisely, Odo," said Jagger.

"But we can't travel all that way in a day, Sally is… not fleet footed."

Preceptor Lucius laughed. "Then we will sell ye a fine horse fer yer mistress. Ye can leave, Sally here. I have people heading south next week. I will have them take her to ye, and ye can tell us how ye fare."

"Odo, this is shrewd," Jagger added. "With a new horse fer Charlotte, we can travel much quicker and it will be more difficult for anyone to set upon us."

Odo looked to Charlotte who was grinning from ear to ear.

"Very well, so be it."

"I will arrange with the marshal to have suitable horses selected for Charlotte to choose from. I wish ye all to spend the night here, eat with us, enjoy yer time and then ye can leave in the morn. Yer can't stay in the village with all that coin. What say ye?"

Odo could only agree or risk upsetting his wife and Jagger.

CHAPTER TWENTY

It didn't take Birney Beekman long to find the trail of Herdsman Odo Read. In Taunton's inns, people still talked about what happened during Steward Cederic's manorial court, and without appearing to be meddlesome, he learned that the herdsman escaped conviction for horse theft and he and his woman were seen riding towards Combe Templariorum the previous morn. He was only a day behind, but what business did the herdsman have in Combe Templariorum? Certainly it had naught to do with Templars, perhaps he was visiting family, thought Birney. With some urgency, he headed towards Combe Templariorum.

Reeve Petrus slept and Cathal watched protectively over him. The plan was simple: provide nutrients and water to the reeve in small amounts every few hours and let him return to sleep with a concoction of infused herbs he'd added to the reeve's portion of the rabbit stew. As the fili knew, the special blend of herbs would make Petrus drowsy and make him sleep. The longer he remained unmoving, the quicker he would heal, provided the wounds weren't corrupt. As Petrus slept, Cathal kept the humours balanced by monitoring his body temperature. When cold, he stoked the fire, threw saddle blankets over him and when hot, gave him water and used wet cloths to cool him down.

He improved the makeshift shelter, made it sturdy and completed the roof and walls by binding leafy branches tightly together and tying them securely to a crude but sturdy wooden frame. The weather would change, and Cathal expected that rain and winds would arrive within the next day or so.

Occasionally the reeve would stir and moan. The pain breaking through sleep. During those times Cathal fed him, gave him water and changed the poultice. With traps set and firewood gathered, Cathal lay beside the fire and slept. He was exhausted and had hardly closed his eyes since he'd found the reeve.

Behind the preceptory were the stables, fenced yards and outbuildings. Men, squires, sergeants and knights were everywhere. Horses were being groomed and prepared for riding, while others were being rubbed down and watered after being out training. Beyond the stables, pigs, goats, sheep and even some cows were penned. Chickens pecked for hidden delicacies and roamed the yards with tenuous freedom. Odo leaned against a fence that encircled a large round enclosure called a lunge pen and stared wistfully at the cows a short distance away.

As promised by Preceptor Lucius, the marshal arranged for half a dozen suitable horses to be viewed, the first being led into the round enclosure by a squire. Odo felt Charlotte stir, she nudged him. Jagger, beside Odo watched the large roan mare being led in. It was a beautiful horse, not as large as Amica, but a fine horse. The squire allowed the roan to run around the enclosure with the encouragement of a whip.

A chestnut gelding was next, and Odo knew Charlotte was having difficulty choosing.

Jagger pointed to the first horse, the roan mare. "That is a good horse."

Odo nodded in agreement. Charlotte gave no indication of her preference.

Two more horses were led in, each was allowed to run. Finally another bay coloured mare entered the enclosure. This horse was remarkable different. Its head was wedge shaped, its tail position was high and its neck, proudly curved. This mare wasn't as large as Amica, and as it pranced around the lunge pen perimeter it turned its head and gave Charlotte an inquisitive look as it passed her.

Odo turned to Jagger. "I have never seen a horse such as this."

"Aye, this is an Arabian, a special horse indeed and bred for its great stamina and endurance. Some men say these horses are intelligent and very gentle."

"Is beautiful and so unusual, it looks like it poses for us."

Charlotte was captivated by the Arabian.

"Have ye made up yer mind? Or do ye require the good marshal to present another two dozen beasts before ye," teased Odo.

She elbowed him in the side. "I cannot take my eyes away from that one." She pointed to the Arabian.

Marshal Hughes stepped over. "The Arabian takes yer fancy, Mistress?"

"Aye, it appears delicate, yet has a strength," she answered.

Marshal Hughes nodded. "These are wonderful horses, and a wise choice."

Jagger nodded in agreement.

The marshal indicated for the other horses to be removed, leaving only the Arabian. The squire held the Arabian by a rope

"Release the rope let her run," Charlotte requested.

The marshal nodded to the squire who allowed the Arabian the freedom of the enclosure, and stepped out. Charlotte, still dressed as a male with breeches and a capuchin, nimbly climbed the fence, took a few steps into the ring and watched the horse.

After a few moments the Arabian began to trot around Charlotte in ever decreasing circles. Charlotte was talking to her, but Odo couldn't hear what she said. Intelligent and curious, the mare stopped and took a few steps closer to Charlotte, her ears pricked forward. They stared at each other, Charlotte stood unmoving. Her words only for the mare. The Arabian took another small step forward, and sniffed her. Odo wondered who was choosing whom; it looked like the Arabian was selecting who would be its new owner and not the other way around.

Charlotte lifted a hand and allowed the mare to sniff, then casually she stroked the horse's nose. She began to walk around the animal, her hand softly stroking the neck, shoulders, back and rump.

"Careful," advised the marshal.

She ignored the comment. Odo was surprised, Charlotte had never displayed this type of bravery in front of a horse before, she'd always been a bit timid, especially in front of Amica. Even though the stallion was a dangerous horse, he'd never threatened Charlotte. Yet here, Charlotte was walking around an unknown, high-spirited animal without fear.

She arrived back at the mare's head. Then without a word she walked towards Odo, the Arabian followed. Odo and Jagger both grinned.

"Would ye like to ride her?" asked the marshal.

"Aye, if it is of nay bother to ye," responded Charlotte eagerly.

The road leading to the preceptory ran alongside the Templar training field. Many people travelled the road and some stopped to watch the beautiful Arabian mare and the unusual sight of a woman with golden-coloured hair ride around the field. Charlotte didn't show off, she wasn't considered a great rider, but she was moderately competent. At first she walked the Arabian and spoke to her, then they trotted briefly. Odo could tell she was nervous and he was surprised at her resolve. She urged the mare into a canter, and lastly feeling a little more confident, she allowed the Arabian free rein and they galloped from one edge of the field to the other.

Birney Beekman watched Charlotte ride the Arabian around the field with no more than mild curiosity. He saw a small group of men watching her. He saw an older man, a Templar knight, who pointed and gesticulated from time to time. There was another man, a huge giant of a man dressed as a sergeant and between them was another young man, a commoner, *probably a servant*, he thought. It didn't occur to Birney that the man he sought was in fact the man he'd just seen. Certainly commoners had no business with Templars, so after the pleasant distraction of watching the attractive woman ride, he continued on his way.

Charlotte face was flushed. She rode the Arabian around the same field where Templar knights had trained the previous day, she couldn't stop smiling. "I would like this horse, if it is possible?" She turned to Odo and gave him a smile.

"Aye, I will inform the preceptor," the marshal responded.

"And a suitable saddle and tack?" Odo added.

"A smaller and lighter riding saddle?" offered Jagger.

"Of course."

"Does she have a name?" asked Charlotte.

"I believe they call her 'Noor,' it means, light," the marshal added.

"Noor, what a beautiful name. Noor," she slowly repeated. "I will keep this name for her." Her face was bright with tears.

"Come, let us visit Preceptor Lucius and discus the price."

Marshal Hughes and Jagger walked a step ahead of Odo and Charlotte and were discussing horses. Odo turned and bent down to whisper to her. "Why do ye weep?"

She stopped and faced him. "Because this is the first time in my life I have owned anything, and ye allowed me to choose myself without sticking yer beak in and telling me what to do."

"Why would I? This is yer horse, ye will ride her and ye need to be happy."

"I am happy, Odo. Don't yer see?"

Odo looked sheepish. *Then why weep?*

Early the following morn, ten fully armed Templar Knights and accompanying sergeants departed Combe Templariorum. With them rode Jagger, Odo and Charlotte atop Noor. She was excited at the thought of riding her new horse and the three of them set out, along with the Templars, in high spirits.

Preceptor Lucius insisted his knights accompany them for part of their journey. Their presence, he maintained, would provide a powerful deterrent to any highway men or brigands who wished to waylay the three travellers.

Minus the cost of Noor, Odo's coin was distributed equally amongst the three of them. The amount was too heavy for one person to carry alone. With the memory of the unpleasantness in Taunton still fresh in Odo's mind, he asked the preceptor for a proof of ownership document for Noor and a copy.

Late the previous evening Odo spoke with Jagger after Charlotte retired to the chamber assigned to them by the preceptor.

"Are ye still determined to ride with us?" he asked as they nursed a tankard of ale.

Jagger looked serious and didn't reply immediately. Finally he looked towards Odo. "I have nowhere else to go, Odo. What I have seen and experienced these last two days is beyond belief. Ye are a good and honourable man and I see an unexplained need to keep watch over ye and keep yer safe."

After all that had happened to him recently, Odo saw the wisdom in what Jagger suggested. It would cause people in Mellester to question the giant, and possibly some would believe Odo to be living above his social station. He would deal with that at the time, but for now, Jagger's presence was comforting, and he liked him. They shared similar thoughts values and ideas, yet came from remarkably different backgrounds. "Then I welcome ye into our family and am grateful to ye, Jagger."

When Odo and Charlotte were finalising all the details with the preceptor and issued with a new Templar warrant for the four hundred and ninety two pounds still held by them, after the cost of the horse was deducted, Preceptor Lucius asked about Jagger. Odo explained in detail how they came to be acquainted and how Jagger offered to ride with them and keep them safe.

"I asked about Jagger," informed the preceptor. "because an unusual young man like him is memorable. What I have learned is that Jagger is a good person, he has fine qualities and is a unique and superior soldier, better than most, and that includes knights. He would make a superb Templar. Ye are fortunate to have him in yer service. I believe he is loyal and can be trusted. I spoke with him earlier and told him all he needs to do if ye encounter any difficulty, is to send word to me. I will do what I can."

Odo listened attentively. "I am still surprised why ye wish to help. Why do ye do this? I know ye explained, but it is so unusual."

"Yer father was a Templar, Odo. Ye are not a commoner, but of noble birth. I cannot change what happened to yer throughout yer life, and Brother Odo did what he thought was best in how ye were raised. From what I've seen, Brother Odo made a wise decision."

Charlotte was rivetted.

"Ye showed us honesty and integrity, we value that. What we want, is to see yer succeed, do well and do all ye can to help those in need. From what I know ye have always done that. Now ye have the means to make a difference."

Odo swallowed.

Amica's instinct as a stallion was to lead, and Odo had to fight to keep him back and allow the Templars to ride ahead. They charged through the countryside, two abreast in a long column. The ten fully armed knights, sans lances, rode at the column's head, followed by Odo and Charlotte riding side by side. Behind them rode Jagger on his powerful destrier. Ten sergeants brought up the rear.

It was exhilarating! Charlotte had never experienced this before; she turned frequently to Odo and grinned broadly. Noor was proving to be a gentle animal and already Odo could see a bond developing between the two of them. To his surprise, it was Charlotte who was adjusting and changing. He knew she had strength, but now she began to blossom in ways he could never have imagined, he felt proud of her.

Other travellers hastily made way for the quickly moving procession as the miles fell behind them. They stopped frequently to allow the horses rest and drink. Charlotte didn't allow the templar sergeant to take Noor and water her. She insisted that she do this herself. Odo laughed. Amica wouldn't allow anyone other than Jagger and Charlotte near him, so the three of them each took care of their own horses.

It was midday, dark clouds rolled in and the weather was beginning to change. The knight commander approached Jagger and informed him they would be on their own; this was where the Templars said farewell.

Odo and Charlotte gave their thanks, and before long the Templars had disappeared. For the first time in days, Odo felt vulnerable.

Jagger looked skywards. "We shouldn't tarry, rain is coming."

CHAPTER TWENTY–ONE

As customary, Birney Beekman arose early and walked through the township of Combe Templariorum. No one he'd spoken too had seen the herdsman. He'd hoped a casual walk through town and visiting stables would provide a clue to his whereabouts, after all, how many black stallions could there be. As he approached the Preceptory he witnessed a commotion as a company of Templar Knights departed. He immediately recognized the black stallion, and then the flaxen haired woman riding the beautiful Arabian. He'd never met Odo Read, but was given a fair description of the horse he rode. In itself, unusual for a commoner. He could have kicked himself, they were the same people he saw the previous day and now they rode with the protection of Templars. The black stallion and the clothing of a commoner was unmistakeable, it was the herdsman and his woman. But where they going?

Birney quickly returned to his lodgings, retrieved his horse and set out after the procession. Unfortunately, his horse was unable to maintain the pace set by the Templars and he fell further and further behind. From the direction the armed group travelled, he guessed the herdsman was returning to Mellester Manor.

The instructions given to Birney were quite explicit; the herdsman was to meet with an unfortunate accident away from Mellester Manor. If the herdsman, as he guessed, was returning home then his task was essentially over.

Failure wasn't something Birney took lightly and the bonus for completing his mission was significant. He allowed his tired horse the opportunity to satiate its thirst, looked at the darkening sky and arrived at a decision. He would go to Mellester and wait for opportunity. Patience was always rewarded, and Birney was a patient man.

Priest Benedict stood at the pulpit of Mellester's church and surveyed the empty seats. He felt contemplative and then glanced up at the newly completed roof. It looked wonderful and he was thrilled. The roof had been in need of a major repair and the Bishop's generous contribution made it possible. Never mind the threat from Sir Hyde that encouraged the bishop to loosen his purse strings. After completion, the last man had packed his tools and moved off days ago, and with bad weather approaching, the church was now a dry, safe haven for his parishioners if needed.

Earlier a messenger arrived and delivered a missive from Bishop Immers. It was typically brief and succinct and requested that he make haste for Exeter to meet with him. In light of all that had transpired recently, a meeting with the bishop didn't bode well for Mellester or Herdsman Odo.

One thing Benedict didn't want to do was abuse the trust of his parish and work against an honest and likeable young man to satisfy the unholy needs of a rapacious bishop. The dilemma was an ethical conflict.

Priest Benedict looked down at the ambo and the heavy bound collection of holy manuscripts that sat upon it. He stroked the cover lightly, almost sensually with his fingers, then with both hands opened the substantial volume. Latin, old Latin, *Vetus Latina*, words written in traditional flowing script stared up at him. It gave him pause, and he questioned his scared duty to minster to the people. His moral conscience was stirred.

He sighed, closed the book, hefted it under his arm and walked back to the rectory. As ordered, he would depart for Exeter immediately.

Odo, Charlotte and Jagger rode into Mellester Manor just as the sun descended behind shadowed forests and hills beyond. They attracted curious stares from villagers, mainly because of the horse Charlotte rode and the giant who rode a destrier that trailed them. People waved in greeting but it was plainly obvious Mellester was suffering. They rode through the main street and on towards their home and byre.

Thrilled to see their daughter return unharmed, and somewhat surprised by the beautiful horse she rode, Cheesemaker Gerald and Agnes stood happily in the doorway to their shoppe and waved. With a shout, Charlotte promised to visit them shortly.

To Odo's relief their home and the others ravaged by fire had been rebuilt. Apprentice Daniel, full of vigour and excitement welcomed them enthusiastically and then froze – he stared open mouthed when he saw Jagger.

"Open the bloody gate, and close yer gob." yelled Odo with a big grin.

Daniel peppered them with questions and wouldn't give them any respite. He fell in love with Noor and claimed he'd never seen a more stunning and beautiful horse. He went to take the reins and begin to rub her down when Charlotte interceded and threatened him with violence if he as so much touched her. Odo and Jagger laughed. Daniel, red-faced, looked to Odo for help.

"Ye have been told, Daniel," said Odo, "I can't touch her either."

As Daniel fetched water and feed, all three horses were rubbed down and taken care of.

"Where is Reeve Petrus?" Odo asked.

Daniel shrugged, "We have not seen him fer days."

"Perhaps Steward Alard knows. Jagger and I will go and see him now while Charlotte visits her family. See the byre is secure," Odo advised.

After being on horseback all day, it felt good to walk and stretch. Odo and Jagger walked through the village and then up the carriageway to the manor. A man-at-arms at the doorway to the hall looked at Jagger with uncertainty and some trepidation.

"I wish to speak with Steward Alard," Odo announced.

The guard tore his eyes from Jagger, nodded and disappeared inside the hall. He returned moments later and invited the two men in. Steward Alard stood near the dais with a welcoming smile.

"I'm pleased to see yer safe and sound, Odo, we were worried." He looked up at the immense form of Jagger, "And I see ye have a new friend."

After introductions were made, Odo recounted his ordeal in Taunton and then he told of their experience at the Templar Preceptory. He did not tell the steward how much coin the Templars gifted him. Steward Alard listened attentively and shook his head. "I thank ye, Jagger. Odo needs looking after, he has a way of attracting trouble, and I can only hope ye will keep him and Charlotte safe."

"I will do my best, Steward Alard."

"Where is Reeve Petrus? Daniel says no one has seen him?"

"I know not where he is." Steward Alard shook his head. "I confess, I am beginning to worry, for he has not sent word."

"Does Cathal know?" Odo asked.

Jagger's head whipped around to stare at Odo.

"Well, yer see, Odo, Cathal went to Ridgley Manor to tend to Sir Hyde, but Steward Baldric tells me after Sir Hyde became stable, Cathal disappeared. So both Cathal and the reeve are missing."

"Cathal?" asked Jagger. "The same seer, the sage healer in France?

"Aye, it is he."

"Why is he here in Mellester?"

"He just decided to come here," replied Odo.

"But why? The man is special, he is gifted and revered, and spoken of as a great and wise man."

"Because of him," Steward Alard inclined his head towards Odo. "He came here because of Odo, and yes, Cathal is a great man and loved here by all in Mellester, even if he has a habit of vanishing."

Jagger kept his mouth closed and looked at Odo.

"Could the reeve and Cathal be together?" Odo asked, ignoring Jagger.

"Reeve Petrus came to me and said he'd be gone for two days. But not where he was going, I know not where, and he hasn't returned or sent word."

Odo looked thoughtful. "And what of Mellester, how fares the village?"

Steward Alard's expression changed. "All is not hale. I have not had coin to pay the millwright and his men. As of yesterday, all worked stopped at Falls Ende. Ye see Odo, the coin those men earn is spent in the village, the coin passes from one man to another. With no coin, people can't buy food and they suffer with empty bellies. Yer crops won't be ready for weeks. I am at a wits end."

"How much do ye need to see work continue?"

"Six pounds would see the men busy for a few weeks."

Odo chewed his bottom lip. Then fiddled with his hands beneath the table an extracted a bulging purse. He emptied a considerable amount of coin on to the table top and counted. Steward Alard watched in fascination.

"Here is ten pounds, use this to resume work on the mill."

"Odo! Where did– is this from, the Templar warrant?'

"Aye, Steward Alard, it is."

"Then this is a prest[8], and ye will be repaid," offered the steward with a warm smile of gratitude. "Is good to see yer back, and is good to know Jagger here will keep an eye on yer. Be careful, Odo, don't go carrying so much coin around. If yer want yer can leave it here where it is safe," the steward advised.

Jagger nodded in agreement.

"Aye, best yer kept this quiet fer now, don't go telling anyone where the coin came from," Odo added.

"Agreed."

"Steward Alard, what can ye tell me about Frisia?"

Jagger leaned forward to listen just as rain began to fall.

The first drops of rain pitter-patted on the ground, the beginning to

---

8   *Loan*

what he knew would be some nasty weather. The fire was well alight, and large logs burned hungrily. Cathal wasn't concerned. He collected enough wood to last days and he kept it dry inside the enclosure he'd built for the reeve.

Reeve Petrus woke occasionally, consumed by pain and injuries that devastated him. When awake, Cathal did his best to ensure the reeve drank and ate. Petrus wasn't always obliging and at times required forceful administering.

As far as he was concerned, the reeve's wounds appeared to be mending and if previously defiled and corrupted, they now lost the redness and inflammation and were beginning to heal. The splints tied to the reeve's leg needed to be loosened from time to time; the danger was in making them too tight. The broken ribs were easier to administer to with the use of a leather belt that offered support to his chest and prevented risk of further injury when he moved.

Cathal hoped that when the weather eased and the reeve was stronger, then in three or four days he could construct a litter and risk having one of their horses drag it and the reeve to the nearest home or settlement so he could send word to Steward Alard in Mellester. The juddering over rough ground was the biggest concern.

He wasn't inconvenienced by tending to the reeve. Cathal didn't see it as a burden or an obligation to care for him, he saw it simple terms, much like how he viewed the world. He *could* help the reeve, therefore he *should* help the reeve. If the Irishman saw it as fulfilling a duty, then that duty was to mankind. Put aside personal feelings and thoughts and do the job required of him. Of course he liked Reeve Petrus, he was a good and caring man, a companion, but all men are worthy of help, not just a friend.

When the reeve soiled himself, Cathal cleaned him. He didn't judge or find the task distasteful. The job needed to be done and he was able to do it. So be it. Cathal's *determinist* outlook on life was bound by similar principals.

His own demeanour was affected by other outside influences. He now knew Odo was in imminent danger. The urgency to find assistance and send word to Mellester wasn't because he feared for the safety of Reeve Petrus, his need to find help was so that he could come to Odo's assistance, and this responsibility sat heavily on his shoulders.

Heavy rain drops spattered on glowing embers, the wind, now more present, began to whip through the fire and sparks shot up into the night sky. Inside the small hut, Reeve Petrus mumbled, his torment obvious, but even with all the herbs that Cathal could find, it wasn't enough to subdue all the pain. Cathal spooned small portions of easily digestible food into the reeve's mouth then followed by water. He yelled out in pain, but his cries, borne on the wind, vanished and soon he was asleep again.

The Irish fili lay down on the platform beside the reeve, lost to the simplicities of life.

CHAPTER TWENTY–TWO

"You are dripping!" exclaimed Bishop Immers as Priest Benedict strode wet into his officium.

"Aye, Yer Grace, obviously our Heavenly Father, did not read yer missive and delay the rain while I journeyed here," replied Priest Benedict with a smile. He removed his cloak and gave it a vigorous shake, splattering droplets of water harmlessly around the room and then handed it to a waiting cleric. He turned back to his superior and an extended pudgy hand.

Bishop Immers did not find the priest's comment appropriate. His face soured.

Priest Benedict ignored his superior's churlish expression and as protocol required, kissed the episcopal ring. "I came as soon as I could Yer Grace." He dipped his head in respect.

"It took yer long enough," grumbled Immers as he returned to his seat to sip wine from a goblet.

Priest Benedict remained standing and waited. A seat wasn't offered.

Bishop Immers placed the goblet on a table and leaned back in his chair. "Now then, how does Mellester fare?"

"Ah, um, Yer Grace, the church roof has—"

"I have no interest in fatuity," the bishop waved his hand, "what *is* important to me, and should be to ye is the tithes – or lack of. What say ye, why is it ye are not doing God's work and obtaining tithes as ye should?"

"Mellester suffers, Yer Grace, food is becoming scarce. Since the murrain–"

"The murrain! The murrain, I am toil–worn over it!"

Priest Benedict couldn't help himself and shouted in a paroxysm of emotion. "Mellester was pillaged, outlaws stormed in and looted the entire village, Yer Grace. There–is–no–coin!" He knew he'd gone too far and steeled himself for what would follow.

Bishop Immers glared. A nerve on his cheek twitched. "Have ye finished?"

"Fergive me Yer Grace, I am weary, wet and–"

"Enough of yer drivel, what of Mellester, how will the steward turn things around now they have no reeve?"

No reeve? thought Priest Benedict. *No reeve, what is this*? He coughed, a brief moment to buy some time. "I, uh, believe, Mellester Manor will look to purchase new cows after the equinox, Yer Grace," he said after a quick recovery.

"From whom and where will this coin come from? I hear Mellester can ill afford to even pay wages to honest God fearing masons, let alone livestock. Work on Falls Ende has stopped," the bishop smirked. "Who will pay fer a new herd of cows? Where will coin come from to finish the mill?" He raised an eyebrow in question.

Benedict looked at the bishop and remained silent.

"The Church will have to augment and come to the aid of a manor in need," he shook his head in the guise of disgust. In actuality, that was exactly what Immers hoped would happen. "Again, commoners come to depend on the Church for salvation while unavailing lords seek to restore their fragile sense of worth by doing battle across the ocean and abandoning their manors to the bedevilled. What do lords care of manors when what commoners really need is a firm guiding hand – and that is *yer* undertaking, something ye can't seem to do." He glowered at the priest, then took another hefty pull of wine. "The Church is their saviour, that's what it is. Always has been – always will!" Immers finished his tirade with a self-satisfied smirk.

Priest Benedict exercised all his self-control to not speak his mind.

"Have ye nothing to say, or have ye forgotten God's work and all yer responsibilities to this diocese?"

Benedict shook his head, his face displaying contempt for the man seated in front of him. "I have nothing to say to yer."

Bishop Immers saw the patent enmity from the priest's body language and expression. He leaned forward, the chair creaked ominously. "Nothing–to–say? Nothing to say! I fear ye have lost yer calling. Ye disrespect the Church, and by doing so shame the apostolic succession of bishops and all who succeeded them – me included! Ye have caused me offense, damn ye!"

Priest Benedict knew he'd gone too far and was too late to turn back now. He couldn't sit idly by as Immers continued his unholy rule over poor manors that needed the Church's hand in support. "Nay, I honour God, and all that is divine. I have no respect for the man who stands vainly in the shadowed glory of ministerial priesthood and Pharisaism[9], the same

9   *The doctrine or practices of the Pharisees, especially strict observance of the traditional and written law.*

man who sits here before me now, so consumed with imperiousness and privilege over piety and righteousness-"

Immers heaved his bulk upright as quickly as he could and rose to his feet, his face incandescent red in uncontrolled fury. He sputtered before finding his voice. "Away with yer, the Church has no need of ye." He pounded his fist on the table. "Begone! For ye are a...a...a proselyte!"[10]

Benedict held the bishop's gaze, just long enough to show he wasn't intimidated and then smiled in satisfaction at seeing the bishop's fury. He slowly turned and grabbed his wet cloak from the astonished cleric who held the door open and gratefully left the officium to the sound of Bishop Immers hysterical rantings that pursued him like a yapping dog through darkened corridors.

A temporary break in the weather offered the ex-priest a brief reprieve from even more rain, but it did little to alter the despondency and loneliness of a man with a broken heart. He returned to his wagon and wanted to escape the toxic confines of the cathedral and Exeter and never return. With some vigour, he obsessively wiped his lips on his sleeve – more of a symbolic gesture to remove the last vestiges of the bishop from his body lest it defile his soul.

His life would forever change, no longer part of the Church he loved, no longer with a sense of Christian purpose. He allowed the horse to find its own way, he didn't care, as long as it was away from that despicable man. Benedict seethed, yet he found some satisfaction in speaking his

---

10   *A person who has converted from one opinion, religion or party to another.*

mind to Immers. But satisfied or not, this unforeseen predicament posed a new set of problems. Unguided, the horse and wagon lumbered along unfamiliar roads.

Despair was not a good companion for Benedict, it was a sentiment he was unused to. He thought back over how many times he had witnessed greed, seen the bishop exalt in power – all for self-gain and prosperity.

The horse and wagon plodded along in a random course and Benedict cared not.

Were all bishops the same? he wondered. Did the Church put itself before the base needs of those who needed help and to be saved? Where was God when called upon, where was God to right the wrongs? After the environs of Exeter were far behind, Benedict's simmering emotions finally erupted, he looked skywards to the heavens and dark clouds that rolled overhead and yelled in pent up frustration, anger and helplessness. "Where are you!"

Taking advantage from the respite in the weather to forage for food and herbs, Cathal stood upright when he heard the pitiful cry. His robes flapped against his legs, and his hair whipped across his face as he looked at Benedict atop the wagon. "What took ye so long?"

In surprise at seeing Cathal so far from Mellester and here… Benedict was speechless. His impassioned plea forgotten, his mouth opened, but no reply was forthcoming.

Cathal turned and began to walk away, "Come now, Benedict, we have much to do."

Benedict was struck when he saw the condition of Reeve Petrus. Cathal was spoon feeding the reeve inside the shelter he'd built. "Where did ye find him?"

"In the ditch, he was left for dead – perhaps he was."

"Can we move him, take him back to Mellester?"

Cathal shook his head. "Alas, nay, not yet. He is too weak, the journey will finish him off."

"Then to Exeter?"

"Ye think he will be safe? It was men from Exeter, the bishop's henchmen who did this."

Benedict clenched his hands, his knuckles turning white.

Cathal glanced up and saw his pained expression. "Ye think yer God has forsaken ye, abandoned ye because ye stood up to the bishop?" he asked as he slipped another spoonful of mush into the reeve's mouth.

Benedict held the gaze of the Irishman. "What do ye know of the bishop and my feelings?"

Cathal smiled. "How is it that ye came here – to this forlorn place? Did ye wander here because ye had a map? Nay, methinks not. Ye came because yer God gave ye a purpose, he had a task fer yer and ye were too caught up with yer self-pity to see it."

"Yer God? Ye say, yer God, do we not have the same God?"

Cathal shrugged, "Perhaps, I know not. Does it even matter? Ye place too much faith in the man with the ring and men like him - bishops, fer they are just men. Ye are naïve to expect mere men to act with righteousness you are so fond of preaching. Perhaps yer faith should be directed to just honouring yer God. Learn not be fearful of Him, love and work in His name and ignore the body of the Church that ye have placed so much faith in." The Irishman's blue-green eyes bored into the Benedict's, "Remember – men have weakness, God has none."

Contrary to all he'd ever learned, the Irishman's secular advice rung in his head. Benedict looked down at the sorrowful sight of the reeve and shook his head... Cathal's words ... he spoke the truth ... they were like a pealing bell, an awakening. He swallowed, thought a moment and realised he was being selfish and turned his thoughts back to the injured reeve. "What do ye think we should do?"

"We must wait a few days. Petrus will be stronger and he can then be moved in the wagon. But we risk being attacked. The bishop doesn't want Reeve Petrus to stand in the way of the Church and Falls Ende. Go back to Mellester, to Steward Alard, and bring help and then return with the wagon. Bring blankets, many of them." He paused and looked into Benedict's eyes. "Bring Odo."

"Odo?"

"Aye, bring Odo. Ye must bring him."

Benedict nodded. "Will ye be safe here? What else do ye require?"

"I have everything I need."

It was an uncomfortable ride to Mellester Manor and Birney arrived wet and grumpy. He found lodging easily, it wasn't difficult, he was the only guest. However a good sleep changed his disposition and the following morning, he set out to explore.

The village was pleasant enough, he admitted to himself, but an air of misery pervaded everyone. Pretending to be interested in the mill, he asked a few discreet questions and soon learned whose land the mill sat on and where he lived. He walked casually past the newly built cruck house and noticed the large extended byre and the stunning horses grazing in one of the fields. This herdsman was peculiar indeed. It was plainly obvious the murrain had devasted this manor, the conspicuous absence of cows a blatant reminder as to the tenuous existence of common folk and their dependence on livestock.

In the distance, across one of the fields, he saw a group of people standing and talking. Although too far away to see detail, he noticed one man, larger than the others. The same man, the sergeant, who rode with the herdsman. Why? And he recognised the flaxen-haired woman, the same woman who rode the Arabian, then one of the other men in the group must be the man he sought.

Birney decided to walk to the Falls Ende grist mill, have a look and keep a wary eye on the herdsman.

Odo stood and looked at the earthen mounds that covered the large pits where his precious herd was buried. It tore him apart, and he knew it was as tragic an event as anything he'd ever experienced. The pain was real and lasting. Unconsciously, his hand went to his head where he'd suffered the wound in his home the evening they'd culled and burned his herd.

No one spoke; it was obvious to all how Odo felt, even to Jagger, who only now was fully appreciating Odo's loss.

Charlotte edged closer to Odo and linked arms, her presence offering comfort. Daniel stood a short distance away with Huntsman Seth and watched.

With a heavy sigh, Odo looked up. He'd come to a decision, and would discuss it with Charlotte at first opportunity. "Come, let us go to the mill and see how work progresses."

The five of them began to walk along the river bank towards Falls Ende and the mill. Seth and Jagger were in a friendly debate that broke the morose spell that hung over them. As usual, Seth's high-spirited antics provided laughter and even Jagger, normally stoic and contemplative, couldn't help but join in which encouraged Seth even more. They were fast becoming friends.

Odo nudged Charlotte and whispered into her ear. "See, now Jagger looks happy, laughter suits him."

As they approached Falls Ende, a man, a stranger, not dressed as a guildsman, suddenly broke from the conversation with the master mason and walked away, back to the village.

"Hail, Master Mason Mundy," greeted, Odo. "I apologise fer disturbing yer chat," Odo inclined his head at the quickly disappearing stranger.

"Hail to ye, Odo, and Charlotte," the mason returned the greeting. "Aye, he was a strange one. Asking questions, seemed like he knew ye, Odo."

Odo shrugged, and then introduced Jagger.

"We might be needin' someone the likes of ye," stated the mason with a laugh after appraising the giant accompanying Odo and Charlotte. "We have some big stone blocks to move."

Jagger nodded, his face broke into a grin, "Be happy to help, Master

Mason."

"And work is progressing?" asked Odo.

"Aye, we had a setback, but all is hale now," replied Mundy.

Although he never said so, Odo knew he was referring to the coin he gave to Steward Alard to pay wages.

Jagger was looking at the back of the stranger walking quickly away. "And yer don't know that man?"

Mundy shook his head. "Never seen 'im b'fore."

The group left Falls Ende to return to the village, and Odo continued to introduce Jagger to stunned villagers. Few had seen such a large man and most were instantly suspicious of him but remained polite, although a little standoffish. It didn't bother Jagger who was used to stares and finger pointing.

Odo decided to pay Steward Alard another visit; hopefully he had word on Reeve Petrus. Both Daniel and Seth had work to attend to, and Jagger wanted to familiarise himself with Mellester while Charlotte went to visit her family.

"Steward Alard is waiting for ye, Herdsman Odo," informed the man-at-arms when he approached the manor. Odo was surprised. The door swung open and Odo entered Mellester's great hall to find Priest Benedict and Steward Alard in deep conversation. Both men didn't appear to be in jovial spirits and Odo walked towards them with growing concern.

"We've been searching for ye, Odo," informed the Steward without pleasantries. "Sit." He waved a hand to a bench where the priest sat.

Odo did as told, nodded to Benedict and waited for the steward.

"Benedict has found the reeve, he is severely hurt and near death."

Odo gasped.

"Cathal tends to him but the reeve needs to be brought back to Mellester," informed the steward matter-of-factly.

It was with immense relief to know that Cathal was with him. "What happened?" Odo turned from Steward Alard to Benedict.

"Cathal believes he was set upon by outlaws in Exeter when–"

"Exeter! What was he doing there? What outlaws?" Odo interrupted Benedict.

"Why he was there we don't know, I suspect he went to see Bishop Immers," added Steward Alard.

"Over the pillaging of Mellester?" Odo asked.

"Aye," the steward turned to Benedict for confirmation and then continued. "But there is more, Odo. Benedict had an altercation with Bishop Immers; he is no longer in the bishop's service as a priest."

Odo turned to Benedict, and despite his less than devoted feelings for the Church, gave him a sympathetic look. "And the reeve?"

"He is some distance from Exeter, where Cathal found him, but Cathal believes Petrus was dumped in a ditch where the scoundrels believed him dead. Cathal, as usual, managed to be there in time. However, he says that outlaws will likely attack and kill the reeve if they find him to be alive."

"Then we must go to him, immediately," Odo's voice rose.

"Odo, take a breath and rest but a moment," admonished the steward. He gave him a stern look. "Cathal insisted ye come too."

Odo nodded. "Very well, then we should go."

"He told me, that ye are in danger, Odo," added Benedict.

"Danger? From whom or what?"

"I know not, and ye know Cathal, Odo, he speaks in riddles. He told me ye must come to him."

"When do we leave?"

"In the morn. I have not the soldiers to spare, perhaps six men-at-arms, and an injured knight is all I can offer. Benedict will go, with ye and yer new companion that makes about ten men, plus Cathal."

"Can we take Huntsman Seth?"

"Aye, good idea, that gives us another good man with a bow."

"I will leave here soon with the wagon and ye will all catch up to me on the morrow," added Benedict.

Odo was silent as he thought. He knew the wagon was slow and it was wise for Benedict to depart before them. He looked across at Steward Alard. "Charlotte will want to come and help Petrus."

"No Odo, she cannot go!" The look on the steward's face was resolute.

Odo didn't argue.

CHAPTER TWENTY–THREE

Charlotte argued.

"Cathal believes outlaws will try to kill the reeve. This journey is no place for a woman, Charlotte," Odo appealed.

"Reeve Petrus needs care and–"

"Priest Bene – uh, Benedict and Cathal are there to see to him. Steward Alard is correct; this is too dangerous."

Charlotte folded her arms across her chest and glared at him.

"This isn't my idea, is the steward's, take it up with him," he advised, knowing full well she wouldn't.

"And ye agree with him?"

"Well…"

She spun and stormed out the door into the byre.

Odo slumped in his chair and breathed out.

Daniel and Odo were making a few changes to the byre and building an extra stall to accommodate Sally after she was returned by the Templars when Jagger strode in.

Odo looked over and recoiled in shock. Jagger was covered in blood and dirt. "Are ye hurt, what happened?"

"I was helping the mason move stone blocks as I promised him, then later, I saw the tanner needed aid to hoist the sheep he slaughtered. He was having some difficulty."

"Why would yer do that?" Odo was grinning. Jagger would endear himself to the villagers by his generous hand.

"They needed help. What was I to do? The tanner was alone and was struggling, I lent my back, to help," Jagger replied.

"And of Brom?"

"Ah, the simpleton, he was having nothing to do with it. He wouldn't help his father."

Odo looked thoughtful. "That was his last sheep wasn't it?"

Jagger nodded, "Aye, it was."

The food situation in Mellester was a dire. Odo shook his head. "Ye did well, Jagger, I'm sure Tanner Haelan be grateful to yer." Word would soon spread about his generous and kind nature. Odo informed Jagger of their trip to rescue the injured reeve.

Jagger looked pensive. "Odo, that man we saw earlier talking with the master mason, ye remember?"

"Aye."

"He's been asking questions about ye all over Mellester. I think we need to be careful, and Charlotte too."

"Have ye seen him again?"

"Nay, but Steward Alard says Charlotte should stay in the manor until ye return."

Odo looked thoughtful. "Aye, I will talk to her."

"Talk to whom?" Charlotte walked into the byre and slid an arm through Odo's. To his relief, her previous mood seemed forgotten

Nor did she protest when he explained. It was a wise decision, she agreed. On seeing the state of Jagger, she told him to not return until he'd cleaned himself and shooed him away.

Word spread throughout Mellester that a small group of men would depart the next morn to bring back the reeve who was seriously hurt. It was inevitable that Birney would also eventually hear the same rumour, and additionally, the news that the herdsman would also be part of the group. When the assassin saw the priest depart in his wagon, he made it his business to find out why and soon learned that the wagon was for bringing the reeve back to Mellester, it all made sense. It didn't take long before he learned that the group of Mellester riders would meet up with the priest the next day.

Birney also knew that he'd been asking too many questions and overstayed his welcome in Mellester. It was time to leave and with a plan in motion, he followed the priest from a discreet distance and remained undetected. He would wait until the following morning before he made an appearance. He doubted anyone would recognise him from Mellester, especially after a change of clothes.

His plan was simple and effective. He had a potent poison that would kill quickly. All he needed to do was approach the herdsman and scratch him once. The plan was quite simple. He would slip a small piece of shaped metal with a sharp protrusion that extended out, over his finger and then pull on a glove over the top. The sharp end would poke through the glove and once dipped in poison, he'd be ready. He'd get close to the herdsman, pretend to lose his balance, then for stability reach out and accidently scratch him. He would apologise profusely, disappear, and before the day ended, the herdsman would be dead.

The riders left Mellester, spraying mud in all directions as they rode to catch up to Benedict some distance ahead. Steward Alard and Charlotte watched as they rode away.

"It was Bishop Immers who tried to kill Reeve Petrus, was it not?" she asked the steward.

The steward shook his head. "It is likely he did, but there is no proof, Charlotte. The bishop takes precautions to ensure he is not implicated."

"What can we do to keep ourselves safe, if it is proven that the bishop is behind all these things–"

"Charlotte, ye must be careful what ye say." Steward Alard looked around to safeguard that no one was listening. "The Church rules supreme, even the king has difficulty when dealing with the Pope. In Mellester, as in all manors, the Church cannot be questioned. Ye put yerself at great risk to speak out against the Church–"

"But Immers is not a good man–"

"Charlotte, hold yer tongue," warned the steward. Ye must not utter these words. If someone overhears ye..."

Charlotte looked up at him, her big blue eyes sparkled.

He couldn't scold her. Of course he knew what she meant, he felt the same, but there was nothing he could do. He bent low and spoke quietly. "Even if there was proof of the bishop's activities, what will ye or can ye do? Who will ye go too? We are not nobility, we are simple Freemen and have no voice."

Like many knights who fought for King Henry II in France, Sir Jarin Babenberg was another wounded casualty. He suffered a severe gash in his side from a pike and was fortunate not to succumb to sepsis and die. When healthy enough to travel, Sir Jarin returned to his small fief on lands granted to him by Sir Hyde, not far from Mellester, to rest and recover. When summoned to fight for the king in Ireland, Sir Jarin was unable to heed the call, but eagerly hoped to join the king soon.

Sir Dain still suffered from a wound he received while trying to rescue Charlotte and it was doubtful he would ever retain full use of his arm. Unable to lead the mission to retrieve the reeve himself, Sir Dain asked Sir Jarin if he was well enough to command a small group of men and return the severely injured reeve back to Mellester. He informed the young knight that there was a high probability they would be attacked by outlaws during their quest.

Eager to impress the lord, and very mindful of the fact that this was his first role as a commander, Sir Jarin readily accepted. It was with some gravitas that the young knight undertook the task.

Shortly after leaving Mellester Manor, Sir Jarin, riding at the head of the small formation, pulled his horse to a stop. "I will not lead a rag-tag gang of rootless wanderers without some order!" Sir Jarin shouted. When he had the full attention of all nine men under his command, he walked his horse around the group. "Mellester's men-at-arms will ride tightly, two abreast behind me, and not like a gaggle of geese" he continued. He paused when he came alongside Seth and saw his bow. "A huntsman?"

"Aye, milord, and good one," he said grinning.

"I will be the judge, but an archer, even if he is a huntsman could be useful. Ride behind my men." He turned his gaze to Jagger. "Who are ye? Ye are a sergeant?"

"No longer, sire," replied Jagger.

"Then ye will ride at the rear," stated the knight dismissively after taking a moment to appraise him.

"And ye?" he raised a gloved hand and pointed at Odo. "What are ye, a commoner, doing here, and on such a horse?" He gave Odo no time to answer. "I will not have ye prevent me from completing this mission. If ye fall off, we'll leave ye. Understood?"

"Aye, ye will not have any problem with me, milord," Odo replied respectfully.

"Ye will remain last, ride beside him." The gauntleted hand swung to Jagger.

Sir Jarin turned away and Odo gave Jagger a questioning look. The giant shrugged.

Sir Jarin's squire moved to the front of the column as ordered, and with a doleful expression, the knight and nine mounted men under his command continued on their journey in some semblance of martial order.

Benedict spent a very comfortable night sleeping on and beneath a pile of blankets on the wagon. He expected the men sent by Steward Alard to catch up with him late in the morn. He was somewhat surprised when a voice called out to him in greeting shortly after setting out. A single man on a hackney rode up alongside the wagon.

"Hail to ye this fine morn," said Birney Beekman. "Is a pleasant day to be out, is it not?"

"Aye, after rain comes sunshine, and I welcome it's warmth," replied Benedict.

Birney rode alongside the creaking wagon in silence.

"Where ye headed?" asked Benedict after a while.

This was a question Birney anticipated. "Not far, a little further," he waved his hand and pointed randomly in a general direction somewhere ahead of them. He hoped the herdsman and men would catch up to them soon.

Benedict didn't object to the company, it was nice to have someone to talk with. They chatted amiably about this or that, and the morning passed quickly.

They rounded a bend and directly ahead Odo recognised Benedict and the wagon, although he couldn't identify the stranger that rode with him. Sir Jarin signalled the column to stop and approached the ex-priest. "Who rides with ye?"

"I am Birney Beekman, at yer humble service, milord," replied Birney with a smile before Benedict could answer.

"Where is yer destination?" asked the knight with barely concealed annoyance.

"Not far, few miles along the road and I will take my leave."

"If ye wish to ride with us, remain at the rear," ordered Sir Jarin.

Birney smiled, and looked back to see the herdsman and the giant. This was going quite well, he was pleased. "Thank ye, milord." He turned his horse and rode back as the knight spoke quietly to Benedict.

Jagger watched the stranger carefully as he rode up to them and nodded in greeting.

Birney was perplexed. The horse the herdsman rode was astonishing, as fine a stallion as he'd ever seen. Why and how would a commoner know how to ride, and where would he have obtained such a prized beast? When the abbot requested his services and explained what needed to be done, he'd not mentioned these details. He could see the young herdsman was not extraordinary in any way, yet rode with a giant as a companion, a military man. For what reason did he ride to Combe Templariorum? Obviously it had nothing to do with anything in the town other than the Templars, so what business did a herdsman from a small manor have with Templars and did the bishop know?

With a signal from the knight, the column began to move, but at a slower pace dictated by the speed of the wagon, and they rode in silence. Sir Jarin rode at the column's head followed by the wagon, and lastly everyone else trailed. This gave Birney time to prepare. By riding at the very rear, no one was watching him. He reached behind and with one hand opened the flap of a bag tied to the rear of his saddle and found his gloves.

He slipped his left hand into one glove, and then extracted a small sharp pointed object from a pocket and pushed it over his forefinger on his right hand. He then slid his hand into the glove. The pointed object poked through, almost invisible to anyone looking,.

The wagon lumbered on, men relaxed and began talking amongst themselves.

With care, Birney extracted a small clay vial. He pulled the stopper and dipped the sharp protrusion from his finger into it, then replaced the stopper and put the vial safely back in his pocket. Heedful to not scratch himself, Birney was now ready. "That is a fine horse ye have," he shouted to Odo who rode ahead of him.

Odo pulled Amica to stop and waited for the stranger to ride up.

Seeing what Odo was doing, Jagger turned away from the group and allowed the stranger to ride up alongside Odo. He then positioned himself directly behind the stranger and looked at the horse the man rode. It was a bay mare. Normal in all respects except this horse had one white sock on it right rear leg, making it distinguishable. The other three legs did not have any white fur around the fetlocks and were all uniform in colour. He'd seen such a horse in Mellester recently in stables belonging to the inn.

"Aye, he is a beautiful animal, I call him Amica."

Birney eyed Odo's thigh, this was where he would inflict the lethal scratch. "Amica? I am not familiar with that word, does it have a meaning?" He edged his horse a little closer to the larger stallion and the herdsman. He gave a quick look behind, and saw the giant watching him.

"Cathal!" cried Benedict.

All heads turned to face the Irishman who unexpectedly appeared from behind a tree.

This was it, now or never, thought Birney. Taking advantage of the distraction he leaned across and began to extend his right hand.

"Nay!" yelled Jagger, and spurred his horse forward to come between Odo and the stranger. His larger destrier responded nimbly and lunged forward, slamming into Birney's hackney with its shoulder.

The much smaller hackney stumbled and for balance Birney withdrew his arm so he wouldn't fall.

Releasing the reins, Jagger leaned across and before the hackney or Birney could recover, grabbed the stranger by his clothing and heaved him from his horse. Birney tumbled to the ground yelling. All heads whipped around to stare at the drama at the columns rear. Startled, Amica leapt forward and Odo had to hold on and fight to control him.

Jagger leapt from his horse onto the ground and unsheathed his sword, his intentions very clear.

"What are ye doing?" yelled Sir Jarin. "Sheath ye sword immediately, ye hear me!"

Jagger ignored the command and moved his sword tip so it was beneath the chin of the stranger.

"Sheath it!" Sir Jarin rode up. "Now!"

"This man was about to strike at Master Odo," Jagger hissed. He kept his gaze on the stranger and ignored the knight.

"I have done nothing, milord, why did he attack me?" appealed Birney trying hard to look indignant. He sat on the ground, both hands hidden behind him for support; the sword mere inches from his neck.

Cathal ran up.

Jagger hadn't moved, his sword held steady.

"If ye don't put the sword away, I will run ye through, so help me God!" Sir Jarin, dismounted, his own sword unsheathed and held in the ready position. "Obey me, sheath yer sword, sergeant!"

Cathal was watching intently, studying the stranger. "Wait!" With speed that surprised everyone, Cathal's leg shot out and kicked the arm of the stranger. Unable to support himself, Birney fell backward and Cathal pounced on him, pinning his right arm to the ground. Birney tried to struggle and fight off the Irishman. Seeing what Cathal was doing, Jagger stepped forward and with his weight and strength quickly immobilised him.

"What are ye doing?" cried Sir Jarin.

Cathal held up Birney's gloved hand, the sharp point obvious to all. "Methinks poison."

With Amica under control, Odo could only watch dumbfounded and broke out in a cold sweat when he heard Cathal's words.

Sir Jarin looked from the stranger to Odo.

With the help of the men-at-arms, Cathal searched Birney Beekman and soon discovered the vial of poison, a collection of lethal knives and other strange potions and tinctures. "I have seen this before... one scratch and from this potion and a man dies quickly," he informed Sir Jarin.

"What business does an assassin have with a lowly herdsman?" asked the knight.

"Perhaps ye are too quick to judge, not everything ye see has clarity."

"Certainly not from some distance," Sir Jarin answered, warily.

"Then step closer so ye can see before ye condemn, yer own life may last longer," offered Cathal.

Sir Jarin didn't know what to say. Like many who'd seen battle in France, the legend of the Irishman known as Cathal was often talked about. Some called him a druid, others a seer. Whatever he was, he commanded respect. The knight pondered Cathal's words.

A little distance away, Jagger stood with Odo who was still pale.

"Thank ye Jagger... I, I would never have guessed. How did ye suspect him?"

"I searched the village for the man, the same man who talked with the master mason and walked away when we arrived at Falls Ende. I thought that strange. I could not find him so I searched all the stables. That horse," he pointed to Birney's hackney, "was in the stables, and I remembered the sock on its rear leg. I found it strange to see that same horse here, and yet the man was a stranger to us all. I did not know what he would do, but when he reached out, I knew something was amiss," he shrugged.

Benedict walked over. "Are ye hurt, Odo?"

"Nay, just a little flustered, is all."

Cathal walked away from the knight and approached Odo, "Ye were fortunate, Odo, ye were moments from death." He looked at Jagger and nodded, then turned back to Odo. "Yer new friend serves ye well, take care of him because it won't be the only time he saves yer life." He turned and looked back down the road. "Come, the reeve has been alone too long."

Jagger looked surprised. "And that is Cathal?"

Benedict offered a rare smile. "As I am learning, there is much to that man."

Odo managed to laugh, "Aye, and ye will get used to him and his prophetic riddles. I have placed my trust in him. As ye will learn, he has answers before questions are asked. He is a friend and as good a man as any, he is wise, a puzzle, and can bring tears to yer eyes, fer he can sing like no other."

"We will take the assassin back to Mellester, let Sir Dain question him," ordered Sir Jarin. Already the men-at-arms had Birney trussed up in the rear of the wagon.

CHAPTER TWENTY–FOUR

Sir Jarin, Cathal and Benedict were crouched around the reeve. He lay still, his chest barely rising and falling – he was a man fighting to stay alive. For those who saw him, he looked as if he was shrouded in the pallor of death. How he remained alive this long was a mystery, yet remarkably Cathal had worked miracles. Odo tried to get a better look at his friend, but Sir Jarin pushed him away. "What are ye doing in here? Begone with ye, make yerself useful and bring wood," reprimanded the knight.

Odo backed out of the small enclosure.

"Ye might want to show him a little more respect," advised Cathal to the knight.

"He is a commoner–"

"He is also a man, a good man. Would do ye no harm to remember that," counselled Cathal sternly.

Odo was desolate. The reeve looked like death. His cheeks sunken, his face pale, he didn't look like he would survive the day, let alone the journey to Mellester in a bumpy wagon. An unknown voice suggested they should be digging a grave and not trying to move a corpse.

Sir Jarin posted guards around the campsite perimeter, and two men were sent to scout the outlying area. Odo was fetching wood as ordered when Jagger walked up also carrying an armful. "Seems the knight has little love fer ye, Odo," stated Jagger.

"He knows me not, he would treat all commoners this way," Odo replied as they walked back to the camp.

Jagger could see how Odo was affected by the reeve's condition. "Is he a good man, this reeve?"

"Aye, none better, he is also a friend. Ye would like him."

"And what of Cathal, why is it he asked fer ye to be here?" Jagger asked.

Odo shook his head, "I know not, I have yet to have a quiet word with him."

It was decided to return to Mellester the following day. Meanwhile Sir Jarin ordered the men to create a number of crude fascines that would serve as defensive structures in the event they were attacked during the night. He'd been diligent in his role as commander and ensured every precaution had been taken to protect them. Even the wagon was tipped on its side to provide a safe screen. It would be easily returned upright if they survived the night. He put men on a roster and rotated them frequently; he'd even sent a scout to hide on a high piece of ground where he could observe distant comings and goings. Given their predicament, there was nothing more he could do.

Odo and Jagger had been tasked to help with building the fascines; no one was spared a job and they worked hard until darkness signalled the end of a long day.

It was late, and everyone was resting when Cathal found Odo near the fire. "Where is yer friend?"

"Jagger? He is on lookout duties."

Cathal nodded. "I knew his father–"

"What?"

"Aye, Jagger Lippe, a huge man, much like his son. Was shot in the arse by an arrow."

Odo couldn't help himself and laughed.

Cathal tried to look stern and failed.

"How did ye know his family name? Jagger has never spoken to me of this."

"Do ye ever question why the wind blows and from which direction it comes?"

"Aye, I have, many a time, but have no answer fer ye," replied Odo with a smile.

"Then do ye lose sleep in worry fer yer lack of knowledge on why it is so?"

Odo gave the question some thought before replying. "Nay, for it matters not."

Cathal turned from the fire and looked into Odo's face. "Ye are in great danger, Odo." He scooped up a handful of dirt and let it pour through his fingers. "What happened today is like one grain in a handful. I can help ye only so much, Jagger came to ye in much the same way I did–"

"But why? What have I done? If I'm in such danger then should I go into hiding?"

This time it was Cathal's turn to think carefully. He looked back into the reassuring orange glow of the fire. "Ye need to do what ye feel here, Odo." Cathal touched his chest. "Be yerself, don't let people like Sir Jarin beat ye down. He is a good man, but his mind is set on what he has been told to believe." He picked up a stick and poked the fire. "Ye have more coin than ye can ever spend–"

"But how–"

Cathal raised a palm. "Do what ye feel is right, the path ye choose will always be the right one." He stood. "I must see to Petrus."

Birney Beekman was resourceful; during the night he managed to loosen the bonds that held him and slipped quietly away. No one saw him leave and he left no tracks. When it was discovered that he'd escaped, it was too late, there was nothing anyone could do. Sir Jarin didn't have spare men to go searching for him and it was unlikely he would make a second attempt on Odo's life with no weapons or horse.

When the sun rose, the wagon was returned upright to its normal position and the small group prepared to leave the camp after they moved the reeve. With Cathal fussing, the men-at-arms carefully lifted the reeve and the bed that he lay on, and slowly moved the contraption to the wagon. Petrus groaned and grunted as he was being jostled but otherwise he slept. He was placed on blankets and straw, made comfortable and kept warm. The sun was only just beginning to share its warmth when Sir Jarin gave the order for the group to ride for Mellester Manor. It would be a long slow journey.

Sir Jarin decided to send Odo and Jagger to scout ahead; it was an easy and logical decision. While Seth the huntsman with his hunting bow was best suited to help defend, his own men were better equipped to guard the reeve. The herdsman had proved himself on horseback and few horses would catch the black stallion, not to forget the herdsman's enormous friend who seemed more than capable of dealing with any problems they may encounter. He watched them ride off.

Perhaps Cathal was correct, thought the knight. The herdsman was unlike any he'd previously encountered. He was quick witted, eager to lend a hand, and yet wasn't overwhelmed or cowered in the presence of his betters. He admitted to himself that Odo was a likeable fellow, and people treated him as an equal – a ridiculous notion.

Odo and Jagger crested a small rise dominated by an old ash tree. Other low growing trees covered one side of the slope and disappeared down into a gully. It was the highest point for some distance and gave a reasonable unobstructed view in all directions.

"We should remain here for a while," Jagger advised after their horses were hobbled. "This is the best place to observe." He walked to the edge of the trees on the far side of the hill and looked down into a thickly wooded valley. "And be good place to conceal men," he added pointing into the gloom.

Amica snorted and tossed his head. Odo looked over towards him. Something agitated the stallion. He walked over to calm him down. Perhaps the hobble was too tight; he bent down to remove it when suddenly six men charged out of the trees swinging swords.

"Odo!" yelled Jagger in warning.

Odo was some distance from Jagger, and already he could see him twirling his sword a blur of white steel as it clashed with the attackers. Two men ran past Jagger and headed directly towards him. He was totally defenceless. Amica tossed his head, pulling on the reins in Odo's hand.

The stallion began to turn to face the oncoming threat. Odo dropped the hobble and leapt up onto the stallion, spurring him forward. He remembered that day a few months ago when Charlotte was kidnapped and Amica had charged and killed the fleeing man.

Jagger had his hands full but seemed to be holding his own against the outlaws. Already one man lay bleeding on the ground, and it looked like more would follow. The giant never kept still and moved quickly, almost randomly which made it difficult for the outlaws to launch any serious coordinated attack.

Odo felt the stallion tense. Amica knew what to do and he let the horse have its way. The stallion lunged forward and collided with the first outlaw sending him flying on his back. He was trampled underfoot as Amica powered past leaving the man screaming in pain. Odo hauled on the reins to turn the courser around. The remaining outlaw slid to a stop and stood uncertainly, with his sword raised in the air.

Amica needed no urging and leapt forward towards the waiting outlaw. With the reins loose in his hands, Odo held tightly onto Amica's mane. The horse quickly closed the gap and at the last moment turned. Odo nearly flew from the stallion's back as Amica locked his front legs, twisted and kicked. The outlaw stood no chance. Unable to swing his sword at the swiftly moving courser, the powerful rear legs struck the back peddling outlaw in the ribs. The sword flew from his hand as he fell backwards clutching his chest.

Risking a quick glance towards Jagger, Odo saw two more men on the ground. Blood flowed freely from fatal wounds. One eviscerated man with his entrails hanging loose was trying to place them back in his stomach.

The remaining outlaw had enough and turned to flee. He took two steps before he fell with Jagger's knife embedded in his back.

Around them, six men lay in pooling blood. Jagger was bent over, his hands on his thighs sucking in lungful's of air. Four men were dead, or about to die, the other two were severely injured. It was unlikely they would survive the day.

"Are ye hurt?" Odo yelled as he rode over. He slipped from Amica's back. He too was breathing hard.

"I, I am well," gasped Jagger. "And ye?"

"Unhurt, but, but what we will we do with these men?"

"Yer horse… is well trained. A warhorse…" Jagger looked at the black stallion with new found respect.

Odo looked at Jagger; never had he seen a man move with such poise and ease and wield a sword in such a violent and destructive manner. He looked down at his hands, they shook. He sank to the ground still holding the reins to his horse. Amica nudged him in the back.

Jagger straightened and walked to the only outlaw capable of talking. "Who sent ye? Tell me now, and I'll finish ye quick." His sword mere inches from the man's chest.

The outlaw coughed. Blood spurted out of his mouth. He held his stomach, panting like a dog.

"Who sent ye?"

"A–Abbot An–drew, Ex–et–er," he managed to say. He looked up at the giant, his eyes pleading for mercy.

Jagger nodded once, then pushed his sword effortlessly into the outlaw's chest. It was over.

Odo retched. It was all a bit much.

The last surviving outlaw met with the same fate. By the time Sir Jarin and the others arrived, all six outlaws were dead.

Sir Jarin stared aghast at the carnage. He shook his head in disbelief as he walked from body to body. He stopped in front of Jagger and raised his head to look into the giants eyes. "Ye did this?"

"Nay, sire, I had help," he inclined his head at Odo who had partially recovered and stood beside him.

"Ye are unarmed, how could ye have helped?" Sir Jarin's voice rose.

"I was on Amica, he–"

"The stallion is a trained warhorse, milord," interrupted Jagger.

Sir Jarin's expression softened, he knew, he understood. "Ye both did well, ye have my thanks. He turned to walk away then stopped. "How many men did ye battle and slay?"

"It was four, sire."

"Four armed men?"

"Aye. But they were just poorly trained outlaws"

"Did any of them talk?"

"One did, said they were sent by Abbot Andrew in Exeter," offered Jagger.

"Exeter's abbot?" The knight looked thoughtful. "Are there more?"

Jagger shook his massive head. "We saw fleeing men in the distance afterwards. They won't be bothering us anymore."

He nodded and walked to the wagon where Cathal watched. "I pray I never have to fight him," he said quietly as he watched the sergeant. He spun and faced his men. "I want them buried, with haste, see to it! The herdsman and sergeant can rest."

Cathal watched Sir Jarin carefully. *He was learning.*

They resumed their journey and arrived back in Mellester the following afternoon. The reeve was taken to the manor where Steward Alard arranged women to care for him under Cathal's supervision. The journey took its toll on Reeve Petrus; many believed he wouldn't see the light of the new day.

CHAPTER TWENTY–FIVE

The people of Mellester weren't happy, food was becoming scarcer. Fights broke out between neighbours who were lifelong friends. Accusations of theft were common place and Steward Alard and Sir Dain had their hands full keeping order and settling disputes.

During their absence when they were with the reeve, the Templars, true to their word, delivered Sally. She was healthy and fat and it was obvious she'd enjoyed the company of Templar horses. Odo was grateful they'd kept their promise and cared for her. She was a gentle animal, and a good calming influence on the high-strung Amica and Noor.

Jagger was insistent that he give Odo and Charlotte riding lessons. Each day under his tutelage the couple learned the finer points of horsemanship. He made them ride using their legs to guide the horse and to keep their arms and legs held tight to their body and not flapping like an injured duck. Even after a week the improvements were noticeable. The horses, trained to respond to rider leg commands, became easier to handle and riding became more enjoyable for them. Both Charlotte and Odo suffered daily from aching leg muscles.

With no cows, there wasn't much for Odo to do except think. One morning he rose earlier than usual and wandered up to Falls Ende and stared into the cold depths of agitated white-water and sharp rocks. He always found solace here. While the thunder of cascading water was violent to some, to Odo it was calming and it was here he found peace.

"There is beauty in nature, is there not?" came a voice.

Odo turned to find Cathal watching him. "I think Falls Ende reminds me of when I was a child, carefree and without a concern in the world," he replied.

Cathal stepped up to stand beside him. They both watched the dark river water spill over the edge and disappear into the gloom below. The ever present spray billowing up and away to descend like a perpetual mist.

"I find all of nature esoteric," replied Cathal. "Is like a book of existence but without words, fer all of life's questions have answers within nature – if ye care to look."

Odo pondered Cathal's cryptic utterance, the early morning silence disturbed by the tumult of water pummelling on rocks far below.

"I am leaving for Ridgley Manor, I need to wait on Sir Hyde," Cathal said, changing the subject.

"Aye, it would be heedful to do that. Do ye know, how does the lord fare?"

"I think ye should come with me."

"What? I have no calling at Ridgley Manor."

"Perhaps ye should tell Sir Hyde of yer plans."

Odo's head whipped around. "What plans?"

"Do ye think it would be wise to inform the lord of what ye want to do?"

Odo laughed. "How is it ye know so much? Can nothing can be kept from ye when I know not myself? What mystical powers do ye have that always gives ye the answers?"

Cathal remained silent.

"Are ye a druid? Did ye kill a frog and cast a spell to read the minds of men?" Odo shook his head in consternation.

Cathal's eyes were firmly fixed on Odo's, his expression serious. "Nay, Charlotte told me, she came to me for counsel."

Odo turned away and began to laugh, he never saw Cathal's smile.

"Remember Odo, if ye don't ask the question, ye will never get the answer. How ye ask the question becomes the key."

"I apologise, Cathal. It was wrong to ridicule ye. Ye are a good man, a wise and a dear friend and always help me to keep both feet on the ground. I thank ye."

Cathal placed a hand on his shoulder. "I leave in the morn with the sun. I'm sure Charlotte will enjoy the journey." He turned and walked away, his robes flapping, and his hair flying in all directions.

Charlotte, excited about the plans, was up early and had Noor groomed saddled and ready before Odo woke. Cathal, Jagger, Odo and Charlotte departed Mellester as the sun rose and arrived in Ridgley Manor a few hours later. Even Cathal enjoyed the ride, his own horse showed surprising speed and endurance as Charlotte constantly urged them to ride quickly.

Odo was taken by her, his love for Charlotte was consuming and it took all his self-control to not whisk her from her horse and lay with her on a bed of long summer grass beneath a warming sun. Upon the Arabian, she came alive, her eyes sparkled with energy and life, her golden hair shone. When she looked at him and smiled, his heart melted. Seldom had he seen her so happy. She was like a new woman, euphoric and vibrant.

He'd known her his entire life; she was different from all the other girls and he'd always loved her. Now as his wife she was blossoming. He wasn't jealous, he wasn't unhappy to see the pleasure she received from being on Noor and enjoying life, it made him want to give her more. He couldn't stop smiling.

On arrival at Ridgley Manor, Cathal immediately went to attend to Sir Hyde; the loss of his arm had serious remedial implications and even severe emotional ones. For a knight to lose an arm was unthinkable. A one-armed knight couldn't fight, he was incomplete and ineffectual as a warrior and no one was more aware of this than the Irish fili. Cathal was genuinely worried and hoped he could keep both the lord's wound and mind free from foulness and corruption.

Word came quickly. Sir Hyde wanted to see Odo and Charlotte the following morn, they were to stay at the manor as his guests and he wouldn't hear otherwise. Jagger would stay with the men-at-arms.

With time on their hands, they went to see Herdsman Searl. Odo would talk to him about his plan.

A man-at-arms swung open the heavy door and Odo, Charlotte and lastly, Jagger walked in. Odo recoiled. The powerful lord sat slumped on a chair and a blanket lay across his shoulders. His formerly full grey beard was now white and sparse, ageing him. His eyes, once intense and bright, looked lifeless. He'd lost weight, his skin sallow and the hand that lay in his lap trembled. Cathal sat near him and mixed a potion with a mortar and pestle. He looked up at the visitors, but said nothing. Steward Baldric was seated at a desk and rose quickly, offering Odo and Charlotte a welcoming smile. A man-at-arms stood at the door.

Charlotte could barely constrain herself, such was the transformation of the lord. Despite his frail appearance, Sir Hyde's voice broke the spell of despair, it was authoritative, clear and immediately they were reminded of the great man he still was.

"Welcome Master Odo, and Charlotte," he dipped his head but did not rise from his seat. "You look radiant, a delight to this weary body."

"Milord, is good to see ye have recovered, we were concerned fer ye," she replied.

Odo was still moved by the sight of Sir Hyde. He couldn't find words.

"Flatter me not, I'm a worn-out warrior." He looked down at where his right arm used to be and then focused on Jagger. "And who is this? The man I've heard so much about? Step forward, let me see ye."

Jagger stepped around Odo to stand beside him, his face expressionless. "Milord." He dipped his head in respect.

"I know of yer family, and I have heard much about ye since ye came to Mellester."

Jagger smiled at the acknowledgement and allowed the lord to continue.

"Why is it ye have attached yerself to this scoundrel? Ye know he brings trouble where ever he goes?" Sir Hyde tried to laugh, but ended up coughing. Cathal looked up.

"I have no answer, milord, it just feels the right thing to do."

This time Sir Hyde managed a laugh. It ended with a wince and a sharp intake of breath "I understand, we've all felt it." He looked at Odo.

"Cat got yer tongue?"

Odo found his voice. "I'm sorry fer what happened to yer, milord. It seems so unfair."

Sir Hyde's eyes flashed briefly. "War isn't fair, Odo, men like me fight to keep people like ye safe. We face injury and death every day." He swallowed and fought to control the stabs of pain that wracked his body. "I wouldn't change a thing … I have been fortunate … fer I am alive."

"We are all fortunate to have ye alive," added Odo with sincerity.

"And barely," the lord added. "Be seated. Now tell me… Mellester has also suffered greatly; this is of concern to me."

Odo recounted the murrain, the steps Reeve Petrus took to prevent the scourge from spreading. How Mellester was plundered by outlaws. He told Sir Hyde about the reeve's injury and how he was still in serious condition but hoped to see him hale and hearty soon. Sir Hyde listened attentively, although Odo knew the lord was probably already aware of what he'd said.

"Poor Petrus. And Mellester is afflicted?"

"Aye, milord, food is scarce, no coin, villagers fight and argue." Odo shook his head.

Sir Hyde mumbled.

"Pardon me, milord, I did not hear" asked Odo

"Bishop Immers." It wasn't a question, it was a statement.

Odo kept his mouth closed lest he say something about the bishop that would see him in trouble.

"Then how does work on the Falls Ende mill progress?" Sir Hyde looked at Odo, a small smile played across his face masking his pain.

"Master Mason Mundy is doing well, there is much work still to do."

"But Odo, ye haven't told me everything. I understand ye have some new friends, Templars."

Odo paused, surprised at the revelation. "Aye, it seems that way." He looked down at his feet.

The room was quiet and Sir Hyde kept his gaze firmly on the herdsman. "I understand ye are responsible fer the coin the masons received to continue to work on the mill."

Odo looked up. "Aye, milord."

"How can a herdsman pay the wages of masons to work fer weeks on the mill?"

Odo felt the gaze of everyone on him. He felt uncomfortable. He recalled the preceptor's advice and warning, and said nothing. Reticence filled the room.

"I will see yer loan repaid," offered Sir Hyde, breaking the awkward silence.

"Nay milord, it was a gift."

The lord shook his head. "And I hear ye have gifted yer land to grow food for villagers."

Odo nodded. "Some, milord."

Jagger listened intently. This was the most peculiar conversation he'd ever heard between a powerful lord and a herdsman.

Sir Hyde shifted in his chair. The movement caused him to flinch. With his hand he grasped the stump hidden beneath the blanket as he tried to reposition. Charlotte wanted to go over and help. She didn't and could only observe.

"We will speak more on this on another day. I grow weary quickly."

He paused for a moment as another shooting stab, shot up his non-existent arm. "I admire ye fer what ye have done, Odo. Now, tell me, what is it that brings ye, Charlotte and Sergeant Jagger Lippe to Ridgley Manor?" His watery eyes settled on Odo as he waited.

"I want to go to Frisia and buy deierie cows, milord," Odo blurted out.

Jagger's head spun around to stare at him.

Sir Hyde began to laugh, and again and it ended in a fit of coughing. Cathal came over to rub the lord's back. When Sir Hyde was again in control, his face flushed, "Odo, forgive me," he gasped, "I do not make light of yer desire to travel to Frisia to purchase cows, I am amused that this idea can only come from ye. Now tell me, what is it about Frisia and cows that has yer interest?" He turned to the man-at-arms. "Find Herdsman Searl, bring him here."

Odo expected that Sir Hyde would have consulted with Herdsman Searl and had him prepared and waiting nearby.

"They are larger than our cows with a calm and gentle temperament. They produce much more milk and meat, and they are just more productive." Odo stood. "Frisia is the only place where we can buy them, for they are found nowhere else." Everyone in the room listened carefully as he explained. "I want to buy thirty cows and a bull—"

Sir Hyde raised his hand. "Odo, Odo, do ye realise the cost? Ye can't go traipsing around Frisia and just round up thirty cows and a bull. Ye will need ships to carry that many animals back to England, people to help and protect yer animals from outlaws. This is a serious and expensive undertaking."

Odo stopped his pacing and looked at the lord, "Aye, milord, I am aware of this. I can pay for this and hire good men to help me."

"They might be costly, you may arrive and find ye have not the coin…"

"I can pay, milord, whatever the amount."

Steward Baldric sat up at Odo's revelation. His brows knitted together in puzzlement.

Sir Hyde shifted his gaze and stared at a tapestry on the far wall as he stroked his beard. Charlotte reached up and pulled Odo back down to his seat. Finally Sir Hyde spoke. "Have ye spoken to Herdsman Searl?"

"I have, milord."

"What say he?"

"He wishes to have some of these Frisian cows too," replied Odo with a smile.

"God help us," muttered Sir Hyde. "And ye wish fer me to help pay for these cows, is that it?"

Odo shook his head, "Nay, milord."

"If I also have these cows then this will be competition fer ye."

"Nay, far from it, I expect to buy yer surplus milk."

Sir Hyde looked mystified.

"I don't have pasture for so many cows, ye do, so in a way if ye purchase cows ye are helping me."

A quick knock on the door and it swung open. Herdsman Searl walked in with cap in hand. He looked uncertain.

"Ah, Searl, is this true, are these Frisian cows that much better?" asked the lord, forgoing pleasantries.

"Aye milord, they produce much more milk than our cows, and also we get a lot more leather."

"How many of these cows do ye want?"

"As many as possible, milord."

Sir Hyde ran his fingers through his hair. "Ye will need to take men yer can trust, Odo. Who will go with yer?"

"Apprentice Daniel, then there is–"

"I will go," interrupted Cathal.

"So will I," added Jagger.

"Benedict may come, and he knows cows," Odo added enthusiastically.

"I wish to go too, milord," requested Herdsman Searl.

"I'm going!" said Charlotte in such a way everyone stopped and looked at her. She shrugged, daring anyone to challenge her.

Steward Baldric coughed once. "Odo, how will ye transport all that coin? Ye risk being robbed."

"Aye, ye are correct, Steward Baldric, ah, I will have enough men with me to keep my purse safe."

Sir Hyde raised an eyebrow at the revelation and looked at Jagger. "Is that so? Odo, I think yer idea is sound, it will alter Mellester's fortune. It could also help Ridgley Manor. Let me first discuss this with Steward Baldric, Herdsman Searl and Ridgley's reeve. How soon do ye wish to leave?"

"Ah, soon, milord, before the weather turns. I'm not fond of the ocean and the longer we wait the rougher the seas. I cannot graze the cows at Mellester until after the equinox, or so Cathal says, so until then I will arrange grazing near Exeter."

"He speaks wisely, milord," offered Cathal. "It will be safe to bring cows back at the equinox, enough time will have passed and the murrain will not bother us anymore."

CHAPTER TWENTY–SIX

"In the war against the Welsh," began Jagger, "a man-at-arms was struck by an arrow shot at him by a Welshman from a bow just like this." He held the bow in a meaty paw and waved it around to emphasize his point. "It went clean through the iron *chausses*[11] that protected his thigh, entered his leg and then through the skirt of his leather tunic. It then penetrated the seat of the saddle and lodged into his horse, driving so deep that it killed the animal."

Both Huntsman Seth and Odo looked incredulous. "Nay, ye jest," scoffed Seth.

The three of them stood on the other side of the River Eks, well away from Falls Ende at the fringes of the forest. Earlier Odo explained how he'd received the gift from a remorseful outlaw before he died in the pillory. Jagger marvelled at the finely crafted bow and explained how his father also owned a Welsh long-bow such as this and he had learned how to shoot, but lacked the patience in training to improve his accuracy. "Takes years," he explained.

"Go on then, show us," challenged Seth.

Jagger pointed up the path. "See that far away tree with the crooked trunk?"

Seth and Odo squinted to see. "The one with the dead branch hanging?"

11   *Part of a knight's armour. Close fitting coverings to protect the legs and feet.*

Seth asked.

"Nay, further, beyond."

"That is so far," Odo stated. "Surely ye can't hit a target at that distance?"

"I think it's about two-hundred and fifty paces," estimated Jagger as he notched an arrow onto the bow-string.

With practiced ease, he positioned himself as taught; his feet were in the right place, his shoulders back. He leaned back until his back was perfectly straight and then with powerful arms and shoulders slowly drew the bowstring back until it touched his cheek. He raised the six-foot bow to the correct height, shut one eye, elevated the bow a little and took aim. Not yet satisfied, he raised the bow a fraction, then let the bowstring slip through his fingers. The noise startled Odo; he didn't expect the sound to be so loud.

The arrow flew in a slight upward arc, its fletching keeping the arrow true and stable while in flight. It was almost too quick to see, then on its zenith, the arrow began to dip a little before it slammed into the trunk of a small tree about three paces from the one he aimed at.

Seth was doubled over in delight. "I'd never have believed it if I hadn't seen it." With that he ran down the path. Odo ran after him and the giant followed at a measured speed.

"Two-hundred and fifty-six paces," Jagger told them when he arrived.

The arrow was embedded deeply into the trunk of a tree and couldn't be pulled out.

"Careful not to break it," said Jagger extracting a large knife he used to cut the wood away surrounding the arrowhead. "Well-made arrows are difficult to come by."

"You should take this bow with us when we go to Frisia," suggested Odo.

"Is a shame Steward Alard will not allow me to go,' Seth said despondently.

With a grunt, Jagger finally pulled the arrow from the tree, he inspected it carefully. "And who can use this bow except me? I don't see a use fer it."

"If ye could hit something," taunted Seth.

The giant turned to the grinning huntsman. "I will practice each day, and since ye are so sure of my aim, I will have ye stand here. Then I will aim at ye and ye can tell me how to adjust. If I hit yer, then we'll both know the arrows fly true."

Odo laughed. "It's time to return, Steward Alard wishes to see me."

The pain from Sir Hyde's amputation tormented him. At times it was unbearable – the agony consuming. Every sinew and fibre in his body seemed afflicted. A simple cough sent spasms down his shoulder to the stump where it exploded, almost blinding in a searing eruption of intense, debilitating hurt. The only relief came from Cathal who brought mysterious potions that eased the torture somewhat. But the Irishman couldn't be here with him at his side constantly as Petrus was also in need of his valuable skills.

Sitting around doing nothing wasn't an option, decided the lord. He needed to focus his mind on other things, a distraction. His sleepless nights were dominated by thoughts of Bishop Immers, and the things he had done to the good people of Mellester. What for? To satisfy a need to own Falls Ende? It was only a mill, and arguably would provide a steady income to Mellester and Ridgley Manors. He understood the attraction Falls Ende had for the bishop. But to cause and inflict suffering on innocent people to fuel the need for coin and power was beyond belief.

Yet the bishop had insulated himself well. All his illicit activity went through the abbot. Perhaps the abbot was how he could frighten the bishop into leaving Mellester alone.

He called for his confidante and administrator. When Steward Baldric arrived, Sir Hyde sat with his eyes tightly closed fighting the agony. He opened them slowly and breathed deeply, "It can't last, Baldric, surely the pain must leave my body soon."

Steward Baldric looked at his lord with sympathy, "I hope so too, sire."

Feeling more composed, he indicated for the Steward to take a seat. "I want ye to go to Mellester fer me and speak with Steward Alard. Tell him I want five of those damn cows and I will send Herdsman Searl and his apprentice to accompany Odo. Find out how much coin he wants and I will send a purse with Searl."

"As ye wish, milord."

"Now then, talk with Steward Alard and find out all ye can on who was behind the plunder of Mellester. If Reeve Petrus can talk, ask him, who it was that tried to kill him."

Steward Baldric nodded.

"And the ex-priest…"

"Benedict," milord.

"Aye, Benedict, he'll know something. I want facts and details, not opinions unless they're supported by fidelity, understand?"

"Aye, milord."

"I want ye back here in three days, before Master Odo leaves fer Frisia."

"Three days, milord."

"Aye, then I want ye to invite Bishop Immers to Ridgley Manor, but he must not arrive here until Master Odo has already departed, perhaps the next day."

"And the reason for his visit, sire? I'm sure he wishes to know."

"Tell him it's about Mellester. I expect Bishop Immers will be chaffing to help Mellester from its plight and take Falls Ende as his price. No doubt he'll believe we seek the Church's help." Sir Hyde began to laugh, then stopped abruptly when another stab of pain shot down his arm. After a moment he continued. "I was just thinking about Immers' reaction if he knew all that Master Odo has done to help Mellester. Mellester will survive, Baldric, mark my words, and it will be because of that young man Odo Read."

"Where did he receive all the coin, from where, sire?"

"Aye, I wonder. I suspect it isn't his coin, it might be he uses Templar coin and buys cows fer them. Perhaps Steward Aldric can enlighten ye. Now, two more things. I need to speak to Cathal as soon as possible. Please find him and send him here."

"And the other?"

"Send my sergeant to me."

"Yer sergeant? Sergeant Chanse?" asked Steward Baldric with

surprise.

"The same."

"Aye, milord, anything else?"

"Nay, ye have enough to do." Sir Hyde leaned back and closed his eyes. "Oh, how I yearn for Sir Gweir."

It seemed like only moments before Cathal stood before him. "Ah Cathal, that was quick, Steward Baldric found ye then?"

Cathal looked puzzled.

"Never mind. I have some questions. Can ye recount to me about the assassin and how he intended to kill Odo?"

Odo's preparations were well under way, he'd purchased hackneys for those who'd ride with them and had no horse of their own. His trip to Ridgley Manor was useful in that regard as the thriving manor had more options for him to buy what he needed. Certainly Jagger was satisfied with the supply of arrows he bought from Ridgley's finest fletcher. He insisted the arrows were for training only and he wouldn't bring the longbow with him to Frisia.

The steward even sent a messenger to a small manor not far from Exeter and arranged for him to graze his Frisian cows there when they arrived back in England. Then, after the equinox, when it was safe to bring the cows to Mellester, Odo organised extra land to graze them on as he didn't have enough pasture for all the cows he intended to purchase. Steward Alard went out of his way to help.

Odo hired men to rebuild fences and repair broken stone walls. He'd even had the byre extended again to accommodate bigger cows.

Mellester had a buzz, a feeling of excitement, and while food was scarce, the stone masons working at the mill were again spending money in the village, as were the people Odo hired to complete the work and repairs he needed.

Charlotte suggested they build a new home, a proper house. It didn't need to be big, just comfortable and secure. Odo gave the matter some thought and decided they would look together at suitable locations once they'd come back from Frisia.

The people of Mellester knew that the return of cows would bring fortune back to their village. Not a soul spoke harshly about Odo, for they all knew their future hinged on the success of his journey.

Many questioned where the coin was coming from, most guessed that the venture was being financed by Sir Gweir and Sir Hyde. They didn't care, all they wanted was to see their little village prosper and return to normal. A few wise men, supported by copious amounts of mead, even suggested that the Templars were behind it all. Since the Templars first visited Mellester, things had begun to change for the better. The Templars brought them fortune and were blessed, whereas, the Church was conspicuous in its absence.

"I feel sad that I won't be alive to see this fine cathedral completed." Bishop Immers walked down Exeter Cathedral's nave, hands clasped behind his back, towards the chancel. Behind him, at a respectful distance, two clerics trailed. Beside him, Abbot Andrew struggled to keep pace, his own foot still causing him grief. "The new cathedral will have the most beautiful vaulted ceiling. Perhaps from heaven I will see it completed, eh?

What say ye, Andrew?"

"I think from heaven ye can revel in its splendid glory and receive worthy accolades from joyful angels, Yer Grace."

Immers looked up towards the heavens. "Aye, yer might be right, Andrew." The sound of their footsteps echoed inside the expanse. He stopped at the pulpit and turned to face the abbot. "Yer man, he failed and the reeve still lives."

"I have not received word from him and news from Mellester is hard to come by." Abbot Andrew shrugged.

"Another waste of coin. But all is not lost. Finally, I've been summoned to Ridgley Manor," Immers raised an eyebrow at the indignation of a lord beckoning for a bishop. "Although, poor Sir Hyde suffers from the loss of his arm, so it is understandable he is unable to travel here. We are compassionate men are we not, Andrew?"

The abbot concurred with a nod and a smile.

"I believe the Church will be able to help the wretched people of Mellester and Sir Hyde wishes to negotiate. Falls Ende will be ours, Andrew."

"When will ye leave for Ridgley Manor, Yer Grace?"

"On the morrow. I will bring Mellester's new priest with me. I hope he is more loyal to me than Benedict, that treacher!"

CHAPTER TWENTY–SEVEN

It would take two days of hard riding to reach South Hamtun and Odo was determined to put as many miles as possible behind them on their first day. The group left Mellester beneath a bleak morning sky. A few villagers and children waved and wished them well on their journey, some even threw flowers. Odo was excited, his exuberance and enthusiasm spreading to everyone. It was an almost festive atmosphere as they departed Mellester Manor.

As before, when he and Reeve Petrus rode for France, Odo intended to ride to South Hamtun and find the Frisian cog and its owner, Hilke, who took them to Herosfloth, and arrange with him to give them passage to Frisia.

To a certain degree he was dependant on Jagger. The sergeant was well travelled and wise beyond his years. As he'd discovered, Jagger was contemplative and not prone to impulsiveness. Not only was his physical presence reassuring, he was proving to be a valuable and trusted friend and advisor.

His previous trip to France to see the king was the only time he'd travelled so far away from home. The dangers were very real, it would be a perilous journey. Had he taken enough steps to ensure their safety?

Eight of them would travel together, including Charlotte and himself. Odo was doubtful that Cathal would go, however, with the help of scullery maids, he had collected enough of the required ingredients to ensure both the reeve and Sir Hyde had an adequate supply of his special potions. To Odo's surprise, the Irishman was waiting in the village that morning and greeted them with barely a nod. For the seer, it was just another day. Benedict was also with them; the likeable ex-priest had a knowledge of cows and farming that would prove useful. Herdsman Searl and his apprentice Usher arrived from Ridgley Manor and were as excited as anyone to set out on this unusual adventure. Odo knew having the older and experienced herdsman with them would ease the his own burden.

His ever faithful and reliable apprentice, Daniel, would also be an asset. He had enough skilled people to handle cows, however, Jagger wasn't satisfied. As he pointed out, no one was armed, none could fight. How could they defend themselves if outlaws attacked?

Jagger was concerned that they couldn't defend themselves if they encountered trouble; wisely he suggested hiring a few experienced and capable fighters in South Hamtun. Dependable men who wouldn't run from a fight and act as a deterrent to any would be robbers. It would cost, but there wasn't any other option and Odo readily agreed.

One person wasn't with them and Odo truly missed his presence. Reeve Petrus lay on a cot in Mellester Manor under the care of Mother Rosa and the watchful eye of Steward Alard. In the days preceding their departure, Odo visited Petrus and was pleased to see his condition had improved somewhat, although still he could barely talk. Odo spoke excitedly of his journey, he told Petrus of his plans to bring back cows from Frisia, but the reeve fell asleep and Mother Rosa told him to go.

On the day before departure, Odo wanted to visit the reeve again, however Steward Baldric from Ridgley Manor was with him and again

Mother Rosa adamantly shook her head. She wouldn't allow him to see his friend. She gave him a big hug and told him to be careful and to take care of Charlotte and bring everyone back safe. Odo left the manor feeling sad.

Against all advice, Sir Hyde refused to take any of Cathal's potions. He insisted that he needed his senses clear and focused for his meeting with Bishop Immers, and no amount of persuasion would alter his mind.

Bishop Immers finally arrived at Ridgley Manor and as Sir Hyde waited for Steward Baldric to escort the bishop to his day room. Another wave of pain shot down his arm and he closed his eyes tightly to control the agony that coursed through his body. The man-at-arms at the door looked on helplessly. Sir Hyde knew he could control the torment and after a few slow, deep breaths, he finally began to feel more composed.

A quick knock on the door preceded the bishop's entry. He was followed by two attending clerics and of course Ridgley Manor's own ageing priest, Kirby. Bishop Immers decided not to bring Mellester's new priest; it was better if Sir Hyde was not familiar with him, he told Abbot Andrew. Steward Baldric entered last and was surprised to see the lord looking alert and attentive. However, the bishop's reaction was less than considerate.

"Oh, dear God, you look dreadful," blurted out Bishop Immers as he held his hand out for the lord to kiss the episcopal ring.

Sir Hyde didn't kiss the ring. "Forgive me if I do not show respect to your exalted position, Bishop Immers, sadly it causes me great pain to do so."

Steward Baldric knew that Sir Hyde wasn't referring to his injury.

"Please be seated." Sir Hyde inclined his head at the only vacant chair in the room positioned directly in front of him. The other chair was for Baldric, at his desk.

Bishop Immers withdrew his arm and looking at the simple chair, his nose twitched. It had no padding and looked like it had been dragged up from the kitchens – which it had. "Perhaps we could have some other chairs?" the bishop asked, and gave Steward Baldric a scornful look. The other clerics looked uncomfortable and fidgeted. Priest Kirby stood near the door and appeared uninterested. No one offered to find a better chair.

"Fer this discourse, I would prefer we speak alone. Of course my steward will attend to me if needed, and if Yer Grace prefer to have Priest Kirby remain, then I find that acceptable." Sir Hyde stared at Immers, daring him to contradict.

Bishop Immers wasn't enjoying this very much. He fully expected a warmer welcome from the lord, with hat-in-hand, and appealing for the Church's compassion and pecuniary assistance.

On cue, the man-at-arms swung open the heavy door, a less than subtle invitation for the two clerics to leave. Bishop Immers swallowed thickly and reluctantly eased himself down onto the uncomfortable hard seat.

"I hope yer journey was without incident, Yer Grace?" Sir Hyde courteously enquired.

"Ah, nay. Although I admit I thought to be received with a little more cognizance, after all, I am a Bishop of the Church, do I need yer to be reminded?" He shook his head, his displeasure evident on his face..

Sir Hyde fought back another stab of shooting pain and ignored the rebuke. "Yer Grace, it uh, troubles me to bring this to yer attention, I'm sure ye have more important things to do like tend to the woeful and administer to yer various parishes."

Bishop Immers offered his first smile of the day.

"However, Mellester Manor has suffered greatly as a result of murrain, I'm sure ye've heard."

"Indeed, tragic," tut-tutted the bishop as he attempted to look sorrowful.

"And while Mellester's lord, Sir Gweir, battles valiantly in Ireland alongside King Henry, I feel it's my honour and duty to step in and provide a guiding hand to assist Mellester in whatever way I can. I'm sure you understand."

"The good people of Mellester are fortunate that are ye able to do this, even with yer, uh, affliction." The Bishop was pleased with the direction of this conversation, despite the uncomfortable chair that was digging into his back.

"To add to Mellester's woes, outlaws entered the village and plundered it. They robbed the villagers who were already feeling the effects of the murrain. Women were raped, houses pillaged. The people of Mellester have nothing left, Yer Grace. All valuables were taken!" Sir Hyde fought to control his emotions, the pain temporarily forgotten. His eyes clear, glared at the bishop.

"Aye, uh, news reached me of this tragedy–"

Sir Hyde's voice took on a hard edge. "Sadly, since then, Mellester's reeve succumbed to a rather savage and cowardly attack in Exeter, and although he recovers, this is just another crisis Mellester faces. Without his expertise, the challenge facing Mellester only increases."

Bishop Immers managed to look shocked at the news of the reeve's injury. "Then we shall pray for a swift recovery for the reeve, Sir Hyde."

Bishop Immers fully expected Sir Hyde to begin making a plea as to why the Church should come to Mellester's aid. He leaned forward on the chair to alleviate his discomfort and in anticipation of the entreaty.

"Aye, I'm sure ye will. However, I have discovered some interesting news that affects ye."

"Oh?" This time the look of puzzlement was genuine. The bishop leaned back.

"Aye, as pursuant to my duties, I made some inquiries and discovered that all these unfortunate happenings, excluding the murrain, are linked to Abbot Andrew. I believe he is well known to ye? A close acquaintance, I'm told."

The seat was causing numbness in his thighs. The bishop shot to his feet. "Abbot Andrew is a pious, God-fearing man! It isn't possible for him to be associated with the violence ye describe, utter nonsense. Ye have been misled, milord. I suggest ye take yer baseless accusations elsewhere rather than besmirch the name of the Church and my thriving diocese."

"Sit down!" ordered Sir Hyde. The strength of his voice surprised everyone as it resonated around the room. Immers could only obey. The lord waited for the bishop to be seated before continuing. "Ye also had a visit from some of yer colleagues, Templar Knights, seems they were displeased with ye–"

"How dare ye–"

"Sit down!" again commanded Sir Hyde as the bishop made to stand.

The man-at-arms at the door tensed and Priest Kirby frowned but kept his eyes averted.

Sir Hyde had only heard rumours, and wasn't sure what the Templars had spoken to the bishop about. After a lengthy discussion with Steward Baldric, they decided it could only be to deliver him an admonition, a warning. "Sir William Marshal, 1st Earl of Pembroke and I are acquainted. I feel it my duty to report to him any concerns I have." Sir Hyde sat a little straighter, his pain forgotten. He'd never met the famed Templar commander, but Immers didn't know that. "While ye keep yer hands clean, Abbot Andrew soils his…"

Priest Kirby raised his head and risked a peek at the bishop.

Bishop Immers face was scarlet and he fought to control himself. While Sir Hyde may have lost an arm, he hadn't lost his ability to instil fear.

"I predict– Yer Grace – that yer relationship with Abbot Andrew will end. Ye will act in the Church's best interest or suffer a similar fate – and best ye remember that. Leave Mellester alone!" Sir Hyde gave the man-at-arms a quick look. "Take heed! Now ye may leave."

"By what right do ye have?"

Sir Hyde turned away, the meeting was over.

The door swung open. Priest Kirby stepped out of the way as Bishop Immers, in outrage, ran from the room. The priest gave a flicker of acknowledgement to the lord before he followed.

Sir Hyde tried to stifle a laugh. He shook his head. "How is it, Baldric, that one rapacious man with so much power can cause so much misery to many?"

Steward Baldric rose from behind the desk. "Milord, ye must be careful, the bishop may be all ye say, but he is still a bishop."

"He can't go to the Pope, he can't do anything. By doing so draws attention to his own less than Christian deeds."

Bishop Immers was furious, and vowed he would never set foot on Ridgley Manor ever again. Consumed by rage, he set out to return to Exeter immediately but the thinly veiled threat by the lord was vacuous and had absolutely no effect on him.

Chanse, Sir Hyde's trusted sergeant, loitered in Exeter near the cathedral and within sight of the abbey. He waited patiently for Abbot Andrew to make his way to the local inn where he would have his habitual and nightly tankard of mead.

Darkness had only just descended over Exeter and according to the instructions given to him by his lord, Sir Hyde, Chanse had to complete his unusual task early this evening, before the bishop returned. Chanse had already been in Exeter two days and knew the abbot would make an appearance at any moment.

He was fully prepared and had already slipped the unusual glove on his hand, the metal protrusion poking through the finger. He'd dipped it in the poison carefully, exactly as Cathal precisely instructed.

From a moral standpoint, Chanse had no qualms about completing the grim task Sir Hyde asked of him. Petrus Bodkin was a dear friend, a mentor; he'd looked after him and helped him when he first arrived at Ridgley Manor as a young squire all those years ago. Knowing that the abbot was behind the attempt on the life of Petrus, as well as the pillaging of Mellester Manor, was motivation enough and Chanse was determined to seek vengeance for his mentor and lord.

The abbey door opened, and with the aid of a stick, the abbot stepped through and began his slow walk to the inn as he typically did. Chanse paused for half-a-dozen heartbeats, then began walking towards the unsuspecting abbot. He feigned a slight totter; their paths would cross at exactly the right place.

"Hail to ye, good sir," said Chanse, as their approach intersected. The sergeant paused, blocking the way of the abbot and swayed unsteadily. Earlier, he deliberately poured mead over his capuchin and he smelled potent.

Abbot Andrew looked at the stranger with suspicion. *Another drunkard*, he scowled.

"Fer the life o'me, I can't find me lodgings," offered the sergeant as he looked around bemused. He stumbled once, then a second time. He reached out to steady himself, the gloved hand extended.

In reflex, the abbot went to push the stranger away to continue past, but the hand of the stranger scratched him on the wrist. "What have ye done!" exclaimed Abbot Andrew withdrawing his arm quickly and looking at it. It was too dark to see clearly, but a small rivulet of blood was already partially visible against his pale skin.

Fulfilling his role as a drunk, Chanse fell to the ground in a tangle of legs and curses. "Forgive me, good sir..."

Abbot quickly limped away muttering, happy to be rid of the man.

Chanse stood and carefully removed the glove and stowed it in a small bag that hung from his belt and disappeared into the darkness.

The abbot's nightly ritual of sharing a tankard of mead with the locals was cut short. He was feeling poorly. He returned to the abbey earlier than usual and went to sleep.

His body was discovered the following morning when he didn't arise for matins.

Bishop Immers arrived back in Exeter in a foul mood the same night. His disposition didn't improve when he was informed that Abbot Andrew had passed away while he slept. The shock of Andrew's unexpected death hit him hard. Sir Hyde's parting words echoed in his head. He was convinced Lord Hyde was behind it, but how? For Bishop Immers, the stakes had changed. He'd need to be more careful … perhaps Mellester Manor and Falls Ende just weren't worth it.

The following morning Bishop Immers received word that Herdsman Odo and a group of men had departed Mellester for Frisia to purchase cows. Immers glared at the cleric. "And how would a herdsman from a small hamlet find the resources to travel to Frisia and purchase cows? Do tell!" The bishop managed a laugh.

The cleric shifted uncomfortably, "Yer Eminence, I know not, but they have already left Mellester and ride fer South Hamtun where they will seek passage to Frisia."

"Ye are mistaken, it can't be, off with yer."

Pleased to be excused, the cleric bowed and backed away.

CHAPTER TWENTY–EIGHT

South Hamtun proved to be captivating for Odo's crew as they entered the busy town. Heads rotated in all directions to take in the unusual sights. Odo, Jagger and Cathal had been here before, and like a seasoned traveller, Odo smugly explained the tall building with the spire was Saint Mary's Church, he pointed out the inn where he and Reeve Petrus spent the night, and showed them where all the huge ships were tied up. Within a short time they'd secured lodgings and stabled the horses. Cathal went off to seek old friends and disappeared into darkened alleyways, while the others were eager to explore and wander the town. Odo, Charlotte and Jagger headed towards the docks to find the Frisian Cog and Hilke.

Screeching gulls heralded their arrival at the waterfront. The large birds noisily competed for entrails as fishermen cleaned and gutted their morning catch and then threw waste offal into the river. Solicitous, hand-wringing merchants dressed in fine clothes presided over cargo being loaded aboard ships, while others fretted anxiously as their goods were unloaded onto waiting wagons and carts. They barked out commands at the luskish, admonished the slothful and yowled in perturbation if they believed men were being unnecessarily rough with their valuable merchandise, but of the Frisian called Hilke, there was no sign.

Odo, Charlotte and Jagger wove through the turmoil, they side-stepped past men carrying goods, avoided uncurbed wagons and after a warning cry from Jagger, nimbly evaded having something heavy dropped on them. Odo asked a man wheeling a bale of wool on a handcart if he knew of Hilke. Helpfully the man pointed further up the river. "Ye'll find his ship up there," he pointed, then hurriedly carried on his way before he was squalled at.

They found the Frisian cog easily enough; since Odo had spent most of his voyage to France leaning over the side emptying his stomach, he recognized the ship immediately. It sat neglected and alone, rocking gently against a wharf, no sailors scrambling about the deck and lines. It looked to be in a state of some neglect. Neither Jagger nor Charlotte looked impressed.

Again Odo asked a passing man if he knew of where he could find the Frisian owner.

The man leered at Charlotte and finally he gave his full attention to Odo. "Hilke will likely be where he's always at when not up 'ere," he stated helpfully, then gestured to a building back down towards the main waterfront area they'd just left. "At the 'King's Arms.'"

Odo was pleased, although his companions weren't convinced. "Come."

They followed Odo to the inn and entered the less than majestic establishment. It was gloomy and filthy inside and it took Odo a few moments for his eyes and nose to adjust. With the huge figure of Jagger looming over him, all conversation stopped and heads turned to stare. He scanned the patrons as best he could and quickly saw a face he recognized. "There he is." With Charlotte in tow, they approached the ship owner who sat brooding and alone in a corner.

Hilke looked at Odo, then Jagger and furrowed his brows.

"Hail to yer Hilke, do yer remember me? Petrus and I sailed on yer ship a few months ago, yer took us to Herosfloth in France."

The sailor's brows were still knotted. Then recognition dawned, "Jakob!" he broke out in a warm smile

"Nay, I am Odo, do ye remember me?"

Hilke studied the young man before him. "Ah, aye, ye were *siik*[12] the whole voyage, but of course." He waved to a seat with a well-used clay pipe he held, inviting them to join him.

Odo introduced Charlotte and Jagger and all three sat at the long bench opposite the sailor as conversations resumed around them.

"I saw yer ship, it uh, looks forsaken."

Hilke's generous smile vanished. He shook his large head slowly from side to side. "I need a new mast. We sail into bad storm some weeks past, the mast, it crack and I do not have a fat purse to have new one, ye understand? *Fernield*.[13]" His eyes squinted in the gloom at Odo. "Why ye wish to know this, ye want me to take ye back to Herosfloth, I cannot do."

"Nay, nay, I want ye to take us to Frisia."

"Frisia!" Hilke began to laugh. "Frisia, why ye want this?"

Odo leaned forward. "We have nine horses we wish to take to Frisia and eight men–"

"Perhaps six more," added Jagger.

"Aye, maybe fourteen men. Then I wish fer ye to wait and I will buy cows and have ye take us to Exmouth in Devonshire," finished Odo.

---

12   *Frisian - Sick*

13   *Frisian - Broken*

Hilke's face turned serious. "*Wêr*[14] in Frisia ye wish to go?"

Odo shrugged. "I was hoping ye could help. I want to buy thirty-five cows and a bull. But I do not know where in Frisia and hoped ye would know."

"*Well dan.*" He scratched his head. "Perhaps Geestendorf, is not town like this, is small farming village on coast, perhaps ye can buy cows, *Ik know net*[15]." He shook his head again. "But this many cows and horses, ye will need *trije* ships, uh, three big ones."

"Can ye find two more ships if yers is fixed?"

Hilke gave the matter some thought. "Aye, but not here, we must first go to Delfzijl, in Frisia, there we will find two ships. But Odo, this will cost much. Ye have coin?"

Odo nodded. "How much to have yer ship fixed?"

Hilke inclined his head. "Two pounds, *net mear*[16]. But this is expensive fer ye, aye? And when to leave?"

"Soon as ye can," stated Odo. "I wish to talk to yer about the entire cost of everything, even the other ships."

"I cannot speak for other ships, but can tell ye what I will cost," added the Frisian.

Jagger was listening intently and decided this was a good sign, the man was at least being honest. The Frisian was right, he couldn't speak for the other ships. Odo would need to negotiate with each ship owner individually.

---

14   *Frisian - Where*

15   *Frisian - I know not*

16   *Frisian – Not more.*

A price was agreed upon with Hilke and Charlotte counted out two pounds for the repairs. It was a lot of money, and she was understandably nervous. Hilke would receive half the amount for passage prior to sailing after the ship was repaired, minus the two pounds. He would need coin to provision his ship and the remainder when they departed Frisia for Exmouth.

Hilke drained his tankard, slammed it down on the table and stood. "Wim!" The inn fell quiet as all patrons turned expectantly to the Frisian.

A heavy-set man stood.

"*Wy go, gather de manlju[17]*!" yelled Hilke.

The man gave a toothless smile and began issuing instructions and half a dozen more men rose from their seats and began filing out.

They all stood on the dock.

Hilke looked at Odo. Maybe tomorrow on tide we leave, is good?"

"Thank ye Hilke."

"Bring horses at midday." His clay pipe bounced up and down as he spoke.

Odo, Charlotte and Jagger left Hilke to work on his boat and began to walk back to the inn.

"What is so special about this ship?" Charlotte asked.

"Do yer see inside, the deck is flat, not curved. This makes it easy for animals and this type of ship can carry much weight," offered Jagger.

"And how much does a Frisian cow weigh?" she turned to Odo.

---

17   Frisian – We go, gather the men.

"From what I heard, as much as half a ton each. But the problem is not the weight in each ship, it's the space. According to Hilke, we can put as many as twelve cows and three horses plus food for the animals in each ship."

They began walking back to their lodgings. People were everywhere. Young children tugged at their clothes with grimy hands held out, appealing for food or coin. Adults with missing limbs or gross deformities cried out for charity. Jagger was busy shooing them away. "Don't pay them any mind, ignore them," he warned, "otherwise they'll be all over ye."

It was like a mob, and they congregated in the centre of town. Odo felt someone tug his capuchin and wouldn't let go.

Jagger saw and quickly swatted the hand away. The woman yelled out in pain.

Charlotte felt pity for the starving beggars and wanted to help but there was little she could do. When the woman yelled she turned her head to look. Charlotte stopped and froze. "Grace? Is that ye Grace? Oh dear God, Odo, its Grace!"

The beggar woman stared, and appeared momentarily confused. "Charlotte, Odo? What brings yer here?" she finally replied. She was thin and dirty, her hair a tangled mess and her clothes torn and ragged. The man seated in the filth beside her looked up and Charlotte recoiled. *It was him, how could she forget..*

Odo saw her reaction and stepped between her and the man he was only just beginning to recognize.

Seeing the reaction, Jagger leapt back to protect them both.

"Wait" cried Charlotte, having regained her composure, "I know them both."

Jagger looked unsure.

"We know these people, Jagger, Hearth-Wife Grace is from Mellester, the man with her is the brigand, Tedric," she said.

"Watch him, Jagger," warned Odo.

Jagger stepped closer to Tedric, but the former outlaw made no attempt to flee and remained seated in the filth.

The last time Charlotte saw Tedric he was being pilloried for his role in kidnapping her. Unlike his brother, he survived, and on his release, Grace took care of him and nursed him to health. It was Tedric who was accused of killing Priest Durwin and believed to have taken Grace as captive before he fled. Neither had been seen since.

"Are ye hale, Grace, were ye taken captive?" Charlotte asked with concern.

Grace stood. "Dear Charlotte, yer a sight fer sore eyes. Nay, Tedric is a good man, he never took me from Mellester, I chose to go with him."

"But he killed the priest," added Odo.

"Aye, Priest Durwin was scum." Grace turned her head and spat. "He struck me, Odo, he beat me over and over again. Tedric came to my help and saved my life fer Durwin would've killed me because I discovered he was stealing church coin. It was me who told Tedric to leave and I wanted to go with him. I am his woman now." She looked down at Tedric who sat dejectedly, her expression softening as she smiled briefly before exhorting the priest. "Priest Durwin was a wicked, evil man, truly hedge-born."

"Is this true, Tedric? Does Grace speak the truth?" Odo asked.

"Aye, is as she says. I killed Durwin, and I'd do it again if my Gracie was in peril."

"Then how did yer end up here?"

"We did a little graft here and there, we got a ride in a wagon carrying wool to South Hamtun. But we couldn't always find work. Gracie didn't want me to do bad things, so I didn't steal – have been good."

Charlotte studied them both. She turned away and whispered to Odo. "Can I have a word with yer?" She pointed, "over there."

"Stay here," he said to Grace and Tedric and then walked a few paces away with Charlotte.

"Can ye hire Tedric? We'll need Grace to help cook. Tedric is a fighter, but is he good enough?"

"Are ye sure, Charlotte? This man kidnapped ye … I don't know."

"He paid the price, he did his turn in the pillory, even before he and his brother were pilloried they apologised, remember, it was his brother who gave ye his bow."

"Aye, that he did." Odo chewed his lip as he considered Charlotte's request. "Let me talk to Jagger, if he says the man has skills, then we'll hire him." They walked back to Jagger and Odo pulled him aside and explained Charlotte's idea.

Jagger gave the suggestion some thought. "Let me take him to the stables at the inn, I will see if he can fight. If he can, then I suggest we hire him, he's a big strong man."

"Aye, that he is."

They walked back to the Inn and Charlotte helped Grace clean the filth from her, while Odo, Jagger and Tedric went to the rear of the building to the stables. "I want ye to show Jagger yer fighting skills, Tedric. If ye can fight and obey Jagger, I will hire ye and Grace. She can help with the food. I need some fighting men."

Tedric looked at Odo. "Thank ye Master Odo. I'll do m'best, I will."

Jagger rummaged around and found two pieces of wood, equal in length that would serve as dummy swords. He handed one of them to Tedric. "Do yer utmost to hurt me, Tedric." He stepped back and took a couple of mighty practice swings. The wood swooshed dangerously through the air and wisely Odo took a couple of steps away to avoid being struck.

Tedric felt the weight and he too took a couple of swings. "I don't want to hurt ye."

Jagger laughed, "Do yer best." He leapt forward and the wooden sword arced down towards Tedric's kidneys.

Tedric was quite physically nimble, more so than his mind, thought Odo. He was impressed how Tedric seemed to be very intuitive and fluid. He'd seen Jagger fight and knew the sergeant was holding back, however, it was Jagger who received the first blow on the arm. It hurt and he gasped.

"Are ye alright?" asked Tedric looking worried.

Odo tried not to laugh.

"Just fight!" Jagger insisted through clenched teeth, and launched a flurry of moves and spins that caught Tedric off guard. Tedric fended most of them, but couldn't maintain his defence against the bigger, stronger and more skilful man. He sat on the ground rubbing his shoulder and his arm simultaneously. Jagger was breathing hard and stood over him. "Where did ye learn to fight?"

"Me brother, he taught me, he did."

"Can ye use a bow?"

Tedric shook his head. "But I can grapple."

Jagger smiled and stepped over to Odo. "He is a natural fighter, caught me ill prepared. He is much better than most, a lot better, strong too."

"Do ye wish I hire him?"

"Aye, if we can control him."

"I will talk with Grace first," Odo replied.

"We will need to purchase some weapons," suggested Jagger as he rubbed his sore arm.

Jagger put the word out he needed capable trustworthy men who could fight. The next morning, he put a dozen men through their paces. Six stood out as being remarkably better than anyone else and he released the other six men. He spoke to each at length, and once finished he let another two of them go. Including Tedric and Jagger there were now six men in Odo's small army and three of them could shoot a bow with accuracy. None had horses, but that was of no concern to Jagger. He wanted men on foot. If horses were needed, Odo agreed to rent or purchase them once they arrived in Frisia.

As promised, each man would receive a shilling in wages and the entire group met at the dock at midday just as the last of the stores were carried aboard Hilke's ship. The tide was turning and Hilke was keen to depart. With horses loaded and everyone aboard, Hilke's newly repaired ship slipped its tether from South Hamtun and headed for their first port-of-call in Delfzijl, Frisia.

Odo and Charlotte watched South Hamtun fall away. "How long will it take to get there?" she asked.

"Hilke says three and half days if the wind holds up," he replied. Already he was beginning to feel queasy. He held his face to the wind – it helped a little. "Then another day from there to Geestendorf."

Cathal wandered over. "Yer look a little pale, Odo."

Odo just looked at the seer and said nothing.

"Chew on this." He held out his hand.

"What is it?"

"Matters not if it makes ye feel better, is this not so?" He raised an eyebrow. "If ye must know, its ginger root."

Odo took the small piece of root and held it to his nose, then took a tentative nibble.

CHAPTER TWENTY–NINE

The cog lumbered through a moderate swell, and at eighty feet in length and twenty-five feet in beam, the heavy ship effortlessly shouldered aside an endless parade of rolling green waves. The ship creaked and spoke like it was a living, breathing entity. The men who crewed this fine vessel always referred to the ship as 'she.' She had a personality the crew explained; some days she behaved and at other times she transgressed. Sailors were superstitious and were attentive to her fickle moods. Today, beamed Hilke, she was in fine spirits, she sailed fast and responded easily to the fine adjustments of her huge mainsail.

Earlier, with Odo, Daniel and Jagger's calm demeanour, the horses were brought aboard and secured into small sturdy stalls that the crew previously assembled. They were given food and water and appeared unaffected by being on a ship in a gentle, undulating ocean. If the conditions worsened, the horses were protected in their stalls and could even lean against the sides of their pen for stability.

For Charlotte, the experience was life changing. She saw a world beyond the confines of Mellester and her father's cheese shoppe. There were people who spoke strange languages, looked and behaved differently, and the way some were dressed was, in her opinion, ridiculous and garish. She was used to the way men looked at her, but in South Hamtun, it was unsettling and even hostile at times. Probably because she was dressed in breeches and not as women normally do, she thought.

Jagger was proving to be more than a trusted friend; his company and presence was a strong deterrent for anyone seeking to take advantage of them and both she and Odo valued the loyal sergeant more and more with each passing day.

He became more relaxed and grew in confidence; he smiled, laughed frequently, and lost some of the staidness he first brought with him when he came to Mellester. It was obvious to everyone he revelled in the responsibilities he assumed, and warmed himself to Odo and Charlotte's closest friends. Cathal, forever the augured exemplar, took kindly to Jagger and when time allowed, they would engage in deep philosophical discussions. The two most unlikely companions were becoming close friends, and certainly Cathal was becoming his mentor.

When still in South Hamtun, Charlotte insisted that Grace and Tedric discard their rags and she purchased new clothes for them. Without the constraints of a bleak future, and their self-esteem buoyed and motivated with the hope of a normal life, they lost the cloud of severity from their vagrant lifestyle and made themselves useful. Tedric, not gifted with intelligence, was intensely loyal and when given opportunity proved himself eager to contribute. When he put a foot wrong, Grace was there to ensure he wouldn't do it again. With infinite patience, she explained and guided him and seemed to instinctively know how to reach the dark vacant recesses of his mind. In turn, he responded positively and doted on her; he loved Grace as everyone could see, and as a couple they were truly suited for each other. A few years older than Tedric, Grace was a bastion, she provided strength and hope to them all. No wonder Priest Oswald had her as a hearth wife, mused Odo.

Of similar age and many shared common interests, Benedict and Herdsman Searl, paired together and could frequently be heard sharing good natured banter while Daniel, and Searl's apprentice, Usher, were tied at the hip.

The four armed men hired to protect the group kept to themselves and were respectful and friendly. Jagger had done well and Odo and Charlotte were pleased.

As the cog sailed in a northerly direction towards Frisia, all aboard were in good spirits. Even Odo's stomach settled down and he tried hard to enjoy the strangeness and vulnerability of being on a small craft, bobbing on the wide expanse of ocean that stretched far into the distance.

From time to time Bishop Immers thought it best to visit manors in his diocese and show Church support, especially when a priest was lazy and was not diligent in collecting tithes as required. A visit by him often worked wonders and provided enough divine guidance to spur motivation and increased offerings.

Including Mellester, there were four other poorly performing manors in his diocese which had also been struck hard by the murrain. They were all neighbouring manors and the bishop felt it was time to call on each of them. Despite the recent warning from Sir Hyde to stay away from Mellester, he decided he would visit anyway. In his role as bishop, Immers felt Sir Hyde had no business telling the Church what it could and couldn't do. Additionally, the information provided by his cleric that the herdsman was travelling to Frisia, had been confirmed. This left the bishop with more questions than answers; his curiosity was piqued.

There was also the matter of ordaining Mellester's new priest, Aylwin, and more than anything, Bishop Immers was keen to see the progress on the construction of the Falls Ende grist mill. He brought his normal gaggle of clerics with him, including a number of men-at-arms for security.

Selecting a new priest had been taxing . The bishop wanted someone with unquestioned loyalty to him and who would report back on worthy developments within the manor in a timely way. After the debacle of Durwin, who was far too ambitious for his own good, Immers wanted a more moderate presence, but not too moderate like Benedict who was the other extreme. Bishop Immers' face soured at the thought of how Benedict, after many years of loyal service and dedication, had turned on him and the Church so easily.

Priest Aylwin was the obvious choice. He was certainly pious, and well liked by all. He had a good relationship with people and would never go against the wishes of the Church. After all, thought Bishop Immers, Aylwin would not want the information he had on him to be made public, it would affect the standing and honour of Aylwin's rather wealthy family and cause them untold misery and dishonour. Aylwin obviously knew this, and for that reason, he was subservient and obedient. He turned to look at the priest and was again satisfied with his decision.

His small troop arrived at Mellester, and once the bishop inspected the newly renovated church and rectory, he decided to pay a visit to Falls Ende. He'd never seen it or been there before and felt it was high time he became familiar with his future acquisition.

Mellester was without a regular reeve; its lord was fighting for the king elsewhere and the manor was being administered by a lowly steward. This was convenient for Bishop Immers; he could wander through Mellester with impunity.

He directed his entourage to proceed to Falls Ende. As they passed through the village, he noticed a few hostile stares, children ran alongside the wagon shouting and he noticed a few grimy faces peering from behind darkened doorways. A Mellester man-at-arms patrolling the hamlet ran up to the manor to report the bishop's unexpected arrival to Steward Alard.

On reaching Falls Ende, a portly man strode up to meet them.

"Who are ye?" asked the bishop foregoing pleasantries.

"Hale to ye, Yer Grace. I am Master Mason Mundy." He respectfully lowered his head. "And to what do we owe this unexpected pleasure—"

The bishop peered down his nose at the man. "I wish fer an update on yer progress here, make it quick, ye are taking valuable Church time." A cleric gently assisted the bishop down from the litter.

"Had I known ye would visit with us—"

"I'm not here for a visit or to exchange banter, I wish to know the progress yer making," interrupted the bishop testily.

Mundy cleared his throat. "If Yer Grace would like to come this way, I can show ye." He waved an arm and indicated the bishop should lead.

Large boulders of various sizes lay scattered around the site. Masons hammered away, patiently shaping them with large hammers and oversized chisels. As the group walked closer to the precipitous edge of Falls Ende, the roar of cascading water increased, everything was wet and damp. "Careful where ye step, Yer Grace," warned Master Mason Mundy.

The bishop stood back from the edge and peered down where large stones had already been carefully positioned against the sides of Falls Ende, creating a foundation from where other stone was layered upon and built up. Much work had already been done but there was still a lot of work to do. Each stone was carefully lowered in position and masons suspended by ropes completed any further shaping before they were permanently set in place.

"The Falls Ende mill will be a large mill, Yer Grace!" shouted Mundy over the noise.

Immers nodded. The dampness made him feel a chill. He turned to walk away and Mundy followed a step behind. Once near his litter, Immers turned back to Master Mason Mundy. "This is costly is it not?" Before the mason could answer, the bishop continued. "Are yer men being paid honest wages?"

"Aye, Yer Grace, they are."

Immers raised an eyebrow in surprise. "And paying tithes?"

"I believe so, Yer Grace."

Bishop Immers scowled. "And from where is the coin coming from to pay fer this?"

"Sir Gweir and Sir Hyde have made provisions, all is well."

Immers mumbled.

"I beg yer pardon, Yer Grace?"

"I said, that's not what I heard."

Master Mason Mundy shrugged.

"Ye have held me up long enough, I have Church affairs to conclude." Immers waited for a cleric to assist him back onto the horse litter.

At Mellester Manor, Steward Alard looked down at the tiny figures in the distance. *Why would the bishop come here*, he wondered? He knew as soon as the bishop departed, Master Mason Mundy would report to him. He felt a knot of worry in his stomach.

As the bishop's small group left Mellester, he failed to notice the empty pastures or the looks of hunger and need on the faces of commoners. He didn't see their pain, feel their suffering, nor spare a thought for how the murrain and pillaging had affected nearly all those who lived in the manor. Instead, Bishop Immers was consumed only by the desire to obtain title on Falls Ende. Now that he'd seen the mill site, and the surrounding land the herdsman squatted on, he wanted it even more. Sir Hyde, Sir Gweir and that vexatious herdsman, be damned.

They'd been travelling for some time and were finally approaching Exeter when a commotion disturbed the bishop's contemplation. "What is it?" demanded Immers petulantly.

One of his men-at-arms rode up. "Yer Eminence, a knight insists on offering ye a greeting."

"Who is this knight?"

"Sir Kasos, Yer Grace."

The horse litter that Bishop Immers rode upon continued for a few more steps. The Bishop was trying to place the name and failed.

"Yer Grace?"

"Very well, have him approach, keep close."

The four horses carrying the litter stopped and the bishop waited impatiently. A few moments later a swarthy unkempt knight approached on horseback. A man-at-arms rode either side. "Hail to ye, Yer Eminence," greeted the knight. "I am Sir Kasos and we have met on more than one occasion." The knight dipped his head in respect.

Bishop Immers still didn't recognize the knight, his name unfamiliar. "Where did we meet?"

"Some time ago, Yer Grace, at Mellester Manor, a feast when Sir Wystan was lord."

Bishop Immers remembered now. "Aye, ye were friends with Sir Borin."

The knight's face clouded over. "Aye, is a shame he was taken from us."

Bishop Immers saw the brief flash of the knight's eyes at the mention of Sir Borin. "And what are ye doing now ye have no liege?" he asked innocently.

"I will return to my family in Hellen[18], Yer Grace."

Bishop Immers looked at the man closely, his inquisitiveness aroused. He had a thick, black and very full beard, his hairline was extremely low with bushy and prominent eyebrows that shielded dark nervous eyes. The bishop had an idea. "Perhaps if ye have nothing of importance requiring yer duty, ye might wish to serve the Church briefly?"

"Ye are most generous, Yer Grace, how can I be of humble assistance?"

"Come see me on the morrow." Bishop Immers gave a subtle nod to a man-at-arms and the horses pulling the litter moved on.

---

18   Greece

CHAPTER THIRTY

All heads faced forward and looked out over the bow of the Frisian cog towards the smudge of a distant sail that appeared over the horizon some moments before. There were many other ships on the ocean, mostly coastal traders, plying backwards and forwards and loaded with valuable goods and merchandise. A collision at sea was always a possibility and it was prudent for these ships to sail clear and avoid each other.

When the lookout first hailed a warning, the sight of just another ship created no real special interest. For Hilke, he wanted to know in which direction the ship was headed so he could steer clear of them. However, another yell from the sharp eyed lookout created some concern. The distant ship had altered course and appeared to be heading towards them.

Wim, Hilke's second-in-command and sailing master was conferring with him on the best course to sail when the lookout yelled out again. A second ship was now visible on the horizon and was also headed this way. Both men looked at each other, unspoken words in full agreement. *Pirates*.

Pirates in these waters weren't uncommon and Hilke had encountered them before, but never more than one ship at a time. Turning tail and running wasn't an option. The Frisian cog was a transport and not built for speed. They would be caught quickly, no matter what direction they sailed.

Hilke ordered a slight course change which would slow their convergence with the two mystery ships and bring them closer to the coast of France and hopefully to other ships who could come to their aid if they were attacked.

Hilke called for Jagger and Odo and calmly explained what was happening. Already the two distant ships had separated and if their course remained unchanged, each ship would bear down on them, likely one each side.

Of value was their cargo; valuable coursers were certainly worth a lot. Hilke knew the pirates couldn't transfer the cargo from one ship to another, so they would likely board the cog and take control of her and kill anyone who tried to stop them.

Hilke asked the lookout to count how many men each ship carried. The sharp-eyed sentinel, now high up the mast, informed them each pirate ship appeared to have fifteen, maybe eighteen men aboard.

Jagger explained that they had enough experienced fighters to put up a spirited defence if they fought only one ship at a time. If his fighters all hid behind the high gunwales of the cog, then they had the opportunity to surprise the pirates, board their smaller ship and launch a quick counter attack. However, success depended on Hilke's ability to manoeuvre the cog at exactly the right time.

"Try to avoid the first pirate ship and steer away, directly towards the other one, which hopefully will force it to sail a little wider, then quickly come about and turn back into the first ship. A minor collision at the bow wouldn't hurt," he added. "At that moment we will leap aboard. The other ship hopefully will over-shoot and need to turn around and come back. Ye must avoid the second ship, Hilke," insisted Jagger. "Best if ye sailed up one side of the ship we are fighting, turn and come back down the other side. They will not expect us to attack them. Hopefully we can all come back aboard quickly. I can spare only one man, an archer to launch fire arrows at the sail of the second ship at the same time. God willing, we might even be able to disable it."

Hilke nodded. "Aye, I know what ye want, and it will be so."

They still had some time before the pirates were upon them and already Jagger had his armed men hidden from view and crouching behind the gunwales. Wim brought up a bucket of pitch from below that the crew used to seal planks and prevent leaks, and Jagger had his men wrap cloth around half a dozen arrows and dip them in the pitch. A crewman would set each arrow alight once Archer Stuart had the arrow notched, and he would then aim for the mast of the second pirate ship. Jagger explained that the mast would burn and hopefully set fire to their sail. With luck, he hoped, it would keep them busy and slow them down enough until they could successfully overcome and take control of the first pirate ship. It was a risky plan, and Jagger knew trying to hit a swaying mast from a moving ship was not an easy task. He wished he had more seasoned fighters.

Vehemently protesting, Odo, Charlotte, Grace, Daniel and Usher were sent below and out of harm's way from errant arrows or fighting. Jagger double checked his men were prepared and ready; there was little else they could do but wait. Benedict and Herdsman Searl were each issued a rusty but sharp sword from Hilke's small armoury. Cathal refused to be armed and claimed he would still do his share of fighting – if needed.

Two of Hilke's crew also crouched with swords, out of sight behind the gunwales to lend a hand.

They waited.

Finally they heard a voice from the fast approaching pirates, "Lower yer sail! Heave to! Lower yer sail!" The pirates hoped intimidation alone would be enough to force the Frisian cog to obey their commands and surrender.

The cog tried to avoid one of the pirate vessels, just as planned, then suddenly, Hilke pulled on the tiller and the bow of the heavy cog swung quickly towards the approaching and smaller pirate ship. "Brace!" he yelled, and the cog slammed into the other ship with a crunch. The cog lurched and the horses stumbled and scrambled to regain their footing in the stalls below.

Simultaneously, Jagger and his men leapt up and began climbing over the gunwale and poured onto the smaller vessel from the cog. Already the distance between both ships was widening as Hilke bore away to avoid tangling the rigging of both ships. As planned he would come about and sail down the other side, but first he needed to build up speed.

At the same time as the cog collided with the first pirate ship, Archer Stuart rose with his first notched arrow. With the bucket of pitch safely out of the way, the arrow was lit and he took careful aim and shot at the mast of the second pirate ship. It was a hurried shot and combined with some nerves, the arrow hissed past the mast and disappeared into the ocean some distance away.

Jagger and Tedric were the first to leap aboard the first pirate ship. For a brief moment the pirates were shocked at the sight of the sword wielding giant that landed on their boat. When Tedric landed beside Jagger with a feral yell, it broke the spell and they charged. Jagger's men followed. They were vastly outnumbered, but Jagger believed the pirates were not well-trained and his own skilled men outmatched them easily. The sound of clanging swords and screams drifted across to Hilke who was frantically trying to build up speed so he could tack. Below, Charlotte cringed and held Odo tightly.

The second arrow went the way of the first and also missed the mast. Unfazed, Archer Stuart forced himself to relax and notched another.

The horses were unsettled and began to panic. The unnatural movement of the quick turning cog, the sound of clashing steel and men yelling made them nervous. They would hurt themselves if they didn't settle down.

Odo pried himself from Charlotte. "I must go to the horses, stay with Grace." He looked at Daniel and Usher, "Come."

He scrambled down to where the horses were. The whites of Amica's eyes told him the feisty stallion was frightened. Daniel and Usher each went to other horses to calm them. Amica recognised Odo with a snort and then to prove a point, kicked out at the wooden rail that prevented him from backing out the stall, but the sturdy wooden rail held firm. Odo was genuinely fearful; at any moment pirates could leap aboard and begin killing everyone. From below in the cog's hold, he could hear men fighting but could see nothing. He put the fear out of his mind and focused on the black stallion and slowly began rubbing his neck and speaking softly. The stallion continued to stamp its feet and toss its head. Realising he needed to do more, Odo quickly removed his capuchin and with care and soothing words, he gently placed it partially over Amica's head, covering only one eye. The uncovered eye could see only him. Amica responded immediately and began to settle down. Sally, in the adjacent stall, was nervous too, but

Odo's presence alone was enough to calm her. He was concerned for Noor, the Arabian, and looked back behind him. There was Charlotte perched on the railing that separated each stall, successfully soothing her horse. Combined with Daniel, Usher and Charlotte's help, all the horses soon settled down and became manageable.

The second pirate ship had completed its turn and began to chase down the cog which was some distance ahead. The heavy cog slowly gathered speed and headed towards the stern of the first pirate ship where Jagger and his men fought.

The primal sound of men fighting for their lives drifted down to Odo and he was petrified. His heart beat furiously as he tried to overcome and control his dread and focus on the horses. He continued to talk to Amica in a soothing, calm voice and stroke his neck. He turned his head to check on Charlotte; she looked up at the same time. Their eyes met and locked – he could see the fear etched plainly on her face.

Archer Stuart had a third arrow notched and drew the bowstring back. This time he took his time, anticipated the movement of the cog and waited for just the right moment. He judged it perfectly and let the bowstring slip from his fingers. The flaming arrow arced away leaving a trail of black pungent smoke as it sped to it target. Archer Stewart allowed himself a smile as he saw the arrow bury itself into the mast. Flaming spots of pitch splattered everywhere and small flames immediately began licking up the mast. Within moments the sail ignited. Too high up to reach and douse the flames, the pirates began to lower the sail so they could extinguish the fire, but as the sail furled, it only made it worse and the fire spread. With no sail to propel them forward, the second pirate ship quickly lost way and began to drift. One pirate aboard the wallowing vessel also had a bow and began shooting at the cog. Arrows began clattering onto the deck; it was a token gesture born from frustration, and the pirate was far from a marksmen. Fortunately no one on Hilke's ship was hit.

Hilke now had sufficient speed and tacked at the stern of the first pirate ship to come down its far side and stop to pick up Jagger and his men. He risked a quick look to assess their situation. The second pirate ship was dead in the water and posed no immediate threat, it trailed by about four boat lengths. The first pirate ship was now in the middle, between them and the second ship. Hilke grinned, they were safe from archers.

Once the cog no longer heeled from its turn, Odo felt a gentle bump and as the cog came alongside the first pirate ship, the sound of clashing swords had stopped. Odo removed the capuchin from Amica's head and looked up and waited for pirates to leap down onto him with bloodied swords raised.

Jagger and Tedric took the brunt of the pirate attack. But fighters the pirates weren't. They were sailors, armed seamen with no training or skill and certainly no match for the giant and Tedric. By themselves, and in the confined space of the deck, the two of them could have fought all the pirates with ease. With a yell of frustration, the pirates dropped their swords and raised their arms in surrender. Not one of Odo's men were hurt or suffered an injury. Five pirates lay bleeding on deck and four were dead.

"Fire the sail!" yelled Jagger, wiping his blade on the dead pirate's clothes. "Throw all weapons overboard!" He waited until the sail was alight and the last of his men were safely back aboard the cog before he left the pirate ship. They wouldn't be sailing far without a functioning sail and plundering helpless ships without weapons.

Hilke was sweating profusely, a combination of fear, exertion and relief; they'd all been very fortunate and came away from the brief skirmish unscathed and alive. His crew felt the same and everyone was jubilant. Most were huddled together and talking about the fighting skills of the fearless giant. The pirates never stood a chance.

Odo was still looking up when the face of Jagger appeared and he breathed out a sigh of relief.

"All is well Master Odo; these pirates won't be troubling us no more."

"Anyone hurt?"

Jagger grinned and shook his head.

Odo playfully grabbed Amica's ear and whispered to him. The stallion snorted then lowered its head and began looking for food.

Jagger and Hilke decided to leave the second pirate ship alone. With decorum restored, and in high spirits, Hilke turned the cog around and continued on their way to Frisia.

Impervious to sea spray and wind, the solitary knight stood near the prow of the converted galley as it effortlessly sliced through the mild swell. Its perfectly designed narrow beam and shallow draft was ideal for a quick passage in the current sea state. The knight flinched and turned his head away as another errant wave sheeted over the bow and onto the deck, dampening the spirits of anyone unable to seek shelter. Familiar with the nuances of such a ship in the open ocean, it didn't impede the men aboard from doing their arduous work. Long sweeps dipped into the water with precise timing as oarsmen bent their backs and pulled tirelessly. Aided by sails suspended from two masts, the galley was making good time as it headed for the fishing village called Amstel in Guelders.[19]

The knight wasn't interested in the spectacular panoramic seascape laid out before him; his insidious mind was focused on the unusual mission he'd accepted from Bishop Immers. His instructions were quite precise and he was to personally hand a missive to Bishop Laninga, of Utrecht, and then wait for his response and counsel. With guidance from Bishop Laninga, he was to discover from where Herdsman Odo Read obtained his coin, then disrupt and thwart him from fulfilling his quest in Frisia. If opportunity presented itself – *kill him*, insisted Immers, but do not implicate the Church. As a reward for this task, he'd received a fair purse, with a promise of more if he succeeded. According to Bishop Immers, Bishop Laninga was an old and trusted friend, and would be quite amenable in assisting him.

Bishop Immers explained to him in some detail that local lords in Devonshire had prevented the Church from obtaining title on a piece of land it deemed derelict. This land, known as Falls Ende, was illegally tenanted by the young herdsman, Odo Read and his woman.

Sir Kasos grimaced. Although he'd never met or seen the herdsman, he was familiar with the recent turmoil in Mellester Manor and the unfortunate and violent death of his friend Sir Wystan, Lady Constance and another close friend, Sir Borin. He had no love for the unworthy usurper, Sir Gweir, who'd been bestowed the manor by the senile lord, Sir Hyde, or the troublesome herdsman who'd been at the centre and cause of

19   A region, one of many, that comprised of what is now known as The Netherlands.

all Mellester Manor's recent turmoil. If not for the herdsman, his friends would still be alive this very day.

The knight felt the motion of the vessel change as a course alteration was made; they were nearing their destination. The bow swung around and he ducked as the galley slammed into another wave and threatened him with a soaking.

Conveniently, Bishop Immers had not bothered to inform the knight of the warnings he'd received from Sir Hyde Fortescue and the Templar Knights. If he had, Sir Kasos may have put aside his personal feelings and thought very differently about pursuing this quest.

Through the sea haze the knight could already discern a township in the distance. He thought again about Bishop Immers' instructions, but his own need to see the herdsman suffer far outweighed the bishop's and the purse he offered. He turned from the bow and went to prepare to disembark; soon he would be ashore where he would rent a horse and immediately ride for Utrecht.

CHAPTER THIRTY–ONE

Sir Hyde Fortescue refused to take any of Cathal's potions since the day Bishop Immers came to see him. He'd not lain about in a sorrowful stupor of despair as he had done since his return from Ireland; instead, he began to walk the manor. Each day he strolled a little further and greeted people he knew and cared for. He lost the unhealthy sallowness of being indoors for weeks at a time and forgot about the pain that ravaged him. He still felt the occasional searing stabs that shot up his arm, but they were manageable and grew less with each passing day. The people of Ridgley Manor were joyous to see their lord again. Rumours of his death had been rampant, but now their lord once again exuded confidence and power, even if his lower arm was missing from just above the elbow. It didn't matter to them, what was important was their lord of the manor; their protector was again looking after them.

While Sir Hyde smiled and chatted amicably with villagers, his mind was elsewhere. A messenger from Mellester Manor informed him that Bishop Immers had been there and casually inspected the Falls Ende mill as if he were the land-owner. He'd arrogantly asked about the work and cost, and did so in a blatant show of disrespect without first honouring the manor's lord by presenting himself to the steward and informing him of his intentions. In Sir Hyde's opinion, the bishop was already counting coin, despite the warning he'd given him.

He'd made it perfectly clear to Immers to stay away from Mellester.

The bishop's disregard was obviously a subtle message intended to demonstrate he no longer respected or feared him.

Directly behind Sir Hyde walked Steward Baldric and two men-at-arms, and at his side, holding on to his only hand walked Amy, Steward Baldric's daughter. The two had a special bond, and he loved her like the daughter he never had. Her tiny perfect hand completely enveloped by his heavily scarred and calloused paw seemed incongruous, yet to the lord, she provided balance in a world that was brutal and savage, where the weak, through no fault of their own, often struggled to survive. Amy represented his conscience; she made him aware of things, flowers, animals, and nature - beauty and goodness where previously he saw none. She marvelled with childish glee at things he'd long ago dismissed and deemed insignificant or unimportant. He was envious of her naivety because she saw nothing but virtue in the world, much like Odo and Charlotte did.

Was Odo weak and doomed for failure? In the past he would unequivocally have thought so. His opinion wasn't personal, it was nothing more than a simple fact of life. But now, more than at any time before, he saw Odo and Charlotte as not just commoners or survivors, but strong principled people who created goodness around them. It was infectious and drew kindness to them. He looked down at the beaming face of Amy and smiled with deep paternal love. He hoped she would grow to be like Odo and Charlotte and would be spared the harsh realities of manor life and the ugliness and unfairness of an early death through sickness and hard work.

Sir Hyde greeted merchants, offered them good tidings and received well wishes for his health. A few brave souls said a few kind words and commiserated over the loss of his arm. It mattered not to him, he wasn't offended. When Amy first saw the missing limb, she frowned and said in a loud voice, "Ye have another!" The philosophical simplistic words of a six year old struck him hard. He vowed at that moment he would protect Amy and others like her from leeches like Bishop Immers. For those who sought to take advantage of their nobility and position and use it unjustly against commoners would suffer by his hand – his only hand.

He's spent the best part of a day in discussion with Priest Kirby. They talked candidly about many things, mostly about his revelation of the symmetry, harmony and beauty around him he'd never acknowledged to himself before. He asked the old priest where God fit into this. Why was it a six year-old girl made him see things so differently? In reflection, Sir Hyde mused, the wily priest didn't say much, he listened attentively and occasionally asked the odd question. Just as Priest Kirby told him they would, the answers he sought came from within.

Bishop Immers was indeed a powerful adversary, he had the undisputed support and backing of the Church, while he, lord of the manor had the king's ear. It was time that King Henry heard about the bishop's blatant attempts to wrest Falls Ende from Odo and possess the grist mill that he and Sir Gweir had so heavily invested in. The stakes were too high now, and the king may even have a solution. When he'd departed Ireland under a cloud of death, King Henry said he would visit him when on his way back to France. Meanwhile, until then, Bishop Immers needed to be tempered.

Amy slipped out of his grasp and ran off to play with a girl about her own age. He stopped to watch and felt the presence of Steward Baldric as he stepped up beside him. The two men watched the girls play in quiescence. The sight of the two girls innocently playing drew attention to the evil that needed to be eliminated. "Come Baldric," said Sir Hyde, breaking the silence, "we must put our heads together and find a way to curtail the bishop's unholy ambitions."

The land was flat, surprisingly so. There were no rolling hills like in Devonshire or other parts of England he'd seen. Odo commented this to Hilke who stood aft on the cog as they approached the fishing village of Delfzijl in Frisia.

Wim was at the tiller, and giving Hilke a well needed break. They slowly sailed past a series of small islands, then turned into a bay. Fishing boats glided by and many fishermen waved in greeting as the *koggership* slowly headed towards the village.

"Frisia is flat land, is good fer *afgrøder*," replied Hilke.

"Afg...?"

"Uh, *Engelsk*[20]... crops for food," added Hilke.

Odo noticed the Frisian's eyes never stopped moving, he saw everything, missed nothing. While Wim stood at the tiller, Hilke, as a good captain should, observed him and everything around them carefully.

Ahead, many boats and ocean going vessels of all sizes and types were tied to a long dock, and Odo quickly recognized ships similar to Hilke's. Odo pointed, "Are those the ships we want?"

"*Ja*. Perhaps, we shall see," replied Hilke.

The ocean was dead calm, barely a ripple disturbed the surface. The

---

20   *Frisian - English*

cog was barely making way and rather than head towards the dock, Wim altered course and began to sail wide. Hilke nodded in approval.

"Where are we going?" asked Odo. He expected to sail directly to the pier.

"We need wind, more wind out here, then we turn in," informed the Frisian.

Odo nodded but didn't really understand. He followed Hilke's gaze as he looked up at the sail. It flapped once, twice, then filled a little. They barely moved. The sail, snapped as it caught the wind, then filled, and Odo felt the sensation of movement again.

Charlotte came up and stood beside him. "Is so different than England, looks peaceful," she said quietly. They watched as the crew made preparations to dock. Already men on the pier looked to be ready as the cog altered course again and turned towards the fishing port. With nary a bump, the cog came alongside and was quickly made fast to sturdy bollards.

Instructions were given to replenish water and food for the horses. They wouldn't stay long, informed Hilke, the tide would turn soon and he wanted to follow it out. Leaving Wim in charge, Hilke walked along the dock and disappeared amongst the buildings.

Standing on dry land felt peculiar, commented Charlotte as they waited for Hilke to return. They stood on the pier stretching their legs; Jagger never more than a step or two away from them. He was vigilant and for anyone with hostile intentions, he was menacing. He told Odo that it would be better if he did not wear armour, for doing so, he said, would risk intimidating farmers. Odo and Charlotte were so used to seeing him wearing chainmail and without it he looked so different.

It was some time before Odo saw Hilke walking towards them with two men who looked identical to each other. Each man had an enormous stomach and an even larger thick bushy beard that grew in every possible direction, hiding their mouths.

"How do they eat?" Charlotte whispered.

Odo shook his head in wonder.

Jagger stepped closer to Odo. "*Gemels*[21]."

"I've heard of them but never laid eyes on any before, are they normal?" Odo asked.

"Odo!" exclaimed Charlotte and elbowed him playfully in the ribs.

"I expect so, but ye can never be sure," Jagger warned with a grin.

"Odo, this is Fyt and Gys; they each have a *koggership* like mine," Hilke said as he walked up.

Odo nodded respectfully but couldn't tell them apart. All he knew was the one on the left was named Fyt and the other on the right is Gys.

"They have agreed to help ye out but first they have to pick up some goods south of here. They will meet us in Geestendorf in seven days if ye have coin and can pay them for the journey to Exmouth."

"How much to take thirty–six cows to Exeter in England?" asked Odo with confidence he didn't feel.

Fyt and Gys looked at each other and said nothing.

"They want three pounds each," said Hilke speaking for the brothers.

---

21   *Slang for twins.*

Three pounds was a lot of coin. Odo shook his head, "Nay, is too much."

Fyt and Gys again turned to each other in perfect synchronization, then again looked at Hilke who seemed to know their thoughts.

"Two pound each," quickly countered Odo.

Charlotte looked up in surprise at his assertiveness.

The beards parted slightly to reveal small mouths and both brothers spoke simultaneously. Other than Hilke, no one knew what they were saying although Odo heard the word 'Sterling.'

Hilke shook his head. "Not enough, Odo."

Odo shifted his feet looked as if he was ready to walk away. "Two pound and ten shillings each, and another five shillings each when both ships are safely unloaded in Exeter," stated Odo with finality.

The beards parted again and at the same time the brothers both spoke. "*Ja.*"

"Sterling?" questioned Hilke.

"*Ja,*" replied Odo using the only real word of Frisian he knew.

Fyt and Gys looked genuinely happy and Odo believed they were smiling; it was difficult to tell but the beards expanded outwards offering him a clue.

"*Ja,* is good, now we must leave or we miss the tide," Hilke grumbled and walked towards his ship.

The brothers dipped their heads in acknowledgment, swung their prodigious stomachs and beards around and shuffled away.

"Charlotte linked her arm through Odo's. "I'm proud of ye Odo, ye did well."

"Let's hope they show up in seven days time."

CHAPTER THIRTY–TWO

St. Martin's Cathedral dominated Utrecht, and Sir Kasos had no difficulty in locating the landmark church. Once inside, he marvelled at its majestic beauty. Never before had he seen such an awe-inspiring building; it was breathtaking and an interminable reminder of Church dominance and supremacy – a belief he fundamentally supported. Five separate churches were joined together to form the shape of an elongated cross and he stood at its very centre. He slowly spun and looked up in wonder at the unique Roman design, the towering columns and superbly crafted arches. The sound of footsteps broke the spell and he reluctantly dropped his gaze to an approaching priest. "Hail to ye."

The priest halted and looked at the travel-stained knight with imperiousness; he didn't speak but inclined his head in question.

"I seek Bishop Laninga, where is he found?"

The priest's mouth tightened. Ignoring the man he went to step around when a hand on his shoulder forced him to stop.

Perhaps the priest doesn't speak English, thought Sir Kasos. "Bishop Laninga? Uh, *raison d'être. Attendre, s'il vous plait*." spoke the knight using imperfect French.

The priest looked at the offending hand on his shoulder with indignation. Sir Kasos quickly removed it and fished for the introduction letter given to him by Bishop Immers. He handed the document to the louring priest and waited.

The priest unrolled the document, read it once, then looked up at the swarthy knight. "Wait here," he instructed in perfect English.

Sir Kasos continued his appraisal of the Cathedral while the priest vanished into the gloomy recesses. After an age, he heard footsteps as a different priest approached.

"Sir Kasos? Forgive me for the wait, please follow me."

He followed the priest through a labyrinth of corridors, dusty chambers and upstairs to a sizeable room with a large table dominated by an assortment of scrolls and a pile of thickly bound books. Candles burned and a flickering yellow light cast moody impressions against cold stone walls.

"His Excellency will be with ye soon," said the priest and backed out of the room.

He didn't have to wait long before the priest returned, closely followed by a tall elegant man, with an enormous hooked nose that he presumed was the bishop. Confirming his prestige, the man extended a hand and as protocol required, Sir Kasos dropped his left knee to the floor, bent his back and kissed the episcopal ring. "Bishop Laninga, is truly an honour," he said when again standing.

The priest remained near the door while the bishop moved to the other side of the table and settled into a stout hand-carved chair. He stretched his legs, crossed them and clasped both hands across his midriff. "I hope yer journey was without incident?"

"Thank ye, Yer Grace, it was damp but uneventful."

"How does Bishop Immers fare?" smiled the bishop. "Forgive me, please be seated." He unclasped his hands and waved to a small hardbacked box chair.

Sir Kasos eased himself into it and faced the smiling bishop. "He sends salutations, Yer Grace, and hopes ye are hearty and hale."

"Bishop Immers is a good servant to the Church; I have known him for many a year and he is a warm–hearted generous man."

While the bishop's accent was thick, he spoke well and his English was easy to understand. "Aye, he said the same about ye."

"Now…" Bishop Laninga leaned forward. "why is it ye have come all this way to see me? How can I be of assistance to my old friend, Sir Kasos?" He smiled graciously.

"Yer Grace, Bishop Immers trusted me to bring this missive and he told me to wait fer yer counsel and guidance." He rose from his seat, leaned over the table and handed the bishop the scroll given to him by Immers.

Bishop Laninga broke the seal and read through the document three times before he placed both arms on the table and shook his head. "It appears the good nature of Bishop Immers is being taken advantage of, is this not so?"

"Aye, Yer Grace, it is."

"The local lords have been less than kind to the Church and it appears this impertinent herdsman is having his way. I find this shameful and disrespectful to not only Bishop Immers but to the Church as well."

Sir Kasos nodded. "I have no fondness for the herdsman or those Devonshire lords, Yer Grace."

The priest at the doorway stirred.

The bishop scratched at something on his neck. "Frisia? What does a simple herdsman want in Frisia, and why would the lords grant him coin and allow this?"

"That's what Bishop Immers hopes ye can help find out, Yer Grace."

The bishop looked perturbed. "But if it were anywhere else but Frisia..."

"I don't understand, Yer Grace," replied Sir Kasos surprised at the bishop's response.

"Because Frisia is still full of pagans and nullifidians."

"But the Church—"

"Aye, the Church ... Frisia is Christian in name only and since many there still believe in their pagan Gods, my reach there is somewhat restricted. I am Frisian, and yet even my old neighbours were heathens." He scratched again. "To help Bishop Immers, I will need to call on others who support the Church. Pious and devoted men with influence, there are but a few."

Sir Kasos looked crestfallen.

"Where is this herdsman bound?"

"I believe it is Geestendorf, Yer Grace, and may have already arrived."

Bishop Laninga frowned, "Geestendorf? There is nothing there but herrings and cows."

Sir Kasos looked at the bishop. "I'm sure Bishop Immers would be grateful fer whatever assistance ye can provide, Yer Grace."

"If he is in Geestendorf already, then ye need to be there quick. Come see me on the morrow, I will think upon this and arrange passage fer ye." He rose from his seat, the meeting was over. "Have ye somewhere to rest yer head fer the night?"

"Nay, Yer Grace, it was my duty to first come to Utrecht and speak with ye," replied Sir Kasos.

Bishop Laninga continued to scratch. He turned to the priest, "See Sir Kasos has a bed and is fed."

The priest respectfully dipped his head and stepped away from the door to allow the bishop to pass then followed him out. "Wait here," he said over his shoulder.

Alone again, the knight reflected on his meeting. Bishop Laninga was no man's fool, the easy going attitude masked a fertile and devious mind, of that he was certain. Bishop Laninga controlled an expansive diocese and couldn't manage it effectively if he wasn't shrewd.

After showing the knight to his accommodation for the evening, the priest hurriedly left Utrecht's grand cathedral and disappeared into the streets.

If Delfzijl was a small fishing village, then Geestendorf was tiny. The only pier was just large enough for Hilke's cog to tie alongside after another boat was moved to create space. Locals, all villagers, came out to see the big ship enter the bay and welcome Hilke who was obviously known and liked. When he stepped ashore he was warmly greeted like a returning conquering hero.

The first thing Odo noticed and couldn't keep from staring at were the cows that grazed on thick lush grass that grew almost to the water's edge. They were much larger than he expected, and the colouring... even Charlotte laughed when she saw them for the first time. They were white with irregular black splotches all over their bodies. "Are they diseased?" she asked.

Cathal stood alongside her and offered his opinion. "I have seen these animals before, this is how they are, these markings tell the breed apart from others. These are the cows ye seek, Odo."

Odo was grinning. "I have never seen animals like this."

Hilke returned from greeting everyone and walked up to Odo.

"How soon can we go to the local manor and speak to the lord about buying cows?" Odo asked excitedly.

Hilke shook his head. "Here there are no manors or lords, each farmer or *ploegg*, a landowner, is his own man and is responsible only to himself. If he is bad or done wrong, then he must come before a *redjeven*." Hilke could see Odo was confused. "A *redjeven* is chosen by many *ploegg*, to keep order and ensure freedom."

"Then do I need to speak with this *redjeven*?" Odo asked.

Hilke shook his head, "Nay, the *redjeven* has no business with a *ploegg* if no laws are broken by him or ye. The *ploegg*, or landowner is free to do as he pleases."

"It seems so simple," Charlotte added.

Jagger nodded. "I have heard of this but thought it fanciful talk."

"Be warned, Odo, men here are covetous of coin just like in Devonshire, do not be fooled by their freedom, for they are bound to gold and silver as any man," counselled Cathal.

Odo looked thoughtful. "I will be careful, and this is why I have ye all here with me."

Cathal mumbled something unintelligible and with his bag slung over his shoulder wandered off.

Now that fresh food was available from the village, Grace was preparing to cook a meal aboard the cog to feed everyone. Odo knew it would take some time before it was ready and he was impatient to begin. "Can we visit a farm now?" he asked.

Hilke considered his request and smiled, "Ja, there are farms close."

Jagger asked Tedric to accompany them and felt no need to bring more guards. They set off at a brisk walk and they all agreed it felt good to be on dry land again and stretch their legs. Charlotte was at Odo's side, along with Herdsman Searl. Hilke walked in front and Jagger and Tedric, both armed, followed closely behind. They passed through the village and were already surrounded by flat fields and the unfamiliar sight of black and white splotched cows that grazed peacefully. Some cows raised their heads in curiosity and watched as the small group of men walked past. Odo saw two men digging in a waterfilled ditch in the distance and pointed them out to Hilke. It was no different here than in Mellester he surmised. Work, milking and making repairs. He may be in a different country, but the life of a herdsman was the same everywhere.

The group paused as Hilke shouted a greeting to the farmers. Both men looked up and waved in reply and one man downed tools and walked over towards them.

After the introductions were made, Hilke explained that Odo was a deierie farmer from England looking to purchase cows. The farmer, introduced himself as Haro Sikma, and gave Odo close scrutiny, and then turned his attention to Jagger and Tedric with suspicion, it was obvious he wasn't impressed that a herdsman was in the dubious company of armed men.

Odo could sense the man's unease. "Tell him I have coin because I want to buy cows, and these men behind me are friends and are with me to see I am not plundered by outlaws."

Hilke dutifully translated and the farmer visibly relaxed. Many Frisian words were similar to English and Odo found he could understand the odd word here or there.

The farmer turned to Odo and prattled off a sentence too fast for him to understand.

Hilke dutifully translated. "He says, why come here, are cows in England not good?"

"They are smaller than yer cows and produce less milk," Odo replied.

After Hilke translated, Haro again studied Odo carefully before speaking again.

"He asks how many?"

Odo smiled, and held up both hands with fingers spread, then again two more times, lastly he held up one hand. "Thirty-five and one bull."

The farmer raised his eyebrows in surprise.

Hilke again spoke to the farmer. Odo understood the word *stirk* the farmer used and he nodded enthusiastically. "He says he can sell you two stirks, that is all, his farm is too small to sell ye more, he says other farmers will sell to ye."

"I wish to inspect them first, perhaps on the morrow?" Odo replied after a nod of agreement from Searl.

"And what is a stirk?" Hilke asked.

"Is a cow aged between one and two years old."

Arrangements were made to return to the farm the following day. They said farewell and turned around and headed back to the village and a meal Grace was cooking.

Sir Kasos arrived in Geestendorf aboard a small fishing boat, his passage gratefully arranged by the good bishop. He saw the cog tied to the pier and guessed it was the same ship the herdsman had hired, but he didn't see him anywhere. Perhaps that was a good thing, he thought. Neither he nor the fishing boat attracted any unwanted attention and after thanking the fisherman he set about finding a horse to rent. Bishop Laninga gave him the name of a man, a wealthy merchant who was also a *redjeven* who would do the bishop's bidding without question, however the man lived a few miles inland from Geestendorf in another much larger village.

The innkeeper had horses for rent and after a little haggling over the tariff, Sir Kasos rode from Geestendorf.

It was dusk when he rode up to large house owned by the prosperous merchant and friend of Bishop Laninga in the town of Schiffdorf, about five miles from Geestendorf. A young servant girl answered the door and he politely introduced himself and asked to speak with Antonius Richter. She looked uncertain and nervous and seemed reluctant to disturb her master. He showed her one of the scrolls with Bishop Laninga's seal. She dipped her head in subservience and said something unintelligible that he thought meant *wait*, and shut the door. It seemed like an eternity before the door was thrust open and a tall thin man filled the space. He didn't appear thrilled at being roused.

"*Ja?*" questioned the man. His eyes narrowed in suspicion at the dark complexioned stranger.

Bishop Laninga assured him that Antonius Richter was fortunately fluent in English. "Please excuse the intrusion, I am Sir Kasos, and ye are *Mynhear*[22] Richter?"

The man stepped out from the doorway and cast a quick glance either side of the knight to determine if he was alone before he answered. "*Ja.*"

"I come at the bequest of Bishop Laninga, I bring greetings and a message." He showed him the scroll which was quickly snatched from his hand.

"Come inside," coldly snapped the merchant after he studied and verified the bishop's seal.

Sir Kasos was seated in a large room near the fire. Other people lived here, he heard children and the voice of a woman who he believed to be the merchant's wife, but they were in another part of the house and he never saw them. By the light of a candle, he waited while Antonius read the bishop's message.

Finally the merchant looked to him. "Bishop Laninga is a good man, a good bishop and a good friend. It is my duty to come to the aid of the Church when in need."

The merchant's accent was thick, similar to the bishop's, but at least his English was easily intelligible. Sir Kasos nodded in agreement.

"What the bishop asks me to do is– uh, difficult, because we must first

---

22   *Frisian for mister.*

learn what this– *Koe boer*[23] is doing here in Frisia. This will take time. He also asks that I provide ye with food and lodging. I will make arrangements fer ye to sleep and eat at the hostelry here in Schiffdorf. It is a short walk, not far."

"Thank ye *Mynhear* Richter."

"I will have men inquire in Geestendorf in the morn, and then we will decide what to do when we learn more, *ja*?"

"We do not have much time, *Mynhear* Richter–"

"I will do what I think is best!" interrupted the merchant. His eyes met and held the gaze of the knight, without flinching.

"Of course, forgive me, I am weary," offered the knight hoping to placate him.

"Femke!" bellowed the merchant without looking away.

Within moments the servant girl appeared, her head bowed.

The merchant spoke to her harshly, again she dipped her head and backed away towards the door, opened it and was gone. It was obvious to the knight she was extremely frightened of Antonius Richter.

"She will arrange fer ye to have a bed at the inn, ask for Klaes."

"Thank ye, *Mynhear* Richter."

"This *koe boer,* ye want to, uh, stop him from whatever he is doing here?"

Sir Kasos nodded. "It depends on why he is in Geestendorf, if we can prevent him from succeeding in his task..."

"Tell me why, I wish to know this?"

---

23   *Frisian – Cow farmer.*

CHAPTER THIRTY–THREE

It felt good to be on Amica, and the stallion was equally thrilled to be able to stretch his legs after the confines of the cog. Everyone was mounted except for Odo's guards who walked behind at Jagger's insistence.

As arranged, Odo first visited *Boer* Haro Sikma, the deierie farmer he spoke to the previous afternoon. After a thorough inspection, Odo purchased two stirk, young cows about a year and a half old for three shillings each. He made another arrangement with Haro to be able to keep the cows secure in a field surrounded by water-filled ditches. As the day progressed, Odo purchased more cows from other deierie farmers; he would bring them to this holding field until it was time to load them aboard the cogs when Fyt and Gys arrived. He was excited and his exuberance was infectious and everyone was in good spirits.

As he'd hoped, the Frisian cows were remarkably different than the cows in England and it wasn't just their unique colouring. These animals could be milked more often and each cow could produce up to five buckets of milk a day, sometimes more. *This would keep Cheesemaker Gerald busy,* thought Odo. Their meat was lean, they calved more frequently and despite their size, these cows had a friendly, curious nature. This was a dream come true and Odo couldn't stop smiling.

It was late morning when Sir Kasos was summoned to attend to *Mynhear* Richter at a tannery, one of many businesses he owned. Antonius wasted no time in explaining what he'd learned.

"Your *koe boer* friend is in Frisia to buy cows." *Mynhear* Richter frowned. "He has a fat purse, and is buying every cow he can. Tell me, Sir Knight, why is it that a young farmer has so much coin to spend and why is it he travels with armed men?"

The stench of urine used in tanning leather was overpowering. It was deliberate of *Mynhear* Richter to bring him here to make him feel uncomfortable and queasy. Sir Kasos swallowed. "With yer help, that is what I have come to find out. We would like to see him fail in this, *mynhear*. Is there a way to prevent him from buying cows or returning with them to England?"

Richter shook his head, "Nay, not unless he has done something wrong."

Sir Kasos looked up at the tall Frisian. "Is there is way that he, uh, could have done something wrong?"

"Bishop Laninga has asked me to help him; I think this is important to the Church both here in Frisia and in England..." Richter looked away and seemed to be lost in thought. After a moment of hesitation, he turned to face the knight. "I will help, it is my duty to the Church to do this but will I will not do this unlawfully. Is this what the bishop requires of me?"

This isn't going well, thought the knight. "Preventing the herdsman by any possible means may suit the bishop, Mynhear Richter."

The Frisian pointed a finger at the knight and opened his mouth to speak. He paused in reflection for a moment before he spoke. "I will do what I can."

In spite of the sickly stench of urine, Sir Kasos breathed in deeply, squared his shoulders and met the piercing gaze of the wealthy merchant. "Aye, *Mynhear* Richter, this is what the Church wants, but ye must understand, I or Bishop Laninga cannot be seen to be involved."

Mynhear Richter shook his head. It was plainly obvious he had no fondness for the knight or for the task asked of him.

The day was long and tiring, but for Odo, it was rewarding. He found a young bull he liked but the farmer was reluctant to part with it. After some haggling, the farmer asked Odo to return the following day as he would think on it overnight. Without Hilke's local knowledge it would have made the job so much more difficult. He proved to be invaluable and both Odo and Herdsman Searl were grateful. Odo purchased a number of healthy stirks from local farms and they were heading back to the ship, while apprentices Daniel and Usher herded the newly purchased cows towards Haro Sikma's holding field just outside Geestendorf. Not one farmer declined to sell Odo cows, although it was impossible to buy more than four from any farmer at a time. More frequently they were sold just one or two.

Night was fast approaching and already elongated shadows marked the time for them to return as the sun slowly dipped towards the horizon. Jagger didn't like the thought of them travelling during darkness and was anxious to return to Geestendorf as quickly as possible.

On Hilke's advice they had travelled some distance throughout the day and purchased a total of nineteen cows. Two were already in *Boer* Haro's holding field. All were deemed to be in perfect health and condition by Odo, Searl and Cathal, and with apprentices Daniel and Usher, and occasionally Odo and Herdsman Searl, when needed, they drove the cows back towards Haro Sikma's holding field.

Jagger was edgy and instructed three men to follow behind, two more were positioned directly in front of the group and one man was sent forward, well ahead of the group to scout for any problems. Earlier, Cathal expressed some concern that all was not well and that everyone should be alert and attentive. There could be some trouble, he predicted.

They were not far from the holding field when a dozen men silently approached from the other side of a water-filled channel that bordered the road. Charlotte saw them first; her sharp intake of breath alerted the others of their presence. Immediately Jagger and Tedric turned their horses to face the threat. The sound of unsheathing swords disturbed the peacefulness of the Frisian countryside. Sensing danger, a horse impatiently stamped a hoof, another snorted in agitation. Without hesitation, Jagger barked out an order and his men reacted with urgency and quickly descended towards Odo and Charlotte to offer protection. Unfazed at the interruption, the cows lowered their heads and foraged for food as Daniel and Usher quickly returned to the group for safety.

There was little Odo could do but anxiously watch until he knew what the strangers wanted. He had placed all his trust in Jagger to make the best decisions and keep them safe. From what he saw, the strangers weren't mounted and at the first sign that their lives were threatened, he and Charlotte could easily gallop down the road towards the village for safety. "Be ready Charlotte, just as we talked about, if the need arises we will flee," he whispered as Jagger and Tedric each took up a defensive position between them and the strangers.

"Ask them what they want," instructed Jagger to Hilke.

Cathal sat astride his horse and watched attentively.

Used to yelling at his sailors, Hilke's voice was strong and authoritative as he questioned the strangers.

One man, the group's leader, with his features hidden by a rag, answered strongly in Frisian accented English. "Ye will all depart Friesland on the morrow. Leave the cows and yer coin will all be returned to ye!"

Hilke needed no prompting to reply. "Why must this be so, what have these people done except purchase cows and deliver coin to yer hands? They have done no wrong!"

The stranger repeated his announcement and didn't elaborate.

"Who has instructed ye to do this?" yelled Jagger. "Are ye afraid to speak truthfully?" He urged his horse to take a step or two closer to the strangers, hoping to see their faces, weapons and armour. Like the leader, they all had their faces covered.

Again the stranger shouted across the narrow water-filled channel separating both groups. "Depart Friesland, leave the cows and yer purse will be returned!" Having delivered his message, he turned and briskly walked away into the early evening gloom, his men followed a step or two behind.

Jagger rode closer to the ditch hoping to see in which direction the men were headed, but already it was too dark to see any distance with clarity. He returned to Odo. "Those men are not soldiers, but labourers with poor quality swords. None has armour or protection and we are not in any danger, although I think we need to hasten this mission."

Odo turned to Cathal for his thoughts.

"It is as he says, those men present no threat to us, but there may be others who do. Jagger speaks wisely, best to hurry with this Odo."

"What say ye, Jagger, are these men just foolhardy or should we heed their warning?"

"These men pose us no risk, their swords are old and rusty. I would fear them more if they fought with rakes, spades and pitchforks, swordsmen they are not. Finish what ye came here to do, Odo, but we shouldn't tarry," he advised.

Led by seventeen cows, the group pressed cautiously on.

"I will leave two men to guard the herd overnight, Master Odo," advised Jagger, " But on the morrow, we do not have enough men to come with us and leave men to guard yer cows."

"If ye can pay them, I can ask some of my men to stand watch over the herd," volunteered Hilke.

"I think ye should do this Odo," said Jagger.

"How many men can ye spare?" Odo questioned Hilke.

"Four, not more."

"Then two men to guard the cows, and the other two to add to our numbers?"

"It will help, especially if they can wield a sword," offered the sergeant.

"I will arrange fer this when we return."

Sir Kasos paced backwards and forwards in frustration. He shook his head at what Antonius Richter had done. "Ye have alerted them, they will expect trouble now and we have lost our advantage."

"What we have done, Sir Knight," spat *Mynhear* Richter, "is offer them a choice. This was an honourable decision by me, and one I stand by."

Sir Kasos stopped and looked at the tall Frisian. He opened his mouth to speak.

"They may yet heed our warning and depart," added the Frisian quickly.

"And if the cog does not sail with the morn tide with the Englishmen aboard?"

Antonius inclined his head. "Then where are they most vulnerable?'

The knight remained silent.

"Their cows!"

"And do ye believe that yer farmers with old, dull swords can overcome experienced soldiers?"

"The men I will send can easily overcome a handful of Englishmen."

"And ye will now send men to fight the Englishmen?" Sir Kasos looked up towards the evening sky and hoped for some divine assistance. He took a deep breath, then exhaled. "Do not underestimate these men, the giant, he is one to be respected, and do ye know who else accompanies the herdsman, *Mynhear* Richter?"

Antonius shook his head.

"An Irish seer known only as Cathal. I have seen this man in France, he is spoken about in hushed whispers, men fear him, yet welcome his healing hands. Some say he is a druid–"

"And ye know who is on my side?" interrupted the Frisian angrily, a vein pulsed on his neck.

"Ye have a company of armed knights?" hoped Sir Kasos.

"Almighty God! We do not fear a heathen or his spells, for Christ is with us." Antonius crossed himself. "May the blessed Virgin Mary watch over us all."

Sir Kasos turned away in frustration. Perhaps *I should do something myself*, he thought. He looked back over his shoulder. "Where are these cows being held?"

"At *Boer* Haro Sikma's farm, at the edge of Geestendorf," replied Antonius.

"I will watch the herd first," said Odo, surprising everyone. "They are my cows, I am a herdsman and that is what herdsman do," he finished with finality.

"I agree," spoke Charlotte. "We will do our fair share of the work too. I will keep watch with Odo."

"Those men will return–" began Hilke.

"Not this eventide," Jagger added with a wry smile. "On the morrow they may, but not this eventide, fer they suggested we set sail in the morn so they will not come. We must take them at their word."

It was quite dark with only a waning crescent moon overhead. Stars twinkled boldly, high above them like a canopy of suspended flickering candles in a near cloudless sky. Odo sat, leaning against a wooden gate with a blanket draped over his shoulders and Charlotte leaned against him, she also had a thick blanket covering her to ward off the chill and damp. Periodically they would walk the perimeter of the small field and then return to the gate where they talked quietly.

Odo knew Jagger was out there somewhere watching over them both, even after Odo insisted he remain on the boat. Jagger just shook his massive head defiantly and said nothing. The giant was completely selfless with his loyalty and dedication and Odo and Charlotte commented on this frequently. Unbidden, Cathal brought the subject up on more than one occasion and claimed Jagger was drawn to him like a moth to a flame, and nothing, no power on this earth, could prevent or stop it or him.

Raised voices caused Odo and Charlotte to sit up. From the direction of the farmer's home they could hear a commotion. Charlotte pried herself from Odo's arms and allowed him to stand. There was barely enough moonlight to provide illumination and Odo couldn't see anything.

Charlotte rose wearily and yawned. "Is the farmer having a squabble with his woman?" she asked as she repositioned the blanket around her shoulders.

"I can't tell … perhaps it is nothing." Odo squinted into the darkness. "Someone is coming."

Charlotte looked into the blackness. Again there were raised voices. "Two men come. I think one is Haro," she added, "I recognise his voice."

CHAPTER THIRTY–FOUR

Sir Kasos gave the farmer another shove. "Take me to where the Englishmen keeps his cows," he hissed.

Boer Haro Sikma didn't understand English and he wasn't partial to being woken late in the night by a sword-wielding stranger. From the odd word here and there that he understood, he presumed the late night caller wanted to see the Englishman's cows. Why he didn't come during the day like decent folk, Haro couldn't fathom. The sharp point of a sword provided motivation but no answers.

There were few fences in this part of Frisia. No stone walls or hedges that were commonly found in England. Land was precious and because it was flat and low, it was susceptible to flooding and storm surges. Even farmers' homes were built on man-made elevated mounds of earth called *terps*. Water-filled channels and ditches divided fields which made navigating from one field to another in darkness treacherous, especially if you didn't know your way around. Sir Kasos needed the farmer to help him find the Englishman's cows.

As Haro led the way, Sir Kasos saw the dim silhouette of two people waiting at a gate. He gave the farmer another push forward.

"Haro?" questioned a male voice.

Haro Sikma began to reply when he was struck by the knight.

"Who are ye, what do ye want?" again came the voice from the darkness.

After ensuring the farmer wasn't going to flee, Kasos took another step closer to the gate to better see who challenged him. He kept his face partially turned away as he slowly edged closer.

"These cows belong to me, I have purchased them. Why are ye here in the middle of the night?" Odo took another tentative step towards the stranger hoping to see who it was. *Where was Jagger?*

As he approached, the knight recognized a female form; they were both here. *This was the English herdsman and his woman*, grinned, Sir Kasos. It was fortunate indeed.

"What are ye called, yer name?" the herdsman asked.

A woman's voice carried across the fields. "Haro! Haro!"

"Fenja! *Gean werom*!" yelled Haro, warning his wife to stay away. He took a hurried step towards her and was grabbed by the tall knight and yanked backwards. He slipped on the damp long grass and fell heavily, the back of his head hitting the gate post with a sickening thud before his momentum carried him sideways and he slid into the water-filled ditch.

Jagger was quickly approaching and even with the dim light of the moon, he witnessed the outline of the stranger hurl the farmer into the gate.

Odo reacted quickly and leapt for Haro. The gate ended at the water's edge and Odo was able to ease himself around the gate post and into the ditch to reach the fallen Frisian farmer.

Sir Kasos was losing control of the situation quickly. This wasn't what he'd envisioned when he first set out this evening. All he intended to do was kill as many of the herdsman's cows as possible. He drew his sword, hoping to quickly end his dilemma, solve the bishop's problem and run the young Englishman through, but the looming outline of the approaching giant quickly changed his mind.

"Master Odo?" Jagger yelled.

"Jagger!" Charlotte cried. She backed away from the tall stranger. "He has a sword!" she added, hoping to alert Jagger.

Sir Kasos wasn't a particularly brave knight, he'd fought in many victorious battles, although never with distinction, but he was no fool either. He couldn't remain here and fight the giant in darkness and hope to win. Best to live and fight another day. He spun and ran into the darkness just as Haro's wife, Fenja arrived. She saw Odo bent over her husband.

By the dim light of the waning crescent moon, Odo was close enough to see the horror etched on her face.

Jagger arrived in time to hear her yell, "*Myn Haro, wat hawwe jo dien!*"[24]

"Haro is dead," said Odo barely above a hoarse whisper.

Sunrise saw a group of people gathered on the dock beside Hilke's *koggership*. No one had slept much since the incident during the night and Jagger was again questioning Odo and Charlotte about the stranger who'd come to Haro's field. "I am vexed that this man spoke English and wasn't a Frisian." He shook his head and looked to Cathal for any advice. "Why would an Englishman be here and be after Odo's cows?"

"Nothing would surprise me, it could even be Bishop Immers who is behind this, he is the only one with reason," said the Irishman.

---

24   Frisian. My Haro, what have you done?

"Are ye sure he was English, Odo?" asked Benedict.

"Nay, I never saw him well, but he was tall and while he spoke English, I saw nothing of his features as he kept his face hidden. I can only tell ye that much."

Jagger turned to Charlotte.

She shrugged. "Odo was closer to him than I; all I saw was his outline and then the flash of a sword."

"And now a man is dead," Odo said despondently.

Grace had prepared some food and everyone sat down to eat.

"What of Haro's woman?" Odo asked.

"She is with family," Charlotte replied.

Odo sat on a box with elbows resting on his knees; he looked down at the rough wooden planking of the pier. "Why must innocent people die? Haro had done no wrong."

Benedict stepped over to console him when a clamour aboard the ship caused all heads to turn. One of Hilke's crewman pointed.

Hilke stood and looked where the seaman indicated. "It is Fyt and Gys!"

Odo rose from his seat. Sure enough, two Frisian *koggerships* were entering the small bay. Charlotte stepped up beside him and put her arm around his waist and held him tightly. "Is good news Odo, now we can begin loading the cows and return home."

A Templar Knight upon an impressive chestnut stallion rode into Mellester, the red cross, vivid against the travel-stained white mantle he wore. He was accompanied by his sergeant, dressed completely in black.

Both men were travel-weary and exhausted. They ignored the curious glances of peasants, and with purpose made their way slowly through the village, past the square and Cheesemaker Gerald's Cheese Shoppe and stopped outside Herdsman Odo Read's cruck house.

"Ye won't find Odo, if its 'im yer lookin' fer, milord," informed a villager as he dipped his head respectfully. The folk of Mellester were used to the Templars and no longer feared them. They knew the Templars were their friends. A small curious crowd began to gather.

The knight nodded thoughtfully and turned his attention up towards the manor. "Has yer lord returned from Ireland?" he asked.

"Nay, but Steward Alard is at the manor, sire," offered the villager helpfully.

The knight and sergeant swung their horses around. "Thank ye." The knight humbly lowered his head in thanks and rode back through the village with his sergeant following close behind. Within a short time the templars were seen riding up the carriageway towards the manor house.

"I wonder what's all that about then?" asked a villager scratching his head.

The man-at-arms at the door to Mellester's great hall looked uncomfortable as the Templar Knight, with spurs jangling, strode confidently towards him. The knight paused at the door and gave the guard a smile. "I am here to see ... I believe, uh, Steward Alard?"

Word reached the steward that a Templar Knight was in Mellester and was on the way up the carriageway to see him. He was already in the hall when the man-at-arms entered with the knight following closely behind.

"Welcome to Mellester Manor, Sir Knight." He gave a nod to the guard who remained near the door. "How can I be of assistance? Please, rest yerself."

The knight removed his gauntlets and eased himself slowly to a seat. Alard could see the man was weary. "Have ye eaten? A scullery maid was nearby. "Fetch wine and bring food, please," he asked.

"My sergeant, he is seeing to the horses..."

"We will see he and yer animals are taken care of," assured the steward.

The knight exhaled, a long drawn out breath laced with tension. He looked at Steward Alard. "Forgive me, I am Sir Peter of Gaunt and I am here at the bequest of Sir William Marshal, whom I'm told ye are acquainted with."

"Indeed, and an honourable and good man," replied Steward Alard.

"I was hoping to talk with Mellester's lord, Sir Gweir, but have been informed he is still in Ireland."

"Aye, and we all wish he was here."

Sir Peter glanced around Mellester's hall. "Sir William has a vested interest in this region, the templars have considerable land and we wish to see it prosper. In addition, the well-being of Odo Read is of concern to Sir William and information has come to light that greatly perturbs him."

Steward Alard raised his eyebrows in interest and took a seat opposite the knight. "Oh? Is Odo in jeopardy?"

Sir Peter turned his attention back to the steward and shrugged his shoulders. "We don't know, perhaps."

Steward Alard looked thoughtful. "And how does this affect Mellester?" He leaned forward and whispered so only the knight could hear. "The templars have been more than generous to him."

"We believe…" Sir Peter also lowered his voice. "that the Bishop of Exeter has a personal feud with Odo Read, and this has to stop."

Steward Alard looked worried. "Then he is in peril."

"We do not know fer sure, and hoped he'd returned from his venture to Friesland by now, and a villager told me he is still away."

"Aye, he hasn't come back yet, the lad is a worry."

The templar shifted position. "What I wish to know are details about Bishop Immers, what can ye tell me about this feud?"

Steward Alard sat upright and looked uncomfortable. He took a moment to formulate his thoughts as the knight looked on. "Sir Peter, I am but a freeman, it is above my position to comment on these things. Ye would be best to see Sir Hyde Fortescue, Lord of Ridgley Manor, he can talk freely and is more than intimate with those details ye seek."

Sir Peter held the gaze of Steward Alard as if assessing him. He knew the steward was correct, it would be improper for him to comment. "Very well, we shall do this and visit Sir Hyde. Can we impose on yer generosity and rest here fer the night, we have travelled from afar?"

Hilke instructed Wim to take his *koggership* out into the bay which allowed room for Fyt to bring his ship to the dock. Already crewmen were creating sturdy pens where cows would be constrained during the voyage. Food was being loaded aboard and Herdsman Searl, with a watchful eye, ensured the work was done to his satisfaction. Odo and the rest of the group departed to purchase the last of the cows and a bull, while Apprentice Usher and Daniel went to the holding field to bring the cows down so they could begin loading them aboard Fyt's ship. As soon as they were aboard, Fyt would depart with the tide and continue on to Exmouth and as arranged. Herdsman Searl and Apprentice Usher would go with them.

Benedict and Apprentice Daniel would go aboard Gys's ship when it was loaded. Already Gys was building pens on his ship for the cows while still anchored in the bay.

Odo wanted to be at the dock to oversee the building of the pens and loading of the cows, but both Jagger and Cathal advised him that they needed to leave Frisia as soon as possible and he should focus on buying the last of his cows. Herdsman Searl was more than capable, they reassured him.

He wasn't used to speaking to a group of people, and most certainly he was uncomfortable being the man they turned to for guidance and direction. On Charlotte's prompting Odo addressed his small group of friends and soldiers and informed them that today they would purchase the last of the thirty-five cows and a bull, then immediately herd them to Geestendorf where they would be loaded aboard Gys's koggership. The sooner they could accomplish this task, the sooner they could return home. Everyone understood what was required of them and his men began preparations. With Hilke as their guide on a borrowed horse, they set off to the next and hopefully the last few farms.

With his only arm, Sir Hyde Fortescue held a goblet of wine to his lips and paused briefly as he studied the youthful templar knight who sat with him in a small private chamber at Ridgley Manor. The elder knight was alert, his mind keen and curious to the reason for the templar visit. Templars did not make unannounced visits on manorial lords, much preferring to keep to themselves.

"Ye are spoken of as a good, honest lord, Sir Hyde, and I'm sure Sir William regrets not being here to speak with ye personally."

Sir Hyde inclined his head slightly in acknowledgement but said nothing.

Sir Peter took a healthy swallow of his wine before continuing. "Our order is in possession of considerable lands scattered throughout southern England. As ye do, we wish to keep the peace and ensure the lands are farmed and productive."

"Of course," nodded the older knight.

"We find ourselves disheartened that the Church has been unable to manage its affairs in, uh, certain areas."

At this revelation Sir Hyde sat more upright and placed the goblet on the table and faced his unexpected guest.

The knight chose his words carefully. "It is difficult for us to determine exactly, and to what extent this neglect has affected local parishes, but we listen and we hear things from time to time."

Sir Hyde nodded, encouraging the templar to continue.

"With yer help, Sir Hyde, we hope ye can shed some light on the activities of the local bishop."

"Immers?"

"Aye, the Bishop of Exeter."

Sir Hyde pried himself from his seat and stepped over to the barely smouldering fire. He kept his back to the templar as he considered the implications. He spun, his eyes glared at the templar. "To what end?"

Taken by the reaction, Sir Peter was unsure how to proceed.

"Well?" snapped the lord.

Surprised at Sir Hyde's response, the templar knight decided to trust his instincts and push cautiously on. "Sir William has little faith that the bishop is acting in the best interest of the Church and is allowing a personal feud to interfere with management of his diocese."

Sir Hyde laughed, but it contained no mirth. "So ye can help the bishop, is that it? I never thought I'd live to see the day when I was called upon to grant a boon to the Church to assist Bishop Immers in his time of need."

The templar looked uncertain and shook his head. "Nay, sire, Sir William wishes to inform the Pope of Bishop Immers' unorthodox behaviour and have him censored if not removed as bishop."

Sir Hyde broke in to a broad smile and breathed out a sigh of relief. He returned to his seat and took a generous pull of wine before he replied. "Forgive me, I thought…"

Sir Peter raised a hand to forestall an apology. "My error, sire, I was not clear."

"How can I assist ye?"

Sir Peter relaxed. "Is Bishop Immers involved in a personal feud with a freeman from Mellester, Herdsman Odo Read? Is this man known to ye, Sir Hyde?"

"I am surprised ye know of him. Before I answer, tell me how ye came by the herdsman's name?"

"He did a great service to the Poor Fellow-Soldiers of Christ and from the Order of the Temple of Solomon. We are eternally grateful to him and will be forever in his debt."

Sir Hyde had his goblet to his lips and almost spat out the wine. "What say ye? What is this, I know nothing of this service!"

"We feel it best that Master Odo's service to us was not made public."

"Then I think it best ye begin to tell me, Sir Peter." Sir Hyde called for more wine and the templar knight told of the pyxis.

Sir Hyde wiped his eyes, he'd laughed so hard and for so long, servants, unsure of the noise came to investigate. "And I believed Odo was going to Frisia to purchase cows for the Templar farms, using yer coin, not his own." He shook his head in wonder. "Young Odo is indeed a fortunate man." He paused a moment as he digested what he'd learned.

The Templar watched on in quiet amusement.

"Then what ye say is Odo Read is a noble?"

"Milord, Herdsman Odo Read, or Odo Brus, the younger, is indeed a noble."

"And Odo knows this, he is aware of it?"

"Aye, but it has affected him not, he remains unchanged and is content to farm cows."

Sir Hyde was dumbfounded. "Although I shouldn't be surprised." He shook his head and turned back to the Templar. "However," his voice turned serious, "he has endured much and suffered greatly and certainly Bishop Immers has played a role in this, and continues to do so."

"Aye, and these are the details Sir William wants. Aye, he knows much already, but your voice could support Sir William's conviction that Bishop Immers is an unholy man who is ignoring his Episcopalian responsibilities and intent on destroying Odo to gain title to Falls Ende at whatever the cost."

"But there is more, is there not? Ye wouldn't be here to just tell me about Odo and the injustices he has suffered, what have ye not told me?" The blue-grey eyes of Ridgley Manor's lord bore into those of the younger Templar knight.

Sir Peter looked uncomfortable and it was obvious he was reluctant to share. Unable to meet the piercing gaze of the elderly lord, he turned away and thought through his options. He cleared his throat and turned back and held the lord's eyes. "We believe if King Henry were to find out that a bishop had overstepped the bounds of his authority and took advantage of his, uh, exalted position to–"

"Fill his own purse?" interrupted Sir Hyde.

"Aye, then this may further fuel tensions between the Holy See and King Henry."

"Of course, now this is beginning to make sense to me, please, Sir Peter, continue," invited Sir Hyde.

"Already there is much talk about the King's unhappiness with the Church. King Henry has made no secret that he wishes clergy who have committed crimes be punished under his laws and not just the precepts of the Church. The Pope disagrees. If the King were to hear of what Bishop Immers continues to do, then..." Sir Peter shrugged, leaving the sentence unfinished.

"So ye want to solve this problem quietly, without alerting the King?"

Sir Peter nodded and drained his goblet.

Sir Hyde chewed his bottom lip as he considered the implications. He recalled his last visit from the bishop and the malice he felt for the despicable man. "Bishop Immers has become my nemesis."

Sir Peter saw the flash of anger in the eyes of Ridgley Manor's lord.

"I have no desire to come between the Church and the King and inadvertently incite tension, certainly I have no want to see animosity develop between them. However, Bishop Immers has impinged on the affairs of Mellester Manor and coveted more than salvation for its poor inhabitants. Sir Peter, Mellester Manor is a small and poor hamlet, the people who live there are good hardworking decent folk; they need all the assistance they can get." Ridgley's lord repositioned himself and thought of young Amy and how he wanted her to grow up in a place where justice and fairness prevailed for all, and not a privilege of birth right. He looked the Templar knight squarely in the eye. "I will help, but battle the Church I cannot do without support from the King. The Templars are better equipped to deal with Bishop Immers than I, if ye feel ye can do this and keep King Henry out of this mess, then Sir Peter, ye have my support."

Sir Peter smiled, acknowledging the lord. "Milord, ye do not do battle with the Church, only an aberrant bishop."

"But ye wouldn't be here if there was no immediate concern."

The Templar knight nodded and looked away.

Sir Hyde took a deep breath, his eyes slowly focused intently on the young templar knight. "Then Odo has met with strife in Frisia?"

Sir Peter nodded. "We believe him to be in some peril, milord."

CHAPTER THIRTY–FIVE

Charlotte screamed in fright. She tried to turn Noor around and go to Odo, but a man stepped up and tightly grasped the reins of her horse and held a sword to her chest. "Odo!" she yelled hopelessly, but there wasn't anything she could do.

Already Jagger was leaning over the neck of his courser as it galloped up the narrow road towards them. Villagers scattered out of the way as he thundered past. He'd been cleverly distracted by a few men posing as locals who deliberately blocked the road, preventing the herd from advancing towards Geestendorf. In frustration, he and Tedric rode to the front of the herd to move them when they first heard Charlotte scream. Tedric, also on horseback, did his best to keep up with Jagger, but it was too late for them to help Odo.

A stranger had come up beside Odo and yanked him backwards off Amica, then dragged him, fighting and struggling, back towards other armed men who silently rose from the bank of a water-filled channel. They quickly encircled Odo preventing anyone from reaching him and slowly the group of Frisians began to back away.

Amica was agitated and began fussing. The stallion posed a risk to the retreating Frisians and a man foolishly tried to grab the reins to lead him away, but the stallion pivoted nimbly, one rear leg cow-kicked outwards and struck the unsuspecting man hard. He crumpled to the ground clutching his leg. In panic, he desperately tried to crawl away before he could be savagely kicked again. Hilke, who rode a borrowed horse, was speechless. His head swivelled from side to side as he tried to make sense of what was happening.

Completely surrounded by armed men, Odo was held tightly around the throat and dragged away from Charlotte who was yelling frantically. Seeing the charging form of Jagger quickly bearing down on them saw a change of heart from the men. The one holding Noor released the bridle and hastily retreated back to the safety of his friends. Charlotte was about to spur Noor forward to go to Odo when Jagger arrived, cutting her off.

"Charlotte, return to Geestendorf, quickly, it is not safe here." His courser slid to a stop and he leapt off, his own sword already unsheathed and glinting in the late afternoon sun. "Release him! Release him now!" he bellowed and took a threatening step towards the ring of men surrounding Odo. Moments later he felt the presence of Tedric as he leapt from his horse and stepped up to stand beside him. More of Odo's men were running towards them but, they were still outnumbered.

Charlotte looked uncertain and turned to Odo who was being choked. "Go! Go now!"

She didn't know what to do.

Benedict who'd been at the front of the herd finally arrived.

"Benedict, take Charlotte back to the cog, alert the others, quickly," instructed Jagger without tearing his eyes from the Frisians.

She had no intention of riding away and leaving her husband behind.

Astride a borrowed horse, Benedict leaned over and grabbed the reins to Noor, "Come, Charlotte, ye are at risk." Protesting loudly, Charlotte had no option as Benedict led Noor away. She looked back, over her shoulder as they headed towards Geestendorf less than half a mile distant.

Jagger assessed the men who held Odo. They looked competent but they weren't knights. One man, tall with a dark complexion, had a look of a fighter, but strangely he hung back and didn't look eager to become involved. There was a woman with them, he recognised her as the wife of Haro, the dead farmer.

The group's leader, obvious by his deportment and arrogance, glared at Jagger. With confidence and the surety of superior numbers supporting him he took a single step forward, "Ye have no right to challenge my authority, I am a *Redjeven*, and duly elected to oversee our laws in this part of Frisia, leave, go now!" he commanded.

Jagger fought to control his fury. "Why do ye hold Odo, what has he done?"

Haro's wife, Fenja, angrily shouted something Jagger couldn't understand.

"She says, this man," the leader pointed to Odo, his accent thick but comprehensible "killed her husband, she saw him over the body. She recognized him and we will take him so he can face the penalty for his crime."

"Nay, nay, ye are wrong, there was another man, he pushed the farmer and he fell hitting his head. Odo was trying to help, not kill him. Odo isn't a killer, he is a herdsman," appealed Jagger. He looked from the Frisian leader to Odo who was still being held tightly around the throat and couldn't speak. "Who are ye, what is yer name?"

"I am *Redjeven* Antonius Richter, and this area is in my jurisdiction.

Leave Frisia, go back to where ye come from."

Up to now, Hilke had remained quiet; he dismounted and cautiously approached Jagger. "It is as he says, *Mynhear* Richter has authority," he nervously whispered.

Jagger spared a quick glance around to evaluate his options. Cathal was riding towards them which strengthened their small force, but they were still heavily outnumbered. The Frisian *Redjeven* and his men were slowly backing away and taking Odo with them. He needed to act, and quickly. He indicated for Tedric to take three men and quickly circle behind the tight group of Frisians to prevent them from leaving. He knew once they had taken Odo back to the village, it would take a miracle to free him. At present, the only thing slowing them down was the man Amica kicked, he could hardly walk. He spoke softly to the archer and told him to keep an arrow aimed at the tall dark man. Something about the man bothered him and in a fleeting thought wondered if the tall stranger was the same person who pushed Haro.

"Ye have the wrong man! It was another who killed the farmer, an Englishman but not with us!" Jagger yelled. He took a step or two closer hoping to push through the ring of men so he could release Odo. One overconfident Frisian stepped forward to stand in front of Jagger, blocking his path and took an ill-advised swing at the giant with his sword.

Jagger was fighting to control his rage and he acted instinctively. Driven by frustration and anger, he pivoted his body and with pure strength and speed, his sword, which had been pointed down at the ground swung up with all his might. With a horrendous crash of steel, the inferior Frisian sword snapped cleanly. The numbing blow caused the Frisian to drop what remained of his weapon and clutch his stinging hand. With an open palm, the giant stepped forward and casually thrust him aside.

As ordered, Tedric and three others, with swords drawn, positioned themselves behind the group. The Frisians were trapped, they'd have to fight their way past.

Wanting to leave as quickly as possible with their prisoner, Antonius Richter turned around to find their escape blocked by four armed Englishmen.

In anger at having their retreat impeded, one man yelled and raised his sword to strike at Tedric. For a skilled fighter like Tedric it was easy to defend, and in reflex, he just extended his sword to block the slash. With all the attention focused on the Frisian swordsman, no one saw Sir Kasos give Antonius a sudden and unexpected, violent shove. Caught unawares, he stumbled forward as Tedric tried to deflect the Frisian blade. Unable to stop his forward momentum, Antonius fell onto the point of Tedric's outreached sword. The blade fatally pierced his chest and he collapsed to his knees. The Frisians all froze and could only watch in horror as Antonius Richter fell face down onto the road. He lay unblinking, unmoving – he was dead. Haro's wife, screamed. Not a man moved, everyone was stunned except Jagger who shouldered aside the nearest Frisian and head butted the man holding Odo.

With a huge fist, Jagger grabbed Odo's capuchin and hauled him away from danger, while he stood his ground, daring anyone to reattempt to grab him. Cathal was the first to step up and stand at his side; he carried no weapon but bravely stood in a peculiar stance beside the giant. Tedric, in shock at what had just happened, reacted before the Frisians could respond.

Urging his men, they quickly ran around the group to stand alongside Jagger and the Irish seer.

While they still outnumbered the Englishmen, the Frisians could see the men who stood before them were seasoned fighters; the giant who glared defiantly at them was just outright frightening. Without their leader their decision was easy and not a man amongst them was foolish enough to retaliate. Wisely they picked up the dead *redjeven* and withdrew.

Stewart the archer was the only person to witness what the tall stranger had done. He stood slightly to the side and still kept an arrow aimed directly at him.

"We will be back," snarled a retreating Frisian. "We will come back for him!"

Odo easily quieted Amica down and climbed into the saddle while he waited for Jagger. He was frightened and his body shook, but he didn't ride away. He watched the Frisians as they slowly withdrew, occasionally someone would yell something, but he couldn't understand what they said.

When they were far enough away, Jagger turned and for the first time Odo saw the battleface of the giant. Gone was the affable friendly face of his friend, instead, he saw the hard lines and hooded piercing eyes of a seasoned warrior. "I'm sorry Master Odo, t'was my fault, I shouldn't have left yer side." He shook his head in disgust at his perceived mistake.

Odo took a deep breath to calm his frayed nerves. "Thank ye, ye all did well." He coughed and then grimaced, his throat still a little tender. "It wasn't yer fault, Jagger, it was mine. Fer I never saw the man come up beside me. I am to blame, and it will not happen again." He held Jagger's penetrating stare and nodded his thanks.

"It is well to blame oneself," said Cathal as he walked to his horse, "But looking forward, not back will set a man's mind on the right path. No one is at fault, but I grieve for the man who died."

"It was the tall man," said the archer, "I saw him push the Frisian. It was not Tedric who killed him, it was the tall one with the olive skin."

"And *who is* that man?" said Jagger to no one in particular.

"He was armed with a fine sword, t'was the sword of a knight, but he never unsheathed it," Tedric added.

"We must hurry back to Geestendorf and load the cows, they will be back and there will be more of them," Jagger insisted.

Those without horses began to run, while the others stayed in a tight group and rode together driving the cows as quickly as possible to the seaport village of Geestendorf where Gys and his ship waited.

Sir Kasos was quite pleased with himself. When the Frisian woman complained to the *redjeven* that her husband was killed by the Englishman known as Odo, Antonius Richter decided they would set out after the Englishmen and insisted Sir Kasos accompany them. He protested and reminded Antonius that his role was purely that of an observer and should not play any active part. In truth, he was concerned he would be recognised by the herdsman, his woman or the farmer's wife. As it turned out, it was a needless worry and no one had seen his face the previous evening. His protestations made little difference to the stubborn *redjeven* and he was forced to go with them.

The knight felt Antonius was weak, and perhaps too principled, and if questioned, the Englishman herdsman may easily have convinced the Frisian of his innocence and be allowed his freedom.

When he saw the Frisian strike at the Englishman with his sword, the opportunity was too good to miss and it was easy to push Antonius into the path of the Englishman's sword. Now that the dear friend of Bishop Laninga was dead, the Church may take a different approach. Two people had died by the hand of the Englishmen, and it was unlikely the Church would ignore the deaths, especially if he recounted to the bishop all the details.

Sir Kasos knew he must return to Utrecht as soon as possible and report the crimes so Bishop Laninga could take all necessary steps to begin retribution and have God's justice served.

When Odo and his group arrived back in Geestendorf, he was pleased to see Fyt, along with Herdsman Searl and Usher, had already departed with a shipload of cows for Exmouth near Exeter. Already, the last remaining cows and food were being herded aboard Gys's *koggership* which was now tied alongside the small pier. Hilke's ship was still in the bay and would be loaded with all the horses once Gys's ship had moved to make room.

Odo was shaken, his throat was still sore and Charlotte was distraught. They both knew that fortune had smiled briefly on them and they were lucky, but the day was not over yet. If they had any questions about the loyalty of Jagger, today's event dispelled that doubt. He had proved himself yet again.

Jagger posted lookouts well up the road and if the Frisians came, as he fully expected they would, then he would have advance warning and time to get Odo and Tedric to safety. Encouraged by Hilke, and Jagger's looming presence, the pier was a hive of activity as men quickly loaded, cows, food and supplies aboard Gys's ship.

It would be some time before the tidal ebb turned, and Hilke suggested once his ship was loaded, they wait in the bay for the tide. It would make it difficult for the Frisians to mount an effective attack, he insisted, if they were safely aboard the ship and in the bay.

Sir Kasos readied his rented horse in the village of Schiffdorf. As he completed cinching the saddle he could already see a large group of men assembling. Many carried swords, some pitchforks and others wooden staffs, one man even carried an oar, but one thing was clear, these Frisians were furious that *Mynhear* Richter had been slain and they sought retribution. He counted nearly two score; however, he knew it would make little difference how many men rallied. The English herdsman had a highly organised and effective group of men with him, he doubted they'd still be in Geestendorf when the mob arrived.

He mounted his horse and rode unseen from the town of Schiffdorf, towards Utrecht where he'd report the brutal slayings to Bishop Laninga.

CHAPTER THIRTY–SIX

One of Jagger's lookouts came barrelling down the narrow road to Geestendorf on horseback. The horse slid to a halt and he ran for the dock to find Jagger. The last of the cows were secured aboard Gys's ship and already Gys had the dock lines untied and the fully loaded ship slowly began to inch out into the bay. Hilke was aboard his own ship and was waiting for room before he could come alongside the dock to begin loading the horses.

"They come, Jagger," yelled the man when he found the giant. "There are over two score armed Frisians coming this way."

"What weapons do they carry?" he asked calmly.

"Mostly swords, no armour, many have pitchforks and some with staffs."

"Horses?"

The guard shook his head. "They walk."

"How far away are they?"

"At least six *mileway*'s[25]"

Jagger scratched his head as he thought. "Leave yer horse and gather the other men, have them set up defences near the outskirts. We will try to delay them."

The guard nodded and ran off.

25   *Unit of medieval time measurement, equal to the time it takes for a man to walk a mile, approx 20 min.*

Tedric was helping Odo and Charlotte with the horses when Jagger approached. "As expected the Frisians come. Archer Stuart and I will try to slow them as much as possible, ye must not tarry and load the horses as quickly as possible."

Odo's expression was grim. "Aye, we will do our best, Jagger. But ye can't stop two score men."

"We will do our best to slow them down enough to give ye the time ye need," Jagger explained. He eased his bulk into the saddle of the rented horse and Archer Stuart followed suit. With a wave, they galloped down the road.

Already Hilke was easing his ship into the newly vacated space alongside the dock. Gys had anchored his ship in the bay, and was waiting until late afternoon, when the tide was favourable to hoist sail and leave Geestendorf.

Including Cathal, Odo's men each held a horse in preparation for loading, and a pile of food and water was stacked on the dock ready to be hauled aboard. Once the cog was securely tied to the dock the horses would be led down a ramp into the ship and finally the crew could begin loading food and supplies. Odo held Amica and was at the rear of the line, as the black stallion would be the last horse loaded. It would take time to secure all the horses so they wouldn't injure themselves during the voyage and no one was sure if they could do it in time before the Frisians arrived. It all hinged on Jagger and Stuart.

Frisia's featureless, flat landscape made it easy for Jagger and Archer

Stuart to see the large group of men walking up the narrow road towards Geestendorf. Jagger could see they walked with determination, fuelled by the conviction they were just and acted within the tenets of Frisian law. Jagger acknowledged to himself that if their roles were reversed, then he would likely be doing the same. These men weren't the enemy and he certainly had no quarrel with them except for the mysterious man who'd killed Haro. As he surveyed the hostile mob that approached, he saw no sign of the tall, olive-skinned stranger and he wondered again if he was the man responsible for Haro's death.

He pulled his horse to a stop about twenty yards from the approaching men. "Where is the tall one, the man with the sword?" he yelled across the narrow gap separating them.

One man took a step forward. "We have come for the herdsman and the other man, the fighter," he answered with a sneer, ignoring Jagger's question.

The Frisians looked grateful for the respite from their walk; many leaned on an assortment of unconventional weapons and wiped their brows as they rested.

"We respect yer laws and wish ye no ill will," Jagger responded. "But the herdsman did not kill the farmer. It was another man, a man we could not identify for it was dark. As fer the *redjeven*, Mynhear Richter, he was pushed onto the sword of my man by the tall one who isn't with ye."

This revelation produced a series of simultaneous conversations as the Frisians discussed the giant's claim. "That is why ye must hand them both over to us," replied the Frisian leader. "They must account fer their actions and face fair penalty."

"Look, yonder, two men on horses!" yelled Stuart Archer.

Jagger shifted his gaze and looked beyond the Frisians at two men who rode towards them at an easy canter. His mouth tightened. Already he could see that the approaching horsemen were not farmers, they were knights. This changed their situation somewhat.

The Frisians all turned to look behind them and also saw the approaching men and they began to yell in encouragement. With their confidence boosted, their yells soon turned hostile and they began to act more aggressively.

"Return to yer farms, we have no quarrel with ye, the man ye seek is the tall one," Jagger shouted, hoping to pacify the group. He turned his horse and stepped away to keep separation. The two knights drew closer and he could see these men were armed and experienced warriors. He knew the sensible option was to retreat and keep trying to delay their advance into Geestendorf. Again he urged his horse to turn away and create more space from the Frisians.

He caught the movement from his peripheral vision, but it was too late to respond. A shortened axe, much like a hatchet, spun through the air and struck his horse, embedding itself into the animal's right shoulder with a sickening thud. The horse screeched in pain and stumbled. It tried to regain its footing and failed. Jagger had only an instant to free his leg before the wounded horse lurched and fell heavily to the ground, driving the axe deeper and causing even more damage. The Frisians stopped their yelling and watched as the horse writhed helplessly on the ground. Blood streamed from its wound and the panicked animal tried unsuccessfully to stand.

Jagger managed to safely leap from the horse and successfully dodge its flailing legs. The wound was mortal and the horse would bleed to death in agony. Sparing no thought to the angry Frisians, he leapt for the horse's neck and slid across to lay over its head. He spoke soothingly and immediately the animal calmed down, but the blood flow was too great and he knew the horse had to be put out of its misery. As the Frisians watched with curiosity, Jagger pulled a lethal blade from his belt, a cross-hilt dagger with razor sharp edges and quickly ended the stricken horse's life.

He slowly stood and turned to the man who threw the axe and held his gaze. Jagger shook his head at the senseless death of the horse. Feeling shame, the man looked away and Jagger sheathed his bloodied knife and turned to the archer. "Return to Geestendorf, bring all the available men to meet me. Together we will slow their march."

The archer looked uncertain. "You'll be alone… ride with me."

"Go, hasten, we don't have time," responded Jagger as the emboldened Frisians began to step closer. He backed up to maintain a safe distance between them.

The archer swung his horse around and galloped away leaving Jagger alone with the angry mob.

He turned his attention back to the Frisians as he thought about the dead horse. "Why was it necessary to kill a valuable horse? Return to yer farms, begone!" He moved away from the dead horse and the coppery smell of blood.

Many of the Frisians didn't speak or understand English, but all the men understood the tone and intent behind the giant's words. Many looked uncomfortable, uncertain and shifted their feet nervously. The arrival of two armed knights immediately changed the mood.

"We have come to bring two men to face justice!" yelled one knight in French accented English. He nudged his horse a step closer. The Frisian group parted allowing the mounted knight room.

"Ye have the wrong men, we came here in peace to purchase cows, not to kill. It was another man who did this, not the herdsman ye seek," responded the giant. He looked up at the knight and assessed him carefully. In reflex his hand reached across and grasped the hilt of his sword. After a moment's pause he turned to walk back towards Geestendorf.

The ship had barely been tied to the dock before a ramp was positioned, allowing the horses to be loaded. One by one, each horse was led to the ramp, Noor and finally Amica bringing up the rear. All heads turned to the sound of a galloping horse as Archer Stuart rushed recklessly past the guards Jagger posted and through the township towards the dock.

"Is Jagger, he faces two knights and two score men, his horse was killed and he wants all armed men to go to him," shouted Archer Stuart breathlessly.

Odo looked towards Charlotte. There were no spare horses and his men could only travel on foot. He knew the giant needed help immediately and he knew he was the only one who could do it.

Charlotte knew what he was thinking. Their eyes met. "Be careful," she silently mouthed.

Odo needed no further urging and without a word, pulled the stallion from the line and vaulted onto its back. "Give me yer reins," he instructed the archer who'd already dismounted. With a spare horse for Jagger, he charged out of the village.

As a dark cloud passed ominously overhead, Cathal looked solemnly up at the heavens and shook his head.

Bishop Laninga took another pull of wine and looked over the rim of his goblet at Sir Kasos. His mind worked furiously as he contemplated what he'd been told. Antonius Richter had been a lifelong trusted friend. They'd grown up shoulder to shoulder, laughed, cried and even been punished together for the mischievous deeds of boys. Now Antonius was dead, killed needlessly by a cowardly English swordsman. To make matters worse, the herdsman had killed a simple farmer, why? The bishop couldn't fathom... perhaps they'd been haggling over coin, over the price of cows.

The bishop placed the goblet firmly back on the table, making its contents slosh over the lip and pool beneath the ornate vessel. "Have ye doubt, are ye sure these two men are responsible fer the deaths of the farmer and Antonius Richter?" He held the gaze of the dark-complexioned knight and stared into liquid pools of blackness. "Speak now, or forever hold yer tongue."

"I was there, Yer Grace, I witnessed everything." The knight had the sense to break eye contact by dipping his head in supplication.

The bishop wasn't convinced; something about the man irked him. He would mull over the dreadful news before he made up his mind. "I will think upon this, come to me on the morrow and ye will receive instructions and an epistle."

"As ye wish, Yer Grace." Sir Kasos lowered his head, then turned quickly and exited the room.

The bishop remained motionless long after the knight departed. A myriad of thoughts and emotions flowed through his consciousness as he dwelled upon the unfortunate circumstances of his friend's untimely death and the role of the mysterious knight.

Ebel Laninga was conflicted. Part of him wanted no part in antagonising the English and he preferred to just mourn the passing of his dear friend. Yet he also felt a sense of duty, first to the Church and his friend Bishop Immers of Exeter, and to see justice done in the name of Almighty God. His face reddened and with clenched fists he hammered on the table upsetting the goblet which fell to the floor with a clatter. An attending priest ran into the room fearing something tragic had happened.

"Fetch me a scholar, and be brisk about it," ordered the bishop before the priest could enquire.

CHAPTER THIRTY–SEVEN

"Halt!" ordered the knight in plain English.

Jagger slowed, but continued to walk towards Geestendorf. He could hear the sound of many men following him. They were close, but he felt no fear. The unmistakeable scrape of a sword unsheathing changed that feeling and he felt the hair on his neck rise. He took another step and stopped, then slowly turned. One of the knights had dismounted from his horse and now stood directly behind him with his sword in the on-guard position. This wasn't an invitation to talk, the knight intended to engage. "What reason have ye, Sir Knight, to challenge me? Since my horse lives no longer and I have done no wrong? I wish only to peacefully return to the village."

"Ye are obstructing us," spoke the knight, his accent thick. "Defend yerself!"

Jagger wasn't wearing any armour; his chainmail lay in a heap on the deck of Hilke's cog. He had only his sword and dagger and was disadvantaged by a fully armoured knight, sans helmet and shield. "Perhaps ye should reconsider." As yet he had not drawn his sword, but his hand lay on its hilt. Already he could feel the heat rising throughout his body in preparation for what was to come.

Without any further warning, the knight slashed. Jagger stepped back as the blade whistled past his stomach.

Generally knights are trained to stab with their swords as a slash will have little effect on quality armour. They aim for parts of the body that are unprotected and hope to inflict as much damage as possible on those areas. As Jagger had no protection, the knight felt confident he could easily slash and kill the large Englishman with ease, while his opponent didn't have that luxury. In normal circumstances, it was an unfair engagement and without chivalry.

As the sword's momentum swung the knight around, Jagger unsheathed his sword in a single practiced motion. He held the sword with an unusual grip. One hand on the pommel and the other on the hilt. This hand position offered the offensive swordsman more accuracy and Jagger stabbed at the exposed shoulder joint. It was a quick move and certainly unexpected. Driven by the force of Jagger's immense strength, the sharp point of the sword drove deep into the joint of the armour and into the shoulder. The knight cursed and stepped back. Blood began to freely run down his arm.

The other knight who watched the fight with amused interest atop his courser suddenly leapt down. This was not what they expected. The Frisians backed up in a half circle.

The clash of steel was loud, and each man defended blow after blow. The knight was weakening and while Jagger had done little more than inflict a relatively minor wound, he nevertheless hoped the knight would yield. He had no desire to kill him, for doing so would further enrage locals and put Odo and Charlotte in even more danger.

An idea came to mind. He quickened the speed of his attack and with pure strength, forced the hapless knight to turn; now his back was to the water-filled canal that ran parallel to road. Step by step the knight was driven backwards. Each time he tried to twist away, Jagger countered and forced him closer to the water.

The knight's face was twisted in agony. He was tired and weakening and the increased tempo of the strikes against him strengthened in power and speed. The giant was more than impressive, he was fearless and without weakness. The knight took another involuntary step backwards and his foot slipped on the edge of the road. The big man parried a weak lunge, and then pushed the knight. With arms windmilling and a loud cry, the knight fell backwards into the canal.

Jagger stepped back and away, he took a deep breath and prepared himself for what was to come next. As expected, the other knight decided to challenge him.

"See to yer friend, and I will walk away," Jagger spoke, offering the knight a choice to save face.

The closest Frisians ran to the canal to help the wounded knight. The slippery sides of the canal and weight of the armour proved too much, the knight was in danger of drowning.

The second knight shook his head, his mouth twisted into a feral snarl and his sword arced through the air to strike at Jagger's shoulder. It was easy to deflect and Jagger's sword met the fast moving blade with a loud clang. Older and wiser, the knight showed more skill and Jagger needed to be careful. He decided to end this fight quickly as he was beginning to tire, while his new adversary was fresh. Their swords met again and again, the noise disturbing the peacefulness of the Frisian countryside.

Both men fought with poise, their feet and movements almost graceful as they parried lunged and struck with ferocity. It was like a choreographed dance, except there were no minstrels, only death or dismemberment awaited the loser.

Odo rode as fast as he dared, the trailing horse unable to keep pace with the powerful stallion. The flat countryside made it easy for him to see the group of men in the distance, and as he rode closer, he heard the clash of steel upon steel. He pulled Amica to a stop, still some distance from the group of men but close enough to easily see the large form of Jagger as he twisted and spun, his sword flashing in the afternoon sun. His opponent, also a large man, was lithe and quick. Odo was no expert at sword fighting, but he'd witnessed enough to see that Jagger appeared to have the better of the man.

Odo's heart was racing. Even though it looked like Jagger would survive as victor, the knight was fighting for his life. Anything could happen.

With unbelievable speed and dexterity, Jagger defended another strike and then spun, sidestepped and anticipated from where the knight's sword would be. From an overhand position, Jagger's gleaming sword arced downwards and struck the knight on his sword arm, carving a deep gash lengthways, almost the full length of the arm. The knight dropped his sword as he cradled the injured limb. The fight was over.

Jagger was breathing hard, he was exhausted, having fought two knights and bested them both. He'd had enough. He straightened, looked at the Frisians who stood silently dumbfounded and turned to walk away back to Geestendorf. He raised his head and in the distance saw Odo with a spare horse and smiled.

Caught in the emotion of the violence, Odo's heart was still beating furiously. He was about to ride up to him when a Frisian stepped from the mob, and from only a few feet away, launched a pitchfork at the exposed unprotected back of Jagger. Thrown with considerable force and without armour to deflect the missile, the sharpened steel tines of the farming tool easily penetrated Jagger's clothing and embedded deep into his body. The force of the impact drove him to his knees, the look of total surprise etched on his face.

Odo froze, his mouth opened in horror as Jagger tried to stand. Bitter in defeat, the vanquished knight with the injured arm picked up his weapon and strode purposely towards the giant. He raised his sword and twisted his body. The finely honed blade descended in a blur and severed Jagger's head cleanly from his body. The knight spat and casually turned away to have his wound attended to.

Odo couldn't move. He was in shock and sickened.

Over half the Frisians turned and began to walk away. They too were disgusted by what they had just witnessed, this wasn't what they had come here to do. The man who threw the pitchfork stood alone and watched as Jagger's blood flowed freely into Frisian soil.

The remaining men finally realised that one of the men they sought was sitting astride a horse about thirty yards away and with a shout began to run towards him.

Odo retched, and then again. He couldn't move. Without realising it he'd dropped the reins to the spare horse which was now foraging for grass on the side of the road. He was traumatised and his body began to shake. The Frisians bore down on him, their yells alerting only the black stallion who stood nervously waiting for a command.

The approaching mob was drawing closer. The courser sensed something amiss; he took a jittery step, then another, and then with his mind made up, bolted. There was only one direction to run and that was back to the seaport village of Geestendorf.

Purely in reflex Odo hung on. Unencumbered without a saddle or being restricted by the spare horse, Amica stretched out and thundered down the road. The stallion passed the men Jagger called for without slowing, and left them scratching their heads and wondering what had happened. With nowhere to run, Amica slid to a halt near the dock. Odo sat immobile and dazed.

"Odo! Odo!" cried Charlotte. She ran from the dock towards him.

Cathal had just secured his horse aboard the ship and he leapt onto the dock when he saw Amica and Odo pull up.

He sat astride Amica, unmoving. His eyes unfocused, he said nothing.

"Where is Jagger, Odo? Tell me, where is he?" she asked.

Cathal froze.

Slowly he lifted his head, and looked into her eyes. "He, he's dead. Jagger is dead."

CHAPTER THIRTY-EIGHT

The tonsured clerk sat benignly in front of Bishop Laninga with ink-stained fingers delicately clasped together. His pale and pasty coloured skin a clear indication of his profession as a scholar and little time spent outdoors. Before him were a pile of thickly-bound books and scrolls, all reference materials he used to complete the unusual task given to him by the bishop. He sat with the confidence and self-assuredness, his lipless smile, condescending if not mocking to those unfamiliar with his quirks, for those who knew him accepted his oddities and peculiarities in favour of his sharp and agile mind.

The bishop changed position in his chair, his fingers steepled as if in prayer, pressed against his chin as he contemplated the exhortation given to him by the scholar.

The clerk inclined his head, a silent reminder he waited, if not impatiently for a response.

Bishop Laninga removed his hands from his chin, placed them both flat on the table and focused his eyes on the clerk. He'd made up his mind; it was time to take matters further. "See to it. I want an epistle outlining the course of action the Church will take to proceed against the herdsman, ensure it is ready to give to Sir Kasos when he calls. He will deliver it to Bishop Immers."

The clerk's lipless smile expanded. "As I advocated, Yer Grace?"

The bishop sighed, "Aye, the herdsman, Odo Read will stand trial before the bishop's Consistory Court in England, under the jurisdiction of Exeter's diocese. I believe this sensible course of action will ultimately see this distasteful matter and the meddlesome herdsman receive his comeuppance." The bishop rose. "The knight will be here soon, make sure yer arguments in the missive are plain."

"As ye wish, Yer Grace." The scholar dipped his head.

The bishop made to leave then stopped and turned back to the scholar. "I just had a notion." He raised a forefinger skywards to emphasise his point.

The scholar's eyes followed the direction of his finger and felt a fleeting moment of dread.

"Perhaps it would be in the Church's interest if ye went to Exeter and presided as Court Chancellor. However this decision ultimately rests with Bishop Immers." Laninga smiled. "Regardless, ye shall accompany Sir Kasos to England," he looked at the cleric. "Ready yerself, Silas."

Odo sat on the deck of Hilke's *koggership* as it sailed from Geestendorf, already the green pastures of Frisia falling into shadow many miles behind them. Charlotte sat at his side and did her best to console him. It did little good, he was unresponsive and in shock.

"We must give him time, Charlotte, his mind must reconcile the violence and loss." Cathal leaned against the rigging smoking a clay pipe. He pushed his own feelings temporarily aside, for his heart also ached with the loss of Jagger Lippe, but he would honour the giant in his own way, in solitude when they arrived back in Mellester. "Give Odo all yer love, fer he needs it."

Charlotte's tear streaked face looked up at the seer. She said nothing, but her pained look spoke for everyone. She turned away from him and positioned herself closer to Odo, her head resting on his chest.

Grace and Tedric also watched and it looked as though Grace would go to her and offer comfort. Cathal shook his head. "Leave them a while, they need each other."

Night descended on the koggership, and Hilke was pleased to have sailed clear of the islands that dotted Frisia's coastline. Already the bow of his ship rose and fell to meet the swell of the open ocean ahead of them and he relaxed a little as Wim spelled him on the tiller. He walked over to Odo and Charlotte and saw they still hadn't moved. "Fetch a blanket," he commanded.

Because the Church preached against gluttony and weakness of the flesh, Bishop Laninga frequently chose to eat in his chambers where he could enjoy, with exclusivity, rather liberal portions of what should have been, as advocated, a conventional and moderate light supper. This evening, his housekeeper prepared a fine roasted pheasant along with a relatively new dish called pasta, and a variety of vegetables to satisfy his discerning palate and empty stomach.

It was without guilt that he stared ardently at the steaming bowl, however, being a pious man, the bishop hurriedly mouthed an abbreviated silent prayer of thanks before reaching for a succulent pheasant leg that caught his eye. With the finely cooked appendage firmly grasped in his hand, he raised the leg and opened his salivating mouth when a knock at the door interrupted what could have been a euphoric moment.

With the sound of the knock still reverberating around his chamber,

Bishop Laninga was too incensed to respond. It mattered not how he felt, for the door was thrust open and two men strode confidently into his private chamber. His housekeeper stood meekly in the open doorway looking apologetic. She needn't have worried, few people could or would have attempted to prevent two Templar knights from entering.

If the bishop's mouth could have opened further, then it surely would have.

"What is the meaning of this!" shouted the bishop, the pheasant leg only inches away from his gaping maw.

"I am Sir William Marshal, 1st Earl of Pem–"

"I know who ye are, damn it."

"–and this is Sir Peter of Gaunt."

"Ye have overstepped yer bounds and authority, I don't care that of yer indulgent position, I have guards–"

"They're a little occupied at the moment, Yer Grace." The two Templars took another step forward and stood at the table's edge looking down at the bishop who wielded the pheasant leg in his fist like a club.

"I shall make a complaint, Templars or not, ye have gone too far!"

Sir William ignored the threat. "We have need of a knight called Sir Kasos; we understand ye have spoken with him some days past."

"I know of no such knight." The pheasant leg was reluctantly returned to the bowl.

"Do not speak mistruths to us, for we are emissaries of His Holiness. It would serve ye very well to assist us in our time of need. We seek Sir Kasos, where is he?" Sir William's eyes were mere slits. The unwavering intensity of his gaze was too much and the bishop looked away.

"Where is he?"

Bishop Laninga swallowed. "The man ye seek is, uh, he is gone."

"Gone, gone? To where has he gone?"

Sir Peter walked around the table to stand at the bishop's side.

"He has returned to England this very day."

Sir Peter turned to his commander in silent question.

"Why has he gone, fer what purpose has he hurried away?" Sir William asked, his suppressed anger threatening to boil over.

"Has he gone to see Bishop Immers?" asked Sir Peter.

The revelation shocked the bishop. How could these men have known? He nodded, "What business is this of Templars?" he asked, his voice lacking confidence.

Sir William leaned forward and placed both hands on the table. "What is he seeing Immers fer, does he have a missive?"

Laninga took a breath. "He travels with a monk, a scholar, who will advise Bishop Immers on how to proceed with a Consistory Court where a mere herdsman will face the compassion of the Church's judgment. It is nothing."

Sir William straightened and turned his back on the bishop as he stepped away in anger. "Ye fool, ye've been deceived by Immers, he–"

"He's a trusted friend and a devout bish–"

Sir William shook his head as he stepped back to the table. "Bishop Immers is a lecherous, thieving and avaricious deceiver who will face His Holiness and answer fer his misconduct." Sir William raised a hand and pointed at Laninga. "And ye are riding on his shoulders – and so shall ye fall."

"Nay, this can't be, I have known Bishop Immers fer years. And, and, the Consistory Court is just, the herdsman needs to face retribution fer his crimes, he killed a farmer..."

"He did no such thing," added Sir Peter. "The farmer was killed by Sir Kasos and the *redjeven* was killed when Sir Kasos pushed the poor man onto a sword. Ye've been choused."

Bishop Laninga's eyebrows furrowed as he looked with doubt from one man to the other. "How do ye know?"

"Because witnesses saw," answered Sir Peter with contempt.

"Why should Templars care about a lowly herdsman?"

Sir Peter looked up at his commander who nodded in response. "Are ye familiar with Odo Brus?"

"Of course," nodded the bishop, his light supper forgotten.

"Well, that *lowly* herdsman, isn't quite so lowly, he is the only son of Odo Brus."

Bishop Laninga raised his eyes. "Then his mother is...?"

Sir William nodded

"Mary, Mother of Jesus! What have I done?" and then he crossed himself.

To be continued...

Books
by
Paul W. Feenstra

Published by Mellester Press.

Boundary

The Breath of God (Book 1 in Moana Rangitira series)

For Want of a Shilling (Book 2 in Moana Rangitira series)

Falls Ende eBook series

Falls Ende – The Oath   (eBook 1)
Falls Ende – Courser   (eBook 2)
Falls Ende – The King   (eBook 3)

Falls Ende – Primus Book 1
(Print version of eBook compilation 1, 2 & 3)

Falls Ende – Secundus Book 2

Please visit my website and join my mailing list for news and updates.

www.PaulWFeenstra.com

Facebook Paul W. Feenstra

Instagram PaulWFeenstra

Twitter @FeenstraPaul